THE POWER

Books by James Mills

NONFICTION

The Underground Empire
On the Edge
The Prosecutor

FICTION

The Power
The Truth About Peter Harley
The Seventh Power
One Just Man
Report to the Commissioner
The Panic in Needle Park

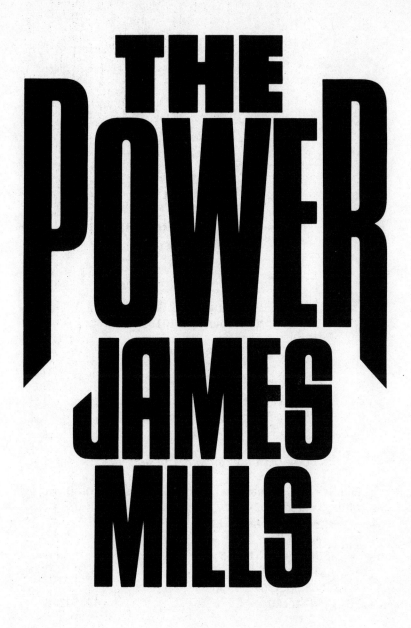

THE POWER

JAMES MILLS

WARNER BOOKS

A Time Warner Company

WARNER BOOKS, INC., 666 FIFTH AVENUE,
NEW YORK, NY 10103

 A Time Warner Company

PRINTED IN THE UNITED STATES OF AMERICA
FIRST PRINTING: SEPTEMBER
10 9 8 7 6 5 4 3 2 1

BOOK DESIGN BY SIGNET M DESIGN, INC.

LIBRARY OF CONGRESS CATALOGING-IN-PUBLICATION DATA
Mills, James, 1932–
      The power / James Mills.
        p.   cm.
      ISBN 0-446-513938
      I. Title.
    PS3563.I423P69   1990
    813'.54—dc20   90-50278
                                                        CIP

FOR
SUZANNE

1

T*HE WATER IN THE PINK* marble bathtub was still steaming, and if the man's nose had not been below the surface Jack Hammond might have dragged him out and started mouth-to-mouth. But Hammond was a good enough physician to know a dead man when he saw one and a good enough spy to know that police take a closer look at people who move bodies than at people who merely discover them. So Hammond fished out a Winston butt floating beside the corpse—it was the least he could do—put it in the crystal ashtray on the floor by the tub, and stepped back into the bedroom.

Staring out at the sun-drenched lawn sloping down to the Mediterranean, he telephoned the front desk and asked for a security man. Then he punched nine for an outside line, dialed twelve for Information, and said he wanted the number of the American embassy in Paris. Before the operator could answer, he changed his mind and hung up. If the Antibes police did a toll analysis on the phone, it wouldn't do for them to find a call to the embassy. The important thing right now was to wait for the cops, give a statement as finder of the body, and avoid entanglements that might complicate his departure for Moscow.

A young man in white trousers and pink Lacoste polo shirt appeared hesitantly in the doorway.

"Security?" Hammond asked. It was a very classy hotel. George Cox always went first class.

"Yes, sir. May I help you?"

Hammond nodded toward the bathroom.

2

THE DRIVE ALONG THE MED-
iterranean coast from Antibes to Monte Carlo should have
taken an hour. But Hammond was rounding the Bay of
Villefranche, trying to force the image of George Cox's
body out of his mind, when he spotted a dark blue Ferrari
Dino in his rearview mirror. The car had been in the
parking lot of Cox's hotel, and he had seen it again near
the hospital where they took the body. Would an intelligence service use such a conspicuous automobile?

A man at Washington's Dulles Airport as Hammond prepared to depart for Nice had lingered close enough to hear
Hammond's conversation with the check-in girl. When the
girl asked if she could help him, the man walked away
without speaking. And eleven hours later, as Hammond

emerged from the international baggage-claim area in Nice, two pairs of men had watched him approach the Hertz counter. Leaving with the car keys, he looked back through the crowd to see them in conversation with the clerk.

It had all been rather obvious, but not so blatant as the blue Ferrari. They had wanted to be seen, wanted him to know that he was watched. Hammond did not enjoy spy games. "If they're trying to piss me off," he thought, "they're doing a good job."

Hammond took a left at Cap d'Ail and climbed the narrow winding road up the mountain to the *grande corniche*. The detour would add half an hour to the trip, but he wanted to see if the Ferrari stayed with him. It did. When he stopped at a traffic light, the Ferrari, driven by a young man in a red-and-white-striped, open-neck shirt, tried to crawl up his tailpipe. Hammond jotted down the plate number.

At the Hôtel de Paris in Monte Carlo, the Ferrari passed him and continued down the hill out of sight. Hammond tipped the doorman fifty francs to look after the rented Renault, settled in the leather-chaired bar at one of the window tables overlooking the casino, and ordered a double Chivas Regal. He raised the glass to George Cox, or at least to the memory of him, and took a long sip. It was the first time he had experienced the death of an agent he actually knew, and he didn't like the feeling. He was a physician, after all, a healer.

Disentangling himself from the cops in Antibes hadn't been that difficult. They had wanted to know, of course, how Hammond had happened to be in George Cox's hotel room when he found the body. The lady at the desk took care of that—Cox had left instructions to give Dr. Hammond a key whenever he arrived. At the hospital in Antibes, the chief of trauma gave a preliminary cause of death as cardiac arrest. No fluid in the lungs. No foul play. Natural causes.

That gave Hammond a sick feeling in his stomach. If there was one thing Cox's death wasn't it was natural. Supernatural would be more like it. Hammond's wife, Carol, would have said I told you so. Anything supernatural, Carol ate it up.

It was late afternoon and the bar filled with solemn old men and women, richly dressed, sitting alone at separate tables. They've come to Monte Carlo to die, Hammond thought, carrying with them their gold, their memories, and their pride. He smiled at a stoop-shouldered man with a gold-headed cane, but the man pretended not to notice.

Hammond returned to his drink and set his mind on Carol. He thought he could identify the exact moment when his life—invariably successful but never, somehow, quite successful enough—had finally edged out of control. He had foolishly left his attaché case open on the dining room table where he was working. She had walked in and seen a pile of newspaper clippings with headlines like "Human Parts Buried at Satan Church," "Cult Worshipers Murder Boy," "Stanford Student Talks to the Dead."

"What's that?" she asked, shuddering.

"Just some nonsense," he said, stuffing the clips back into the case. "We're studying psychopathic behavior."

Two weeks later, tired and distraught after an all-night meeting at work, he had screamed at Carol for bringing home a book called *Modern Magic: The Age of the Psychic*.

"Why did you do that?" he had yelled.

"Why not?" She stopped cold, her arm halfway into a sweater. He never raised his voice. "Why are you so angry?"

"I thought you were intelligent, and now I find you reading junk like that."

"Maybe it's not junk."

"Maybe it's not—Carol, are you crazy?"

He'd grabbed his coat and attaché case and headed out the door, leaving her standing there openmouthed. Why was he so angry? If only he could tell her. He was a scientist, but everything he did these days seemed anti-science. His outburst had been wrong, unfair. It wasn't her fault. Sweating with fear and guilt, he got in his car, put the attaché case on his lap, flipped open the lid, and stared at the document that filled it—three hundred pages that were threatening his life.

TOP SECRET   MAG CHANNELS ONLY

DEFENSE INTELLIGENCE AGENCY

PSYCHOTRONIC WARFARE: SPIRITUAL ACCESS

Prepared by U.S. Army
Medical Intelligence Office
DST-03447/82/018

TOP SECRET   MAG CHANNELS ONLY

That had been thirteen months ago, and now here he was in Monte Carlo, mourning the death of a CIA agent and investigating a Soviet psychotronic operation code-named Spectrum. What Spectrum's specific objectives might be, no one knew, though destroying President Reagan was not a bad guess.

Hammond had started out as a neurophysiologist, did consciousness research for the National Institute of Mental Health, served in the army during the Vietnam War, wrote a report for the Surgeon General's Medical Intelligence Office on Soviet advances in paranormal (the Soviets called it psychotronic) warfare, and ended up as a scientific intelligence officer for something called the Monday Afternoon Group. MAG, as they called it, was a four-man control team from the Central Intelligence Agency, the Defense Intelligence Agency, the National Security Agency, and the White House overseeing U.S. research into the intelligence and military applications of paranormal phenomena. Some people said they were practicing witchcraft. It was perhaps the most secret research group in the government.

Ten days ago in Washington, Hammond had been driving Carol to a friend's house on his way to the Foreign Service Institute for an advanced Russian class. She had started again about wanting to know why he'd been transferred to Moscow.

"I'm going to be the embassy doctor."

She raised her hands, fingers splayed, in the gesture of ineffectual anger that had endeared her to him when they first met at a party three years ago. "Don't *tell* me that. That's crap and you know it. I want to know what you're doing."

Her camel overcoat was missing a button. "You ought to get that—"

"You tell me we're going to Moscow so you can be the embassy doctor, go from a world-class neurophysiologist to treating cuts and colds. I *know* that's not true. I married a doctor, Jack. A researcher, okay. But not some kind of spooky . . . I don't know what. You're off on trips all the time and I don't know where. Men come by the house and wire up the doors and windows. I get some secret number to call while you're away. I'm scared, Jack. I've got migraines. I can't sleep."

She was dark-haired, small, with a round, pretty face and a temper inherited from her mother. Their marriage had started falling apart two years ago when she found out he wasn't going to be a respectable country-club doctor like her father. She hadn't understood why he'd served in Vietnam (he could have stayed in school), or went into research, and she didn't like his working for the government. She wanted him to have a nine-to-five Manhattan practice, an East Side town house, weekends on Long Island, vacations abroad, and pots of money. Just like her father, one of the dullest men Hammond had ever known.

They drove for a minute in silence. They'd had these arguments before, and he hated them. He hated them because they hurt her, and there was nothing he could do about them.

"Why are we going to Moscow, Jack? Tell me. What are you doing? What's *happening*?"

He took one hand off the wheel and laid it on her knee. She pushed it away.

"I'm going to Moscow to be the embassy doctor."

Six months earlier, after his blowup over the *Modern Magic* book, he had made the mistake of trying to share with her the peculiar strangeness of his work, of searching for the scientific basis, if there was one, behind the claims of mystics, healers, satanists, voodoo witches, Hindu priests, and other odd characters dredged from the psychic depths. He hadn't told her much, but she had run off and repeated it to her horoscope-reading friends. They were fascinated. The occult was fashionable. Astrology, I Ching, crystals, channeling. They had nothing else to do.

Not long after that he discovered his wife had been seeing a "spirit guide," a sunken-cheeked, wide-eyed fraud who lost no time in persuading her that his so-called power could be communicated physically. She made love to him, went home, waited for Hammond to get back from work, dissolved in tears, and confessed. He forgave her.

She did it again, and this time her unexplained absences and late nights with "friends" made admission unnecessary. They separated. After several months, they came back together, promised mutual fidelity, and tried to pretend that nothing had happened. But her affairs continued.

Then four days ago, a week after their quarrel in the car, she had announced that she was not going to Moscow with him. She would file for divorce in the Dominican Republic. He was upset, but not surprised. At least they had no children.

3

Y*URI ANDROPOV, TALL,*
gaunt, bespectacled, sat in the green-wallpapered study
of his one-bedroom apartment six stories above Moscow's
ten-lane Kutuzovsky Prospekt and thought about the happiest day of his life. Ten months ago, huddled against the
numbing cold in Red Square, he had seen the body of his
predecessor, Soviet president Leonid Brezhnev, dropped
into a hole. It had been like watching the interment of
eighteen years of rot and depravity.

The corrupt old man had died of a heart attack just one
flight up from this apartment, in the middle of breakfast

with his wife, Viktoria. No more would Andropov be kept awake by drunken parties in Brezhnev's full-floor apartment and the neighboring home of his drinking buddy, General Nikolai Shcholokov, minister of the interior, boss of Soviet police.

By sundown the night of Brezhnev's death, the Politburo had selected former KGB chief Andropov as the new general secretary. Two days later the Central Committee made it official, and the next day Brezhnev went into the ground.

On the windswept top of the red-granite Lenin mausoleum, Andropov removed his fur hat, handed it brusquely to a Brezhnev crony ("Hold the hat!"), and made his funeral speech to a freezing audience of Soviet officials, military troops, and the largest throng of foreign leaders ever assembled in Moscow. He could not pick out American vice president George Bush, but he knew he was there and looked forward to seeing him at the reception after the funeral. Bush had been CIA director while Andropov was KGB chief. Now Andropov, chief of state, had surpassed his former adversary. As he peered into the crowd, Andropov reflected that it would take an assassin's bullet to restore the equality.

Brezhnev's alcoholic son was visible, as was his willful, overweight fifty-four-year-old daughter, Galina, her flabby face marked by a lifetime of corruption and a series of bizarre sexual liaisons—marriage to a trapeze artist, elopement with another circus performer, another marriage to her bodyguard, and a scandalous relationship with a flashy, degenerate circus character called Boris the Gypsy.

Andropov, a man who wrote poems to his wife and considered two glasses of vodka a drunken debauch, had already taken care of Boris the Gypsy and had plans for other powerful figures whose security had died with Brezhnev. Lefortovo prison was waiting, and so was the firing squad. Two solemn-faced KGB agents, posing as bereaved family members, were at Galina's side now, just in case she planned some outburst for the benefit of the international television audience.

After the funeral speeches, Andropov and his protégé Mikhail Gorbachev paraded down the steps of the mausoleum and around to the grave behind. Galina, her brother, and Brezhnev's widow kissed the corpse on the forehead. Two funeral attendants lifted ropes to lower the coffin into the grave.

And then something suddenly went wrong. The previous day, as the shoddily built coffin was raised to the catafalque for the lying in state, the bottom had fallen out; and Brezhnev's corpse tumbled through. Now, when the two attendants seized ropes supporting the new, steel-reinforced coffin, they found the load too heavy. One of the men lost his grip. The coffin pitched into the grave with a splintering crash that echoed through the stillness.

Watching on television, millions of Soviet citizens, inheritors of a long tradition of supernaturalism, took the violent descent as an occult comment on Brezhnev's reign. Nor was the symbolism lost on Andropov, who, though not a superstitious man, had for the past five years watched KGB-controlled scientists reach secretly into the realm of the mystical and psychic.

And while it was true that this was the happiest day of Andropov's life, it was also true that he had never felt more threatened. As he cast the first shovelful of earth onto the coffin, he knew that of all those present only Gorbachev was aware of the calamity that faced them.

4

HAMMOND ORDERED AN-
other Chivas Regal in the bar of the Hôtel de Paris and
thought about his only other visit to Monte Carlo, a visit
that had led finally to this, mourning the death of a friend
and colleague.

It had been last July, a month after discovering his wife's
first infidelity. He had been across the street from this bar,
in the famed Monte Carlo casino, standing at a craps table
watching a young woman with a red ten-thousand-franc
plaque on the Don't Come line.

She was about twenty-seven, tall and lean, with the
beauty of a fashion model, rich black hair over bare

shoulders, flat tanned cheeks, square chin, full lips alive with a smile that could have melted the dice she rattled in slim, delicate fingers. But despite the smile, her green eyes betrayed a shyness, a vulnerability, as if she might be unaware of the power of her charm.

At first Hammond thought it was her extraordinary beauty that had attracted the crowd around her, but he quickly discovered it was more than that. She had been winning with a consistency forbidden by the law of probability. With unaccountable frequency, the dice left her hand, hit the felt, rolled, stopped—and she raked in more chips. Only the unyielding arm of her escort, a solid, baggily dressed Russian, was finally able to pull her away from her success and admirers.

The next morning Hammond had been astonished to see the woman standing behind a podium, delivering a paper to the same gathering that had brought him to Monte Carlo, the Second International Congress on Psychotronic Research. With her hair in a bun, no makeup, and a speaking style as stern as her appearance, the shyness and vulnerability were absent and she appeared to be exactly what the program said she was, a Soviet scientific delegate named Darya Timoshek. The only thing that related her to the gorgeous young lady of the night before was the topic of her paper: "Quantum Theory Applications to Psychokinesis Placement Experiments." Either she was extraordinarily lucky, or she'd been willing those dice to come up winners.

Which it might be, Hammond didn't know. As a scientist, he was generally contemptuous of mumbo jumbo, but as the American intelligence community's premier expert on the paranormal, he had grown less contemptuous than he used to be. In the weird world of quantum mechanics, where scientists routinely took for granted particles traveling backward in time, electrons vanishing on one side of a barrier only to reappear inexplicably on the other side, and electrons perceived before they existed, you tended not exactly to accept the impossible, but at least to give it a hearing.

Hammond's surprise at seeing the woman on the podium had nothing to do with the change in her appearance from the previous night. It was her identity. Darya Timoshek was the purpose of his trip to Monte Carlo, a rare Soviet bird that he, as an American intelligence officer, had come to observe and study.

He took a copy of her paper back to his hotel room and read it before lunch. One paragraph particularly caught his interest:

> The path taken by cubes bounced down a gangway onto a table can be influenced paraphysically. This will be seen from the following treatment of the mechanics of cube bouncing (see Fig. 2).

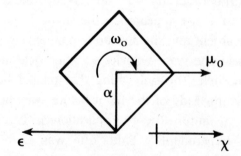

Figure 2. Diagram of quantities used in the derivation of the mechanics of cube bouncing.

Hammond smiled. He wondered if Monte Carlo casino officials ever thought of craps as cube bouncing.

Darya's paper also discussed psychotronic effects "on electronic equipment and thermodynamic systems." At that Hammond decided to pass it to Admiral Ralph Whitmore, MAG's NSA representative, a man obsessed with the threat of psychotronics to NSA's code-handling computers. If a human mind could move a gambling die, it could surely sabotage a computer chip.

Hammond had lunch at the Vigie, an open-air restaurant on a rock jutting into the Mediterranean, approached along a garden path from a hotel and beach. To help attract his bird's attention, to make himself as appealing to Darya Timoshek as she was to him, Hammond had brought with him to Monte Carlo Steve Burkholzer, an American psychobiologist who was to deliver a paper on biological-deterioration reversal techniques, a ridicule-deflecting euphemism for psychic healing. The KGB, which controlled all East Bloc psychotronic research, was reliably reported to have acquired a sudden and intense interest in healing. This was not uncommon for a Russian—they had a long history of that sort of thing—but it was surprising in the pragmatic, defiantly unsuperstitious KGB. So Hammond was there with Burkholzer and his healing paper as a decoy, a piece of bait. Neither man had ever met Darya Timoshek, but they had heard about her supposed brilliance as a psychotronic researcher.

The white-jacketed maître d'hôtel gave Hammond and Burkholzer a table under a parasol near the railing overlooking the sea. Burkholzer was a skinny young man with a right arm paralyzed in a motorcycle accident, and a long face and easy drawl that reminded Hammond of Jimmy Stewart. He directed a CIA-funded "private" mental clinic near Macon, Georgia, where twenty-four men and women were studied for psychic potential. The researchers, though no one ever put it in writing, were looking for saints and mystics. Burkholzer, a charismatic Christian who spoke in tongues, never doubted that such people existed. And if they existed, might not their powers be of some value to the United States government?

The answer to that question was a resounding, richly funded *yes*. Individuals and devices displaying psychic or supernatural ability were what MAG had been created to study and develop. It was MAG doctrine that the Soviets, through advances in the black art of psychotronics, were, as one MAG member put it, "recruiting the devil" for military and intelligence purposes. MAG, in its response to this threat, intended to give new meaning to the slogan "God is with us." It was all very clear: Us versus Them, Good versus Evil, God versus Satan.

Clear to MAG, but not to Hammond. As a scientist, he found it difficult to believe, as Burkholzer did, that the supernatural was simply an extension of the natural. And his encounters with religion had fallen far short of producing anything like Burkholzer's faith. When Hammond was a child, his parents had made him go to church. He had hated the vaulted gloom, dreary sermons, incomprehensible prayers. If God existed, surely he wasn't here. Neighbors across the hall in Hammond's apartment house obviously believed they had found him, and Hammond thought perhaps they had. They used to invite Hammond to their Wednesday-night "fellowship meetings," but his mother wouldn't let him go. She wasn't certain what church they belonged to—Baptists probably—and she considered them socially inferior.

One evening Hammond's mother had sent him out to buy milk for dinner. As he passed the neighbors' door he heard singing and stopped to listen. The singing ended and prayers began. There must have been twenty people in there. When the singing began again, he wanted to go in. He felt he had to go in, something told him it was what he should do. He put his hand on the doorknob, then thought about his mother. Dinner was almost ready, and she had told him to hurry. His mother's word was law.

In the end, the law won. He let go of the knob, ran down to the store for milk, and happened never again to be sent past the neighbors' door on a Wednesday evening.

At twelve his parents had made him sing in their church's boys' choir, led by a fat, white-haired tyrant. Hammond would have done almost anything to escape. In a sex education class at school he heard something he didn't completely understand, but it gave him an idea. He told his mother the choirmaster had put his hand on his leg. "Where?" his mother asked. "Here," Hammond said, touching his thigh. It had never occurred to Hammond that she would tell anyone else, but she must have because the choirmaster disappeared. A rumor said he had taken an overdose of sleeping pills. Tormented by shame, fear, and guilt, Hammond confessed the lie to his father. He expected a thrashing, but his father put his arms around him and said, "Why didn't you tell us you hated it? We wouldn't have made you go." After that the choirmaster returned, but Hammond did not. He never forgave himself for what he had done, and never quite got over the shame. The incident proved to him, as church never had, the danger of lying and sin. He wanted to be good. Eventually, without his ever actually making a decision, goodness became his religion.

Four men, arriving in a blue-and-gold-striped Cigarette speedboat, climbed the iron ladder up the rock from the sea to the restaurant. Dripping and grunting, they settled at a table next to Hammond's. One of them, a heavy-lidded, middle-aged Englishman wearing purple eyeliner, accompanied two well-muscled young men with arm tattoos, long hair, white skin, and awkward out-of-place glances suggesting they had only recently been separated from black leather and motorcycles.

The fourth man, wearing a bathing suit that looked as if it had been made in Bulgaria in the 1950s, seemed unhappy to be with the others and as they took their seats gave no indication he even knew them. Hammond recognized him as the husky Russian who last night had dragged Darya Timoshek from the craps table.

Hammond tipped his head toward the table, and Burkholzer glanced over.

"Last night," Hammond said softly. "Our friend's friend."

Burkholzer was the only man in the restaurant not wearing a bathing suit. He had meant to bring one but forgot to pack it. That was not unusual. Burkholzer forgot a lot of things. Even his car, a canary-yellow Lamborghini he cherished, would be lost for days until a parking-garage ticket reappeared by chance under a pile of desk papers. When discussing science or the supernatural, Burkholzer was utterly reasonable, sometimes infuriatingly reasonable. But his personal life teetered constantly on the brink of chaos. He seemed not to care, or even to notice. Hammond feared that eventually Burkholzer's indifference to an ordered life would cost him his job.

Burkholzer lifted a bottle of Domaine Ott blanc de blanc from the wine bucket and refilled their glasses. It was only twelve-thirty, most of the tables were still empty, and they had not yet been to the buffet table for lunch.

Then they saw Darya. Coming along the path from the beach, her wet gold bikini glistening, she spotted the four men and waved. Damp hair flattened against her head made her eyes appear even larger than they had at the craps table. The green irises, surrounded by whites slightly reddened by seawater, were almost luminous. She took a chair between the Englishman and one of the young men, not more than two feet from Burkholzer.

"Perfect timing," the Englishman said brightly, "we just arrived." He introduced the young men, who shook hands solemnly. The Russian stared out to sea.

It was clear that Darya knew the Englishman well, as she did many of the other people who now began to fill the restaurant. Women jangling jeweled bracelets, men with money written in permanent smiles embraced Darya, patted the Englishman's shoulder, and nodded politely as Darya introduced the Russian and the motorcycle boys. She was doing her best to make the outcasts feel part of the crowd.

"She obviously has things they want," Burkholzer said, watching Darya.

"Like money," Hammond said.

"Yes. And a talent with dice—God-given or otherwise."

Hammond groaned inside. If Burkholzer had a fault, it was God. He not only believed in God, he believed in Satan, angels, and demons. Burkholzer had an IQ of 173.

Hammond and Burkholzer filled their plates with poached salmon, ordered a second bottle of wine, and watched Darya accompany the young men to the buffet table. Chatting graciously, she identified the contents of unfamiliar dishes, trying against odds to put them at ease.

"Nice lady," Hammond said.

Darya playfully poked an elbow into the Russian's ribs and shot him a smile, as if to say, "Come on, get with it, have a little fun." His face cracked into a weak grin, then returned to an expression of boredom and disapproval. Hammond couldn't decide if he was a KGB goon—Russian clothes could make anyone look like a goon—or a scientific colleague of Darya's.

A short-haired woman twice Darya's age appeared at the table, greeted everyone in throaty, Italian-accented English, and pulled up a chair.

"Have some lunch with us," Darya said happily. "You're not swimming?"

The woman, wearing a white shirt and dark trousers, had no makeup, shoulders as sturdy as the Russian's, and a clear affection for Darya. Darya played no favorites, showering smiles and conversation equally among the newly arrived woman, the eyelinered Englishman, the motorcycle boys, and the Russian.

"Polysexual," Burkholzer said.

Hammond shook his head. "I'd hate to think it."

Five minutes later Burkholzer, reaching for the butter, knocked his sunglasses case to the ground. He had to move his chair to get to the case with his good hand, but before he could do so Darya had placed it back on the tablecloth.

"Thank you," Burkholzer said, meeting her eyes.

"Je vous en prie."

The smile she gave Burkholzer was so open and childlike Hammond had to wonder for a moment if this could really be Darya Timoshek, the severe Soviet delegate he'd seen behind the podium.

Hammond finished the salmon and decided to have a swim before helping himself to cheese. He refilled his glass, took a long cool drink, then dove off the edge of the rock and stroked lazily in the direction of a float anchored fifty yards offshore.

Halfway to the float, he stretched out facedown and gazed through the clear, blue-green water at the rocky bottom. He heard a faint buzzing, which he took at first for the sound of a distant speedboat. The buzzing grew louder, his vision fogged, and he felt a not-unpleasant light-headedness. The wine, of course. He rolled onto his back and took deep breaths. The sky was such a rich deep blue. The color faded, grew fainter, became brilliant white, then seemed to emit a golden light. The light intensified and shimmered. The shimmering seemed somehow associated with the buzzing in his ears. He felt himself sinking, but pleasantly, and had no desire to regain the surface. The light was ethereal and dazzling, the sound that accompanied it orchestral.

Something touched him between his legs, and a sensation of sexual pleasure pushed the light and music from his mind. Then a pain stung his right arm, and he returned to his senses with the realization that he had been thrown roughly against the float.

"Can you climb up?"

Darya Timoshek had her hand between his legs, pulling him toward the wooden steps at the side of the float.

He coughed and choked.

She withdrew her hand and gave his rump a shove. He grabbed the top of the float and found the ladder with his feet. He climbed up and collapsed onto his belly, coughing water.

"Are you all right?" She boosted herself nimbly to the float.

"Yes, yes." The coarse hemp matting scratched his stomach. "I'm fine."

"You almost drowned."

"I don't know what happened. I was swimming."

"I'll wave for a boat." Water ran from her hair over smooth, tanned shoulders.

"No, no, don't do that. I'll be all right. I'm a good swimmer." He glanced at her and laughed weakly. "I am, really. I don't know what happened."

Her eyes were uncertain.

"It's okay, honestly. I just need to rest for a minute." He sat up. "How did you get out here?"

"I decided to have a swim between courses. It's a miracle I saw you."

"I'm glad you did. Thanks very much."

She sat cross-legged, watching him. He didn't know when he had seen anyone so beautiful.

He invited her to dinner that evening. They went to a restaurant near the casino and ordered artichokes, sea bass grilled with fennel, and a bottle of Puligny-Montrachet. They told each other lies about who they were and what had brought them to the Congress. He said he was a psychiatrist at NIMH and she said she was a neuroresearcher at the Serbenov Institute in Moscow. He knew Serbenov to be a mental hospital and had read an intelligence report (written by George Cox, as a matter of fact) identifying it as the center of a $20-million psychotronic research project. What she really did there, if indeed she worked there at all, was a question he was not naive enough to ask.

"I've read about Kulagina's experiments," Hammond said, testing her candor. A Soviet psychic named Ninel Kulagina was said to have willed a frog's heart to stop beating.

"Oh, many people have done that," Darya said, pushing her hair back from her face. "It's not such a major event."

"Except for the frog."

She laughed. "Yes, except for the frog."

They spoke Russian, and she flattered him on his fluency. "Where did you get it?"

"In college, and I grew up in a Russian neighborhood in Brooklyn."

The Russian neighborhood was a lie. Hard work had honed his Russian when he went to MAG.

It was the first time since Hammond's marriage that he had had dinner alone with another woman. He had never been tempted, by vengeance or desire, to duplicate his wife's infidelity. Nor did what he felt now seem like temptation, for he supposed that in the strictest sense you could not have temptation without guilt. And given Carol's betrayals, he felt no guilt.

The contrast between Carol and Darya only sharpened his awareness of what a mistake the marriage had been.

He was more excited at this moment with Darya than he had ever been with Carol. He had never expected to be excited with Carol. Their marriage had come as the swift fulfillment of an inevitability. She was rich, pretty, Episcopalian, just what his parents wanted. He was well educated, bound for success, a good person, just what her parents wanted. Marriage was taken for granted. Almost before either of them had had time to think, they were at the altar.

Darya was different, an electrical jolt to his brain and solar plexus—beautiful, brilliant, mysterious, full of promised delights and discoveries.

He finished his artichoke and noticed that Darya had not yet started to eat hers. She had meticulously peeled off the leaves, dipped them in the vinaigrette sauce, and arranged them in a precise circle on the rim of her plate around the heart, which she had cut into four pieces.

"That's lovely," he said, wiping his fingers. "When are you going to eat it?"

"I'm not." Her smile was so openhearted he felt embarrassed. She reached across the table and placed the plate next to his. "You love them so much, and I would guess that you never really get enough. Everyone should always have enough."

It was true. He loved artichokes.

Her black silk dress had narrow shoulder straps that held the loose top just barely high enough to conceal her breasts (though not when she leaned forward to present her plate of artichoke). Later, after a few dances in the crowded darkness of a discotheque called Jimmyz, she took his hand and made it clear that the black silk was all there was between him and the warmth of her body.

Hammond was thirty-five years old, rough enough to have grown up unscarred on the streets of South Brooklyn, and built well enough to have played linebacker at Princeton, which he financed with a scholarship, job, and student loan. He had fair hair and owed to a Harvard running back the slightly flattened nose that saved his handsome face from prettiness.

He knew that Darya was no doubt drawn to him for professional reasons that welcomed supplementary delights but never lost sight of the business at hand. He had come to the Monte Carlo conference to exploit her, and she may well have come at least in part to exploit him. He wanted to know what she knew about Soviet psychotronics, and she would no doubt be happy to learn what he and Burkholzer knew about psychic healing and, surely, other U.S. paranormal projects as well.

She left him at their table near the dance floor and returned in a few minutes with a cigar.

"You smoke cigars?" he joked.

"It's for you," she said, her long, red nails delicately removing the band.

He hadn't had a cigar in years, but was touched by this show of affection.

She contemplated the cigar's end.

"Just a moment," he said, and reached in his pocket for a silver penknife.

"It's beautiful," she said, turning the knife in her hand. "Where did you get it?"

In Vietnam, Hammond had pulled a wounded Marine

corporal from a water-filled ditch and carried him under fire two hundred yards before it was safe to stop and apply a dressing to the hole over the man's right lung. Unable to speak, the man had fished the penknife from his fatigues and pushed it at Hammond. His eyes were so pleading and wild, Hammond had thought he'd better take it. He found him two days later, about to be airlifted to a hospital in Tokyo, and tried to return the knife. The Marine refused to take it, again with such emotion that Hammond thought it unwise to insist. Since then Hammond had never been without it.

"It was a gift from a friend," Hammond said, and watched Darya deftly cut a V-shaped hole in the cigar end. She rotated the other end over a match until it glowed around the edges, then handed it to him.

"You do that very well," Hammond said.

"My husband used to smoke them."

"You're married?" He tried to hide his disappointment.

"No more."

He drew on the cigar, curious but not wanting to pry.

"Would you like to hear?" she said.

"Only if you want to tell me."

"When I was sixteen a party boss in the town where I grew up decided he loved me. He was moving to Moscow and wanted to take me with him. He promised to get me into Moscow University. My parents were ecstatic. It was a great opportunity. So I married him. Unfortunately, by the time I finished university and started graduate work, he'd lost interest and divorced me. He liked his girls young."

"I'm sorry."

"Don't be." She smiled at him. "I got a good education. I know how to light cigars."

They left Jimmyz at four in the morning and strolled up the road to the beach-pool-restaurant complex at Monte Carlo Beach. The enormous saltwater pool had been emptied, and a half dozen men, working under lights with brushes, labored to have it glistening by the time the first swimmers and sunbathers drifted in at ten the following morning.

"Come this way," Darya said, and gripped his hand. She led him away from the pool and the workmen's lights, toward the rocky beach, into a darkened row of green-and-white-striped canvas cabanas.

"Have you been here before?" Hammond asked.

"No, just looking for a quiet spot." Her hand tugged him along confidently.

She stuck her head into one of the cabanas, then entered and pulled him behind her. Without speaking, she stretched out on a *matelas* and drew him down on top of her. He heard the rustle of disappearing silk. He kissed her, and began to feel the strangeness. Her lips were too soft, her touch too electric. She pulled him into her, and her body wrapped him in a heavy odor of sensuality so powerful he could taste it. The sound of surf breaking on the beach mingled with the odor and taste into a single, overriding supersense.

The physical sensations grew so dominating he was frightened. Then he felt the end approaching. But there was no end. The pleasure rose, expanded, became unendurable. He opened his mouth, but no words came, only pleasure increasing rapidly to pain.

When the end finally did come, their bodies lurched, but the pleasure-pain leaped to another dimension, exploding from his genitals through the rest of his body, growing through rising levels of ecstasy and fear. He fainted, and when he regained consciousness it was as if the explosion had continued without him, driving him to still greater peaks of what became pure sensation, neither pain nor pleasure. He cried out with what was this time a real scream. He felt her soft hand go gently over his mouth.

When he awoke, it was over. He was beside her on the *matelas*, facing her, exhausted. She was smiling at him, as if she had been watching over him for hours. Her green eyes seemed incandescent in the darkness.

"How long have we been here?" he asked. He was bathed in perspiration.

"About two hours." She was calm, studying him.

He didn't know what to say. "Is it always like that?"

"Did you like it?"

"My whole body—I thought I was dying."

She stroked his cheek with a tenderness as indescribable as the sex had been. "My darling," she said, "it's the way the gods make love."

Before he could respond, Hammond heard a faint sound and saw a shadow move against the cabana's canvas wall. He turned abruptly to find a thickly built man holding back the flap covering the cabana's entrance. It was the Russian who had led Darya from the craps table.

"Andrei, dear," Darya said, "please come in. There's a stool there. Join us."

Her tone and manner made it clear who the boss was. Though the man had insisted that Darya leave the craps table, Hammond saw now that she was the one who really gave the orders.

"Is everything all right?" He spoke in accented English with no hint of threat, as if he had just happened to be passing and dropped in to see how everyone was getting along. Awkwardly, Hammond found his trousers.

"Jack Hammond, Andrei Marchenko."

They shook hands, Hammond aware that his grip was a good deal less firm than Andrei's. When he tried to stand, his knees buckled. What the hell had Darya done to him?

Andrei and Darya exchanged looks, and Hammond became unpleasantly aware that he was in a more or less deserted place—were the pool scrubbers still there?—in the middle of the night with a couple of Soviets, one of them male and well built.

"Jack, my dear," Darya said, "I have to tell you that we know who you are. You are an American intelligence officer, based in Washington, with a specialty in psychotronics."

Hammond did not move or alter his expression. He was struggling to recall everything the CIA had taught him about unarmed combat, none of which he had ever taken the time to practice.

"Don't say anything, darling. We are the ones who want to talk."

She fell silent and they stared at him. Marchenko smiled, a gold tooth gleaming in the back of his mouth. The smile had a pronounced awareness to it. This was definitely not some KGB thug.

"My dear," Darya said finally, "we want to go home with you."

For a moment Hammond thought she had in mind some bizarre sexual threesome. Marchenko didn't seem the type. Reading Hammond's look of bewilderment, Darya laughed and said, "No, no, darling, we don't mean that. We want to defect."

5

I*N THE END, ONLY DARYA* had come to the States. Andrei Marchenko, it seemed, had too much to lose, or perhaps too little courage. Darya, Hammond soon discovered, had nothing if not courage, and her courage drove a boundless ambition. She also turned out to have a self-confidence that even Hammond, who valued that quality himself, found staggering. There was nothing she couldn't do and no obstacle sturdy enough to block her path.

Not everyone in Washington had been overjoyed at Darya's request to be admitted to the paranormal research program. MAG's interrogators were, not surprisingly, divided in their estimate of the genuineness of her defection. But her access to Soviet experiments had been so high most felt that even if her defection was false, the lies she might tell would themselves be of value. And since the Soviets were so far in the lead anyway, there was little she could steal to advance their knowledge.

Darya herself made no bones about her reasons for defecting. She wanted more research money and fewer people looking over her shoulder. Hammond sympathized with that. After more than two months of interrogation, revelations, and negotiations, she was given a virtual blank check, with Hammond as her boss. Hammond guessed she felt that occasional repetitions of what she referred to as "whole-body orgasms, the love of the gods" would keep him in line. He could sympathize with that too. If you wanted researchers of Darya's class—and MAG did—you had to put up with a sometimes irritating level of pride and determination.

Nevertheless, Hammond promised himself there would be no more sex with Darya. Even though his wife, Carol, was in the middle of another affair, and he was seeing as little of her as possible, a sexual relationship between Darya and himself—defector and handler—was out of the question professionally. His determination to keep Darya at arm's length was strengthened by the dominating effect of their first encounter. He wanted the sex, but he did not want to sell his soul for it. A few more of Darya's whole-body orgasms and Hammond would belong to her. He knew that, and he was sure she knew it too.

Darya's love of pleasure and fun, evident in Monte Carlo, was clearly another reason for her defection. She

wanted to remain permanently in the West, to sub-
merge herself in opulence—first-class air travel, grand
hotels, expensive restaurants. It wasn't just whole-body
sex Darya adored, it was whole-body immersion in
every sensual excess the West might have to offer.
Hammond had confidence she would find them all.
And when it came to her personal life, money was not
a problem. She obviously had all she ever needed.
Where it came from was not something she was willing
to discuss.

At dinner one night in a Washington restaurant, her
bare arms still tan from the Mediterranean sun, she said,
"In Moscow even Politburo members, the most privileged,
have such gray, mediocre tastes. It takes three generations
to acquire culture, and they are still on their first."

Darya not only adored sex, a precarious life of survival
in the Soviet Union had taught her to use it—how wan-
tonly, and with what precision and effect, Hammond discovered when she met MAG. The Monday Afternoon
Group was the paramount force in all U.S. paranormal
research, administering a secret annual budget of $210
million and controlling more than four hundred scientists
and technicians, most of whom, because of the compart-
mentalization of the research, were unaware of the true
purpose of their work. MAG alone knew all the secrets,
approved all the projects, signed all the checks. It was a
group Hammond approached with awe. Darya, wearing
a lemon-yellow Dior cocktail dress, approached it with
the high-spirited confidence of Sheba entering the court
of King Solomon.

Aware of her towering pride, and of her contempt for
the bureaucrats who had tried to control her work in the

Soviet Union, Hammond feared her first encounter with MAG. The fear, as it turned out, was justified.

The meeting was held in Vienna, Virginia, just outside Washington, in what the CIA called "the clean bubble" because it was on the top floor of a CIA-owned commercial building whose first floor was occupied by a dry cleaner. Similar to the secure rooms in U.S. embassies, the bubble was composed entirely of transparent plastic, set inside another slightly larger chamber made of metal shielding sandwiched between plastic sheets. The room's transparency, plus electromagnetic radiation in the area surrounding it, was thought to preclude the placement of listening devices.

All but Alex Buford, the White House representative, appeared to regard Darya as one might a uniquely desirable prostitute—eager to have what she came to sell but wary of the price. Buford, a wispy man in a pink bow tie, at least ten years younger than the others, looked so shaken by Darya's imposing presence it was impossible for Hammond to read his thoughts, if indeed he was having any.

The MAG chairman, sixty-four-year-old Ralph Whitmore, director of the NSA, was so thin his gray winter suit hung in folds from his shoulders. Hammond felt close to Whitmore, a Navy vice admiral, partly because the old man's gentlemanly toughness reminded him of his father, and partly because it was Whitmore who had recruited him into MAG. When Hammond had been working in the Surgeon General's office, a DIA colonel he'd never heard of invited him to lunch. A week later Hammond found himself at NSA headquarters talking to Whitmore. They chatted about Vietnam, and Whitmore told him about his son, a Navy SEAL, who had died there. He invited Hammond for a weekend's sailing in Annapolis. When they were on Chesapeake Bay in a thirty-two-foot sloop, Whitmore told him about MAG. Hammond liked Whitmore, and he was flattered and honored to be asked to join such an important operation. How could he say no?

Whitmore explained now that they wanted, first of all, to hear what Darya knew about the so-called Nixon-Carter-Brezhnev question, an ominous series of events that had haunted MAG's collective mind for nearly a year.

Darya crossed her legs, pushed a cascade of gold bracelets up her arm, and clasped her hands on the table. She fixed Whitmore with the intensely respectful gaze of an obedient daughter. "I would like very much to hear about this. I will tell you everything I know."

There was a moment of charged silence. It was clear, at least to Hammond, that Darya's respect for Whitmore did not extend to the DIA chief across the table from her, a crew-cut, hell-for-leather, Army brigadier general named Pfister, whose eyes had already undressed her and whose leer made it evident that his interest was not in what she might have to say but in what his imagination was telling him she might be able to do.

"Before I begin," she said warmly, "I would like to tell you something about myself. I am from Labinsk, a small Cossack town whose people are known for independence, willfulness, perseverance, and generosity." She turned beguilingly to Pfister, who was tapping the table with a yellow pencil. "When I was twelve, I discovered that I had psychic abilities. I was able to see distant objects and people, to foretell the future, to move small objects with my mind. I also had control over my bodily functions, breathing and heartbeat, and could fantasize myself into any state I wished. Whatever sensual desire I had, I could satisfy without assistance."

She still had her eyes on Pfister, whose expression degenerated from lust to smugness. He stopped tapping the pencil and drew circular doodles on the yellow legal pad in front of him. Hammond was having fresh insights into Darya's relationship with the party boss who had taken her to Moscow.

"Thank you," Whitmore said stiffly. "We appreciate knowing that. Now let me tell you something about this Nixon-Carter-Brezhnev problem."

He drew a sheaf of papers from his attaché case, cleared his throat, and began to read. " 'In 1972 President Richard Nixon, on a visit to the Soviet Union, experienced what he later described to the director of the CIA's mind control experiments as unusual feelings. Other members of the presidential party, including Nixon's physician, also displayed inappropriate behavior, including unaccountable weeping. A CIA investigation failed to rule out the possibility of psychic tampering.' "

Darya was deep in concentration, but not, Hammond thought, on Whitmore's words. Her eyes gazed inward.

" 'In 1979,' " Whitmore continued, " 'while in Vienna to sign the Salt II agreement, President Jimmy Carter visited the Soviet embassy. On his return to Washington, Carter also displayed bizarre behavior. Without explanation, he abruptly canceled a major speech on energy policy and withdrew precipitously to Camp David. He invited numbers of experts to consultations there, then took off for visits with such unlikely individuals as a machinist in Pennsylvania and a retired Marine in West Virginia.' "

Pfister's face was flushed. He appeared to be having trouble breathing. Hammond hoped Darya wasn't going to do anything embarrassing, although if it involved putting Pfister in his place he wouldn't blame her.

Whitmore turned a page. " 'Thirty-four Cabinet members and presidential staffers offered their resignations. Carter swung between hand-wringing indecision and inexplicably sudden action. Senator Ted Stevens stated publicly that "some of us are seriously worried that he might be approaching some sort of mental problem." Again, intelligence specialists with a knowledge of Soviet psychotronics speculated that the President may have undergone psychic tampering while inside the Soviet embassy in Vienna.' "

Darya's lips tightened and her eyes narrowed. Pfister seemed unable to take his eyes off her. Buford, the White House man, was clearly aware that something peculiar was happening. Hammond began to suspect the worst.

Whitmore, absorbed in the report, went on reading. " 'A disturbing speech that had been given in 1960 by Nikita Khrushchev supported these fears. "We have a new weapon," Khrushchev said, "just within the portfolio of our scientists, so to speak, which is so powerful that, if unrestrainedly used, it could wipe out all life on earth." In the summer of 1975, Leonid Brezhnev, Khrushchev's successor, underlined Khrushchev's words when he referred to novel weapons systems "more terrible than anything the world has known." Three years later, Col. T. E. Bearden, a nuclear engineer and an expert on Soviet psychotronics, wrote that Khrushchev's remark "probably

referred to extinguishing electrical currents flowing in cir-
cuits by means of virtual state electron-negation patterns
modulated in electromagnetic carriers." What that meant,
he explained, was that "nervous systems can be disabled
to varying degrees, including total disablement resulting
in death." At the same time it was believed that the Soviets
had begun experiments with psychotronic phenomena
ranging from black magic to hyperspatial nuclear how-
itzers, weapons capable of exploding a single nuclear device, then, by paranormal means, duplicating the blast in
any number of other locations.' "

Darya and Pfister were in another world, their eyes
locked on each other, lips half parted. If they'd been alone
they'd have been rolling on the floor.

Whitmore, without looking up, kept going. " 'In 1967,
three years after Brezhnev came to power, a Central Committee secretary named Yuri Andropov was put in charge
of the KGB. KGB research institutes with names like The
Laboratory of Bio-Information and The Institute of Control Problems were rumored to have developed psychic
energy accumulators and other mind control devices.

" 'Five months before Drs. Hammond and Burkholzer
attended the psychotronic congress in Monte Carlo,
strange things began to happen to Leonid Brezhnev. A
scaffolding Brezhnev was standing near during a visit
to the Chkalov Aircraft Factory in Tashkent suddenly collapsed, sending Brezhnev to the ground beneath a heap
of security men protecting him against what they feared
was an assassination attempt.' "

Darya was sweating. So was Pfister. Their chests heaved
in unison, their breathing deep and rapid. Pfister's eyes

were half closed. Everyone but Whitmore was staring at them. Hammond was mortified.

" 'Reports said Brezhnev had suffered a stroke, that he remained critically ill in a coma for days, and could not speak for several weeks. The prime beneficiary of this inexplicable accident was KGB chief Yuri Andropov, whose power expanded greatly during Brezhnev's illness. A U.S. intelligence asset reported that the scaffolding collapse had been achieved psychotronically.

" 'Following a summer of recuperation, Brezhnev experienced another bizarre setback. As he was beginning a major speech, televised live throughout the Soviet Union, it soon became obvious that his words did not match prepared texts handed out earlier.' "

Darya and Pfister were still at it, sweating and heaving.

" 'After seven minutes of consternation, Brezhnev's national security adviser finally hurried to the podium and thrust a pile of papers before Brezhnev. He began again, muttering, "It wasn't my fault." How could the wrong speech possibly have been substituted for the correct one, and how could Brezhnev have failed for seven minutes to notice the error? The embarrassment further undermined Brezhnev's position, and strengthened Andropov.

" 'A study of the Nixon-Carter-Brezhnev question necessarily produces concern for the welfare of President Reagan. If Yuri Andropov's KGB scientists possess the ability to induce crying, provoke manic-depressive mood swings, topple scaffoldings, and switch speeches, what might they attempt with today's Western leaders, including President Reagan?' "

Darya's body shook with three rapid convulsions.

Pfister gritted his teeth, squeezed his eyes shut, and the yellow pencil broke in his fingers. The noise lifted Whitmore's eyes from the report. He looked at Pfister, at Darya, at the other men, then back at Pfister.

"Are you all right, General?"

"Ah . . . yes, sir . . . excuse me . . . I'm fine." He was red-faced, drenched in perspiration. "I'm sorry. I'm fine now." He pulled a pack of cigarettes from his jacket.

Darya ran a hand through her hair and said, "Delightful."

Whitmore said, "I'm glad you enjoyed it, Miss Timoshek. Perhaps you could give us your reactions."

She adjusted the bracelets. "Certainly. I would be pleased to." Her gaze settled on Whitmore. "It's true. The KGB's psychotronic capability was responsible for the events you describe. I myself was involved in the operations against Carter and Brezhnev. But the situation is worse than I think you imagine."

Pfister took a long drag from the cigarette, looked unhappily into his lap, and cast furtive glances around the table.

"The Soviets," Darya said, "are intensively pursuing a theory for the mediation of all paranormal phenomena. The project is code-named Spectrum."

Hammond saw Whitmore straighten almost imperceptibly. Spectrum was something new.

"Why Spectrum?" Whitmore asked.

"You mean the name?" Darya said. "Because it has to do with radiation, with light. And light is truth, is it not?"

Scientists for many years had speculated that extrasensory perception, psychokinesis, clairvoyance, out-of-body travel, and other paranormal phenomena might have their explanation in a single unrecognized force. The discovery of that force could lead to technology able to harness and control it. Intelligence agents, without leaving their offices, would be able to "see" into locked enemy safes, commando teams could materialize inside fortified enemy missile bases and command centers, enemy leaders could be confused, killed, or made to disappear in their own countries and to reappear at an enemy location. Ships, tanks, entire cities, could be "de-existed" by the touch of a button, or even by a thought. An enemy would have but two options—destruction or surrender.

"How far along is Spectrum?" Whitmore asked steadily, trying to conceal his concern.

"That's a big question," Darya said.

No one spoke, and it was evident that Darya had no intention of sharing now, in this room with these men, everything she knew about Spectrum. Perhaps she had no intention of sharing it with anyone, ever. But Hammond knew what his mission would be. Get it from her.

The meeting ended. General Pfister was the last to leave, eager not to display the stain on his pants. But Buford was waiting for him. "You might want to drop those off downstairs," he said, his smirk a perfect match for the pink bow tie.

6

DARYA, ADAPTING LIKE A
chameleon to American research labs, donned sweatshirts
and jeans and installed herself at a National Institute of
Mental Health facility in the Maryland countryside. She
was given an office in Building Six, an unprepossessing
two-story concrete-block structure surrounded by a double ten-foot-high chain-link fence. The fence and other
security measures were supposedly required by the presence of laboratory animals infected with contagious diseases. In fact, there were no dangerous animals and the
security was there to protect research proposals, results,
and experimental data. The research itself was done clan-

destinely at universities and institutes, many of them CIA and NSA proprietaries, in other locations around the country.

U.S. paranormal projects had been divided into two categories, Black and White. Black was anything whose intention was to harm, White was anything whose intention was benign. Mild friction had always existed between the two branches, and Hammond feared that Darya's strong, never-take-no-for-an-answer personality would increase it.

She asked to visit all the projects, both Black and White, and MAG agreed. On a remote farm in the North Carolina countryside, Hammond showed her a pig whose feeding was controlled electronically by a random number generator, a device that should have fed the pig a predictable amount of food over a predictable period of time, like a coin that gives food every time it comes up heads and withholds it every time it comes up tails.

In fact, the pig was getting food far more often than anticipated, as if the coin were coming up heads more often than tails. When the pig was removed from its cage, the machine behaved properly. Put the pig back, and once again there was more food than predicted. The only explanation was that a hungry pig's mind could somehow influence the machine.

When Hammond and Darya saw it, the experiment was being redesigned for use with humans. A human who could be trained to influence a machine mentally (as the pig had done) might be able to sabotage enemy aircraft, ships, tanks, computers, command centers.

Over a lunch of ham sandwiches and Budweiser in the linoleum-floored office of the young Chinese-born project director, Darya claimed that the Soviets had long ago conducted similar experiments. Even in a white laboratory smock pulled over slacks and a cardigan, Darya's eyes, sharp features, and flowing black hair made her look more like a fashion model than a scientist. Her easygoing warmth and quick smile produced something like adoration in the eyes of her young host.

"You might want to know," she said helpfully, "that results were far superior with highly strung females under hypnosis." She stretched a long, lean arm across the desk and refilled the project director's glass with beer. "Stress also heightened the effect. Ten milligrams of B-CCE, and the effect was sixty percent reliable. We had one sixteen-year-old schizophrenic girl who scrambled the mother board of an Apple IIe six hundred yards away in another building."

The project director's look of adoration turned to shock, and he and Hammond exchanged anxious glances. Injections of B-CCE, an extract of human urine, produced complete, paralyzing terror. Researchers called it bottled fear. Administered to a schizophrenic, the consequences could be catastrophic.

"That disturbs you?" Darya said.

"It does a bit," Hammond said. What else were the Soviets doing?

Indeed, what else were the Americans doing? That afternoon, at the same lab, Hammond and Darya watched as a female chimpanzee experienced multiple orgasms for more than thirty minutes while experimenters delivered a weak electric current to an electrode implanted in her brain's septal region. A male chimp enjoyed similar delights from a chemical transmitter called acetylcholine introduced into its septal region through a canula. These experiments were establishing base data for later attempts to influence the septal region by high-resolution, pinpoint psychokinesis. A little well-timed psychic stimulation of an enemy's neural pleasure center might produce disastrously embarrassing results (as General Pfister had learned to his regret at Darya's MAG briefing).

They visited the CIA mental clinic in Georgia where Steve Burkholzer and his team looked for psychic potential in two dozen men and women. "Acquisition teams" attached to MAG's White group had combed bus stations, public parks, skid rows, and mental wards for bag ladies and other crazies who might have mystical abilities.

Burkholzer had once confided to Hammond that he opposed MAG's division of paranormal research into a Black group and a White group. "There is no good magic," he had said, "Black or White. That which is not from God is evil. The occult is evil. Satan counterfeits God's gifts, makes you think they come from God. Satan can enable a spiritualist to heal your illness, and that will look good. He'll heal you, he'll give you knowledge, he'll give you pleasure—but in the end he'll have your soul."

"So why are you working for MAG?" Hammond had asked.

"Because God can work through MAG. Someday our government may need to know where to find someone through whom God will work a miracle."

Now Burkholzer joined Hammond and Darya in director's chairs around a wicker coffee table in his office. He had a cold and spent two minutes rifling through drawers and cabinets for a box of Kleenex.

"You need a keeper," Hammond said. He made it sound

like a joke, but it wasn't. Six months earlier, before Burkholzer moved to Georgia from Washington, Hammond had tried to call him at his apartment. The phone had been disconnected. When he went to the apartment, it was locked. Worried, he finally tracked Burkholzer to a Holiday Inn. He'd forgotten to pay his phone and rent bills, and when he did mail the checks, they bounced because he'd forgotten to deposit his paycheck. Hammond went with him to his office, found the check stuffed into the out basket, escorted him to the bank, then to the phone company and his landlord, and got him reinstalled in his apartment.

"I'm sorry to cause you all that trouble," Burkholzer had said in his Jimmy Stewart drawl.

"Don't mention it. But you ought to look out for yourself."

"It's all right. Really. I'm fine."

And he was, oddly enough. Nothing seemed to bother Burkholzer. He was like an alien from another universe, blissfully ignorant of this world's priorities. He struck up conversations with strangers everywhere, in elevators, restaurants, at bus stops, asked how their families were, if they liked their jobs, where they went on vacation. He invited derelicts home for a bath and dinner, sent money he didn't have to people he read about in the papers. His wife had left him years ago, the IRS was constantly in pursuit for unpaid taxes, banks repossessed his furniture. His personal life was a ruin, but inside, where it counted, Steve Burkholzer was one of the happiest men Hammond had ever met.

"The best way to get yourself diagnosed schizophrenic," Burkholzer told them now, "is to get hauled into a mental hospital muttering about demons, angels, and Satan. But who knows, maybe some of these people do have such contacts, and maybe they can tell us something."

Under his glass desktop, next to photographs of his nieces and nephews, Burkholzer had a quotation from Jesus: "I am the light of the world." He also had a sentence from the Apostle Paul's second letter to the Corinthians: "The weapons of our warfare are not worldly but have divine power to destroy strongholds." Were these the weapons Burkholzer was looking for? He talked about saints with the reported ability to multiply food, as Jesus and Old Testament prophets had done.

Darya listened to this without smile or ridicule. Then she emptied a Styrofoam cup of coffee Burkholzer had given her and said, "An ability to multiply food and medical supplies could be quite an advantage."

"To a combat force, you mean," he said, his lively brown eyes going straight into her. "But what about multiplying moisture or impurities in computers, destroying a weapon's ability to fire, an aircraft's ability to fly? God did many miraculous things to assist the Old Testament armies of Israel."

"So you're trying to get him on your side." She was grinning now, but charmingly, with no hint of mockery.

Burkholzer grinned back, meeting her on her own terms. "What did Paul mean when he wrote that in a vision he had heard 'inexpressible things, things that man is not permitted to tell'? What were those things? Did they have something to do with what we now call the paranormal?"

Hammond did not want to tell Darya, but he knew that here and in two other MAG facilities, at Stanford and Austin, researchers were probing biblical and secular

miracles, among them teleportation, the instantaneous re-
location of objects from one place to another. Could military equipment be teleported into combat zones?

"Healing?" Darya asked the question with a single
word.

Burkholzer looked at Hammond. MAG was in fact
deeply involved in experiments to determine if psychic
healing had battlefield capabilities.

"We don't call it that," Hammond answered. "But we
have had some success with BDR—biological-deterioration reversal techniques."

Darya laughed with delight. "We have the same problem in Russia. Marxists go berserk when they think you're
talking about the supernatural, so the scientists think up
techtalk words like 'psychotronics' and 'biofields.' "

That night, on a flight from Atlanta to Chicago, Darya
took a sip of champagne and reached for Hammond's
hand. She held it a moment, then let go. "What's wrong?"

"Nothing, just a little tired from all the travel."

"You do human research too," she said, guessing that
he was still upset about the Soviets' bottled-fear experiments.

"Human, yes," Hammond said, not looking at her,
"but it's benign. We don't attack their Valium receptors."
B-CCE, bottled fear, worked by binding to the same brain
receptors as the tranquilizer Valium. How could Darya
have taken such experiments so lightly? Perhaps she resisted them at first. To the Soviets they must be routine,
a standard practice not easily overcome. What would he
have done? It was easy to be self-righteous.

Darya clearly did not want to launch into an argument
about experimental ethics. She took his hand again, raised

the armrest that separated them, and snuggled against him. It was a night flight, the lights were out, and most of the other business-class passengers were watching the movie.

"I have always liked your Dr. Burkholzer," she said, "from the first moment I saw you both at the restaurant in Monte Carlo." She twisted toward him and put her other hand in his lap. "Interesting for a scientist to have such a strong religious faith."

It had started to rain, and Hammond saw flashes of lightning out the window. The seat belt sign came on. "I guess they come up against questions that don't seem to have natural answers." He glanced back to see if anyone was in the seat behind them.

"Do you believe in anything like that?" Darya asked.

The plane dropped like an elevator, steadied, then made a violent sideways motion. Across the aisle an elderly woman with white hair, a mustache, and a body so thin she filled only half the seat pulled an airsickness bag from the seat pocket.

"My father used to take us all to church," Hammond said.

Darya's hand kept moving in his lap. His pulse and respiration felt as if he'd just finished a forty-yard sprint. Why was a touch from her better than an hour in bed with other women?

Six years after the choirmaster incident, Hammond had entered Princeton with an undiminished aversion to churches and religion, much preferring atheists who performed good works to believers who did not. An offensive tackle on the football team took him to a Pentecostal service in New York, and certainly it was nothing like the tradition-bound church of his parents. Eyes were closed, hands raised, voices alive with songs and prayers. Something was happening, but whether it was God or emotion, Hammond wasn't sure. The whole thing was mildly embarrassing, and though he found it interesting he never returned.

After med school, when he was at Mass. Gen. doing his residency in neurology, he encountered a few surgeons and researchers who seemed to find it impossible to discuss their specialties without resorting to the concept of a supreme intelligence. When he asked one of them if he believed in God, the answer had been, "Of course I believe in God. I'm a scientist."

He guessed he half believed that maybe there was a divine intelligence. But was this what most people meant when they talked about God? He didn't think so. He had never felt a need for God. If you had brains and balls, and stayed within obvious moral boundaries, there wasn't much you couldn't handle. He believed in self-reliance. Keep control.

"I think if I do the best I can," he said now, "everything will turn out as well as possible. If there is a God, he's not going to punish someone who tried to do his best."

She squeezed his hand. "That's what I think."

Hammond's sincere and often arduous attempts to lead a good and honorable life, while not always triumphant, had paid off. At Princeton he graduated in the top five percent of his class, played first-string middle linebacker, made good friends, and dated whom he liked. But the success had not felt like success. He awoke each morning with a persistent unease, a nagging sense of incompleteness, failure. He did not know what to do about it. Later in the day, at a class or lecture, the feeling usually left him, but then he'd walk into a coatroom or bathroom and when he was suddenly alone in the quiet, the feeling would come back with a rush, and he'd begin to sweat. Who was he, what was he doing, why was he here?

After college the success continued, and so did the sense of failure. Eventually he had decided to tell Carol about it. They'd just consumed two bottles of champagne at a Manhattan restaurant, celebrating their one-month wedding anniversary, and were on the corner of Fifth and Fifty-fifth waiting for a taxi. He tried to make a joke of it. "Why is success such a failure?"

Her answer was typically Carol. "You need to let your heart speak."

"Need to let my *heart* speak?"

"You're a rationalist, trying to make yourself happy with things in this world, but this world isn't where your happiness is."

"Oh, really?"

"Don't smile. You've never recognized the supernatural. You avoid it, you reject it. No wonder you're unhappy."

A taxi pulled to the curb and they climbed in. She cuddled against him. "You know there's more than this world and success, but you won't admit it. So suffer."

She kissed him and grinned. A couple of years later she was up to her ears in magic.

The rain and turbulence ended, but the old woman across the aisle still had the bag to her mouth. She lowered it, wiped her lips with a dirty, rumpled handkerchief, fastened the bag, and rang for the stewardess. No one came. Even in the half-darkness, she looked ashen.

Darya took an airsickness bag from her own seat pocket, climbed over Hammond to the aisle, gave it to the woman, and placed the full bag under the seat. She put her fingers on the woman's forehead, smoothed back her damp white hair, and whispered something that made the woman nod and smile.

Darya returned to her seat and without a word put her hand in Hammond's lap. Credits appeared on the screen and the lights came on. Hammond moved Darya's hand and sat up in the seat.

"Why did you do that?" she said, taking another sip of champagne. "I was about to make you very happy."

"I don't doubt it."

When they landed at O'Hare they rented a car and drove to a Holiday Inn near the University of Illinois at Urbana. Darya wanted to get a double room. Hammond, with a struggle, refused.

He showered, climbed into bed, and turned out the light. After what seemed like a couple of hours of sleep, he half awoke with the sense that someone was beside him in the bed. He turned his head slowly on the pillow and saw Darya. She came on top of him, put her hands gently on his face, and whispered, "Don't move, darling. Let me do everything."

Still half asleep, eyes closed, he lay quietly on his back while she filled his body with pleasure. He was weightless, detached, buoyant in an electric, bliss-charged cloud. After several minutes, he felt as if he were slowly awakening from a sleepless dream. Darya rolled off him.

He opened his eyes, turned to look at her—and saw the white-haired old woman from the plane. She smiled at him, her mustache beaded with perspiration, her warm breath smelling of vomit.

Hammond leaped from the bed, frantically searched the wall, and found the room light. The bed was empty. The pillow beside his own was undisturbed, the sheets there smooth and unruffled.

He went to the door. The chain was off and the door unlocked. The corridor was deserted, silent. He was positive he had locked the door before he went to bed.

He picked up the telephone and dialed Darya's room.

"Yes?" She sounded groggy.

"It's me. I just—I couldn't sleep. I thought—"

"Darling, I'm sound asleep. Not now. Go to bed. I'll see you tomorrow."

She hung up.

He turned on the TV and spent the night watching movies.

The next morning they drove three miles south of Urbana to a private research institute. By the time he finished breakfast, Hammond had managed to convince himself that he'd had a nightmare. He was simply mistaken about having locked the door. He had not been in bed with Darya, and he certainly had not been made love to by the old woman from the plane.

In the car he mentioned the incident to Darya. To his surprise, she did not laugh.

"You should have told me. I would have come to the room. It must have been terrifying."

"It was."

"Has that happened to you before?"

"Never."

"I don't think it's so remarkable, really, with the kind of research you do." She rolled her window down, and a blast of cold air filled the car. "When I was fifteen someone put a spell on me and I had terrible visions. I was sick with a fever, felt insects crawling on me. It was horrible. I went to a shaman and he removed the spell."

"I am not under a spell, Darya." A shaman? Hammond knew he would never be able to comprehend Darya's life as a child.

"How do you know? The old woman on the plane could have done something."

"That's crazy."

"Do you want me to remove it?"

"Remove what?"

"The spell."

"I am not under a spell."

"Let me. I know how."

"No."

"Why?"

"Because it's ridiculous. Forget it."

"You might have the same experience again. Maybe worse."

"Forget it."

The institute near Urbana had a single purpose—to create an object made from time. A twenty-three-year-old female particle physicist had developed equations suggesting that time had energy. Well, if time had energy, then according to Einstein we ought to be able to convert that energy into mass. And if time had mass, we might be able to fashion it into an object. What would such an object look like, how big would it be, how stable? More important, what would we do with an object made from time? Control the world, maybe.

They left that institute and checked into a Ramada Inn near O'Hare. Hammond locked and unlocked his door three times before getting into bed. It took him two hours to get to sleep, but the sleep was dreamless.

For the next ten days they hopscotched the country, looking at projects so bizarre only scientists directly involved in the research itself were likely to think of them without derision. In a stainless steel basement laboratory at Maimonides Hospital in Brooklyn, instruments measured electromagnetic force fields surrounding a young woman who had been clinically dead for eighteen hours. The body was releasing energy, and the energy, measured on the instruments, displayed characteristics identical to those associated earlier with another young woman who had mentally been influencing the path of falling metal pellets. Were dead human bodies capable of psychokinesis?

A CIA project at a private institute in Loma Linda, California, studied the possibility of extracting information— no one wanted to say thoughts—from the brains of dead intelligence agents, friendly and enemy. Should this project be joined with the one at Maimonides?

In the desert not far from Tucson, Hammond and Darya watched psychic subjects draw sketches of geographical objects—rivers, lakes, buildings, and bridges—for which they had been provided only the longitude and latitude.

"I can do that," Darya announced blithely. Hammond wasn't sure she couldn't. That evening he asked her if it was really true.

"To be honest," she said, "I can do some things some

of the time and other things most of the time. There have been periods in my life when it seemed nothing was beyond me, and other periods when I was unable to do anything at all. I don't know why that should be."

Hammond didn't either. Psychic tests to which Darya had submitted when she first joined MAG had all proved negative. Embarrassment and a fear of ridicule had kept him from reporting her sexual capabilities.

Still another experiment, this one in the tree-shrouded Gothic atmosphere of Princeton's Institute for Advanced Study, examined the viability of developing a computer to interpret and record the waveforms of a person's thoughts, enabling those thoughts to continue long after the person and his brain had died. Might that computer then be able to transmit the thoughts to other computers, or to live brains, informing or corrupting them?

At lunch in a bar on Princeton's Nassau Street they ordered hamburgers, and Hammond asked her about a gold ring with a ram's head and woman's breasts that was dangling from a chain around her neck.

"Do you like it?" she asked.

"It's a satanic emblem."

"So what? I think it's pretty."

"Burkholzer wouldn't approve."

"He believes in Satan?"

"Definitely."

"So do I. But Satan's not so bad, really." She took a sip of Heineken, those lovely green eyes watching him over the rim of the glass. "I have a lot of very nice friends who don't find him so bad. And when you look at some of the people who say they prefer God, with crucifixes around their necks, it's not much of a recommendation."

"It's all a little too spooky for me," Hammond said.

"Spooky?" The word made her laugh. "Everything's spooky."

Throughout their tour, Darya had claimed to know very little about Operation Spectrum. She said she thought it was associated with something called universal Fourier components but pleaded ignorance regarding details. Hammond knew she was holding back, but she would loosen up eventually. The more MAG dangled before her its research resources (one of the purposes of this trip), and the more she became immersed in the pleasures of Western life, the more she would be compelled to produce. "Give us Spectrum, Darya, or back you go to Russia."

Traveling from project to project, hotel to hotel, Hammond did his best to increase his professional rapport with Darya, while keeping her at a distance emotionally. As they walked through research labs rank with the odor of liquefied mouse brains, studied the behavior of monkeys with electrical terminals implanted in their limbic systems, toured all the high-tech science fiction paraphernalia of future-probing, she seemed to amuse herself by tormenting him with clandestine touches and amorous glances that put his central nervous system into an adrenaline-gorged frenzy.

By the time they had returned to Washington, his reservoir of sexual resistance was nearly drained. He knew he was thinking like an alcoholic about to fall off the wagon, but he began to wonder if maybe—well, just one more time? And from consideration of surrender to surrender itself was a short descent accomplished by the touch of Darya's hand in the backseat of a taxicab from National airport.

The first weekend back from their project tour, at Dar-ya's Georgetown apartment, Hammond experienced two days and nights of sleepless lovemaking that made Monte Carlo look like foreplay. As Hammond and Darya lay in bed the second morning, Darya said, "Do you remember the first woman you ever slept with?"

"Of course," Hammond said. "Who could forget that?"

She turned on her side and smiled at him. "Tell me."

"I was fourteen years old, very skinny, weighed about ninety-eight pounds. My father always wanted me to be tough, but I was just this scrawny little kid. I was walking home from school and I saw these two guys following a woman. I came up behind them and heard them talking about how they were going to rip her off. They were walking fast, catching up to her. I was scared as hell, but I saw a crate of empty Coke bottles sitting on a stoop up ahead. So when we passed it I grabbed a couple of bottles, and I jumped the guys. They were shocked out of their minds. This skinny kid pounding away with a couple of Coke bottles. They took off, and the woman, who turned out to be about twenty-three and not that bad looking, asked if I'd come into her apartment so she could thank me. I had no idea what was going to happen."

"Did you ever see her again?"

"Never. She scared me even more than the guys."

Hammond spotted a black mole on Darya's right thigh. "You ought to keep an eye on that," he said. "If it ever changes size or color—"

She threw her right leg over his stomach and locked him in a scissor hold. "You'll be the first to know," she said, and bit his lip.

*   *   *

"Whole-body sex, the love of the gods," was not all Darya had in store for him.

"You need to give your right hemisphere a chance," she had told him one evening in a dim, candle-lit Washington restaurant called Chez Maud. "You think too much with the left side of your brain. You're too literal, you see everything as problem solving. Get abstract. Get creative."

Hammond had never considered himself culturally inclined. He was a scientist, after all, and his interests tended toward the practical. But she led him on a relentless pursuit of what she called nonconceptual sensory input. For more than a week, they spent every evening at art museums (visual), concerts (auditory), restaurants and wine tastings (gustatory, olfactory).

"And tactile?" he asked.

"That I take care of personally." She ran a forefinger along his cheek, then pressed the point of the long red nail against the skin until it hurt.

When he was growing up, such things were not considered unmanly, they were simply not considered at all. If someone had suggested forgoing a Yankees game for a visit to the Museum of Modern Art, he would have encountered not ridicule but bewilderment. Hammond's father was a jail guard ("corrections officer," he insisted) at Riker's Island, his brother worked for Con Edison, and his sister was married to a fireman. "I'm the only one who went bad," Hammond joked, "took off for college and med school." But he had never gone *this* bad. Museums and concerts.

Sometimes, surrounded by walls of cubism, he had to

wonder how Darya would react to a heavyweight title fight. Not wanting her to think he was a hopeless case, he never asked. But one bright sunny afternoon he did suggest they forget the art museums and go for a stroll along the Potomac, or picnic in a park, maybe even visit a zoo. "Oh, please, darling, not today," she said. "The sun hurts my eyes."

With Darya he was doing unaccustomed things, experiencing unfamiliar pleasures. He discovered a taste for Chagall and Vivaldi and Armagnac. But most of all, he had to admit, he welcomed the return to her apartment. Nothing approached the sex.

"I guess I'm just a lowbrow," he told her over breakfast in her bedroom. He had been awake since four, unable to sleep, wondering if his attraction for her might be more than sex. Was he falling in love?

"Don't worry." She smiled, stirring sugar into his coffee. "I haven't finished with you yet."

Then she disappeared.

He spent a week in his office polishing the report of their project tour, reliving his moments with Darya, trying to reach her by telephone.

Her secretary said she was in and out of the office, but she was never there when he phoned, and she did not return his calls. Her home phone responded with a recording requesting messages at the beep. He filled it with pleas to call him.

He couldn't imagine what was going on. He had struggled for months to resist her. And now that he had finally given in, had even imagined he might be in love with her, she vanished.

They had argued often about what he saw as her preference for Black research into so-called negative healing, the infliction of injury, sickness, and death. He had seen psychics, using only their minds, stop the hearts of laboratory mice, cause vomiting in squirrel monkeys, and put unsuspecting human subjects into sudden deep sleep. An experiment had even been contrived in which a cat, given a psychosis-inducing drug called taraxein, caused the death of two other cats separated from it by a quartz panel. Preparations were underway for human trials of the cat experiment, in which psychics would attempt first to kill microorganisms, then small laboratory animals, and finally primates.

Hammond had always opposed Black research, and during his tour with Darya he had contrived to limit her knowledge of it. Most disturbingly, he knew that two MAG-sponsored neuroanthropologists studying voodoo and black magic had visited Haiti and Brazil, as well as satanic cults in Kansas and California. Darya had wanted to accompany the researchers on one of their cult visits. He had opposed that idea successfully, or thought he had. Did she do it anyway? Had something gone wrong?

Tuesday afternoon he finally reached her at work. She was on her way out, had no time to talk, could not meet him for dinner. She would call him the next morning.

But she did not. By now he was like a drug addict, Darya-hooked, desperate.

At two A.M. Thursday he was working in his study when the phone rang. "Sorry to wake you, darling. I'm—"

"Where have you been? Why didn't you call?"

"Darling, I've been so busy. You wouldn't believe it. I haven't had a second, and I've missed you terribly. Don't be angry."

"It's all right. When can I see you?" All his fears had been unfounded. She wasn't avoiding him. She had not been attacked by demons. And one thing he now knew for sure. He loved her.

"Are you free for dinner tonight?" Her voice had a delightful, joyous lilt.

"Chez Maud?"

"At eight. I can't wait, Jack. I've missed you so much."

"Me too. I'll see you then."

He hung up and slept so deeply he was late to work.

He was at the restaurant at seven-thirty, telling himself he'd rather wait there than kill time at home. He ordered a double Chivas Regal. At nine he went to the pay phone in the entrance lobby and called her apartment.

"Hello, I'm not home right now, but if you leave a message at the beep I'll—"

He hung up and went back to the table. His impatience turned to worry. An accident? An encounter with a Soviet agent?

He saw the maître d'hôtel heading for the table and knew at once it was a telephone call. He followed him back to the lobby.

"Darling, I'm sorry." She sounded distraught.

"Where are you?"

She didn't answer. Noises echoed in the background.

"Where are you?"

"Forgive me, Jack."

"Where the hell are you?"

"Dulles."

"What're you doing at Dulles?" He felt sick.

"Taking a trip."

"Don't do it, Darya. I'll be there in fifty minutes."

"I have to, Jack, but not without saying good-bye. I don't want you to think I planned it this way."

"What happened? Are you alone?"

"Good-bye, Jack."

She hung up.

He dialed directory assistance and got the number for Pan Am.

"When's the next flight, Dulles to Moscow?"

"Just a moment, please. . . . There are no Dulles-Moscow flights, sir. They all originate in New York."

"When's the next one from New York?"

"We have a flight at—just a moment, please—at twelve-fifty from Kennedy. There's an Eastern flight leaving here at ten that connects."

He looked at his watch. Forty-five minutes. Was Darya doing this of her own free will, or was someone with her?

He promised the taxi driver a hundred dollars if he made it by nine forty-five. They didn't even come close.

7

H*IS GRAY FACE SOLEMN*
and troubled, Soviet leader Yuri Andropov stepped cautiously from the black Zil limousine and crossed the sidewalk to the entrance of the six-story, yellow stone Central Committee headquarters, a mere five hundred yards across Dzerzhinski Square from his old office at KGB headquarters. Not even children's laughter from the wooden sandbox in the park across the street could brighten the drab August Moscow air nor the stern looks of brown-uniformed KGB officers who ringed the car.

He settled his gaunt, lanky body into the black leather

chair at the center of the dais in the new conference hall, emptied a glassful of water at his elbow, adjusted his wire-rimmed spectacles, and looked out over the dour expressions of aging, die-hard Bolsheviks. Were it not for the medals dangling from their black jackets and dresses, these white-haired dinosaurs would have resembled a pack of Hasidic rabbis. How to propel them from the complacency and corruption of the Brezhnev era into the reality of economic necessity? His principal advantage was that none yet realized how little time he had in which to perform this miracle. His purpose today was to deceive, to win their support for his friend and protégé Mikhail Gorbachev, the man he hoped would crush them.

As Andropov listened to Gorbachev give his speech, attempting from the lectern to drive radical ideas into fossilized brains, he could see light beginning to dawn behind the listeners' dreary, half-dead eyes. Yes, they have guessed it. Gorbachev is more than the boss of Soviet agriculture. He is the heir apparent. Should anything happen to Andropov, their fate will be Gorbachev. Already this calculatingly charming man, young enough to be the grandson of most of those in the hall, was shaping an ominous program of *perestroika*, restructuring, and those who wished to survive had better climb aboard.

The future of those who did not climb aboard was easy to predict. Even before Brezhnev's death, Andropov's KGB agents had gone after some of the ailing leader's relatives and cronies. Brezhnev's profligate daughter, Galina, escaped interrogation by checking into the Kremlin hospital, supposedly with a nervous breakdown. Her boyfriend, Boris the Gypsy, lest his flamboyancy lead him to talk too much, was murdered in prison.

With the ailing Brezhnev so fearful of death he was seeing a psychic healer, in defiance of communism's denial of the supernatural, Andropov continued his attack. The day before the leader died, KGB agents arrested two of Galina's best friends. Within sixteen days one had been sentenced to death, and eight months later he was shot.

Andropov bent forward, and a sharp pain stabbed from his back into his right testicle and upper thigh. His eyes closed and he lost the thread of Gorbachev's words. The pain had struck more frequently in the past week, and he dreaded the other horrors that might soon follow.

When Brezhnev's end had finally come, Andropov, elevated to chief of state, really went to work. Sergei Medunov, Party boss of a Black Sea resort, who kept a twelve-apartment brothel for vacationing Moscow officials, was arrested. His parties had often turned into orgies, and the elderly, staid members of the Politburo and Central Committee had displayed politically embarrassing ways of amusing themselves.

Not long after Brezhnev's funeral, while tales of sex orgies still delighted Moscow gossips, Galina's youthful bodyguard husband, promoted to deputy minister of internal affairs, was dismissed and packed off to the Arctic.

At the same time, Brezhnev's old neighbor and crony, General Nikolai Shcholokov, whose drinking bouts with Brezhnev had kept Andropov awake, was fired as chief of the nation's police. The KGB's Lefortovo prison filled with Shcholokov's corrupt cops, two of whom, thrown in with common criminals, were murdered. Sometime later the general himself, dressed elegantly in a medal-bedecked uniform, blew his brains out with a rifle.

And so the purge continued, Andropov using KGB corruption files as a detergent to cleanse the country of eighteen years of decay and mismanagement. Even his solemn black limousine, cruising sharklike and unescorted through the city, seemed a reproach to Galina's yellow Mercedes and the boulevard-clearing, twenty-car entourage in which her father had traveled.

Now Andropov listened painfully to Gorbachev's speech and marveled at the man's finesse. He spoke humbly with the soft, rolled-R's accent of the south, smiling gently, clothing stern rebuke in the bright hues of flattery.

A barb twisted again in Andropov's right testicle. He winced and took another drink of water. The doctors had told him these pains were characteristic of his illness, but now he was experiencing something new. The pain felt —he couldn't quite shape the thought—deliberate, inflicted. Another one struck, and this time the room went dark. The pain ended in an instant, and light returned. The audience's solemn gaze gave no indication that anyone else had experienced the darkness. He almost cried out as another pain hit, accompanied by an instant of darkness. He was filled with a certainty that something or someone was doing this to him. Was he going mad? He waited in terror, but the pain and darkness did not return. He drew a handkerchief across his forehead and struggled to return his thoughts to Gorbachev.

The two men had first met in the Stavropol region of the Caucasus Mountains, a place of lush valleys, towering peaks, and earthbound values uncorrupted by the avarice and cynicism of the capital. Both men had been born there, could remember tales of local shamans and old women whose touch healed diseases, mended broken bones, closed wounds. Religion mixed with superstition, and though neither man professed acceptance of the supernatural, both carried in their genes, if not in their hearts, a heritage of belief.

When Yuri Andropov was four, his father died of typhus during a famine, while traveling in search of food. His piano-teacher mother remarried and died when Yuri was fourteen. He worked as a movie projectionist and riverboat sailor, joined the Communist Party youth organization Komsomol, married another Komsomol activist, and began a political career. Unpretentious, self-educated, a workaholic reader of American classics, he led World War II underground operations against the Finns, choosing as his code name "Mohican."

He and Gorbachev first crossed paths when the young Gorbachev, the local Party boss, greeted Andropov, the KGB chief, as he arrived for a holiday at his nearby dacha. Andropov liked the younger man immediately, was impressed by his honesty, toughness, and sense of humor. He invited him for strolls in the forest, talked about life, politics, and, eventually, the need to rescue their government from corruption and lethargy. The only display of strength and initiative came from the political and religious dissidents Andropov's KGB was at that moment struggling to destroy.

Gorbachev, whose only contact with Moscow had come during twice-yearly visits for meetings of the Central Committee and Supreme Soviet, was uninfected by the debilitating self-indulgence of the capital. Even his mother, despite the local prominence of her son, lived as she had always lived, continuing to till the soil.

Whenever Andropov had vacationed in Stavropol, he made it a point to spend as much time as possible with Gorbachev. And it was not long before Andropov persuaded Brezhnev to bring his young protégé to Moscow as chief of Soviet agriculture. For Gorbachev, it was a step to power, and the favor of a friend whose confidence he never betrayed.

Today, with Gorbachev presiding, Andropov was, in effect, presenting his protégé to this hall full of conservative hard-liners as designated successor to the Soviet leadership. Would they accept him, or eat him alive? Well, no doubt about the dietary habits of some of them. Gorbachev, the threatening youngster, was raw meat.

Grigori Romanov, a ruthless degenerate who would surely be one of Gorbachev's most powerful opponents during the succession free-for-all, lounged in his chair, his hard blue eyes bloodshot, his boyish face haggard with a hangover. At a wedding party for his daughter, drunken guests had smashed glasses from Catherine the Great's priceless dinner service, which Romanov had ordered brought for the occasion to his dacha from the Hermitage Museum.

And then there was Viktor Grishin, the sleazy Moscow Party chief who had arrived today with a gang of aides in seven limousines. When he was chairman of the All-Union Central Council of Trade Unions, his office had had a door leading into an ornately furnished massage parlor.

But Gorbachev's strongest rival would surely be Konstantin Chernenko, burly, white haired, half asleep in his usual baggy blue suit, for thirty years Brezhnev's dull, loyal, obedient flunky. He looked now like Brezhnev's ghost, come back to haunt the chambers of the Central Committee.

Gorbachev finished his speech, and Andropov unfolded his haggard body from the leather chair and, like a man bearing an almost intolerable burden, walked slowly to the lectern. His hands trembled, his mouth tasted foul, he was dying of thirst, and he was desperate to urinate.

Mustering his strength, he spoke forcefully of the future, of challenge, the necessity for change and reform. Quoting a Russian proverb, he acknowledged the need for deliberation. "Measure seven times, for you can cut only once."

But he left no doubt—he intended to cut. As the men and women shuffled silently from the hall, recalling sins that might lodge in the files of the KGB, there were surely many who felt the blade at their backs.

Andropov headed for the men's room reserved for Central Committee members at the side of the hall. As he emerged, he was approached by a somber-looking sixty-year-old man in large horn-rimmed glasses. KGB chief Viktor Chebrikov put his hand gently on Andropov's arm, slowing his movement. "Do you have a moment?"

Andropov listened briefly and said, "In the car."

In the backseat of Andropov's Zil, equipped with thick, nonresonating glass designed to stop both bullets and eavesdropping microwaves, Andropov said wearily, "What is it?"

"Golub's back at Serbenov."

Golub, the Russian word for dove, was the KGB cryptonym for Darya Timoshek, a woman whose hypocrisy and lack of loyalty offended Andropov. He had chosen the cryptonym himself, perhaps because the word also meant pigeon, a bird he shot for sport during his Stavropol vacations.

"Has she been to Spectrum?" Andropov asked.

"Not yet."

"Tell me when she goes. How long she stays, what she does."

8

HAMMOND GAZED AT THE casino through the window of the Hôtel de Paris bar and decided against another Chivas Regal. It had been two months since Darya boarded a Moscow-bound flight at Kennedy airport. Not until she was gone had he realized how much she meant to him, how many things he liked about her—her opposition to men like Pfister, her affection for Burkholzer, her kindness to the old woman on the plane, the ferocious loyalty to her work.

He was haunted with worry. What or who had forced her return to Moscow? Was she in trouble, in prison, in pain? The MAG interrogators who had thought her defection phony were full of unspoken righteousness, gloating quietly. Were they right? Had it all been an act? Had she used him? He longed to see her face-to-face.

George Cox, a CIA agent under commercial cover as the Pan Am general manager at Moscow's Sheremetyevo airport, had been instructed to locate her. A graduate of Groton and Yale, Cox had been a 210-pound bachelor with a fat man's robust good nature, convivial and friendly to a fault. He also had a sharp mind, but raised in a wealthy family on Long Island's north shore, he lacked the street sense and skepticism that would have proved useful in a career requiring him to make rapid assessments of the true motives of charming men.

A so-called "illegal" agent operating independently of the Moscow CIA station, Cox had employed his own communications methods, primarily a satellite-linked, spread-spectrum squirt transmitter designed to resemble a Chinese-made travel clock, which, for added security, he kept concealed in a metal drainpipe outside his bedroom window. Should that system fail for any reason, he could make emergency coded transmissions over the Pan Am office telex.

For six months following Darya's Monte Carlo defection, Cox had been in clandestine contact with Andrei Marchenko, who, though he had had second thoughts about defecting, was not opposed to keeping the lines of communication open.

Marchenko, as Cox discovered, was a staunch Andropov loyalist assigned to military intelligence, the GRU. It was rare, though not unheard of, for the United States to develop a spy as highly placed as Marchenko. His job was to keep Andropov, former KGB chief, aware of whatever psychotronic activity the rival GRU might be up to. In reality, however, Marchenko's tastes and disposition appeared to be more with the United States than with either the KGB or the GRU.

Meeting in small apartments CIA operatives rented on the Moscow real estate black market, Marchenko at first accepted small gifts from Cox, toys and Western clothes for his wife and two daughters, then a color television set, finally cash. Cox had radioed Hammond in Washington that Marchenko "has mentally and spiritually defected to the West—only his body remains in the USSR."

Since Marchenko's background, much like Hammond's, was scientific intelligence, specifically psychotronics, it was hoped he would know about Spectrum. But when Cox had first spoken the word "Spectrum" to Marchenko during a drive around the Moscow ring road, the Russian stiffened, said something irrelevant about the Doritos corn chips Cox had just offered him, and ended the conversation.

Two weeks later, having had time to think the matter over, Marchenko admitted that an operation called Spectrum existed, but he claimed to have no knowledge of it. He did say, however, that the KGB's Fifth Chief Directorate, which suppressed religious and political dissidents, had been told to halt surveillance of a woman who had demonstrated healing abilities at a clandestine prayer meeting. Because it was unheard of to halt surveillance on such a person, and because psychic healing would naturally be of interest to paranormal researchers, Marchenko "surmised" that her case had been taken over by Operation Spectrum.

Cox pressed Marchenko for more information about the healer. At their next meeting Marchenko revealed that she was a widow named Mrs. Leonov and that she had reportedly healed a minimum of nineteen people with ailments ranging from headaches to a broken hip. Four KGB agents—two healthy, two intentionally infected with a flu virus—had infiltrated one of the prayer meetings and asked for healing. She had healed the two with the virus and gently rebuked the other two for faking. She then denounced all four as government provocateurs, which brought the meeting to an abrupt halt.

Marchenko said Operation Spectrum officials were now considering methods of approaching the woman to win her cooperation. A full range of tests might determine her ability to perform negative healing, psychokinesis, and other psychotronic feats. Could her talents be increased and expanded? Could she teach them to others?

Through the simple expedient of telephoning her research lab at the Serbenov Institute, Cox had also established contact with Darya, who, curiously, was not at all reluctant to meet him. She had resumed her psychotronic research, and her earlier defection to the West—which, to Hammond's chagrin, was looking less and less genuine —appeared to have gone unpunished.

Then an event had occurred that diverted Hammond's attention from Cox's cables about contacts with Darya. In November, Soviet leader Leonid Brezhnev died and was replaced two days later by Yuri Andropov. Over the next several months, Marchenko's close association with Andropov propelled him beyond even Darya as MAG's prime intelligence target. Hammond began preparing for an extended assignment to Moscow. Cox, despite his success in developing both Marchenko and Darya, lacked scientific training and was unable to evaluate their information and respond with immediate requests. Hammond had to analyze Cox's reports, then suggest further lines of inquiry.

The State Department doctor assigned to the Moscow embassy was approaching the end of a three-year tour. Hammond would take his place and depend on two assistants to carry the medical load while he maintained liaison with Marchenko and Darya.

Hammond was nearing completion of State Department briefings and CIA instruction in Moscow station tradecraft when he received a troubling message from Cox. Cox demanded an emergency meeting with Hammond, immediately and outside the Soviet Union. For no reason Hammond could imagine, he strongly requested that the meeting take place near Nice, France.

Hammond packed his bags and booked Pan Am flight 83 nonstop New York to Nice en route to Paris and Moscow, planning to assume his duties in Moscow immediately after seeing Cox. But the meeting with Cox never took place, unless you could call the discovery of Cox's body in a hotel bathtub a meeting.

Hammond signaled for the waiter in the Hôtel de Paris bar and asked for his check. All these thoughts of Cox had reminded him of the day twenty years ago when he stood beside the embalmed corpse of a teenage friend who'd lost control of a Ford convertible, and consequently of his life. It had since been part of Hammond's personal code—encouraged by his father, who shared it—that self-reliance was essential to survival. You had to hold your life in your own two hands and not let go. Seeing Cox's body in the bathtub had reconfirmed that conviction.

The waiter brought the check, and Hammond paid it. He had a plane to catch for Paris, with a change there to Pan Am's Moscow flight. He recovered his rented Renault from the doorman and headed for the Nice airport.

9

JACK HAMMOND HAD NEVER
been to Moscow before, and when he stepped out of a
taxi at Cox's apartment house he could not believe his
eyes. A drab six-story dark-brick building squatted with
five others amid dirty snow, gray leafless trees, and garbage dumpsters.

Perhaps he had been wrong after all to insist that he
spend his first few nights in Cox's apartment. As the embassy doctor, Hammond was entitled to an apartment in
the embassy's north wing, but his predecessor had not yet
completed his move from that apartment, and Hammond
did not want to stay in a hotel. In any case, he had thought

living in Cox's home might give him a feeling for the man, for the life he had been leading, perhaps some hint of precisely why and how he died.

But Hammond had not been counting on this. This was a slum. The entrance was unlighted, the stone steps dim and dirty, and frigid wind blew in through broken hallway windows. He took an antique wire-cage elevator to the fifth floor and had to squint through the darkness to find the right apartment among four others on the landing. He turned the key in the lock and stepped into a lightless hall as cold as the steps had been. He closed the door behind him, groped for a light switch, and found it.

The hall, long and narrow, was lined on both sides with stacked boxes of Doritos corn chips and cartons of Skippy creamy peanut butter. Unable to find his favorite American delicacies in Moscow, Cox had evidently stockpiled them from trips to the West. A closet off the hall was jammed with six Panasonic television sets, stacks of cashmere sweaters still in cellophane wrappers, a three-foot-high pile of Jordache jeans, five cases of Hennessy cognac, four cases of Dom Pérignon champagne, and twenty-seven cans of pâté de foie gras. Hammond stared at it. "Bribes," he said out loud, and continued down the hall to the living room.

Dust covered the worn parquet floor, a Phillips TV set, and a VCR surrounded by piles of video cassettes. Hammond stepped into the bedroom, saw an unmade double bed and a desk strewn with technical documents. He picked one up, a study of the effect of psychokinesis on dice, roulette wheels, and slot machines. Beneath it was a study of paranormal influence on dissipative structures —weather patterns, population shifts, financial markets.

He opened a drawer and found monthly statements for a Merrill Lynch brokerage account in Monte Carlo. Hammond recalled Darya's remarkable success at the craps table. Just how close had Cox managed to get to Darya, or vice versa? Hammond was worried, and not just about Cox's relationship with Darya. He remembered Cox's frantic demand for an emergency meeting near Nice, and his corpse floating in the hotel bathtub. In the cold, eerily silent home of this dead agent, Hammond felt watched.

He looked into the bathroom. A Crest toothpaste tube was open on the porcelain sink. A towel and a pair of white boxer shorts lay on the floor. The entire apartment was dirty, unkempt, smelling of dampness. Cox had left in a hurry.

Hammond did a quick, thirty-minute search, assured himself that the squirt transmitter was still in the drainpipe, then sat in the living room on a threadbare red brocade sofa facing the TV set and contemplated the residue of George Cox's complicated life. On the kitchen table he had found a book-sized stainless steel box with a dial, a wall plug, and two wires attached to small silver-colored alligator clips. He couldn't imagine what it could be, but he had brought it with him to the sofa. It was troubling to find such a device in the home of an intelligence agent.

He examined the video cassettes—commercially produced tapes of movies, and Sony tapes with no markings. He slipped one of the Sonys into the VCR, turned on the TV, and felt his stomach drop. Not taking his eyes from the screen, he stepped slowly backward to the sofa and sat down. He knew he was watching the biggest intelligence find of his career.

For some time the CIA Moscow station had been expanding on public rumors of corruption in the Brezhnev regime. Cables were full of drunken parties at the dachas of Politburo members, prostitutes assigned as maids to a dacha occupied by Brezhnev himself, Brezhnev's daughter Galina smuggling diamonds with a circus clown called Boris the Gypsy. But this tape wasn't rumor, it was real. Where the hell had Cox got it?

The question was answered almost immediately. A shot of a large sitting room showed a chandelier, heavy Victorian chairs and sofas, an armoire, a glass-fronted wooden cabinet filled with teacups, and red velvet curtains. Three naked couples danced what looked like a very slow waltz. The men were heavy, bald, in their sixties or seventies. The women were young, pretty.

After several minutes studying the dancers, touching the VCR's pause button to scrutinize their faces, Hammond became certain that one of the men was Leonid Brezhnev. The woman he danced with was clothed only in long blond hair and high-heeled shoes. It looked like something from a 1940s black-and-white eight-millimeter porno film. Who would the other men have been? Politburo members.

Then two other figures, fully clothed, entered the frame. George Cox and Darya. Ignoring Brezhnev and the other dancers, Cox reclined on a sofa, and Darya, dark hair falling to the shoulders of her blouse, knelt on the floor beside him, blocking him from view. After a minute, she stood and moved away. Cox was on his back, an erection elevating the fabric of his trousers, a small stainless steel box sitting on his chest. Two wires ran from the box to the back of his skull. His hand was on the dial, and his body writhed.

Hammond glanced at the box beside him on the sofa, then looked back at the TV. He saw Cox, manipulating the dial, convulsing with orgasm after orgasm. But in Hammond's mind it wasn't Cox. It was an animal, a chimpanzee in a North Carolina research lab. He turned off the TV, went into the bathroom, and vomited.

10

T*HROUGH THE TINTED WIN-*
dows of the black Volga's backseat, Moscow looked even
drearier than usual. The cars were shabby, the streets were
shabby, the people were shabby, even the air was shabby.
They headed out the broad Kalinina Prospekt, past the
Praga restaurant to the ring road, then turned north and
began a slow circuit of the city.

"This car looks like about a thousand official Soviet
Volgas," the CIA driver told Hammond, "and the plate
numbers end in MOC, an official car. But if you tried to
trace them you wouldn't get anywhere, except maybe
back to Nebraska, where we made them."

A scrawny bean pole with a squeaky laugh, the driver wore a dark Russian-made suit intended to go with the official-looking car. "Russian plates made in the USA. How about that? Sorry about the heater."

The Volga was freezing. Hammond shivered inside his overcoat, losing the battle to keep warm. The driver had been introduced as "Frank," as good a name as any. At least twenty-five, Frank looked and talked like an eighteen-year-old, which did nothing to settle Hammond's nerves.

Hammond smiled and said, "Don't worry about it." He had a lot to think about and wished Frank would stop babbling. The video of Cox and Darya was implanted immovably in his mind.

Their route had been carefully selected on a blanket-sized map of Moscow leaned against the wall of an embassy conference room on the floor beneath the CIA's offices. Hammond had had an appointment to meet Jerry Shroeder, the station chief—his cover was DCM, deputy chief of mission, second-in-command to the ambassador—in the depths of the CIA's sacred conclave, but when he stepped off the elevator at the entrance a Marine guard told him to wait.

Hammond had been warned in Washington about Shroeder, a short, wiry, distrustful man not likely to be overly helpful to visitors. And if the visitor was a scientist—well, what could be worse? Shroeder was a pistol-packing derring-do agent of the old school, weaned in Berlin, hardened in Saigon. He was finishing a three-year tour at the Moscow station and would return to the States in a few weeks. Embassy rumor said he was using his diplomatic status to take half of Moscow back with him—czarist antiques, furs, icons. If you need help, Hammond had been told, don't expect Shroeder to do more than go through the motions. You're on your own.

Hammond was made to cool his heels for thirty minutes on a brown leather chair next to a sign informing him THIS AREA UNSAFE FOR SENSITIVE CONVERSATIONS. Well, he knew that. Shroeder finally appeared without apologies. He ushered Hammond not to his own office but to the less secure conference room.

"I had the map brought down here," Shroeder said pointedly, making it clear he did not want Hammond on the secure upper floors. Shroeder, short and wiry as advertised, had a small, round face that was lightly bearded, even in places where hair should not have grown. A monkey's face.

A mosaic of enhanced satellite photographs, the map replaced official Soviet versions, which were intentionally misleading. Shroeder had Frank with him. Pointing out the route they were to follow, Shroeder said coolly to Frank, "If you have companions, don't make the stop."

Hammond didn't know if Frank was aware of the loss of Cox, who was, after all, an illegal with no connection to the station. But he was certain Shroeder knew, and suspected that Shroeder, at this moment, was thinking of Cox. His flat, emotionless tone was chilling. Hammond had written a study of Soviet psychotronic capabilities, had seen the relatively naive U.S. experiments, and he had seen Cox. All in all, he'd have preferred to be back in New York with a private practice in neurology.

After about ten minutes, Frank reached around a large cardboard carton filling the Volga's front seat and withdrew a notebook from the glove compartment. As he wrote in it he said, "We have a couple of SD Zhigulis in our wake."

The KGB's Seventh Directorate, in charge of surveillance, favored gray Zhigulis, small, ubiquitous cars mass-produced since 1970. Equipped with powerful Chaika engines and ballasted rear ends, the SD Zhigulis could outperform all other vehicles in Moscow.

"How do you know they're KGB?" Hammond asked.

"They have windshield wipers." Frank caught Hammond's eye in the rearview mirror. "Most drivers keep the wipers inside the car and stop to put them on when it rains. Otherwise they get stolen. I guess the KGB has all the wipers they need."

For another fifty minutes they weaved through traffic, speeded up, slowed down, lost the Zhigulis, then made a left off the ring road onto Leninski Prospekt and began a series of turns from street to street that placed them finally in a complex of drab, dirty-yellow, six-story apartment houses.

The smell was the same Hammond had encountered everywhere since stepping off the plane. Some said it came from improperly refined motor fuel, some from cheap heating oil, or cheap cooking oil or cheap bath soap or cheap perfume. When he asked Frank what the odor was, Frank said, "Tears."

They parked across the street from an elementary school. Children, bundled against the cold, played in the front yard. There were few cars. No gray Zhigulis. When the street was empty, Frank made a U-turn, drove a block, and parked again. For an hour they drove, turned, parked, waited.

"Here," Frank said during one of their stops, and reached into the backseat with a pack of Marlboros.

"I don't smoke. Thanks anyway."

"Take them. You need a ride in a hurry, wave them at the cars. Anyone'll stop for a pack of American cigarettes."

"How long have you been in Moscow, Frank?"

"Long enough."

When Frank was satisfied that they were not followed, he made his way across the Moscow River to the city's east side, avoiding the ring road. The route was complex, and Hammond began to think maybe Frank really knew what he was doing.

"It's the second week," Frank said, repeating what had already been explained as they stood in front of the CIA map, "so we're on the alternate plan. We're a little early."

During the past two weeks, Marchenko would have kept to a recontact plan routinely agreed upon should anything happen to Cox, his sole contact with the Americans.

Frank drove around the block, checking his watch. Then he placed a copy of *Pravda*, folded into a triangle, on the dashboard by the passenger seat, made a left turn, and approached two men and a woman standing at a bus stop. Frank halted the car four yards from the stop.

A heavyset man in a thick sheepskin overcoat and fur hat, identifiable by a green book carried in his left hand, moved toward the car. He opened the front door, exchanged a few words in Russian with Frank, closed the door, and slid into the backseat next to Hammond. Anyone watching would have thought the Volga's driver was following the Moscow custom of picking up a paying passenger, who, because of the seat-filling cardboard carton, had found himself obliged to take the backseat, normally considered a violation of etiquette.

Two minutes later, with Hammond and Andrei Marchenko safely out of sight in the tinted-window security of the Volga, they entered a narrow street and turned into the deserted, rubble-strewn back courtyard of a half-demolished building. Frank pulled a pair of magnetized license plates from beneath the driver's seat, emerged from the car, and in twenty seconds had placed them over the original plates and returned to the driver's seat.

"Hammond," Marchenko said, a warm Russian smile displaying the gold molar Hammond had noticed when they met in the cabana in Monte Carlo. "I had wondered if they might send you. What happened to George?"

Hammond suspected that Marchenko knew very well what had happened to Cox, might even have had a hand in it. The question meant they were going to have to play games.

"Tell me about Darya," Hammond said.

The sharp awareness Marchenko had displayed in the Monte Carlo cabana was even more pronounced now. "Were you in love with her?" he asked.

Hammond was stunned. "Why do you ask that?"

"I saw the two of you in Monte Carlo. She has many charms."

"Forget that, Andrei."

Marchenko settled into the seat. His thick chest heaved with a deep sigh. "Well, she's back."

"I think I sort of knew that." Hammond grinned, hoping to remove any offense while leaving the suggestion that they abandon attempts at unnecessary deception.

"I mean at Serbenov." He looked at Hammond, his dark eyes teasing. "Did you know that?"

"I assumed it." In fact, Cox had told him. "What's she doing there?"

"Same as usual, I suppose."

Hammond was silent.

"Mostly the stuff you people call Black." He seemed amused at the distinction. To Soviet researchers it was all Black.

Hammond thought he might come to like Marchenko. The Russian had once said he wanted to defect, and whether or not the request was genuine, he had provided intelligence to Cox. Also, he held a job similar to Hammond's. Both men reported to high officials—Marchenko to the highest—and both were essentially scientists. Scientist first, spy second? That was true of Hammond. He wondered what Marchenko's priorities were. He had the feeling that Marchenko too felt a certain closeness. In another world, they might have been colleagues, perhaps friends.

"And Spectrum?" Hammond asked, trying to sound as if that were not the most crucial thing in his life. Reestablishing contact with Marchenko had been important, and finding Darya was important, but neither of those was worth a thing to MAG unless they led to Spectrum.

"What's Spectrum?" Marchenko said, still playful.

Two cars passed in the street and Frank reached to the glove compartment for his notebook. More Zhigulis?

"Andrei," Hammond said with a sincerity he could not have faked had he wanted to, "we only have a few minutes here. Let's not waste them. This is serious."

The suggestion that he might not be serious produced

an immediate change in Marchenko. "Cox was relentless about Spectrum," he said solemnly. "He begged me and begged me. He didn't believe my ignorance. I know almost nothing about Spectrum."

"Mrs. Leonov?" The healer who had aroused interest among Spectrum researchers.

"Yes, I told George about her. I think Spectrum tried to recruit her but she refused. They're probably afraid to make a forceful approach because psychic abilities tend to disappear in the face of coercion. I expect they're a bit puzzled about how to proceed. Would you like to meet her?"

Hammond was startled. "Yes."

"I thought you might." Marchenko grinned, pleased with himself, and dug into his jacket. He handed over a small sheet of notepaper. "The address is hers, the phone number is for the pastor of her church. It's an illegal church, so he may not still be at that number."

Hammond stuffed the paper in a pocket, tried to hide his delight, and immediately changed the subject. "You report directly to Andropov, Andrei. So how can you not know about Spectrum?"

"Andropov is not a scientist. He has only a layman's knowledge of what Spectrum is supposed to do. And anyway, I can't just walk in and say, 'Dear Yuri, tell me about Spectrum.' "

"What about Darya?"

"Yes, what about Darya? Darya controls Spectrum, but Darya speaks to no one, believe me. I don't know how cooperative she was in the States, but I can tell you that here she is as jealous with Spectrum as a bear with its cubs. What did she tell you in the States?"

It was not Hammond's job to answer questions. "And her researchers?"

Marchenko snorted. "A KGB officer approached one of her people—just approached him, there is no evidence the researcher even said a word. And do you know what happened to him? He's in Ukhta, doing reproduction studies on the local rodent population."

"What does she say when you talk to her?"

"I don't talk to her. Not since she returned. She won't meet me."

"Why?"

Marchenko shifted in the seat, taking a moment. "I am too close to Andropov. She was close to him too when she first began, when Andropov was KGB chief and she needed him for her research. They adored each other. Andropov wanted psychotronics, and she was the one who could give it to him. She was sure that when Brezhnev died one of his friends—Romanov, Grishin, maybe Chernenko—would replace him, and Andropov would continue as KGB chief. So she courted the Brezhnevites, all his cronies."

He reached inside his jacket, lit a cigar, and offered Hammond one. "Montecristo. You can't get those in the States."

"Thanks anyway. I don't smoke." He hadn't had a cigar since the one Darya lit for him in Monte Carlo.

"She is very clever," Marchenko said, drawing on the cigar. "She knows what people want and she knows how to give it to them. She used to be at all Galina's parties. I'm sure she was with Galina and her clown in the diamond smuggling and who knows what else. Brezhnev and his friends had great power, they owned the country.

What did she do for them? She has many capabilities, as you found out in Monte Carlo. What a shock when Brezhnev died and Andropov took over and began attacking the old Brezhnevites. Today she is like this"—he held up crossed fingers—"with the Brezhnevites. And Andropov is after them. She is afraid his corruption investigators will get to her."

He cracked his window to let the cigar smoke out.

"If she is no longer loyal to Andropov," Hammond asked, "why does he keep her around?"

"Because now she is indispensable to the psychotronic research, and particularly to Spectrum, which interests you so much. No one can stop her, because if they stop her the research stops. She has compartmentalized everything so no one knows more than the little piece they work on. She is the only one who can put all the pieces together."

For a moment Marchenko gazed out the window at the rubble. "Nevertheless she is worried, I'm sure. At what point will Andropov say the hell with the research, and go after her? If he feels his life's threatened—he does not love Spectrum more than his life. His investigations have everyone terrified. More people are going to be shot. Darya does not want to lose her work, her money—and certainly not her life."

They were silent, a cold winter breeze blowing at the windows.

"Would Darya try to kill Andropov?" Hammond asked.

"Possibly. Especially if her Brezhnevite friends encourage her. What if they threatened to give evidence against her, tell about the smuggling and currency dealings and all the rest she must have been involved in?"

"Could she kill him, if she wanted to?"

"Perhaps. She is a frightening person, Dr. Hammond. She gets a hold over people. When you think of the things she has done—she has killed animals just by looking at them, did you know that? She is someone you don't want to offend too deeply."

"Are you afraid of her?"

"Oh, yes. Certainly. A man with a gun, you know what he can do. You can train to deal with him. But Darya— no one knows what she can do."

Superstitious Russians, thought Hammond. Marchenko was letting fear get the better of his education. "Was she involved in the paranormal operations against Carter and Brezhnev?" She had told MAG she was.

"Involved? She designed them. They were hers. And she has others against Reagan. Her work at Serbenov— they're doing things there you wouldn't want to believe. I haven't seen it, but I've heard rumors, and I know Darya."

"What if I wanted to talk to her?"

"Never." Marchenko hesitated. His cigar was out. In Moscow, even the cigars didn't work. "Well . . . maybe . . . if she thought there was something she could get from you. Who knows what Darya would do? But listen to me, Jack. If Darya agrees to see you, be careful. It will not be just because she feels like having a chat, renewing old times. Remember your friend George Cox."

"What about George Cox? You gave me the impression you didn't know what happened to him."

"Only rumors. Rumors are very important in Moscow. You have your newspapers, we have rumors."

"What were the rumors?"

"That he died. Strangely."

"Did Darya have something to do with it?"

"If you know the research she has done, you suspect her of everything."

"Tell me."

"Not now. I don't want you to think I'm credulous, or crazy. We are scientists, and what she does does not always look like science."

"What's it look like?"

He raised the dead cigar to the crack at the top of the window, looked at Hammond, then pushed the cigar out. "Black." He rolled the window closed.

If what Marchenko said was true, Darya not only knew about Spectrum, she was Spectrum. Hammond did not consider himself a brave man. He wished he knew exactly how George Cox had died.

Hammond managed a smile and looked at Marchenko. Their eyes met and locked.

"I wish I could help you," Marchenko said.

Hammond wanted to believe that. He needed a friend.

11

A *LARGE BIRD—COULD IT* have been a hawk?—broke from a tight circle above the sprawling wooden dacha and soared down the line of snow-covered pines and birch trees to the edge of the Moscow River deep in the valley below.

"I'm dying," Andropov said, watching the glint of sunlight off the water, hoping for another glimpse of the bird.

"We're all dying." It was said with an attempt at light-heartedness, but Mikhail Gorbachev knew what his boss was talking about. Rumors about Andropov's health had become harder and harder to contain since his failure to appear at festivities commemorating the October

Revolution. In the keynote address, Grigori Romanov, whose daughter's wedding party had decimated Catherine the Great's dinner service, had boldly refrained from saying anything complimentary about Andropov. Those who read Andropov's absence as a sign of ill health—he had not been seen publicly since August—picked Romanov and Gorbachev as the most likely successors.

It was now the first week of December, and Andropov's doctor was making no promises. His diabetes was as bad as ever, he had a pacemaker in his chest, and his right kidney had been removed. Local and regional party re-elections were underway, and in March the new Council of Ministers of the USSR would be chosen at the freshly elected Supreme Soviet. After that, Andropov's power to designate his successor would virtually be assured.

"If I can stay alive until March," Andropov said, tightening the fur robe that wrapped him into the aluminum deck chair on the dacha's second-floor balcony, "you will be all right. Otherwise, who knows? Romanov maybe. Even Chernenko might—"

"I don't think—" Gorbachev began to interrupt, but Andropov moved impatiently in his chair and the sentence was never finished.

Andropov had not invited his protégé to the Usovo dacha for commiseration. He did not want sympathy. He was aware that he had faults, but self-delusion was not among them. He knew exactly what he was and what others thought of him. People said he was a confusion of contradictions—aggressive but shy, treacherous but tender, stubborn but resilient, uneducated but well read. He was stoic as a monk, they said, secretive, almost paranoid. As ambassador to Hungary he had coldly betrayed the prime minister, his old friend Imre Nagy, into the hands of executioners. As KGB chief, he had institutionalized the torture of Christians. Yet, he wrote love poems to his wife. How confused everyone was. They feared him because they did not understand him. Well—maybe Gorbachev.

"What were you saying?" Andropov asked.

"Nothing. It's a beautiful valley."

He did not have long to live. If his policies were to continue, if he was to put an end to the corruption of men like Brezhnev, he would have to guarantee Gorbachev's succession. That meant the speedy appropriation of power. It meant major changes in internal policy, a purification of Party bureaucracy, radical alterations in the character of the Supreme Soviet. Could he accomplish this before his death? Could he pass to Gorbachev the vision of a new Soviet Union?

Andropov, drained by the effort of conversation, laid his head back against the fur and fixed his eyes on the sky. He had to stay alive. At least until March. If he did not, the criminals would slither back to power. Everything would be lost. Russia might be lost. A cold breeze blew up from the valley. The hawk was back, high above the dacha, spiraling lazily in the sunlight.

12

THE BROWN MARBLE SCULP-
tures in the Revolution Square metro station were as cold
and lifeless as the people. A train arrived, sad-faced trav-
elers shuffled on and off, the train departed. No one spoke,
no one hurried. The ornate station, colorless people, and
spotless trains made Hammond long for graffiti, transit
cops, unruly teenagers. The Lexington Avenue IRT had
its faults, but at least it was alive. This place was a tomb.

He followed instructions. Enter the station at seven A.M.,
wait for an orange line train, walk to the last car, count
three stops, get off, stand right there, don't move. And
sure enough, as promised, within three minutes he was

approached by a man in a thigh-length sheepskin jacket. The man stood next to Hammond for a moment, then strolled away. Hammond followed. Whatever you do, he had been told, do not speak English.

Looking around, Hammond spotted two sullen-faced women ten yards behind him. Were they KGB? Don't be paranoid, Hammond thought, the KGB can't follow everyone. But would they follow a doctor assigned to the American embassy, even if they didn't know he was a spy? You bet.

Hammond stayed behind the man in the sheepskin jacket up an escalator and through the station to another train. The women disappeared. Hammond scrutinized the eight other people in the car.

His escort again changed trains. After several stops, they disembarked and left the station. The man in the jacket got on a bus, Hammond close on his heels. Hammond recognized none of the other passengers. Still, a serious surveillance would involve any number of frequently replaced followers.

After twenty minutes, Hammond tailed the jacket off that bus and onto another. Fifteen minutes later they were in the country. The road narrowed to two lanes. Birch forests rose from the snow, stark white fields sparkled in the sun, brightly painted log houses with metal roofs and red-brick chimneys sent up columns of gray smoke. After another half hour the bus stopped near a cluster of birch trees, and Hammond and his guide stepped out. The road was deserted in both directions. The bus pulled away, and they were left in the empty silence of the country.

A short walk ahead on the other side of the road a dilapidated log farmhouse stood amid piles of old lumber.

In the front yard hens pecked at patches of brown earth where the snow had been cleared. Hammond heard faint singing, muffled by the fields of snow.

As they approached the house, the singing grew louder. Inside, Hammond was introduced to the owner, a stooped, white-haired woman named Anna. In the main room, fifty people huddled in the cold on wood planks supported by low stools and crates. Another twenty stood along the log walls and overflowed into a kitchen. Young children, cross-legged on the floor, filled the front of the room at the feet of the pastor who had given Hammond the instructions that had brought him here. Fearing rejection if he approached Mrs. Leonov directly, Hammond had called the number Marchenko gave him for her pastor, who had promised to introduce them at this meeting.

The hymn ended and the pastor gestured to Hammond to come forward and sit on one of four chairs at the front. The seat beside him was already occupied by a stout middle-aged woman in a dark brown dress. She clutched a Bible, and she had one of the most radiant, kindly faces Hammond had ever seen. The pastor whispered to her, nodded at Hammond, and she turned with a smile that seemed to warm the entire room. Hammond smiled back. So this was the widow Leonov.

There were two more hymns, a sermon, prayers, another hymn. These were the happiest Russians—the only happy Russians—Hammond had seen since his arrival in Moscow. Hands raised, they sang with a jubilation that contradicted the cold, the cramped room, and the risk of prison.

After an hour, none of the standees had moved, none of the children had cried. Then Hammond sensed that something had gone amiss. There was movement near the front door, people glanced anxiously toward the windows, and the pastor began to give calm but urgent instructions to those around him.

The singing stopped. A commotion erupted at the door. Hammond followed worshipers through the kitchen into the backyard. Blue-uniformed militia officers appeared at the side of the house. If they found him here he would be arrested, interrogated, expelled, his mission in ruins. A young woman with cropped blond hair hurried past him, looked back fearfully at the militia officers, and saw Hammond. She returned, grabbed his hand, and led him on the run to the back of the house and into a tiny windowless shack. She yanked the door closed.

Long before his eyes adjusted to the dark, his nose told him they were in a privy. Despite the cold and their heavy clothes, he could sense the warmth of the woman close beside him. Breathing heavily, she held her finger to her mouth, demanding silence. Her hand trembled, and not from the cold. She looked scared to death.

The singing resumed and Hammond heard men shouting. The music stopped abruptly. More shouting.

"What's—" Hammond began. The stench was unendurable.

"Shhh!" She had the eyes of a drill sergeant.

Out on the road, vehicles arrived, doors slammed.

Now Hammond could see a rectangle of white porcelain on the floor, a large open hole, a role of paper tied to the wooden wall with string. A small triangular ventilation hole was a couple of inches above his head. He stood on tiptoes, put his nose to the hole for a breath of fresh air, then peered out.

The pastor was on his knees in the snow at the back of the house, his hands clasped, eyes closed, face raised to the sky. A blue-shirted militia officer stood over him shouting. The pastor did not speak or open his eyes. The officer put his boot to the pastor's shoulder and kicked him into the snow. Then he reached down, grabbed the pastor under one arm, and dragged him through the snow and slush to the front of the house. The other officers had disappeared. Hammond abandoned the peephole.

He shifted one foot from the wood floor to the damp, slippery porcelain surrounding the toilet hole, hoping to give the girl more room. Despite the odor and cramped space, she was managing to look as dignified as he supposed it was possible for a woman to look while sharing a privy with a man.

The need for silence added to the awkwardness. She gazed at the wall in front of her, anxious not to meet his eyes. He wanted to thank her for hiding him. His foot slipped on the porcelain and she grabbed his arm. He nodded his thanks. She was skinny, tomboyish, scruffily dressed, one of those French urchins who lead downed fliers to safety in World War II films.

After twenty minutes he heard vehicles driving away. Someone knocked on the door. The girl opened it and spoke with a teenage boy. Then to Hammond she said in English, "They've gone."

They returned to the front of the house. Women and children, those who had not been found important enough to be taken, talked excitedly and wept. The young woman said to Hammond, "Their bus and cars were filled, they may be back. We had better hurry."

She led him to the deserted road.

"Is there a bus soon?" Hammond asked.

"No bus," the girl said, "but we will get a ride."

Hammond was wondering about her confidence when a black Chaika limousine appeared out of nowhere. The woman made an up-and-down motion with her hand. The Chaika stopped, the woman exchanged words with the driver and gestured to Hammond to climb in the backseat ahead of her.

"He has taken his boss to his dacha and is returning to Moscow," she said as the car pulled away. "He doesn't want to be paid. He says he is happy to have the company."

"Lucky for us," Hammond said. In the closeness of the car she smelled of soap—strong, industrial, Soviet soap.

She smiled at him with large ingenuous eyes that had lost their drill-sergeant toughness. Her short hair reminded him of recently bald chemotherapy patients. Her skin was as pale as the snow covering the countryside, and her slender face had not yet begun to show the bread-and-potatoes chubbiness of most Muscovite women. The sleeves of her man-sized maroon ski jacket—had it belonged to her boyfriend?—came over her hands. Hammond guessed she was twenty.

"Not lucky," she said. "Blessed."

Hammond put out his hand. "Thanks for the rescue. I'd have had trouble explaining. My name's Jack Hammond."

She surprised him with the enthusiasm of her grip. "I am called Valentina Leonov."

Hammond did not conceal his surprise. "I thought the woman in the brown dress was . . ."

"That is the pastor's wife. She is very nice."

"But I was told . . . Mrs. Leonov."

"Yes, that's me."

"How old are you?"

"Twenty-three."

"Your husband . . ."

"He was at Perm thirty-six."

She seemed to find no further explanation necessary. It was not unusual for religious leaders to die young in the Soviet Union, particularly those imprisoned in the Perm camps.

"I'm sorry," he said.

She smiled, as if to ask if he had more questions. He had a million.

"What happened, just now at the house?"

"We move around, but sooner or later the KGB finds out where we are worshiping, and then the militia comes and tells us we are an unregistered church and we must stop praying. We do not stop, so—well, you saw. Technically we are the concern of the Committee of Religious Affairs, but they work for the KGB and the KGB tells the militia what to do."

"What happens now?"

She held his gaze for a length of time that would have seemed flirtatious had not everything else about her been so businesslike. "They will take everyone to the militia station. They will ask the leaders where we print our Bibles and hymnals. The KGB wants the presses. And they want to know where our money comes from. The leaders will probably be sentenced to three years, some others perhaps for less, some maybe just fifteen days."

Hammond thought of the pastor who had promised to

introduce him to Valentina. He had kept that promise.
"And the pastor is gone for three years?"

"This will be his third sentence. He is not unhappy. It
is a privilege to be persecuted."

"Has he told you—" He remembered the Chaika's
driver and changed the subject. "You speak very good
English."

"I am an interpreter. I studied English at Moscow University, but now I have lost my job. Now I work at GUM,
the department store." She laughed, making fun of herself.
"I sew hats, the fur hats the tourists buy."

They had followed the Moscow-Minsk highway to Kutuzovsky Prospekt, headed for the ring road.

"I have something I would like to talk to you about."
He nodded toward the driver.

She made a writing motion with her hand, and he
reached for his pen and notebook. She wrote an address.

He wrote his own address and telephone number, tore
off the page, and handed it to her. He touched her hand.
Her pale cheeks went crimson.

She told the driver to let him out at a taxi rank near
the Kievskaya metro station. As he watched the Chaika
disappear toward the Moscow River he saw her blond
head lean forward to speak to the driver. Hammond
wasn't absolutely certain he knew what was going on.
That Chaika really had just popped up out of nowhere.

When the car pulled away, Valentina's face was still
burning. It had been like meeting a man from another
planet. His confidence wasn't foolish or naive, and the
familiarity was candor, not aggression. His clothes were

as fresh as if he'd just put them on. His skin looked scrubbed with a brush. He was natural and uncomplicated, so . . . healthy.

She unzipped the ski jacket. She hadn't had feelings like this since the last time she saw her husband. The Chaika stopped, and as she crossed the street, tears froze on her cheeks.

13

*F*ROM COX'S FIFTH-FLOOR
living room window, Hammond could see the snow-covered streets connecting the building to others in the housing complex. As he stood at the window buttoning his
shirt the Monday morning after meeting Valentina, he
spotted a black-bearded man in a beige, thickly lined,
canvas, knee-length coat loitering in the entranceway of
an apartment house across the street. Hammond went into
the bedroom, finished dressing, and returned to the window for another look. The man was still there.

Hammond watched for ten minutes. The man never

moved, except to withdraw farther into the entranceway when anyone emerged from Cox's building.

"Maybe I'll practice my Russian," Hammond said aloud as he donned his overcoat and prepared to leave for the embassy.

Crossing the street, he could not see the man. He was almost to the building entrance when a hand came down heavily from behind on his right shoulder. He turned, caught a glimpse of a fur collar, and was hurled sideways by a blow to his left kidney. He collapsed, pain tearing at his back. A kick caught him in the chest, knocking the wind from his lungs. Unable to breath, he sprawled face-down in the snow.

A face, the lower half covered by the upturned fur collar of a brown leather coat, appeared beside him. From behind the fur, Hammond heard, "You're a doctor. So be a doctor." The English was almost perfect, with hardly a trace of accent.

The man waited, black eyes watching Hammond. Then he repeated it. "You're a doctor. So be a doctor."

Evidently satisfied that Hammond had understood what he said, the man rose, climbed into the passenger seat of a black Volga, and disappeared.

Hammond waited until he had his breath back. He put a hand to his kidney and walked half doubled over back to the apartment. "So be a doctor." Don't be a spook. Forget Spectrum. Yeah, sure. Where was that guy when I took the job with MAG?

When he looked out the living room window, the bearded man in the beige canvas jacket was still there, lurking in the entranceway.

* * *

Finding Darya was not so easy as finding Marchenko. A CIA watcher team, alerted that she was on her way back from the States, had spotted her coming off Pan Am 1072 at Sheremetyevo, saw her met by four KGB officers, then lost her before her Zil limousine hit the ring road. They had tried to surveil Serbenov, but got chased. Where she lived no one knew. It wasn't like Washington, where the KGB, using subverted police contacts, could locate virtually anyone through automobile, telephone, and utility records.

Hammond spent Monday and Tuesday recovering from the kidney punch and trying to find Darya. Tuesday night he fixed himself dinner in Cox's apartment, then decided to make a more thorough search. It was eleven o'clock and he was on his knees in the living room, unscrewing the bottom of Cox's wooden desk, when the apartment's musty odor grew suddenly sweet. He turned to see Darya in the doorway.

"Looking for something?" she said.

He almost dropped the screwdriver. She was wrapped in a floor-length mink coat, and her model's face, the smooth cheeks flushed with the cold, radiated good humor.

"I've just found it," he said, getting slowly to his feet. He was certain he had locked the door.

She dumped the coat on a chair and dropped onto the red brocade sofa as if she owned the apartment. "I thought I'd find you here." She crossed her legs, and even through the beige trousers and white silk blouse Hammond could sense the warmth and softness of that body. She glanced around. "I could never understand why George lived in this dump. I offered many times to get him something nicer. May I have a drink?"

"Help yourself." After months of worry and uncertainty, he could hardly believe she was here.

Darya withdrew a bottle of Johnnie Walker Black from a glass cupboard next to the television set and strolled into the kitchen to get ice. "Join me?"

"You seem to know your way around."

"George and I spent a lot of time together. That was his job, right?"

"Yours too?" There was something different about her, an almost proprietary confidence. She was in her own country now, on her own turf, no longer dependent on the trust and assistance of Americans.

"It's nice," she said, back on the sofa, "when business and pleasure are so compatible."

Hammond took his drink and sat sideways on the sofa facing her. She smiled, as delightfully as if this were Washington and they had just returned from the theater. She raised her glass. "To old times?"

"To the future," he said, with an irony as pointed as he could make it.

"Jack, please—what is it they say?—lighten up. Stop being so American and so professional."

All the questions he had longed to ask—why did she leave, why didn't she ask for his help, how much had she cared for him—refused to come to his lips. He felt like a high school kid who'd mistaken a good-night kiss for love. "How are things at Serbenov?"

She was, despite everything he knew or suspected, even more seductive than before. He could not blame Cox for what had happened.

"The usual." She looked at the dismantled desk. "Find anything?"

"Corn chips and peanut butter."

She laughed and put her drink down. "Jack, I've missed you. I want to explain." She reached a hand toward him, those long delicate fingers, covered with diamonds.

"So explain."

Her hand fell to the back of the sofa. "I had to come home. You'd have done the same thing."

She was seductive but brittle—no longer the warm, confiding Darya beside him on the bed of a George-town apartment. He had loved her then. Whether he still loved her he didn't know. "Then we are not go-ing to have tiresome claims that your defection was genuine."

"No, darling, it was not genuine, not entirely anyway. But my love for you, that was genuine, and still is."

Was it, really? "And your love for Cox?"

"I did not love Cox. I never told him I did. What do you know about that?"

"I know he's dead."

"Everyone dies."

Hammond went to the kitchen for more ice, and when he came back he caught Darya in a moment of unguarded repose. Her eyes were fixed on the Brezhnev video cassette on top of the television set, and her face was as he had never seen it before—lined and harsh, the muscles stiff-ened around the cheekbones, the red lips tightly drawn, cruel.

Then she heard him move, and the charm came back. She rose. "Oh, so that's where it is."

Hammond beat her to it. He had the cassette in his

hand. She pressed against him. "It's mine, darling. I loaned it to George. We used to watch films here."

"I think I'd better keep it. Custody of evidence. The militia might want it when they find out what happened to the apartment's occupant."

She stepped back.

"I'm afraid you're too late, Darya. Why didn't you come earlier? Recover your things."

"It's not important," she said, "the tip of an iceberg. Did you watch it? I don't remember which one it was actually. We watched a lot."

Hammond tried not to let his expression change. "Why are you here?" he asked.

"Looking for you."

"Couldn't live without me?"

"I want to make you an offer."

She leaned against him, and he tried not to meet her eyes. Her gaze, her scent, her presence, made it impossible not to think about what it had been like to make love to her.

He returned to the sofa, struggling to replace thoughts of love with a recollection of the scene he had watched four days earlier on the television set.

"Running away?" she said, following him to the sofa.

"Damned right."

"Don't you want to hear the offer?" They were sitting side by side, facing each other.

"I'm listening."

"I told you my last defection was not genuine."

"Your *last* defection? I don't believe this."

"Do you want to hear or not?"

"Go ahead."

"Things are becoming a little unpleasant for friends of our late leader. Andropov's investigations are causing problems. I may find myself wanting to leave the country suddenly, and if I do I will need a friend."

"Good old Jack Hammond, friend in need. Tell me something, Darya. Your problems with Andropov's corruption investigators—anything to do with Cox?"

"With Cox?" A cocker spaniel could not have looked more innocent.

"I heard you had business dealings. Something about a Merrill Lynch account?"

She studied his eyes, trying to read the depth of his knowledge. "He had some theories we wanted to test outside the laboratory."

"Psychic influence on dissipative structures?"

She brightened. "How did you know?"

"Lucky guess. I must be psychic. How'd it work?"

"Very well, actually." She held out a hand, displaying a diamond-ringed finger.

"Somewhere in your life there's a numbered bank account, am I right?"

"Several. I've been very fortunate."

"Too fortunate, judging from your popularity with the corruption folks. Sure it was all security transactions? Not just a little something else? Smuggling? Blackmail?"

"What makes you think—"

"There's a closet full of Dom Pérignon and foie gras."

"Cox had expensive tastes."

"Tell it to Chebrikov." The KGB chief.

She produced a pack of Winstons and a gold Dunhill.

"Why'd you come over last time, Darya?"

"I thought I could have it both ways." She lighted

a cigarette. "I wanted to live and work in the West, and I thought if I didn't like it I could always redefect, buy my way back with what I had learned from you Americans."

"And you decided you didn't like it."

"No, Jack, I did not like it. Frankly, your approach is all wrong. Your so-called White work, trying to find ways to protect computers, installations, personnel, going for the passive uses. But psychotronics is not a defensive weapon, Jack. We're talking about war. I learned almost nothing in the States. You're too far behind for it to be interesting to me. And there was no way you were going to let me do everything I wanted to do."

"We work on offensive psychotronics too, Darya, and you know it. We're just not that keen on opening our labs to a bunch of voodoo priests and Satan worshipers."

She shrugged. "Don't make fun of it, Jack. A lot of people believe in God, and if God exists, why not Satan?"

He was silent.

"Someday, Jack, I'd like to show you what we've accomplished at Serbenov."

"Accomplished? Is that the right word?"

"Jack, I would like to show it to you. Would you like to see it?"

"Is that your offer?"

"I want your promise you'll help me get out when I have to."

"Darya, if you ever want to mention the word 'defection' again to the United States, you're going to have to prove your bona fides before we'll even listen."

"What would interest you, Jack?"

"Spectrum."

"What if I offered to show you our work with universal Fourier components?"

Fourier components were part of a method for reducing the complexity of waveforms. Universal Fourier components, dealing with extraordinarily complex frequency interference patterns throughout space and time, had a critical relevance to paranormal research. On their project tour, Darya had suggested that Fourier components might have something to do with Spectrum.

"Are you talking about Spectrum?" Hammond asked.

"Perhaps."

"For that," Hammond said with a smile, "I might even go back to bed with you."

"That's what Cox said."

She reached into an alligator handbag with a Hermès gold-logo clasp and came out with a small notepad. She wrote a number on it, tore off the sheet, and handed it to him.

"My phone number. Call and we'll have dinner." Then she said, "May I use the bathroom?"

He nodded, reading the number.

Ten minutes later she had not returned. He went to the bathroom and knocked on the door. There was no answer.

"Darya?"

No answer.

He turned the knob and stuck his head in. The room was empty. He walked through the apartment. Empty.

He stood at the front door, staring at the bolt. The door was locked from the inside. How did she get out? How had she got in? Darya had demonstrated bizarre skills in the past—her lovemaking notable among them—but nothing truly otherworldly. He knew that quantum theory permitted translocation. A particle could be one place one moment and somewhere else the next, without motion. The chance of this happening on the macro level was vanishingly small, but it was not zero. The theory allowed it.

First the seediness of the apartment itself, then the tape of Cox, now Darya's eerie arrival and departure—Hammond did not want to spend the night in that apartment. It was almost one in the morning. He had no friend to call: "May I sleep on your couch?" Moscow hotels did not accept walk-in guests.

He put on two sweaters, an overcoat, heavy boots, and left the apartment.

The neighborhood was deserted, cold, and lonely as the moon. No corner saloons with warmth and conversation. He walked half a mile through the icy gloom to a deserted metro station and found his way to the Intourist hotel on Gorki Street. The bars and restaurants were closed, the lobby empty. He walked down Gorki Street to Pushkin Square and sat on one of the white-slatted benches in the park. No one passed. How could the city be so dead? Where were the late-night workers, the bums, the lovers?

Hammond wondered what was going to become of Darya, Valentina Leonov, Marchenko. And himself. Was Darya's love still genuine, as she claimed? Did he still love her?

He continued to have the strange, disquieting feeling that he was watched. When he had been a captain in the Surgeon General's Medical Intelligence Office he prepared a secret report dealing with, among other things, the apport technique. "The apport technique," he had written, "is a form of astral projection in which the psychic subject transports his 'energy body' to a remote site, then transports it back. Lack of information on Soviet interest in the technique represents a major intelligence gap.''

Was that how Darya had entered and left Cox's apartment? Hammond had seen too many weird things to deny the possibility. He remembered a disturbing conversation he'd had with Burkholzer before coming to Moscow.

"You're strong, aren't you," Burkholzer had said.

"Strong?"

"Physically strong. Intellectually. Morally too."

Hammond had been too embarrassed to answer.

"But this isn't physical, Jack. It's supernatural."

Burkholzer's eyes had made it clear that he wasn't so sure about Hammond's strengths in that department. Hammond hadn't been sure either, and he still wasn't. Coping with the physical world was one thing, but the supernatural world was, as they said, a whole new ball game. Burkholzer's physical life was a shambles, but the supernatural world, even its evil side, he had well in hand. Hammond wasn't even sure that world existed. Bundled now in the cold Moscow darkness, Hammond felt something he had not felt since childhood. He felt unequipped.

He brooded on the bench until the sun came up, then returned to the apartment, showered, and caught a taxi to the embassy. What he needed was a quick trip back to the States.

14

*L*ATE THE NEXT AFTER-
noon, after thirteen hours of air travel, Hammond drove
to Vienna, Virginia, and entered the CIA's "clean bubble,"
in which Darya had briefed MAG. If Darya was really
capable of teleportation—and what else?—and if she was
serious about showing him the Spectrum research, Hammond wanted MAG to know now. He didn't want to be
like Cox, demand an urgent, last-minute meeting, and
end up dead.

Hammond had Steve Burkholzer with him, and together they hoped to demonstrate to MAG the importance
of Darya's apparent psychic ability and her offer to show

Hammond her work on Fourier components and possibly Spectrum.

Most MAG members were intelligence experts, not scientists, so Burkholzer came prepared. Hammond helped him lug a computer, oscilloscope, miniature television camera, and small leather suitcase into the plastic bubble. They put them on the conference table and waited for the other four men to take their seats. General Pfister, the crew-cut DIA chief, was uncharacteristically silent, perhaps not wanting to stir embarrassing memories of his encounter with Darya at the earlier MAG meeting.

When everyone was settled, MAG's chairman, the aging, bone-thin Ralph Whitmore of the NSA, nodded curtly to Hammond.

Hammond described how he had discovered Darya in Cox's apartment, and how she had vanished from the bathroom. "From what we know of her abilities, and of paranormal phenomena generally, we should consider the possibility of teleportation."

Alex Buford, the bow-tied White House representative, threw a teasing sidelong glance at General Pfister.

"Dr. Burkholzer," Hammond said, "has a briefing for us."

"Let's have it," Whitmore said.

Hammond saw Pfister and Buford exchange glances. They had little respect for each other's opinions, but on one point they agreed completely: Steve Burkholzer was a pain in the ass. He knew everything. You absolutely could not win an argument with him, and he was too politically naive to play dumb and surrender to rank. He was only around because Whitmore liked him. Whitmore, who had an engineering degree from the Naval Academy and had studied enough psychotronics to understand the basics, indulged and coddled geniuses like Burkholzer. If they had beggars in their bathtubs, overdrawn bank accounts, IRS agents at the door, so what? Burkholzer had been involved in psychic research longer than anyone else associated with MAG, and he had a deeper understanding of the relationship between science and the supernatural, of the point at which they touched and merged. He also had a unique ability to explain to laymen the arcane scientific underpinnings of psychotronics. That was enough for Whitmore. But not for Pfister and Buford. Hammond was afraid that the day Whitmore left MAG, Burkholzer would be gone too.

Burkholzer reached his good arm into the suitcase and removed a foot-high glass cylinder, which he placed before him on the conference table.

"This is really two glass cylinders, one inside the other," he told the men around him, "and filling the space between them is glycerine, a colorless, thick, viscous fluid, as you know."

He removed from his case a vial of what looked like green ink, and with an eyedropper introduced a drop into the glycerine.

"Now," he said, "we slowly revolve the outer cylinder."

As he did so, the drop of ink gradually stretched out into a green thread. The thread grew longer, thinner, and fainter until finally it had completely disappeared.

"The ink is now enfolded into the glycerine," Burkholzer said. "You can't see it anymore, but you know it's there. Exactly where is it? It's no longer in any single position. It's spread out, nowhere and everywhere."

Pfister, unable to sit still, was clearly ill at ease, as if expecting Darya to materialize with some new humiliation.

"I now have to ask you to consider extensive research, made here and abroad, suggesting that everything that exists today or ever existed or will ever exist is similarly enfolded in an invisible medium. We become aware of things only when they are unfolded out of the invisible medium into our reality."

He turned the cylinder in the opposite direction, and sure enough the thread of green ink began to reappear. The thread shortened and thickened and in a few minutes had re-formed into the drop of ink. It was as if a film of the enfolding process had been run backward.

"For all you know," Burkholzer went on, "I might have enfolded any number of ink images—perhaps of different colors and shapes—into the glycerine before I came here. If that were the case, and I turned the cylinder backward extremely rapidly, they would suddenly appear within the glycerine, as if by magic, out of nowhere. And that is precisely how we become aware of the reality of this world. Enfolding and unenfolding the ink drop in the glycerine is comparable to enfolding and unenfolding an object backward and forward through time and space. Everything exists everywhere at once, enfolded into an invisible timeless medium. A Soviet missile, for example, might not be visible now to us here in this room, but nevertheless a portion of it exists in this room, invisibly enfolded, just as the ink drop existed invisibly enfolded throughout the glycerine. Would it be possible, from what we know, to materialize that missile here in this room? Nice if we could, right?"

Pfister said, "You make all this up yourself?"

"No, sir," Burkholzer answered. "It's mostly the work of a physicist named David Bohm."

A blank look.

"Worked with Einstein," Burkholzer offered.

Pfister looked unimpressed. What the other men thought of all this was hard to tell.

Burkholzer pushed the cylinder aside and said, "When you throw a pebble into a pond, the ripples hit the edge of the pond, create more ripples that move back toward the center of the pond, and all these ripples run into each other and interfere. If you could suddenly freeze the pond, the points at which the ripples interfered with each other would provide information about the weight, shape, and movement of the pebble that caused them. In fact, you might have enough information actually to create a picture of the pebble."

Burkholzer now produced from the suitcase a three-inch square of paper and handed it around the table.

He said, "And that's exactly what this does."

As the men examined the paper, he said, "It's not a picture of a pebble, as you see, but of an apple. It's a hologram, and if you turn it to the light properly the apple jumps out at you and you see it in three dimensions. That hologram was made by capturing the interference patterns made by light waves from the apple colliding with light waves from another source—exactly as the pebble's waves collide with each other."

He reached out his hand and retrieved the hologram. "Now, here's the point." He took a pair of scissors from his case and cut the hologram in two. "One of these halves contains the top of the apple, the other the bottom of the apple, right?"

The men nodded.

"No, gentlemen. Wrong."

He handed back the two halves to be passed around again. As the men examined the pieces of paper, they shook their heads. Pfister held the halves longer than the others, turning them slowly in the light, obviously suspecting a trick.

"As you can see," Burkholzer said, "each half contains the entire apple. The images are a little blurry, but each is of the entire apple. The extraordinary thing is that every point in a hologram contains the entire picture. Just as every point in the glycerine contained ink. What this means is that to form a picture of that pebble we don't have to have all the points where the ripples interfered with each other in that moment of frozen time. We need only some of them. And to see that Soviet missile we don't have to have all the interference points, only some."

If the men had questions, they were saving them.

"Let's say that in addition to tossing a pebble into that pond," Burkholzer continued, "someone is also tossing in old shoes, automobile tires, and tin cans, all of them producing interfering waves, and the pond is a confused mess of waves. We're in an airplane over the pond, and we're looking down, searching for the waves of that single pebble, the waves that will allow us to make a picture of it. How do we identify in all those waves the one made by our pebble? Has anyone a picture in his wallet of his wife or a child?"

No one moved. These were not young sentimentalists who carried around wallet photos of the wife and kids.

"No one?"

Finally Buford tugged from his wallet a color photograph of his wife.

Burkholzer placed the picture on a small easel in front of the miniature television camera. He turned on the camera, the computer, and the oscilloscope. In a moment, wavy green lines appeared on the oscilloscope screen. Burkholzer touched computer keys and adjusted dials on the oscilloscope. The wavy lines twisted, looped, and shaped themselves into a green outline. The computer terminal displayed a series of numbers.

"Do you recognize that?" Burkholzer asked Buford.

"It's my wife," he said grinning. "She looks like the morning after."

The outline on the oscilloscope screen perfectly matched the outline of the woman's face in the photograph.

"What the computer did," Burkholzer explained, "was take the complex curved line that forms the outline of the face and break it down into simple sine and cosine waves, which are represented on the computer terminal in the form of numbers. Those waves, generated by the oscilloscope and added together, then produced on the screen the wave resembling the outline of the lady's face. In other words, highly complex wave patterns can be reduced to a collection of simple waves that can be represented numerically. Your wife's face can be represented by a series of numbers. Those numbers are called Fourier components, and the transformation of your wife's profile into those components is called a Fourier transform."

He paused, but no one spoke.

"So if we're in that airplane looking for wave interference patterns made by a pebble, all we have to do is break down all the interference patterns on the pond into numerical Fourier components and pull out the ones that have the numbers we know belong to pebbles and not to shoes or automobile tires or tin cans."

Again, there was no response.

"In precisely the same way, we could search the enfolding medium of space and time for the Fourier components of Soviet missiles. Or for that matter of anything we like—submarines, tanks, buildings, personnel. We could look backward through time. Everything that has ever existed in the universe has produced lasting interference patterns from the sea of radiation created at the instant God said 'Let there be light.' "

Ralph Whitmore raised a skeletal hand. "That's a dramatic theory. If it's true, how far are we from the technology to apply it?"

"At least three years. The Soviets' Spectrum program may be much closer, perhaps on the brink. Holography and Fourier transforms are simply a way of separating an image from its object—for example, the image of a missile from the missile itself—then viewing the image at a distance. If you think that's impossible, remember that your mind does it every time you remember something. You see the image in your mind, though the object itself is somewhere else, distant in time and space."

Whitmore took a folded sheet of paper from his breast pocket and scribbled a note. "One other thing," he said. "You keep talking about this invisible medium. What do you mean? What is it? Do you know?"

Burkholzer used his good hand to lift the bad one from his lap to the table. "Actually," he said, "there is probably more than one invisible medium. Each is itself enfolded within another, a regressing series of enfolding media. The ultimate medium, the one into which all others, into which everything, is enfolded is not a medium at all. It is—"

"A divine intelligence," Buford said, pleased with himself.

"No," Burkholzer said. "Not a divine intelligence, not a universal intelligence, not a force. It is a Person, the Creator, outside his creation, existing before his creation."

"The G-word," Pfister said sarcastically. "I knew you'd get God into this sooner or later."

"That offends you?" Burkholzer asked.

Whitmore, his cheekbones sharp as blades, said simply, "Please continue."

Burkholzer put his bad hand back in his lap. "This theory does not restrict us merely to observing objects like Soviet missiles. It is not just passive. It is active as well. What we have been saying is that the world is composed of interference patterns—of frequencies, in fact. And just as the frequency of music heard over a radio can be disrupted by a static-inducing electrical appliance in the next room, so the frequency of things in this world can be interfered with by disruptive static frequencies. In addition to seeing Soviet missiles or personnel, you could also immobilize them. If an apple or a pebble is characterized by—if it is the product of—certain frequencies, certain Fourier components, then it will be altered if those frequencies are altered. Now this brings me to the important part."

The men shifted in their chairs. Up to now it hadn't been important?

"And this goes to your question about how long it will

take to develop the technology to apply the theory. In a way, we already have the technology. What all this equipment does crudely"—he waved his hand at the TV set, computer, and oscilloscope—"the human brain does exquisitely. The brain itself constantly performs Fourier analysis on all the interference patterns in the enfolding medium. The universe itself is a hologram, and the brain is part of that hologram. The brain contains all of space and time just as each fragment of the hologram I showed you contains the entire picture of the apple. If you had full access to the content of your brain, you'd be able to see everything—missiles, submarines, your wife at home with the kids. Of course, if that ever happened, you'd probably go immediately insane—or have been insane in the first place. You'd be a real nut. You'd be a mystic."

Buford was shaking his head. "I'm sorry," he said to Burkholzer, "but this is too much. I can't accept this."

"Don't know why," said Pfister, ready for the moment to take any position that opposed the White House man. "Your guy over there won't go to the bathroom without Nancy checking the stars, and the CIA spends twenty mil a year trying to debrief dead agents."

"Not really."

"Read your pinks." Pink-bordered DIA intelligence abstracts were distributed weekly.

"I don't care," Buford insisted. "It's just incredible."

"Wouldn't believe it even if it was true, right?"

"Anyway," Burkholzer went on, "like it or not, that's how the paranormal works, gentlemen. That's how psychics know what's happening on the other side of the world, how they sense the future. And by interfering with the Fourier components of objects or living cells, it's how they heal, or induce illness, or influence the roll of dice —and it's how they could alter the alignment of molecules in a silicon computer chip, or affect the firing mechanism of a nuclear warhead. Their minds are tuned to the universal hologram, they have access to all the Fourier components. It may be how Darya Timoshek got out of Cox's apartment after talking to Dr. Hammond."

Whitmore said, "You think Darya Timoshek's brain is in contact with the supernatural?" There was no indication that he thought this nonsense.

Burkholzer said, "Yes, sir. With Satan."

"And you think a machine might be able to do the same thing?" Again, nothing to suggest that he found this absurd.

"The same thing and more. All human brains perform Fourier analysis, and some, like Darya's, can access the Fourier transforms to achieve paranormal feats. But those feats, performed by humans, are unreliable and unquantifiable. A device like Spectrum will be able to do what Darya does, and do it with precision and predictability. Did Darya really bilocate out of Cox's apartment? Possibly. Could a Spectrum-like device achieve the same thing? Definitely. When it comes to whatever magic tricks she may be playing, Spectrum's in another league. Do computers perform mathematical functions better than humans? We know they do. Could Spectrum do psychotronics better than Darya? Without doubt."

Whitmore thought that over. "And in addition to being able to see and predict, to perform those passive functions you mentioned, do you think Spectrum could also affect such things as the firing mechanisms of warheads?"

"I think Spectrum would be able to do that."

"And Spectrum might be able to alter, to disrupt . . . the health . . . the mental capacity . . . of individuals?"

Everyone in the room knew he was talking about President Reagan.

"Yes, sir."

"What's the earliest possible time the Soviets could have this capability?"

"The earliest, absolutely?"

"The worst case."

"Now."

Whitmore let out a deep sigh. Hammond felt sorry for the man, whose world had just grown vastly more complicated.

15

AFTER LISTENING TO HAM-
mond and Burkholzer, MAG decided that what they had
to say about Spectrum's threat to Western weapons and
leaders was too important not to share. So Whitmore
dragged them around for briefings with Pentagon nuclear
weapons experts, the DIA medical intelligence office, the
chief of the White House Secret Service, and Reagan's
personal physician.

Then Hammond returned to Moscow, and Whitmore
and Burkholzer took off for Europe, where intelligence-
sharing agreements compelled Whitmore at least to make
a show of briefing counterparts. Rome, Bonn, and

London—particularly MI5—turned out to have nothing but scorn for psychotronics, which suited Whitmore fine. He was under no obligation to shove Spectrum down their throats. The fewer people who knew about it the better.

In Paris, Whitmore had an added interest. What had SDECE, the Service de Documentation Extérieure et du Contre-Espionnage, been able to learn about George Cox's death?

At lunch in the secure basement dining room of a white-columned eighteenth-century mansion in St.-Cloud, just outside Paris, Whitmore put the question to Jean-Claude Chapelle, the stout, jowly, pin-striped chief of SDECE.

"Why all the interest in Cox?" Chapelle asked. The room was small, paneled in oak. Burkholzer was lunching with a French physicist at the Sorbonne.

"He was an old friend of mine," Whitmore said, not expecting to be believed.

"Well, as you know, the police found nothing. There was, however, something of interest to us, though in all likelihood it had nothing to do with Cox."

"What was it?" A waiter in a velvet jacket passed a silver tray covered with slices of rare roast lamb. Whitmore hated big lunches and he hated rare lamb. He took the smallest piece on the tray.

"The day before Cox died," Chapelle continued, "a pay phone in the hotel lobby, on which, for reasons of our own, we maintain what you people call a pen register, was used to telephone a villa on Cap Ferrat. The villa is held by a Liechtenstein corporation with so many layered shell companies, trusts, and fiduciaries the true ownership is beyond discovery. The EDF and PTT bills, electricity and phone, are paid by *prélèvement* through an account at a

Crédit Lyonaise branch in Cannes. That bank has also been used a number of times for the withdrawal of cash advances on a Visa card registered to the same Liechtenstein corporation. The signature on the withdrawal *fiche* is always the same and always indecipherable."

"Could I—"

"I just happen to have one with me." Chapelle grinned and drew a paper from his briefcase. "Billing statements on that card show quite a lavish lifestyle. Never anything traceable—hotels or car rentals—but lots of restaurants and nightclubs. Taillvent in Paris a few times, Annabelle's in London, Giannino in Milan, Gaddi's in Hong Kong. Someone with money and a knowledge of how to spend it, someone with lots of friends."

"What's the villa worth?" Whitmore asked as he examined a photocopy of the withdrawal form. It contained an impression of the Visa card, as well as the signature of the individual who had made the withdrawal. The signature, typically European, was nothing more than a series of lines and loops.

"In the thirty-five-million-franc range. Guesthouse, boat dock, park, stables."

"Seven million dollars," Whitmore said, raising his eyebrows.

"Toll analysis on the villa's phone shows multiple calls to Amsterdam, Milan, Hong Kong, Panama, among other places."

"Drugs?"

"Perhaps. Amsterdam could be diamonds. Panama, Hong Kong—maybe money laundering. Subscriber checks on the numbers are still in progress, but I'll be surprised if we find anything. Neighborhood inquiries, and a few discreet feelers among people who have occasion to mix with the owners of property like that, produced interesting rumors."

"Such as?"

"Religious activity—if you could call it that. Satanic rites. People initiated as devil princes. Things like that are not unknown around there in any case."

"I see."

"Of course, any villa hiding behind that kind of elaborate concealment arouses our interest. But I would be surprised if it had anything to do with Cox. The only connection is the phone call from his hotel."

"I appreciate your telling me," Whitmore said. "You never know in these things."

"Exactly."

Cigars were served, and Whitmore allowed the conversation to drift. After twenty minutes he asked if Chapelle had ever taken an interest in the possible intelligence applications of paranormal phenomena, "what the Soviets call psychotronics."

Chapelle laughed. "None at all. A bunch of voodoo rubbish. Though I hear you people look at it from time to time."

Whitmore encouraged Chapelle to elaborate on his disbelief, happy to have an excuse for not briefing him on Spectrum. When it came to possible psychotronic threats against chiefs of state, Chapelle made his disdain for French president François Mitterrand so evident it appeared that he would almost have welcomed a voodoo curse.

That evening, over glasses of Delamain cognac in Paris's Charles de Gaulle airport, Burkholzer tried to talk

Whitmore out of spending the weekend on the Riviera, where Cox had died.

"Don't be silly, Steve," Whitmore said. "You're too superstitious."

"It's not superstition, Admiral."

"You worried about Satan? I don't believe in Satan. And I don't believe Cox died from anything unnatural."

"Then why are you going to Nice?"

"I'm on vacation."

" 'God does not act contrary to nature but only contrary to the order of nature known to us.' St. Augustine said it. Satan too can act contrary to the nature we know."

Whitmore had read the Antibes police report on Cox's death and it was routine, to say the least. Cox had worked for Whitmore, or at least had undertaken MAG assignments through the CIA, and Whitmore felt an obligation to do more than merely read the death documents.

Also, there was Hammond. Whitmore liked Hammond. In some ways Hammond reminded him of the son he'd lost in Vietnam. And it was only because of Whitmore that Hammond had joined MAG in the first place. Maybe a little more knowledge regarding Cox's death would provide some insight into the dangers facing Hammond. So as long as he was in France anyway, why not spend a weekend on the Côte d'Azur? He had honeymooned there with his wife, and until her death from bone cancer a year ago they had returned often for vacations.

"Where are you staying?" Burkholzer asked as they finished their cognac.

"Not sure yet. I'll find a place when I get there."

"I don't believe DIRNSA travels without reservations, and he shouldn't travel alone." DIRNSA was government jargon for Whitmore's job, director of the National Security Agency.

Whitmore shrugged.

"Are you staying in Antibes?" Burkholzer pressed.

"Stop worrying, Steve. I've been in this business twenty-six years."

"But not in psychotronics. The things you don't believe in are the things that can kill you."

"They're calling your flight, Steve."

Whitmore had not only made a reservation, he had specified the room, the room Cox died in. When he walked in, he knew why Hammond had called it the most beautiful view he'd ever seen from a hotel. Rolling lawns sloped straight down to the Mediterranean.

Whitmore refused to allow the bellman to adjust the curtains, explain the air-conditioning, or show him the bathroom. He unpacked his bag, ordered a Jack Daniel's and Perrier from the bar, and sat with the drink at a window overlooking the sea.

When he finished the bourbon, he laid a beige linen suit across one of the king-sized beds. Then he took off his clothes.

Naked, he faced the closed door to the bathroom. He turned the knob, pushed the door open, and looked around. Pink marble bathtub. Crystal ashtrays on the wide double sink.

He turned on the taps, filled the tub, and got in. He loved old European bathtubs, deep and long. He stretched out, submerged everything but his head, relaxed in the warmth, and let his mind wander.

After the MAG meeting, Burkholzer had pushed on him

an inch-thick portfolio of documents jammed with equations, diagrams, and technical language. Whitmore had
an engineering degree, for whatever that was worth, but
mostly he was a manager. Burkholzer was a scientist. It
was his job to know the technical stuff.

Burkholzer was a good man, Whitmore thought, and
a fine scientist, but when it came to the paranormal he'd
gone a little overboard. These brilliant minds immerse
themselves in quantum mechanics, particle physics, cos-
mology, and then they come up for air sounding like
mystics.

Whitmore unwrapped a bar of soap, then changed his
mind and laid the soap on the tub ledge, deciding to soak
a while longer.

Burkholzer had been positively frightening on the subject of nuclear warheads. He'd insisted that Spectrum, or
some particularly adept psychic, could use psychokinesis
to activate the firing systems of American warheads—set
them off as they sat atop missiles in their silos and storage
areas. If the Soviets could detonate our nuclear warheads,
he claimed, they wouldn't have to deliver their own. And
we would have no excuse for launching a retaliatory
strike. Retaliation for what? The Soviets would not have
fired a single missile. It was the one major flaw in MAD,
the Mutual Assured Destruction doctrine. Planners had
never considered it because psychokinesis had never been
deemed possible. Whitmore did not buy everything Burkholzer said, but the thought of American nuclear warheads
detonating where they sat scared him half to death.

"If the brain can fire neurons," Burkholzer had argued,
"why can't it move the molecules in a nuclear warhead
computer chip?" When Whitmore protested his inability

to believe in psychokinesis, that mind could really influence matter, Burkholzer had told him he had a spider on his neck. Whitmore brushed at his collar. Burkholzer said, "How'd you do that? Your mind just moved your arm. Amazing." A little Burkholzer went a long way.

A row of fluorescent tubes over the sink began to flicker annoyingly, dimming every second. Whitmore sank lower into the water and tried to ignore them.

American nuclear weapons experts had told him that Burkholzer's theory, even if correct, was nothing to worry about. Components in the warhead firing hierarchy were too heavy to be influenced by psychokinesis. Psychokinetic capability followed an inverse-square law—the degree of motion decreased as the square of the mass of the affected body. The heavier the object, the less likely it was to be affected by PK. And certain elements in the firing hierarchy were considered far too heavy to be vulnerable to PK. *Considered* far too heavy.

Whitmore's body was so relaxed he could feel the pulse beating in the back of his head. His arms and legs floated serenely in the warm water. The room was silent. The only disrupting element was the flickering of those fluorescent bulbs. The water had grown a bit tepid, and Whitmore thought about turning on the hot tap.

Then he noticed something peculiar. The bulbs appeared to be flickering in time with his pulse. Well, not in perfect time, certainly. He waited, but the pulse beat and the flickers did not drift apart. They were indeed in perfect phase, synchronized throbs of energy.

As he wondered about this, it seemed that the water was getting warmer. He lay perfectly still. The pulse beat in his head strengthened. The brightness of the bulbs increased. The frequency of his pulse and the flickers quickened. Everything was getting stronger and faster. And the water was damned hot.

He leaped from the bath, ran into the bedroom, and stood dripping on the carpet, his back to the bathroom. He heard two popping sounds behind him as the fluorescent bulbs blew out.

Unwilling to return to the bathroom, he wrapped himself in a bedspread and sat by the window, wishing he had another glass of bourbon.

His pulse returned to normal. His fear subsided. He dressed quickly in the beige suit and left the room.

Whitmore drove his rented Peugeot 205 to Monte Carlo, had another Jack Daniel's in the bar of the Hôtel de Paris, and did a lot of thinking. Maybe his pulse and the fluorescent flickers had not really been in phase. They had just seemed that way in the relatively brief time he'd observed them, the way the turn signals on two different cars seem to flash in unison but eventually go out of phase.

Anxiety over his pulse and the flickering fluorescent lamps could have increased his heartbeat and blood flow and further intensified the pulse in his head. And the same anxiety could have led him to imagine that the water temperature had increased.

The whole thing was probably just his imagination. He'd been spending too much time with Burkholzer. He paid his bill and walked past the casino and down the hill to Rampoldi's for dinner.

But he could not get the episode out of his mind. Had something like what happened to him happened to Cox? Maybe they had both been the victim of some sort of high-energy electromagnetic emissions. Maybe an electromagnetic wave had been affecting both the fluorescent bulbs and his heartbeat. And if his heartbeat, what else? Brain rhythms?

He knew that static electricity could illuminate fluorescent bulbs, and he had heard that people living near high-voltage transmission lines sometimes experienced neurological disorders. But none of that seemed to have anything to do with enfoldment, which was what Burkholzer said psychotronics was all about.

Enfoldment and Satan. To Burkholzer everything was supernatural, a war between God and Satan. Satan was an actual creature. The Soviets were using him—or he was using the Soviets—to fight the West. Burkholzer conjured up amusing images of hard-bitten Soviet generals and their American counterparts talking in their war rooms like a bunch of Satanists and Baptist preachers. He made Jesus sound like a personal friend. His view was that heaven existed and no amount of good works could get you in. You had to know God's son and rely on his influence with the Father. Whitmore had asked him, "You believe in Jesus like that? I mean, really? Why?" Burkholzer had said, "For the same reason I believe in mathematics. Because it's true."

Whitmore left the restaurant and climbed into the Peugeot for the drive back to his hotel on Cap d'Antibes. When he turned the ignition key, nothing happened. He tried the lights. No problem. So it wasn't the battery. He tried the ignition again, and this time the engine started.

He took the *bas corniche* along the coast and was admiring the lights ringing the bay of Villefranche when the engine began to miss. Probably something wrong with the plugs. A car closing rapidly behind him flashed its lights.

He pulled over, but the car did not pass. Whitmore stopped for a red light in Villefranche, and the car drew up behind him, almost touching his bumper. It was a dark blue Ferrari Dino. The light changed and Whitmore pulled away, hugging the curb, flashing his right turn signal.

The Ferrari ignored the invitation to pass. The Peugeot's engine was no longer missing. Whitmore speeded up, and the Ferrari stayed within a car's length of his bumper. When he slowed, the Ferrari slowed.

Whitmore hoped to lose the Ferrari in the traffic of the Promenade des Anglais along the Nice seafront. But for the first time in his memory the eight-lane boulevard was almost empty.

Determined not to allow the Ferrari's driver to discover where he was staying, Whitmore continued through Antibes along the coast. In the narrow streets of Cannes the Ferrari's power would be no advantage over the tiny 205.

Whitmore despised this sort of spy-movie car chase business. One of the things he'd liked about Hammond was his insistence that he didn't want to be a James Bond. "I know more about quantum mechanics than secret inks." Whitmore had assured him he'd never get near that sort of thing. Then MAG decided to send him to Moscow, and that meant CIA classes in everything Whitmore had promised Hammond he'd never need to know.

Whitmore passed the Palm Beach casino and drove by the restaurants and hotels of Cannes's Croisette. He turned right, found the narrow Rue d'Antibes, and moved into the line of cars passing sidewalks jammed with shoppers taking advantage of late-night boutiques. The Ferrari was still on his bumper.

What was he worried about? It wasn't as if this were

some deserted country road. He was surrounded by bright lights and scores of pedestrians. He stopped for a red light, put the Peugeot in neutral, set the emergency brake, and walked back to the Ferrari.

He was ready for almost anything, but not for what he found. A beautiful young woman, black hair flowing over her shoulders, stuck her head out of the window.

"I *thought* it was you," she said gaily. "I've been following you all the way from Monte Carlo."

It took him a moment to place her. After all, he'd seen Darya only once, at her briefing with MAG.

"How do you do?" he said. The light was green and horns honked.

"How about a drink?" she said.

What the hell was she doing here? He couldn't risk being alone with her, but if they stayed in public—

"I'll meet you at the Carlton," he said.

"Five minutes."

It took him longer than that to find a parking place. He had to walk five blocks back to the Carlton, and when he got there, the blue Ferrari was in the hotel's drive under the watchful eye of a doorman.

He found Darya at one of the marble tables on the terrace. An ice bucket was already on the white tablecloth, and when he sat down, a waiter lifted out a bottle of Dom Pérignon and filled their glasses. She was in jeans and a yellow V-necked cashmere sweater over a dark Mediterranean tan.

"A bit extravagant?" he said, feeling no need to be overly polite.

"Perhaps, but I have something to apologize for."

She sipped, her eyes sparkling at him over the glass.

The light was soft and a light breeze blew in from the sea. The waiter set down a dish of black Provençal olives.

"Not at all," he said. "America's a free country. People come and go. More so than in some countries."

He had not been all that upset by her redefection. Let the Soviets deal with her complaints and demands. Her appetite for Black research had disgusted him.

"Soviets travel too, certain of us."

"Evidently."

"Anyway, the champagne's not as extravagant as that hotel you're in."

He ignored that and set his glass down.

"Aren't you curious about how I know where you're staying?" she teased.

He gave her what he hoped was a smile as charming as her own. "I expect there are many things you know, Miss Timoshek."

"Please call me Darya. And you are right. Knowing things is my business, same as yours. We just have different ways of knowing."

She ate an olive, looked for an ashtray, found none, and put the pit on the tablecloth next to her glass.

"I must say that your ways interest me considerably," Whitmore said.

"I'm sure they do. For example, I have an impression that you experienced a certain distress earlier."

"You mean in the car? No one likes to be followed."

She wagged her head. She wanted him to guess, without her actually having to say it, that she had had something to do with the incident in the bathtub. Intimidation without admission.

Why play around? She certainly knew he was aware

of at least some of her capabilities. "Did you do that to me in the hotel tonight?"

"Perhaps."

"And Cox?"

She lifted her glass and stared at him, meeting his eyes. After several seconds she said, "Why don't you ask me about Jack Hammond?"

"You want to talk about Hammond?"

"I might be able to tell you some things you should know. Do a little fortune-telling. A woman's intuition?"

Whitmore wasn't going to respond to that.

"He's developing a relationship with a young dissident. I will even tell you her name. Valentina Leonov. And you should thank me for that, Admiral, because you could have trouble there. She is well-known to the KGB. Very well-known. You might even say, associated with them. Forewarned is forearmed."

What the hell was she talking about? Was Darya jealous of the Leonov woman? The spy business was difficult enough without a lot of romantic complications.

Darya had been serious for a minute, but now her eyes sparkled again and she picked up her glass. "I have done you a favor."

"Why this compulsion to help me, Miss Timoshek?"

"Because we should be on the same side. You know about Spectrum, you know what it can do. You think I want to see your warheads blow up? You think I want to see Reagan, Kohl, Thatcher, just"—with the back of her hand she sent the olive pit flying from the tablecloth —"like that?"

A woman at the next table, hit on the shoulder by the pit, turned and looked at Darya. Darya ignored her.

Whitmore waved at the waiter. *"L'addition, s'il vous plaît."*

Darya raised a hand authoritatively and the waiter, who appeared to know her, handed her the check. She returned it with a credit card.

"You can do it next time," she said.

"It will be a pleasure."

They drank, and as one waiter refilled the glasses, another placed before Darya a silver tray with a pen and credit card form. She signed the form and was handing it back when Whitmore, appearing to change his mind, said, "No. I insist. This is on me."

He grabbed the tray, spilling the pen and form to the floor. He reached for the form, covered it with his body, pulled off the back copy, and returned the top copies and the pen to the tray.

"Please," Darya said. "I invited you."

"Very well," Whitmore said, and handed the tray to the waiter.

Whitmore walked her to the Ferrari and watched it disappear up the Croisette. The license number ended in 06, an Alpes-Maritimes registration. The largest city in the Alpes-Maritimes was Nice. A scrap of information lost in the depths of Whitmore's memory burst into consciousness. Crossing his desk with an avalanche of other NSA business had been a routine contact report from Hammond noting the description and plate number of a Ferrari that had tailed him from Antibes to Monte Carlo. The number on the *carte grise* had come back registered to a French name, certainly phony, with a nonexistent address in Nice. The assumption had been that the car was attached to the Nice KGB base.

The drive back to the hotel was an agony. The cashier buzzed Whitmore through an electrically locked door, escorted him to the safe deposit room, inserted his key into the double-locked box, and withdrew. Whitmore took out Chapelle's photocopy of the cash withdrawal slip and held it next to the copy of Darya's payment at the Carlton. The card numbers were the same and the lines and loops of the signatures matched perfectly.

16

HAMMOND SNEEZED AND
started up the darkened steps, littered with empty bottles,
crumpled bags, a broken broom handle. Compared to this,
Cox's home was a palace. He envied Burkholzer and Whitmore, off in Europe briefing counterparts.

Hammond pulled his overcoat collar tighter around his
neck and tried not to swallow. His throat burned, his nose
ran, his head ached, his body wanted to lie down and die.
Five nights in Cox's frigid apartment, plus the night on a
park bench and the nearly sleepless trip to the States, had
produced a raging case of flu. He was a doctor, but what
could he do? Flu is flu.

Blocked nasal passages did not conceal the odor. He stopped on the stone steps to get his breath and spent the moment wondering what could possibly have produced such a stench. It wasn't feces or urine or decaying flesh, although they may have contributed. The smell had age, must have been here for generations, accumulating, evolving, maturing. You could have taken it into a lab, peeled back the years, uncovered the sweat-soaked laborers, vomiting children, unwashed dotards, perfumed whores.

One flight up he knocked on a door. Valentina opened it immediately, as if she had been lurking behind it in the gloom. She pulled him inside and hurried down an unlighted hall. A baby was crying. He caught dim glimpses of objects hanging on a wall—a rusty washtub, a child's stroller.

They entered a tiny, one-windowed room, the door closed, and she turned on a light. Hammond squinted in the sudden brilliance. The walls and ceiling were a glaring white, the varnished parquet floor glistened, everything was as neat and spotless as an operating room. The smell was the same she had brought with her into the Chaika —strong, industrial, Soviet soap. She must have scrubbed the room with it, fighting the stench from the corridor.

"Sit down, please."

There wasn't much choice. Two straight-back chairs stood beside a narrow mattress covered with brightly colored cushions and a yellow spread. He had to sit at an angle to keep his knees from colliding with a low wooden table separating him from the mattress. At his right elbow, an enormous armoire rose almost to the ceiling, as high as the room was wide.

"I apologize for rushing you through the corridor," she

said, still standing. "Some of my neighbors don't like guests. Everyone watches everyone."

"I understand." She was like a small bird, frail but competent.

On a wall hung a white cloth with a blue design sewn into it: three white doves flying above an enclosure of barbed wire.

She placed cups of tea before them and sat on the mattress. Where had she made the tea? There was no other room, no hot plate.

"This is a very old building," she said, "prerevolutionary, the home of a prince, who was my granduncle. My room is really only a corner of what used to be the library. You can see." Molding along the ceiling stopped at what were obviously partitions.

If what she said was true, and her family had descended from aristocracy to slum dweller, it certainly didn't seem to bother her. She was cheerful as could be.

"Five people used to live in this room. My grandparents, my parents, and my aunt. And the armoire. It belonged to the prince. It takes up too much room, but it's become like a mascot."

"It doesn't seem possible that five people could live here," he said. How had her parents made love?

"When I was born my parents and aunt were given another apartment. My father worked for the ministry of agriculture. Then my grandfather died and I received permission to live here to look after my grandmother. That way, when she died the apartment became mine. Otherwise it would have gone back to the state."

"You've made it very pleasing."

"It was nicer when my grandmother was alive. She

looked after things. She read the Bible to me and said prayers with me. She made me very religious."

"My parents tried to do that." He remembered the gloomy church, the choirmaster.

"She had an icon and we prayed before it twice a day. But when she died all that just stopped. It went out of my life. I never even thought about it."

"You seem to think about it now. What happened?"

"That's too long a story."

He handed her a box of French raspberry confiture he had bought that morning at the embassy commissary.

"Thank you. That's very kind."

"Where are your parents?"

She laid the confiture next to the mattress. "They were killed in a fire sixteen years ago, when I was seven. They went to Labinsk to look at a timber mill that had belonged to my granduncle. The mill—you don't want to hear this."

"Yes, I do. What happened?"

"A young man named Viktor who went with them, who worked for my father, said a mound of sawdust suddenly ignited, as if someone had covered it with petrol. But there hadn't been any petrol odor. The fire spread very rapidly. Viktor got out, but not my parents."

"Did you ever find out anything else?"

"A girl was outside, just sort of standing around. Her family had worked at the mill when my granduncle owned it. She was a little strange and had a reputation in the town for magic. Viktor said he thought she had started the fire."

"By magic?"

"That's what he thought."

"What was her name?"

"It doesn't matter. You don't know her."

Hammond thought maybe he did—Darya had said she grew up in Labinsk—but this wasn't the time to press the matter. After a silence, he said, "Thank you for rescuing me Sunday."

"I'm sorry we could not complete the service." Her dark blue turtleneck sweater made her skin appear even whiter, her cropped hair a lighter blond, than it had at the log farmhouse. Her blue eyes were smiling, candid. "I am afraid it was a disappointment for you."

"For me?"

"We are accustomed to it." Her gaze was disarmingly direct, and even after several moments he felt no inclination to look away.

"Do you always meet in the country?" he asked.

"Not always. Sometimes, especially during the week, we meet in Moscow. We have even met here."

"Here? How many people have you had here?" The room could not have held fifteen people standing body-to-body.

"Once we had fifty. Not all sitting down, of course."

He had seen research at Stanford into the multiplication of matter, heard disputes about whether the multiplication of food by Jesus and various saints and mystics had actually occurred, whether it was miraculous or merely the application of a natural principle not yet understood. But the multiplication of space was something else. If time and space are essentially the same thing, as Einstein said, and if time could be converted to matter, as those researchers at the University of Illinois were trying to do, why not multiply space? The idea sounded crazy, but less crazy than some.

"Fifty people in this room?" he said.

"Why not?" Her question, and the look that went with it, were as innocent as a child's.

He shrugged, and they sipped the tea. The silence was not an uncomfortable one. Finally Hammond said, "I don't know what your pastor told you about me."

"He said you wanted to meet me, because of my gift."

"I understand I am not the first to take an interest in your healing."

"You mean the authorities? Many things interest them. I do not speak with them."

"How do you know you can speak with me?"

"I trust you. Anyway, I don't worry about what happens. I'm prudent, but what happens is not up to me. I'm happy."

"What sort of interest did the authorities take?"

"Since I refused to talk to them I never found out. I don't care."

"Do you know what my interest is?"

"No." Her eyes revealed no concern, not even curiosity. She appeared convinced he could not hurt her in any way that mattered. Her ingenuousness persuaded him to take a chance and tell her the truth, or at least a piece of it.

"I'm a scientist, a doctor, and in the United States I study paranormal phenomena. One of these is healing. I'm interested in all kinds of healing—faith healing, spiritual healing, psychic healing. I want to know who can do it, how they do it."

"You are not a believer."

"I believe in God." Well, sort of, maybe.

"So does Satan."

"Then I guess Satan and I have something in common." She grinned at him. "Satan likes us to believe in gods, in the supernatural, in anything that keeps us from the truth."

"Which is?"

" 'I am the way and the truth and the life. No one comes to the Father except through me.' Jesus said that. Satan doesn't want you to believe it."

"But you believe it. Is that how it's possible for you to heal?"

"I can't heal."

"But . . . you have healed."

"Not me."

"All right. But why does God heal people through you and not through others?"

"You would have to ask God." Now the eyes were playful.

"What if you found out that to heal people God uses some natural, scientific principle, one we don't know about yet?"

"How God does what he does is not important to me."

"But what if we were able to discover that scientific principle and use it to heal people?"

"You would not unless God wanted you to."

He decided not to push it. "If anyone came to you for healing, would you do it?"

"I would ask God to heal anyone who wanted healing."

"The head of the KGB?"

"He is perhaps more in need of healing than others."

He shifted from theology to physiology. "How do you feel, physically, when someone is healed through you?"

"Different at different times." She smiled.

"Why do you smile?"

"Because you are afraid to ask what you really should ask."

"What is that?"

"Why don't you ask me to heal you?"

"Do I need it?"

Now she laughed, warmly, affectionately. The laugh alone made him feel better. "You look like a man with a very bad case of Moscow winter."

"Well, you're right there. I may die at any moment."

"Stand up."

She left the mattress and stood beside him, placing her right hand on his forehead, her left on the back of his head. The grip was gentle but authoritative. She closed her eyes and spoke inaudibly in Russian. He realized he was tense and tried to relax. He closed his eyes. Her hands were light, barely depressing his flesh. He waited for some sensation, remembering a healing experiment he had witnessed at Johns Hopkins. The healer's pulse, respiration, and galvanic skin response had escalated dramatically, and the patient had reported sensations of heat.

Her hands tightened around his head for several seconds, then lifted.

"Finished?" he said. He had felt nothing. His throat was still sore, his head still ached, his nose still ran, and on top of it all he felt a slight nausea and a desperate need to go to the bathroom. Suddenly, without warning, he sneezed. "I'm sorry."

"You look a bit pale," she said. "Are you all right?" The failure seemed not to concern her.

"Could I use the bathroom?"

She opened the door quietly and again he was assaulted

by the smell. She pointed to the first of two doors up the corridor. He went in, found the light switch, and closed the door. Dead insects covered the bare bulb hanging from the ceiling. The walls, cracked and dirty, had been painted a dark color that was no longer even a color. The floor was slippery. A chain descended from a cast-iron flush tank hanging precariously from the wall above his head. The porcelain toilet, all but filling the room, was cracked and encrusted with filth. And there was no seat.

Of course she believes in Jesus, Hammond thought. She has nothing else. She has no parents, no husband, no friends but those she finds at church. The Soviet security apparatus could crush her without a thought. She could die in prison, starve to death, freeze in the street, and no one would notice.

He was not going to sit on that bowl. What could he do? There was no toilet paper, only a dirty plastic bag filled with old newspapers.

Someone knocked on the door and he cracked it open. Valentina's hand came through holding a toilet seat. It was white, polished, immaculate, a miracle. He took it.

When he had finished, he removed the seat from the bowl and held it in both hands, staring at it. The flu, the stench, the toilet—he had never in his life felt sicker and more depressed. These people, living in such estrangement they could not even bring themselves to keep a community toilet clean. You had to have your *own* toilet seat. It was a microcosm of hell.

Back in the corridor, he heard a noise to his left and peeked around the corner into a kitchen. An emaciated old white-haired woman in slippers and tattered brown housecoat perched like a bat on a stool, eating from a tin bowl. A large brown cat curled in her lap. The woman spooned a dark, mushy substance into her mouth, removed a half-eaten loaf of bread from under her arm, bit off a hunk, returned the bread to her arm, and took another spoonful. She faced a rusty, dirty gas stove that looked like a relic of the revolution. Behind her were four cupboards, four stools, and four small tables—one for each tenant, nothing shared. An infant's pajamas and diapers hung drying from a string.

Hammond let himself back into Valentina's room and leaned the toilet seat against the wall by the door. It was like entering another world.

"I'm sorry you had to see that," she said. She was sitting on the mattress. "I used to clean everything myself, but the neighbors resented it. It was like I was saying I was better than they were. So I stopped."

"Who's the old lady?"

"Mrs. Koblov. She was in the kitchen? Did she see you?"

"She was and she didn't."

"She's been here longer than anyone else so she thinks the place is hers. Also, she has the only telephone, which helps her in her duties."

"Duties?"

"She's a *stukach*, she reports to a militia sergeant in the next building. She's very kind, really. If she didn't obey the militia they would throw her into the street. She does what she has to do. You can't judge her for that."

"Who are your other neighbors?"

"A young couple with a little girl, and a man who works at a power station. I don't see them. I eat with friends. How do you feel?"

"Not too well, I'm afraid. Now that your church was broken up, what happens?"

"The church was not broken up. We will continue with another pastor."

"I see."

They looked at each other.

"I guess I'd better go home and go to bed," he said.

She smiled, the look in the eyes now hard to read, something between drill sergeant and helpless waif.

On the way down the stairs, peering through the darkness to avoid tripping over litter, he held his breath against the smell. He heard footsteps below. Two militiamen in uniform climbed toward him. As they passed, he recognized the officer who had kicked the pastor into the snow. Hammond quickened his pace and had gone another three steps when one of the officers called to him from above.

Hammond did not have to think. He was certain the officers were after Valentina, and it would not help if they found him here as well. An arrest for "engaging in activities inconsistent with his diplomatic status," along with press reports and expulsion, would put an end to his search for Spectrum. It might also put an end to Valentina.

He ran, sprinting through a small slush-filled park between the apartment house and an elementary school. He rounded the corner of the school and headed up the block to a black Volga with made-in-Nebraska plates parked in front of an Okeon fish market. By the time he got there, Frank had the back door open and the engine revving. Hammond dived through the door, landed sprawling on the floor, and heard the door slam shut as the car lurched forward.

He lay there panting, then pulled himself onto the seat.

"Some milliman back there waving his arms at us," Frank said. "Nothing to do with you I don't suppose."

"Never saw him before in my life."

"How you doing? You okay?"

"Just fine," Hammond said, and then realized with a shock that he was telling the truth. Nothing hurt anymore. The sore throat, headache, runny nose were gone. "In fact," he said softly, "I never felt better." Had she really healed him? Or would he have got better anyway?

"What happened?" Frank asked.

Hammond looked back through the rear window. Two millimen, as Frank called them, had come out of the building with Valentina.

"Some cop chased me. I guess he thought he'd seen me before. Case of mistaken identity."

"Back to the embassy?"

"Frank, if the militia arrest someone, where do they take them?"

"Usually to the local militia station. You wanna tell me who we're talking about?"

"I met a woman back there. They grabbed her as I was leaving. What happens after the militia station?"

"They get released or charged and they go to court."

"Same day?"

"Sometimes. Not always."

What difference would it make if that milliman saw him at the militia station? They hadn't arrested him at the scene. Hammond's word against theirs that he'd ever seen Valentina. And Hammond knew that the longer Valentina was in militia custody the deeper out of sight she would sink into the mire of Soviet bureaucracy. If there was a search for her later, he wanted to be able to say he'd seen her in the militia station.

"Let's stop by the local cop station."

Frank shot him a glance in the mirror. "You sure?"

"Absolutely."

Frank stopped the car, attached a new set of magnetized plates, then retrieved an overcoat from the trunk. "Change into this." The coat was light blue with maroon checks.

Hammond shook his head. "Not my style, Frank. Let's go."

"They saw you in a dark coat, they see you again in this they won't recognize you. That's why we carry it. People remember clothes."

Hammond shook his head.

"It's a fact, Jack. We did a study. Clothes, not faces."

Hammond changed coats.

They stopped at a corner up the block from a blue-and-white, two-story, prerevolutionary building that looked as if it used to be a residence. Hammond walked between stone pillars into a small courtyard filled with gray militia cars, turned left, climbed a couple of steps, and entered a dim corridor that was as cold as the street.

A wood bench ran along the wall on the left, and in a partitioned area ahead of him a milliman sat at a desk behind a glass window. The bench was empty. The milliman was on the telephone.

Hammond started down the corridor, trying to look as if he knew exactly where he was going. An opening door almost knocked him down. He confronted a fat young milliman coming out of the room with Valentina. Her maroon ski jacket hung around her like a tent.

Frank had been right. Even Valentina wasn't sure. She

saw his face, looked at the coat, went back to the face.
Hammond wondered if the cop who had chased him had
departed or was behind one of two other doors visible up
the corridor.

"Looking for a friend," Hammond said in English with
what he hoped looked like a dumb-tourist grin. "I'm an
American, a tourist, you understand? And I was going to
meet a friend, this woman I know? Up the block there.
But she's not there, been waiting an hour, so I thought
I'd just come in and . . ." Keep jabbering, thought Hammond, convince him you're just an idiot tourist.

The cop delivered Valentina to the bench and turned
to deal with Hammond.

"I thought maybe you could help me," Hammond said
to the milliman. "Maybe she came in here and left a
message. Do you speak English? Anyone here speak English?"

It was clear the cop did not speak English. He walked
to the glass window to confer with his colleague, an older
man wearing the two small stars of a militia lieutenant.

"What did they tell you?" Hammond whispered to Valentina. No one seemed to be standing guard. Where would
a prisoner go? Residency permits, internal passports, job
registrations, the inability of local citizens even to obtain
hotel rooms, provided little chance of hiding. The whole
country was a prison.

She perched timidly on the bench. "Nothing. They are
waiting for someone to come."

"Where will they take you from here?"

"I don't know."

The fat cop turned and yelled at Hammond in Russian.

"Sorry," Hammond said. "I thought maybe the young

lady might have seen my friend." He turned to Valentina. "Did you see—"

The cop grabbed him by the shoulder and pushed him to the partition window. The officer on the other side leaned forward to the glass. "What do you want?"

"Oh, you speak English. I was supposed to meet a friend. I—"

"Your papers?"

"I beg your pardon?"

"Papers. Passport."

Hammond made a show of searching his pockets. "Damn. I must have left it in the hotel."

"Your *propoosk*?" His hotel pass.

"With my passport, I'm afraid."

"What hotel?"

"National."

It was a lie, but he could always plead confusion, didn't understand the Russian accent.

"Name?"

"Jack Baker." Don't help them. If he could get out of this without leaving traces so much the better.

"Sit, please." The officer nodded at the bench and reached for the telephone.

In his routine briefing before coming to Russia, what agents called "the country course," Hammond had been told that KGB officers were extremely reluctant to identify themselves officially, preferring to leave to the militia such matters as identification checks, preliminary interrogation, and arrest. Militia officers were permitted to detain people for three hours on the pretext of checking their papers. Hammond was certain he could drag out his identification charade for at least that long, and by then he might have a hint of what they planned to do with Valentina.

Hammond took a place next to Valentina. The fat officer pointed to the opposite end of the bench. Hammond smiled subserviently, sat where he was told, and settled down to see who would come to talk to Valentina.

Fifty minutes later two men in brown leather overcoats walked in, conferred briefly with the man behind the glass, glanced at Hammond, ignored Valentina, and disappeared through a door up the corridor. In five minutes the fat cop summoned Hammond.

Hammond didn't like letting Valentina out of his sight. He had assumed they would deal with her first and he could get a hint where they took her. Now she might be hauled away while he was in a back office.

It was a small room with a scuffed parquet floor, dingy green walls, and single window. A varnished plywood cabinet sat in a corner with a dead plant on top. A heater with an old cloth-covered cord was plugged into an outlet under the window. Two brown leather overcoats hung on a wooden coatrack.

A heavyset man at a small desk by the window waved Hammond into a metal chair.

"Your name, please?" He had heavy, moist red lips and spoke thickly accented English.

"Jack Baker. Yours?"

The man opened a black plastic wallet, displaying a maroon card Hammond recognized as a KGB credential. Before Hammond could read the name the wallet had disappeared into the inside pocket of a brown Soviet-made suit jacket. The shirt was light green, the tie red and blue striped. The guy would have loved Hammond's overcoat.

The other man was in a chair behind Hammond, out of his sight. Hammond recognized the technique. However they might be dressed, they were professionals.

Obeying his training, Hammond turned his chair to give a view of both men. The second sat cross-legged, taller than the first, a bit younger, and his clothes had a slightly more Western touch. The shoes were definitely American, heavy Florsheim brogans. His eyes were large and blank.

"Where are you living in Moscow?" the man at the desk asked.

Living. Not staying. So perhaps they knew or guessed the National was a lie. Anything he said that was true could hurt him. Anything he said that was untrue might incriminate him. They would have to write a report, so the best procedure was to give them nothing to put into it.

Hammond was silent.

"Where are you living?"

Hammond directed a steady gaze into the agent's eyes, and said nothing. Perhaps silence would hasten his return to the bench and Valentina. After all, if he didn't respond, there wouldn't be much to talk about. And if he could get out of here without telling them anything, they'd have no way to locate him later. So far, they didn't even have his name.

"You told the officer you had a friend at the National hotel."

That was a tempting invitation to correct an error. He did not take the bait. Once you start talking they've got you.

"These are simple questions, Mr. Baker."

An appeal to reasonableness. He was silent.

Now the other man spoke, less of an accent. "We could be here all night."

A mild threat, letting him know they didn't have to stay nice forever. This was exactly what he'd been told would happen. Hammond was impressed by the correctness of his training, and disturbed by what it had warned him might lie ahead.

He looked into the man's large empty eyes and said nothing.

"Mr. Baker, you are an American. We have always heard that the Americans are intelligent people. Why can't you answer a few routine questions and then you will be free to leave and do as you like? Why do you want to turn this into something difficult?"

If you answer one simple question, there will be more, then others not so simple. So don't begin. Don't speak.

"How long have you been at the Intourist hotel, Mr. Baker?"

Another enticement to catch them in an error. He shifted his gaze back to the agent behind the desk, and said nothing.

The man stood, shaking his head.

"Well, if that is the way you want it to be, that is the way it will be. You are making a big mistake. We have been very correct with you. I wonder if police in your own country would be so correct. By now they would have beaten you. That's true, isn't it?"

Hammond managed to swallow the word "bullshit" an instant before it escaped his lips.

They led him out and back to the bench. Through a window he saw two millimen putting Valentina into what looked like a metal-roofed, plywood cabin built onto a small flatbed truck. She stepped in through a side door, one of the cops climbed behind the wheel, and the truck pulled out into the street.

So far, they had learned nothing about him. They had not seen his identification, had not heard his name, had nothing from him but his dumb-tourist act when he entered.

He looked at the door and wondered if Frank was still parked at the corner, or if he had moved nearer the militia station.

The KGB men had returned to the office. The militia lieutenant was behind the glass window talking on the phone. The fat cop had disappeared.

Hammond edged along the bench toward the door. He looked back to make sure the corridor was empty, tensed his muscles, and leaped. He made the door in three strides, banged it open, and dashed for the street.

Frank was still at the corner. Hammond saw the Volga's front door fly open. He jumped in, felt the car lunge forward, and heard Frank say, "We've got to stop meeting like this."

"Did you see that truck come out?"

"She inside it?"

"Yes."

"It's a court truck. They're taking her to court."

"You sure? It looked like something—"

"Homemade. I know. They make them themselves. You wanna go to court?"

"Definitely."

They drove two minutes and stopped across the street

from a small five-story, brown-brick building with four stone steps.

"That's it?" Hammond said. It didn't look like a courthouse.

Ahead of them on the corner, a bearded man in a beige, canvas, knee-length coat was about to step off the curb.

"Frank."

"Yeah?"

"That guy crossing the street. You know him from anywhere?" Hammond was sure it was the man he'd seen outside Cox's apartment just before he was slugged in the kidney.

Frank squinted. "No. Don't think so."

"Maybe I'm wrong."

"Moscownoia, the morbid fear that everyone in Moscow's out to get you. It's an occupational hazard."

Frank watched the man stroll down the street toward them. As he passed opposite their car, he gave them a solid face-fixing stare. He was bigger than Hammond had realized.

"On the other hand," Frank said, "he's enough of a thug to be KGB."

The man quickened his stride and lumbered heavily around the corner. "Yes," Frank said. "I'd bet on it. KGB."

Inside the courthouse, Hammond found green walls, a green stone floor, a couple of millimen loitering in the narrow hallway, three women waiting quietly on a bench. Not much light, even less noise. Through an open doorway he spotted Valentina standing inside a waist-high, wood-railed enclosure. Three judges in high-backed black leather chairs faced three rows of empty yellow benches.

A door in the back opened, and a woman entered to whisper to one of the judges. The judges withdrew. In a moment, a milliman led Valentina up the corridor and through an unmarked door. As she came out of the courtroom, she saw Hammond. He winked at her, and she raised her chin. She looked—how could he describe that look? Frightened but confident? Ready?

He went back to the car. "Is there a back exit?"

"Don't think so," Frank said. "They generally come out here."

They waited for more than an hour. Finally, Valentina emerged between two men in dark suits. They climbed into the backseat of a gray Volga and drove off.

"Official plates and KGB electronics," Frank said, watching the car head up the street. He pulled away from the curb, but was blocked at the intersection by a double, articulated bus.

"What's that mean?" Hammond had gained considerable respect for Frank and didn't want to sound desperate, but they were losing the Volga.

"Telephone and new antennas. They just put new radios in their cars and changed the phone scramblers. You wanta stay with the Volga?"

"Please."

Frank pulled a map from his breast pocket and unfolded it in his lap. He picked up a radio handset concealed in the armrest. "Base, Able Two. Nine, thirteen, red."

Twenty seconds later the radio said. "Able Two. Six, twelve, blue."

Frank consulted the map, then passed it to Hammond. "They're on Leninski Prospekt, just entering the ring road."

Hammond looked at the map. Street names were matched with numbers. Six was Leninski Prospekt. Twelve was the ring road. "What's blue?"

"Northbound. You give base the departure coordinates, they pick up the route."

"That's clever," Hammond said.

"Just a matter of identifying the signature of each car's transmitter, then triangulating with satellites. They do it to us too."

In five minutes they were on the ring road. Frank made a left, crossed the river, got another fix from base, took a right, and turned left into a small one-way street called Kropotkinsky Pereulok.

They approached number 23, a dirty-white stone building joining a twelve-foot-high wall.

"Serbenov Institute," Frank said.

As they passed the wall, Hammond caught a glimpse of barbed wire with electricity insulators, gray metal gates, and rising behind the wall, the top floor of an old yellow building with the windows painted over.

"Any reason they'd be going there?" Frank asked.

"I'm afraid so," Hammond said, fear filling his heart.

"Where to now?" Frank asked.

Hammond thought for a moment. "Can you make another pass?"

When they reentered the street Serbenov was on, Hammond said, "Stop on the corner."

Frank turned to Hammond. "You're not going in?"

"Just stop on the corner and wait for me."

"Do you know what they do in that place?"

"I know."

Frank slowed down but did not stop. "Hang on a

second, Jack. Since I've been in Moscow we've had three people disappear. No Americans yet, but it could happen. We never saw them again. The Soviets said they never saw them. They never existed. You know what I mean? Just . . . poof."

"Listen, Frank—"

"And there is no better place to vanish than right in there. That's the number one haunted house in Moscow."

"Stop at the corner."

"Jack—"

"Give me an hour."

Hammond walked past a sign with a red horizontal line drawn through a Klaxon: hospital zone, no honking. No disturbing the patients—except by doctors. Next to the gray metal vehicle gate was a high double wood door. He opened it and stepped inside.

17

HAMMOND WAS IN A RECEP-
tion room with red plastic seats that could have come
from an old stateside Greyhound station. A sign on one
of the dirty-green walls gave the address but not the name
of the institution. If you didn't know this was the Serbenov
Institute, you had no right to be here.

A woman in a brown military uniform lounged behind
a glass window not unlike the one in the militia station.
Beside the window another sign listed the amounts of
food patients could receive from families and the hours
during which it could be delivered. Again, no mention of
the name of the institution.

Putting on his most authoritative face, Hammond ignored the woman and headed for a door next to the window. It was locked. The woman said in Russian, "What do you want?"

"I am Dr. Harold Baxter," Hammond said, as if he fully expected her to understand English. "I have an appointment with Dr. Darya Timoshek." He spoke the name loudly and clearly, hoping it had the power to intimidate.

"Dr. Timoshek?"

"*Da*. Timoshek." He tried the door again, feigning impatience.

"Moment," she said in English, and reached for a telephone. As she did so, he put his shoulder against the wood door and shoved with his full weight. It had not been built to resist attack. Who would want to break into Serbenov?

He ran down a long, low-ceilinged corridor, opened a windowed door at the end, and found himself in a central courtyard paved with cracked concrete slabs swept clear of snow. An orange Zhiguli van and two black Volgas stood side by side next to a garbage dumpster in the dark slush at the entrance to the yellow building Hammond had seen from the street. The most likely place to find the nasty work was behind the painted-over windows on the top floor. Was that where they had taken Valentina?

He hurried through the entrance, up three stone steps, and into a wire-cage elevator. He pulled the gate closed and pressed the top button. As it lurched slowly upward, he heard the entrance door below open and the excited voices of a man and a woman.

He pulled open the gate and stepped into a hallway lighted only by a single window at the end. He moved quickly to the first door and cracked it open, hoping to

172

see patients. He was disappointed. A bespectacled woman looked up from a desk, hesitated a moment in surprise, then said something that Hammond did not understand.

"*Prastyityi,*" he said, and backed out quickly, closing the door.

He heard the rattle of the elevator and knew he didn't have much more time in that corridor. Where was Valentina? He tried another door, and his heart sank. Standing next to a desk, talking to a seated young man in a white lab coat, was Darya.

"Well," Hammond said, hiding his disappointment, "I've been looking all over for you."

Never before had he seen Darya at a loss. She opened her mouth, then closed it. "What are you doing here?"

"I was in the neighborhood so—just a friendly call, colleague to colleague."

"Come with me."

Without a word to the young man, she took Hammond by the arm and led him back into the corridor. She had her composure again, and she did not seem pleased.

A man and woman, six-footers with the bodies of anabolic steroid abusers, appeared from the elevator in uniforms like the one worn by the woman in the reception room. When they saw Darya they froze.

Darya barked something unpleasant, and the pair raced each other back to the elevator.

In her corner office, Darya ignored a large walnut desk and sat in one of two facing black leather chairs. Light came through three windows with dark green velvet curtains. Plants grew in bronze pots on the windowsill.

"This is more like it," Hammond said, looking around. "Power office. Let's everyone know who's in charge."

"What are you doing here?" She tilted her head and smiled, turning the charm tap, back in character.

"I had expected more of a welcome. You invited me, remember? Offered to show me what you've accomplished at Serbenov."

She stared at him, that lovely smile hiding a head full of spinning wheels. Then she went to the desk for a pad and pen, tore off the top sheet, not to leave an impression beneath, and wrote something. She held it in front of Hammond. When he reached for it, she pulled it back. Don't touch, just read. It said: *Don't forget our deal.*

He raised his eyebrows questioningly, and she bent to write something else. When she showed him the paper again she had added: *Your help when I leave.*

They had no such deal. He shook his head.

Aloud, she said, "You want to see our work?"

"I do."

She held up the paper. *Your help when I leave.*

He had to find Valentina. "Listen . . ."

She stood her ground, the paper dangling from her fingertips.

He shrugged, stalling. "What can I say?"

Darya didn't move.

"Darya, we'll talk. That's the most I can promise."

He watched her think that over. If she wanted his help badly enough, she'd take what she could get. He tried to look unconcerned, didn't care if she threw him out or not.

She crumpled the paper and put it in the pocket of her slacks. "This way."

He followed her to the door. "Could we start at the beginning, what happens to patients when they first come in?"

"We'll start where I want to start."

"Certainly. Of course."

They went down in the elevator, along a half-lit corridor, and through a door into a recently renovated building with beige walls, acoustical-tile ceilings, and overhead fluorescent lights. The elevator was modern, and when they stepped off on the third floor they could have been in almost any hospital in the West except for the empty hallways—no staff, no gurneys, no patients, no visitors.

Darya led him through a double fire door to a labyrinth of hallways, and finally into a room with six chairs facing a one-way mirror. On the other side of the glass, two white-jacketed men attached electroencephalogram electrodes to a white-gowned woman strapped to a steel table beneath a ceiling mirror. The mirror was tilted to provide a view of the woman's face. One of the men connected an additional electrode to a bandaged patch on her skull, then withdrew from the room. The other man stood beside the woman, looking down into her face.

"Who is she?" Hammond asked. To his relief, he could see that it was not Valentina.

"She's an epileptic and schizophrenic with a history of violence. This is the first phase of a control project."

The woman's face was taut with anger. Her head raised as she struggled furiously against the leather straps. From a loudspeaker next to a closed-circuit television screen above the one-way glass came the flat voice of a male technician out of sight in another room. "Sixty pulses."

Suddenly the woman's face relaxed, the fury left it, and she smiled. The TV screen came on and they watched the lines of brain waves from the EEG machine.

The man at the woman's side spoke, his voice crackling through the speaker. "What happened?"

The woman's face came alive, and she tittered. She was a changed woman. "You must be doing something to me."

"One hundred forty," said the technician's voice.

The face became animated, playful, even a little coy. "Come on now, you stop that. You're doing something naughty to me."

The technician's voice, as emotionless as the jerky EEG lines on the monitor, said, "We're coming to the start of the changes . . . a fast spindle . . . eighteen per second . . . first in the dorsal right anterior septal, then it spreads to the other septal leads . . . correlated with clinical findings of intense pleasure, particularly sexual. . . ."

By now the woman was writhing and gasping. They watched for half an hour as she went through a rapid series of orgasms. She was still having the orgasms when Darya pointed to the TV monitor.

"See, it's like the spike-and-dome pattern of an epileptic seizure. Very explosive."

Hammond's stomach was churning. Without another word Darya led him briskly from the room, down the hall, and into a ward containing six beds. The only sounds were moans and gasps rising from the patients.

A young man with a thin, ruddy face lay beneath a blue spread, staring at the white ceiling. A thin yellow wire ran from a square bandage on his skull to a stainless steel machine on a wheeled table by his bed. The machine contained an oscilloscope, three analog meter dials, and a six-place digital readout that was steadily approaching seven hundred.

The man was motionless, his bright eyes alive with delight. As Hammond watched, his head rolled and he let out a sigh of pleasure.

Hammond wanted to get out. Where was Valentina?

"We've isolated septal locations associated with each of the senses," Darya said. "The stimulation here is auditory."

When Hammond didn't speak, she added, "He's hearing sounds more beautiful than Bach."

She waited for a response, didn't get one, and pulled Hammond to the next bed. Another man, older than the first, lay with his eyes closed, a thin smile working on his lips. The quick, erratic motion of the pupils beneath the lids resembled the rapid eye movements of dream-filled sleep.

"Visual," she said. "Paintings, theater, film, pornography—delivered directly to the consciousness with no intermediate artistic medium. Look over here."

In a bed behind them, the jaw, lips, and tongue of a dark-haired teenage girl worked with the steady rhythm of a computer-controlled mannequin. A blue hospital towel, folded beneath her chin, caught saliva drooling from the corners of her mouth. Another towel lay kicked into a corner on the floor by the bed. No one moved to pick it up. Darya said, "The best dinner you ever had can't touch what she's tasting at this moment."

Outside in the corridor, she said, "You want to try it?"

"Try what?"

"What they were doing."

"You must be crazy." Then he had a thought. "Have you?"

"Of course. I wouldn't miss it."

"No, thanks."

"Well, I'll give you a little taste later, anyway. Nothing threatening. Don't worry."

She led him into another ward.

"These are the most advanced subjects," she said, dropping any pretext that they were patients requiring therapy.

The ward was identical to the other—six beds, six subjects—but here black crinkle-finish, waist-high machines at the bedsides were controlled by small boxes, similar to the one Hammond had found in Cox's apartment, held by the subjects themselves. The patients appeared oblivious to the world around them, failing even to register an awareness that visitors hovered at their bedsides.

"In the previous ward," Darya said, "we controlled the frequency and intensity of the stimulation. Here the subjects control everything themselves. All we do is turn the devices off six hours a day so they'll eat and sleep. In the early days we had subjects nearly starve to death and others who experienced sleep-deprivation psychosis."

As she spoke, she stopped at the bed of a long-haired man on his back, spindly fingers gripping the stimulation box to his chest. Darya reached for the box, and he jerked it away with a scowl. She smiled reassuringly and patted his leg.

"We have found," she said, "that no other desire survives habituation to one of these devices. We have had intravenous heroin addicts remain with their stimulation box in preference to the drug. Mothers who hear the screams of their child in the next room stay with the box. These sensations go far beyond drug highs. They act directly on consciousness, on the psyche itself, without the need for an intermediary. They make other pleasures obsolete. All you need is the machine."

"If you don't mind slavery."

"Slavery?" She laughed. "These are the happiest people in the world, Jack. Look at them. Every desire is met and exceeded. Who would want to leave?"

She reached for his hand. "Come on, Jack, be honest. Isn't it everything you've ever wanted?"

Hammond wasn't going to answer that. "What has all this to do with psychotronics?"

She stepped toward a door, cocked her head, and said, "Right this way."

In a third ward—it was beginning to look like a production line—two young women and a gray-haired man in green hospital gowns lay on cots. They opened their eyes, glanced at Darya, then quickly closed their eyes again. A fourth man, young and slender, leapt off his cot to greet Darya, pleading with her. She touched his arm, calming him, reassuring him, and ordered him back to his cot.

"He came here yesterday from the last ward," she told Hammond, "and he's not happy about it. He wants to go back. It's a bit difficult withdrawing, but it's supposed to be. Soon he'll be like the other three, quite content."

"What's going on?" Hammond asked, his mind still on Valentina.

"All the subjects, including the first woman you saw, have been screened for psychic ability. After a period of habituation to the stimulation of specific brain locations, the external stimulation is withdrawn and they feel encouraged to try to stimulate the limbic system themselves by psychokinesis. That's what's happening here."

She walked back toward the door.

"They know exactly what effects they're after. They have a powerful incentive to develop their psychokinetic talents. When they succeed, the sensation is its own reward, a kind of biofeedback. After a period of time they become remarkably proficient. The goal is to train them to stimulate not merely their own brain receptors, but the receptors of other people as well. Finally, they'll be able to perform high-resolution PK not only on brains, but on other microcontrol mechanisms. That's the ultimate goal."

With her hand on the doorknob, she said, "Along the way, as they are developing this skill, the neural mechanisms affecting the PK are studied in order to duplicate the process technologically."

Hammond wondered if that meant brain autopsies on sacrificed subjects. Anything was possible in this place.

"So finally," he said, "you'll have a device capable of pinpoint PK on people and machines." Like the firing mechanisms of missiles and warheads.

"Exactly. Come with me."

They took an elevator down one floor and passed through a thickly insulated door into an anechoic chamber, white cones of acoustical foam spiking from the walls, ceiling, and floor. They stood on a plastic grating protruding into the center of the room. Any sound was immediately absorbed by the cones. There was no reverberation. The silence was so profound Hammond could hear blood humming in his ears.

Darya turned a switch on a small aluminum console fastened to the grating.

Hammond heard a faint, low-pitched tone.

"This was one of our earliest experiments," Darya explained. "We were learning to resonate sound waves with certain brain locations, achieve sonic stimulation of those locations. Be still and wait."

The volume of the tone increased, and its pitch rose slowly. After a half minute, the volume started to become uncomfortable. Hammond felt a throbbing in his head. Then the sound stopped. He could hear nothing, but the throbbing continued. He felt a heaviness, a closeness, as if something had filled the air and was pressing in around his head. Darya watched him.

He was about to complain when the heaviness lifted slightly, and he felt a pleasant sensation he could not describe except to say that it seemed concentrated vaguely in the center of his head.

The sensation intensified. It had nothing to do with sound. It wasn't sexual. In fact, it had nothing to do with any of the senses. It was just a wonderful feeling. He did not want it to stop.

"Had enough?" Darya asked.

He raised a hand and shook his head.

She turned a knob.

The feeling sharpened. It was unbelievable. He had never thought anything but sex could be so wonderful.

"We have to go," she said.

"No, no. Just a minute."

"Come on, Hammond, if I don't get you out of here now you'll want to stay forever."

"Please, no."

She flipped a switch, and the pleasure stopped. Hammond stood for a moment, listening to the humming in his ears. He had to catch his breath.

"That was remarkable," he said.

"I thought you'd like it."

Going up in the elevator, still recovering, Hammond had a disturbing idea. What would have happened if she'd let him stay there as long as he liked? He said, "Sonic stimulation of the limbic system. That was one of your earliest experiments?"

"Yes."

"What are the later ones like?"

"More sophisticated. We don't use sound anymore."

"What do you use?"

"That's the most exciting part. I'll explain later, but not here."

Hammond now regretted having revealed his pleasure to Darya. He felt manipulated, compromised. He was more comfortable with Darya when he was angry at her. And he was forgetting why he was here. The tour was over. She'd shown him as much as she was going to.

"Where is Valentina Leonov?"

Darya turned. "Come here," she said, as if she had not heard his question.

He resisted the tug of her hand. "Where is Valentina Leonov?"

He had a terrifying thought. Did Darya have other wards where subjects experienced the opposite of what he had just seen—endless, unendurable pain in countless varieties administered directly to pain centers in the spinal cord and limbic system? Was Valentina in one of those wards?

Darya glanced at him, and he could see the sudden concern in her eyes. He knew he was having a physical reaction to what she had shown him, and done to him. His face and hands were clammy.

"We'd better go to my office," she said, and he followed her toward the door. She looked up. "See that? One of the patients made it."

A framed sign, crudely shaped red Cyrillic letters on what looked like white cardboard, hung above the door. It said, "Heaven on Earth."

When they were back in her office, she said, "Are you all right? You look terrible."

"I'm fine. Where is Valentina Leonov?"

"*Who* is Valentina Leonov?"

"She was brought in here a couple of hours ago."

"So that's why you came here?

"I want her."

Darya laughed. "Well, you can't have her."

"This isn't a joke, Darya. I'm not leaving without her."

"Then I'll have to see if we can find you a bed. You think you can just break in here and demand to walk out with a patient?"

"She's not sick. The cops brought her in."

"Cops do sometimes bring sick people to psychiatric hospitals."

"She isn't sick."

"Then she isn't here. This is a hospital, a place for sick people."

"You must be talking about the staff."

"I'll have someone show you out."

She picked up the phone, and the steroid abusers delivered him to the street.

Valentina was in a small, low-ceilinged room with a wooden chair and a calendar. The calendar, hanging crookedly from a black thumbtack in the wall, displayed a color photograph of the Kremlin. The pages had not been turned for the past two months.

There was nothing else to look at. She sat in the chair, crossed her arms and her legs, closed her eyes and prayed for the men who had brought her here, for herself, and for Jack Hammond. She also prayed for an end to the desires that crowded her mind when she thought of Jack Hammond.

As she asked to be forgiven for those desires, a sense of release, well-being, and thankfulness drew her to her feet, head back, arms upraised. Her fingertips touched the plywood ceiling. She opened her eyes. Something on wheels rattled past the door.

She was sorry Jack Hammond had seen the bathroom and the kitchen. But she was happy he had followed her to court. She had gone to sleep last night thinking about him. Now she might never see him again.

A man stopped outside and called, "Here?"

Another voice farther away said, "Not yet. The next one."

She forced her mind back to Hammond. What was he really like? Footsteps stopped at the door. She wished she knew what was going to happen. The door opened, and a woman entered.

The menace was like a blow. She was beautiful—long black hair and green eyes. The eyes gazed into Valentina as if they too sensed a danger. Valentina had seen men and women who glowed with holiness. This woman radiated evil.

"So," the woman said, "what are we going to do with you?"

"Hello, Darya."

"It has been a long time, my dear. But I must admit that you have never been far from my thoughts."

Nor had Darya been far from the thoughts of Valentina. She had first heard Darya's name from Viktor, the young man who had been with her parents at the time of the timber mill fire. She was seven, Darya ten. Viktor told her that her parents were dead, but she did not believe it, not if dead meant she'd never see them again. He sat her down in the apartment her parents had shared with her grandparents and explained what had happened. Her first question had been, "Why was there a fire?"

"I'm not sure," Viktor had said. He was only twenty, and she saw in his eyes a desire to be honest with her. "I think maybe someone set it."

"Why would they do that? Who was it?"

He told her about the young girl seen lingering near the mill and said her name was Darya. She was the daughter of peasants who worked land that had once belonged to Valentina's great-grandfather. Viktor said villagers, claiming that for generations Darya's family had practiced shamanism, seemed not at all surprised that she should display magical powers, nor that she should use those powers against descendants of landowners she believed had oppressed her ancestors.

"Did you talk to her?" Valentina had asked.

"I tried, but her family said she had gone away. The local militia commander told me she had done things like this before. A teacher who had slapped her was reading a newspaper and the paper burst into flames. No one doubted that she had caused the fire in the mill."

"I want to see her."

"You can't, Valentina. Not now anyway. I don't know where she is, and it's an impossible trip in any case."

Valentina's desire to meet Darya had never diminished. Viktor too must have retained an interest, for eight years later he told Valentina that Darya had enrolled at Moscow University. Together they stood in a hallway outside a lecture hall, and when the students emerged, a friend of Viktor's pointed out Darya. She was wearing Western clothes, laughing with friends, intimidatingly beautiful.

Valentina's reaction was not at all what she had expected. She had thought she would run to her, confront her, demand to know what had happened the day her parents died. But she felt physically restrained, held back. She could only stare.

"Shall we talk to her?" Viktor had asked. He appeared a bit awed himself.

Valentina watched in silence as Darya moved with her friends toward an elevator. Darya was listening to them, her eyes sparkling with delight at what they said.

"Do you want to speak to her?" Viktor repeated.

Valentina, glued to the spot, could not take her eyes from Darya. She seemed to own the world. Then the elevator closed, and Darya was gone.

Riding home on the metro, Viktor said, "What did you think?"

"She was very beautiful. Everyone seemed to like her. She didn't look like a bad person."

"No," Viktor said, "she didn't."

It had been seven years before Valentina ran into Darya again.

"I asked you a question," Darya said now. "What are we going to do with you?"

She took a step toward Valentina and reached out a hand to touch her cheek.

Valentina drew back, praying for protection.

18

AT TEN O'CLOCK THAT
night, eight hours after he left Serbenov, Hammond stood
in half darkness in front of a mammoth eight-story stone
building at 26 Kutuzovsky Prospekt. Car headlights reflected off the snow on the ten-lane boulevard. A militia
officer eyed him suspiciously from the corner.

Hammond walked through the pedestrian opening in
a thirty-foot-high, iron-spiked gate blocking what had
once been a carriage entrance to the interior courtyard.
Inside he passed parked cars, the snow-covered swings
and slide of a playground, and found the entrance he was

looking for. Soviet leader Yuri Andropov had an apartment in this building, and his predecessor, Leonid Brezhnev, had died here.

No one answered Hammond's knock. Shivering in his overcoat and a fur hat he had bought at a Beriozka shop, he waited patiently in the hall. After forty minutes Darya stepped off the elevator.

"I had wanted to materialize in your bathroom," Hammond said when she saw him, "but I haven't quite picked up the knack."

Provided with the telephone number she'd left behind when she vanished from the apartment, Frank had been able to obtain her address. "So far as we know," Frank had confided proudly, "there are only six original telephone reverse books in Moscow. Ours is a copy of the GRU's. Don't ask how we got it."

Darya's arms were full of packages, and she did not appear surprised to see him.

"I'll teach you if you like. Can you get the key, please?"

She shoved a hip toward him and he reached into her mink pocket for the door key. The pocket was warm. Even after his ordeal at Serbenov, the act felt as intimate and exciting as putting his hand inside her blouse.

He followed her through the door, and was suddenly transported. If he'd just woken from an amnesiac sleep he'd have guessed he was in a Sutton Place penthouse. "Where's the view of the East River?"

"Like it?"

She tossed the mink over a Louis XV chair. It was as if Serbenov had never happened.

"Well, it's not Moscow," he said.

The thick beige carpet, silk flowered wall fabric, velour curtains, antique sofas, chairs, end tables, even the door-knobs and light switches—everything had come from the West. He bet there'd be ScotTissue toilet paper in the bathroom. And most un-Russian of all, the room was immense and filled with light.

"Where'd you get all this?"

"A girl needs friends to get along in Moscow."

He wanted to name some of the friends—Brezhnev, Chernenko, Romanov, Grishin, all the old Politburo cronies—but thought better of it.

She ducked into a kitchen, filled a couple of Baccarat glasses with ice cubes from a gigantic Frigidaire, and poured in about four ounces of Chivas Regal. She handed him a glass and looked into his eyes. "To dreams."

She sat sideways on a dark blue velvet sofa, set her glass on an inlaid marble coffee table, and tilted her head to-ward the seat beside her.

He pretended not to notice the gesture and stood beside a mahogany sideboard covered with old English silver.

"You don't need to defect to the West, Darya. You're already there."

"It feels like it, doesn't it? It's going out the door I can't stand."

"In case you're wondering why I've come—"

"Not at all. I'm just delighted you're here. Please sit down. I'm sorry you had to leave my office so suddenly. You were rather insulting, you know."

"This isn't a social visit. I was very interested in your work at Serbenov, and I'd like to see the rest of it. You promised to tell me the connection with psychotronics, and Tuesday night you offered to show me what you're doing with universal Fourier components, by which I assume you mean Spectrum."

She looked away and ran a hand through her hair. "You know what I want in return for all this. Do I get it?"

"I want to see Spectrum."

"Do I get it?"

"If you show me Spectrum, you'll get—well, for a start you'll get my belief that you're serious."

She reached for her drink. "I want your promise right now that you'll help me get out of here, if and when I need to get out."

"I'm not even listening."

She crossed her legs, her foot kicking rhythmically. After a moment she said, "Okay. You saw Serbenov, and I'll show you Spectrum. Because I need you, Jack, and I trust you. You won't betray me."

"You're completely wrong, Darya. I'd betray you in a second."

"You don't give much away, do you?"

"Depends on the recipient. When do I see it?"

"Monday?"

"Fine. And I want Valentina out of Serbenov."

"Oh, no, not her again."

Hammond headed for the door.

"Stop being such a jerk, Hammond. Who is she, anyway? Every American who comes here can't wait to screw a Russian." He put his back to her and turned the knob. "All right, all right. Whoever she is, I'll see what I can do."

He faced her. "You know who she is, Darya, because

she's in Serbenov, and you won't see what you can do, you'll do what you can do."

If that look of black fury wasn't genuine, he'd hate to see the real thing.

"She'll be home in the morning. Anything else?"

"I'll be here Monday at noon. On the dot."

19

OLD MRS. KOBLOV LET HIM
in, stooping, nodding, grinning like a witch, stains and
bread crumbs covering her threadbare housecoat. She
shuffled back toward the kitchen, and Hammond thought
how delighted she must be to have something to tell the
militia sergeant. It was nine o'clock the morning after his
visit to Darya's apartment.

Holding his breath against the stench, Hammond
knocked softly on Valentina's door. There was no response. He knocked again, then tried the knob. It turned,
and he looked in. He entered and closed the door.

Valentina was on her knees in the dim light at the

window. Her right side was toward him, her eyes closed, head raised toward the ceiling, elbows at her sides, hands extended palms up as if receiving a gift. Perfectly motionless, she gave no indication she knew he was there.

Hammond lowered himself silently into one of the chairs, put a paper bag he was carrying on the floor beside him, and watched. Her white nightdress and the reflection from the polished parquet appeared to give her a luminescence. Her breathing was slow and regular.

What was she praying about? What had they done to her at Serbenov? He wanted to talk to her, console her if that was what she needed, hold her. After several minutes, he said softly, "Valentina." She did not move or speak.

He waited another five minutes, then removed from the bag boxes of sugar, salt, and tea, cans of frankfurters and Campbell's vegetable soup, and a dozen oranges, all bought that morning at the embassy commissary. He placed them on the coffee table.

When he looked back she was smiling, but in so soft and natural a way he wondered if perhaps she had been smiling all along.

He was puzzled. Was she happy? Had she enjoyed whatever happened at Serbenov?

Then the impression of luminescence increased, and it was not just the nightdress and the parquet. She was glowing.

Her head lowered, and her hands dropped slowly to her sides. She opened her eyes, saw Hammond, and said, "How are you?"

"I'm fine. How are you?"

"Fine too."

"Excuse me for just walking in. The door wasn't locked."

"It's all right. I'm glad you're here."

"Why is that?"

"I wanted to see you again. I just feel that what has happened has something to do with you." She stood and saw the food. "You didn't have to do that."

"I was happy to. You sure you're all right?" He wanted to put his arms around her.

"Sure." She sat on the mattress.

"Do you want to tell me what happened?"

"Have you heard of the Serbenov Institute?"

"Yes."

"That's where they took me. They have some very unfortunate people there."

"So I hear."

"I wasn't thinking of the patients."

"I've been told they do experiments on people, not very nice experiments."

He waited for her reaction to tell him how much she had seen or experienced. He wanted every detail of every moment, but he knew he couldn't push her. If she didn't want to tell him, there would be no talking her into it.

"They are doing Satan's work there."

"Will you tell me about it?"

"They just asked me questions."

"Then how do you know what they do?"

"I have heard."

"Who asked you the questions?"

"Several people."

"Was one of them a woman? Tall, black hair, pretty?"

"Yes. Do you know her?"

"What did they want to know?"

"If I would help them with their research."

"What did you say?"

"I said I would pray about it and let them know."

Hammond had to laugh. I'll pray and get back to you. He could imagine Darya's reaction to that.

"Then what?"

"No one was unpleasant."

"They've been unpleasant to other people there, Valentina. Believe me."

"Anyway, it wouldn't matter what they did. I'm not afraid. If you love someone"—she picked up an orange—"and they give everything for you, it's good to have an opportunity to show your love too, to suffer a little bit for them. Don't you think so?"

"Who are you talking about, Valentina?"

"I think you know."

"Well, I wish I had your faith."

She was peeling the orange. "You could have it easily."

"I'm afraid I'm not that religious."

"I'm not religious either. Satan uses religion to keep us from God. I just know Jesus."

He wanted to back out of this, but he didn't know what to say.

"Do you want to do it?" she asked him. "Do you want to know him?"

He was embarrassed. "Not right now. What were you praying for when I came in?"

"Nothing." She finished peeling the orange, divided it in two, and handed him half. "I was giving thanks, that I was able to show my love by not being afraid, and that I was given so much more love than I could show. The amount of love—just immersed in love. I can't describe it."

Hammond thought he could. He had experienced its physical counterpart. Whole-body orgasms.

20

AFTER SERBENOV, HAM-
mond was ready for a little light entertainment, but something told him he wouldn't find it at Spaso House, the
ambassador's residence. So when Frank suggested that
Hammond and Valentina accompany him to the Satur-
day-afternoon movie there, Hammond resisted.

"With Valentina?"

"Why not?" Frank said. "Half the people there will be
dissidents."

Given the strained relationship between the United
States and the Soviets, dissidents were about the only

Russians who showed up for embassy functions, and no doubt a good number of them were KGB plants.

"Who'll be there?" Hammond asked. The movies were a weekly event.

"Could be anybody. The ambassador, embassy people, Western journalists, a couple of people from Doskino if the film's good. You'll enjoy it. So will Valentina. What could happen that's bad?"

At least it would be a chance to meet the ambassador, who, despite Hammond's repeated attempts to pay his respects, had kept himself unavailable. Jerry Shroeder, after arranging Hammond's first encounter with Marchenko, had also remained curiously out of touch. The defense attaché, an overstarched DIA colonel who had finally consented to receive Hammond, was aloof and arrogant, suggesting that in a more perfect world physicians would not be allowed to play at spying. As if Hammond wanted to. Even at "the farm," where he was required to undergo CIA training for this Moscow visit, Hammond had run afoul of CIA recruits whose interest in exotic weapons, tradecraft, and communications paraphernalia he failed to share.

Hammond was lonely in Moscow, lonelier even than he had been in Vietnam, lonelier than he had been at the lowest points of his marriage. He was as much an outsider inside the embassy as on the streets of Moscow. Why was it easier to talk to Marchenko, Valentina, and Darya than to his colleagues at the embassy? He hated having to wonder if even Frank, so amiable and helpful, was really just there to keep an eye on him. Some people liked intrigue, thrived on it, enjoyed all the spy games. Hammond hated it.

In the end, it was Valentina who convinced him to go.

"It'll be very stuffy," he told her. "The ambassador will be there, probably his wife, the DCM, all the embassy stiffs, diplomats from other embassies. You want to go through that?"

"It's only a movie," she said. "I would like to go."

"Why?"

"I don't know. Something tells me I should go. I want to go."

They arrived at Spaso House a half hour early, and a white-jacketed butler directed them to a large room with a spectacular cut-crystal chandelier suspended from a domed ceiling two stories above the floor. The room was filled with children.

"*Snow White*," Frank said after conferring with the butler. "They've got folding chairs in the ballroom, if you want to go in and sit down. The movie will start in a couple of minutes." He looked around. "There aren't usually this many people. Everyone in town brought their kids."

They drifted toward the ballroom, and Hammond saw Valentina's face stiffen. He followed her gaze and spotted Darya. She handed her fur coat to the butler and was immediately approached by a short, stout, fiftyish man Hammond recognized as the ambassador, Christopher Puckett. They kissed on the cheek.

"You know who that is?" Hammond said to Frank.

"The ambassador."

"I mean the woman."

"Seen her before. Friend of the ambassador I think."

A very good friend, Hammond thought, judging by the closeness of their bodies as Puckett took her hand.

Darya and the ambassador strolled beneath the chandelier to a door flanked by two false columns. Laughing together, they passed into a sitting room. Hammond held Valentina's hand, and followed.

The room was already occupied by a dozen adults Hammond took to be parents who had less desire than their children to see *Snow White*. Jerry Shroeder was there, huddled with a pair of Frenchmen.

"Our English friends," Frank said, waving at two dark-suited men across the room who looked as if they had just stepped out of a John le Carré novel. Why did English spies always look like English spies? "And German," Frank said, his gaze turning to a stoop-shouldered, scholarly man smoking a cigarette by the door. "All the spooks are here with their kiddie spooks to watch the Wicked Witch."

Darya's entrance had electrified the room. Everyone wanted to shake her hand, kiss her cheek. Puckett stood by beaming.

"She seems to have a lot of friends here," Valentina said. Hammond nodded. He decided this was as good a time as any to accost the ambassador.

"Excuse me," he said, stepping forward, "my name's Jack Hammond. I'm your new medical officer."

Puckett seemed a bit startled, then smiled thinly in an unsuccessful attempt to conceal irritation. He wanted Darya to himself. "Oh, yes, of course. I believe you know Miss Timoshek." So he'd been briefed. What had she told him? Nothing nice.

Darya kissed him on the cheek. "Good to see you, Jack."

"You too. You've met Mrs. Leonov?" Valentina had

said one of her Serbenov interrogators was a tall, pretty, black-haired woman.

Puckett's scrutiny was too obvious. He'd heard of this girl.

"How nice to see you again," Darya said to Valentina, bathing everyone in charm.

Valentina nodded. With her cropped hair and cheap Russian dress she might have been Darya's maid.

"I was just telling Christopher about a pain in his shoulder," Darya said.

"I don't have a pain in my shoulder," Puckett said. "She wants to make the pain go away and there isn't any pain."

"You don't have anything wrong with your shoulder?" Darya insisted playfully.

Puckett's wife, taller than he and considerably more cordial, had joined them. "Of course you do, dear. You told me yourself this morning your shoulder hurt." She grinned graciously at Hammond. "He broke it years ago at Yale."

Darya put her hands on Puckett's left shoulder, and immediately his expression changed from annoyance to surprise.

"So it did hurt," Darya said.

Puckett rotated his elbow and glanced at his wife.

"Better?" Darya said.

"How did you do that?"

Valentina tightened her grip on Hammond's hand.

"Our physicists say it's bioenergy," Darya said, "but an old shaman in Labinsk where I grew up called it magic."

"And what do you think, Darya?" Hammond asked. A

small crowd, sensing amusement, formed around them. Shroeder appeared at the ambassador's side.

"I think it's love," Darya answered, "a universal force living in everything around us."

Music drifted in from the ballroom. The film had started.

"It's in every natural thing," Mrs. Puckett explained, evidently having had this conversation before. "It's in every one of us and we must learn to use it. Darya has helped many of our friends."

"Can she help her?" No one had expected Valentina to speak. Heads swiveled, first to her, then to the child she had pointed to. A dark-haired girl of about six, accompanied by a woman, was walking past the door of the sitting room, on her way to the ballroom.

"Would you come in, please?" Valentina called.

"I don't think—" the ambassador said.

The woman, seeing the ambassador, took the girl's hand and joined the group.

"How long has she been deaf?" Valentina asked the woman.

"All her life."

"What is her name?"

"Tatyana."

"Are you her mother?"

"I'm a nurse."

Valentina confronted Darya. "Heal her."

"How did you know she was deaf?" Puckett asked.

"Heal her," Valentina repeated, the drill-sergeant eyes boring into Darya.

The crowd was large now, people flowing in from the chandelier room. This was better than *Snow White*.

"I really think," Mrs. Puckett said, "that we should stop this. It's not fair to this poor girl."

"You can't heal her," Valentina said to Darya.

In the midst of the growing number of spectators, Hammond spotted the British and German intelligence officers. They wore the concentrated expressions of men who would shortly be putting all this down on paper. Frank was with them.

"Come on now," Shroeder said, coming to Puckett's rescue, "that's enough. We're here to watch a movie." He looked at the nurse. "Take her into the movie."

"No," Valentina ordered. "You said your universal force, or whatever you call it, has healed. So heal this girl."

Darya appeared to have lost her tongue.

"You can't heal her," Valentina challenged.

"Fine," Puckett said irritably. "Then let's stop this right now and all go into the movie." He glared at Hammond.

"Jesus will heal her," Valentina said.

"Now look here—" Puckett said.

Mrs. Puckett put her hand on Valentina's arm. "My dear, we don't want to hurt this child. She has enough problems as it is. I'm sure you mean well, but I do think we should do as my husband says and just go in and watch the movie."

Valentina took one step forward and gently clasped the girl's head, one hand over each ear. The girl gazed up at Valentina, shy but unfrightened, as if expecting a kiss. Valentina closed her eyes, and her lips moved silently.

The girl's knees buckled. The nurse caught her around the waist. The crowd pushed forward. A woman with a Swedish accent at the back of the crowd cried, "What happened? Did she strike her? Why doesn't somebody stop her?"

The nurse lowered the girl to the floor.

"Hammond, damn it, you're a doctor," Puckett said. "Help the child and then get this woman the hell out of here."

Hammond felt the girl's pulse. Normal. Respiration was normal. She opened her eyes, and the nurse and Hammond helped her to her feet.

"How do you feel," Hammond said, forgetting she couldn't hear. The child turned silently to her nurse. The nurse hugged her and looked at the group. "If we could just sit down for a moment."

"Of course," Puckett said. "Certainly. Please, everyone, let's leave them alone. Hammond, are you sure that child's all right?"

"Absolutely."

Puckett glowered at Valentina. "And still deaf?"

"I'm afraid so," Hammond said.

"Then please leave, and take your friend with you."

Out on the street, signaling for a taxi, Hammond said to Valentina, "Can you tell me please just exactly why the hell you had to do that? You damn near got us lynched." A cab stopped and he held the door for her. "I've got enough trouble in the embassy, I don't need—"

Valentina sat rigidly at the window, back straight, tears rolling down her cheeks.

"Oh, no," Hammond breathed. "Look, I'm sorry if—"

He put his arm around her until the crying stopped, then dropped her off at her apartment.

He spent the night in Cox's living room, trying to imagine what the ramifications of the Spaso House disaster might be. He didn't think the ambassador would go so far as to demand his recall, but who knew. At least he still had Whitmore on his side.

Monday morning he was in his office at the embassy medical clinic, a small wooden building in the courtyard, when he heard his assistant, a male nurse, answer the phone.

"For you, Doctor."

Hammond picked up the receiver. In heavily accented English, a man identifying himself as an otologist at Botkin hospital told him that a patient of his, a six-year-old girl named Tatyana Petrakov, had suddenly regained her hearing. And what did Hammond know about it, since Hammond evidently had treated her.

"I didn't treat her," Hammond said, suspecting a KGB setup.

"An official from the orphanage where she lives said you treated her."

"She collapsed," Hammond said, measuring his words, "and I examined her briefly."

"But what about her hearing? She had congenital nerve deafness. Now she hears."

"Perhaps the diagnosis was incorrect." Hammond kept his voice businesslike, unconcerned.

"Dr. Hammond, I made the diagnosis myself. I have known the girl since birth. I have the records. You may see them."

"So what do you think?" Hammond asked.

"She had congenital nerve deafness. Now she hears."

Something in the man's voice—an excited uncertainty—said this was not the KGB.

"So?"

"The nurse said there was a young woman there, who put her hands on the girl's ears."

"That's correct."

In the silence, Hammond felt his heartbeat accelerate.

"Dr. Hammond . . ."

"Yes."

"This girl has been my patient for all of her six years. I know her mother. If you can tell me what happened . . ."

"I don't know what happened."

"But she hears."

Yes, she hears.

"Dr. Hammond, how do you explain that?"

His forehead was damp. He felt a chill.

"Dr. Hammond?"

"It was a miracle."

He said it, but he wasn't sure he believed it.

21

W*HEN HAMMOND SHOWED*
up at Darya's apartment at noon as promised, she led him
downstairs to a deserted underground parking garage.

"Put this on," she ordered, and handed him a black
leather blindfold. It had straps and a buckle and looked
like something you'd find in the closet of a sadomasochist.
A tightly fitting nose cover to prevent peeking, and a distinct odor of tobacco, made Hammond wonder if he was
the first to make this trip in the dark. He anxiously recalled
that Cox had been a heavy smoker.

Darya sat with him in the backseat of the moving car,
but gave no orders to the driver. His anxiety increased.

He was blindfolded, with Darya and an unknown driver, being taken to he didn't know where. If the Soviets had decided it was time to make him tell them what he knew, wasn't this the way they would go about it? The more these thoughts filled his head, the more he regretted having so readily donned the blindfold and entered the car. On the other hand, if he pulled the blindfold off and demanded to be let out, he might lose the chance to see Spectrum.

"Where are we going?" he asked. He overcame the temptation to tell her the deaf girl had been healed. Knowledge was power, not to be given away.

"You know better than to ask that," Darya said. "Just settle back and relax. The trip will be worth it."

No doubt, but for whom?

Hammond gave up trying to memorize their route. But the length of the trip, plus long stretches without turns, told him they were well outside Moscow. So at least they weren't headed for the Serbenov Institute.

The car turned sharply, Hammond heard a sharp metallic clank, and they descended. They parked, and Darya led him by the arm over what felt and sounded like concrete. They entered an elevator. An acute temperature change from the warmth of the entrance area to a severe chill as the elevator went down, then back to warmth, suggested the presence of air-conditioning, which in turn indicated an extensive computer installation. They were deep under ground. Hammond thought of prisons and torture chambers.

They were met by a man who spoke in whispers with Darya and preceded them down a hallway, his heels clicking on the hard floor. They walked straight ahead for what seemed like a good city block, then angled to the left for about another fifty yards, and passed through a series of doors.

Darya led Hammond to a chair, told him to sit down, and removed his blindfold. The effect was negligible, for he was in a completely lightless room. Even with eyes accustomed to darkness during the hour-long automobile trip, he could not make out the dimmest shape. The chair felt like molded plastic, fastened solidly to the floor.

"Are you comfortable?" she asked from the seat next to him.

"Yes. Fine." In fact, he was sweating with fear.

Darya gave a command, and a faint but disturbingly low-pitched humming surrounded him, as if someone were holding small electric fans a foot from each ear. He smelled ozone. His mouth filled with a metallic taste, the same he had had at a MAG project employing high-voltage electromagnetic radiation. The hairs on his arms stood up.

He sat motionless in the darkness. Was this really Spectrum?

Suddenly a sharply defined column of green light, identical to the light emitted by a neodymium-YAG laser, appeared ten feet in front of him. An instant later, the lower half of the column was replaced by the fuzzy image of what appeared to be a striped pillar. As he watched, the fuzziness disappeared, as if someone were focusing the image. The horizontal stripes around the pillar were black at the bottom, then gray, multicolored at the center, gray and black again at the top.

When the focusing was complete and the stripes stood

out sharply, something happened that made Hammond all but jump from his seat. A man appeared in the image, obstructing Hammond's view of the striped pillar. The man, in a dark suit, white shirt, and red tie, hands at his sides, proceeded to count to ten in Russian.

Hammond's fear turned to excitement. This had to be Spectrum. The man was not really there. He was a holographic image. The Soviets had demonstrated a holographic movie in 1976, and others had considered holographic television. But even the most powerful supercomputers would take hours to process the ninety billion bits of information required by a single stationary televised hologram. What Hammond was seeing here—a real-time, moving hologram, complete with sound—was beyond the scope of Western technology.

Darya touched his hand and lowered her head close to his ear. "Fourier transforms for the interference fringes generated by the man," she said, "are computer processed, point by point, into a series of two-dimensional holograms. Those are then combined to produce the 3-D image we're looking at." Hammond nodded, but did not take his eyes off the man. "Holographic phase-conjugate mirrors compensate for wave distortion." She raised her voice. "Vadim? Can you hear me?"

The man responded in heavily accented English. This was a command performance for Hammond. "Yes, Darya. I am here, as I hope you can see."

"We can see perfectly, Vadim. Have you something to show us? We were wondering about the latest news."

Vadim reached into his pocket and withdrew the front page of a newspaper, which he unfolded and held before him.

"Can you read that from here?" Darya asked Hammond.

He squinted and shook his head.

"Go up and read it. Just the date."

Hammond stood and approached the image. The newspaper was *Pravda*. He reached out his hand, and it sliced through the air where the newspaper was. He bent forward and read the day's date at the top of the page.

"Thank you, Vadim," Darya said when Hammond was back in his chair. "Do you have something else to show us?"

Vadim crushed the newspaper page into a tight ball and set it on top of the striped pillar. Then he withdrew from the image.

"Watch this carefully," Darya said to Hammond. "Don't even blink."

Hammond fixed his eyes on the ball of paper sitting on the pillar. Suddenly the paper vanished.

There was nothing to say. It had to be a trick.

After a moment, Darya asked, "What do you think of that?"

"What's to think?"

"It's gone, Jack."

"I can see that. Congratulations. Neat trick."

"No, Jack, it's not a trick. The paper is gone."

The image of the pillar vanished, the column of green light was extinguished, and Hammond found himself once again in darkness.

"Gone where?" Hammond said.

"Let's talk."

Darya replaced the blindfold, took Hammond by the hand, and led him along a corridor. When she removed the blindfold they were alone in a plain, transparent-walled conference room with chairs and a table. It looked very much like the CIA's "clean bubble."

"Gone where?" Hammond repeated.

They took seats on opposite sides of the rectangular table.

"We'll get to that later. First, tell me what you think of the image itself, before the paper disappeared."

"I have a lot of questions."

She sat back and raised her hands in a gesture that said, Ask anything you like.

"Where was the man located?" Hammond wanted to know over how great a distance the images could be communicated.

"I'm afraid you've begun with a question I mustn't answer. I'm sorry. Try something else."

"What is the means of communication?"

He was hoping against hope. If the signal was sent over a wire or microwaves, like a telephone call or television signal, the consequences would not be so great. Given sufficiently powerful computers anyone might do the same. But he feared this was not the case.

"I think you have guessed that," Darya said. She walked to the other end of the table, putting her back to him. "We're talking about universal Fourier components." She would know he was aware of the theory of enfoldment and a holographic universe, everything Burkholzer had explained with his glycerine jar and oscilloscope to MAG. The question was, had she managed to apply the theory, did she have a device that could really pull pictures out of space?

She stopped and turned to face him. "If we here in Russia want to see a table in your living room in Washington, or a table you had there last year, we have only to identify and make visual that table's interference pattern as it exists here today in Russia."

She was talking about tables, but the interest was in missiles, documents, and individuals. Hammond had just seen a man holding a copy of today's *Pravda*. Could Darya just as easily have shown him, and let him listen to, President Reagan at work in the Oval Office?

"We are able to recognize frequency interference patterns in space," Darya said, "to screen them for the desired Fourier components, transform the components into viewable holographic images, and sharpen those images with holographic image deblurring."

Hammond was astonished. Not for a moment had he imagined that such a device was near realization.

"Can you do that only for your friend Vadim and his copy of *Pravda*, or can you see randomly selected targets as well?"

"Jack, we can see anything we want, particularly with laser assistance."

"I'm not sure I understand."

"Spectrum operates by performing Fourier transforms on background radiation—"

"Electromagnetic?"

"I'll get to that. If you want to know what Spectrum can do, just think for a moment of what's achieved by the analysis of laser radiation."

She stopped, evidently awaiting awed appeals to continue.

"Go ahead," he said.

"Light from an airborne excimer laser easily penetrates cloud cover and seawater, as you know."

"Certainly." She could really be insufferable.

"We can scan large areas of ocean to a depth of thousands of feet. By analyzing the laser return from molecules ejected by your submarines, we can tell how many missiles are aboard, how many men, what they had for breakfast. We'll even know if there's a woman aboard, from molecules contained in her menstrual fluid."

"Very impressive."

"You already know that laser radiation can be used to observe electrons moving in silicon computer chips. Well, Spectrum can do that far better than laser radiation. And if Spectrum can see those molecules, Spectrum can divert them. Spectrum can defeat any computer you have, Jack, and every electronic or mechanical device from aircraft control systems to space rockets. With Spectrum, we don't need the lasers anymore. It uses natural radiation present everywhere in the universe. Electromagnetic radiation, electron beams, neutrinos, anything that moves."

Is that what Spectrum *can* do, Hammond thought, or what it *could* do? Do you have Spectrum, Darya? Or are you just spewing theory?

"Vadim was in real time," Hammond said, "unless you've produced your own edition of *Pravda*. What about past time?"

"We have retrieved past images."

Could they sit in on a National Security Council meeting held last month? Theoretically, it was possible. "What about storage?"

"The Fourier components can be stored like any other numerical data. In fact, the entire imaging process, after capturing the interference patterns, is computerized, so saving the images is routine."

"Would they come with you to the West?"

"Why not?"

"How much is there?"

"You can imagine. The information content of the display you just saw represents trillions of bits. But it's stored on holograms."

Holograms smaller than a pinhead could store immense amounts of information. A stack of twenty superthin holograms, masquerading as a period or decimal point (the CIA called them holodots, after their old-fashioned cousins, microdots), might contain a small library. If she wanted to, Darya could probably remove to the West the totality of Spectrum data in a half dozen holodots concealed on a laundry list.

Hammond nodded, trying to absorb the implications of what he had learned.

"But I have something more to tell you, Jack. The universe is a hologram, right?"

"So they say."

"And so is consciousness. Your brain is a hologram. So we're trying now to capture the Fourier components of nonphysical entities."

"Meaning?"

"Thoughts. Ideas."

Darya paused. Finally Hammond said, "Are you going to tell me?"

"If this works—and it *is* going to work—we'll be able to identify individuals with common ideational structures."

"Drop the jargon, Darya."

"Everyone who likes vanilla ice cream will produce distinctive ideational Fourier components."

"You're crazy."

"You think so? Let's go back to where the ball of paper went."

"Where did it go?"

"It didn't go anywhere. It just ceased to exist. Wherever matter goes when it falls into a black hole, wherever a quantum-tunneling electron goes when it disappears at a barrier—that's where that paper went. It wasn't destroyed. It de-existed."

He saw where Darya was headed. It was like the ink drop in the cylinder of glycerine Burkholzer had used at the MAG briefing. By rotating the cylinder, Burkholzer had been able to spread the ink throughout the glycerine, then, by reversing the rotation, to "wind back" the thread into a single drop. MAG researchers had already been able to wind back damaged microorganisms to earlier states, in effect reversing the damage. It was a kind of healing. Was it possible, then, to wind back organisms and objects through time to the moment of their creation, even to before their creation—to "de-exist" them?

Darya was saying that Spectrum technology had already succeeded in doing this. Spectrum could, if you believed her, de-exist material objects. Spectrum also apparently had the potential to identify and locate individuals with certain, highly specific, common traits. Put those two capabilities together and you'd be able to select any individual or group and de-exist it. But he did not believe that was possible. He had had to accept some wild things since going to work for MAG, but this was over the limit.

"Look at this," Darya said, walking to a display easel at the end of the conference table. She lifted the cover to reveal an enlarged photograph of a rat. Beneath the rat was a series of five-digit number groups. "This is an experiment done eighteen months ago. The numbers represent Fourier components for interference patterns produced by the rat's brain."

She flipped the photograph over the top of the easel and revealed another picture of a rat with a series of number groups. This time the rat was in a lordosis posture, the arched-back stance assumed during mating.

"This is the same rat an hour later, after receiving an LRH injection."

LRH was a hypothalamic peptide that produced sexual arousal. Hammond recalled an outlandish CIA suggestion that an LRH-spiked water supply could be used to drive an enemy population into a debilitating, nationwide sex orgy.

"Look at the Fourier numbers," Darya went on. "They're different. The interference patterns of frequencies in the rat's brain change when it's aroused. If we wanted to, we could use this technique to identify and locate all the sexually aroused rats in the world."

She folded the photograph over the top of the easel. "But we thought it would be more interesting to switch to humans. So we decided to try to locate individuals with high brain-dopamine levels. And guess what we found?"

The next display was a map of Moscow with a half dozen small shaded areas.

"The dark parts," Darya said, "are mental hospitals with relatively large numbers of schizophrenics." Elevated

brain-dopamine levels were characteristic of schizophrenics.

She flipped the map and Hammond was relieved to find
no more illustrations behind it. What would have been
next? Was he supposed to *believe* this? Darya was a born
deceiver.

"We are pursuing this research, and we have advanced
far beyond such relatively broad groups as schizophrenics
and excited monkeys."

Hammond nodded. He wished Burkholzer was hearing
all this.

"Let's be frank," Darya said, taking the chair next to
Hammond and leaning toward him. "We can penetrate
consciousness, identify people by what's in their minds.
If we wanted to, we could target all the pregnant teenagers
in London."

"Target?" His head was aching.

"Maybe that wasn't the right word."

If this was true, Spectrum would be able to influence,
or to de-exist if it wished, all American intelligence agents,
or all Western heads of government, or Jews or Moslems
or Christians or, for that matter, anyone with a knowledge
of Spectrum.

"You could take out a population?" Hammond asked.

"Or age group, profession, belief, race. And remember
what you saw at Serbenov. Spectrum doesn't have to de-
exist targets. It can perform high-resolution PK on specific
locations within the target, even inside brains. It has a
highly versatile attack profile."

After Hammond's sonic high at Serbenov, Darya had
mentioned sophisticated experiments that "don't use

sound anymore." Now he knew what they used—enfoldment technology, Spectrum. In other words, Spectrum could pick out particular people and, by using psychokinesis to alter cells in the brain or other organs, influence their behavior or kill them.

"How many people have access to Spectrum?" he asked.

"A lot of people work on the pieces, but they don't know what they fit into or how they fit. I'm the only one who's seen the whole puzzle and knows where all the pieces go."

"And you have it all on holodots?"

She nodded, a very self-satisfied nod.

"Where are they?"

"Don't be silly, Jack. They're my insurance."

"Tell me something," Hammond said, suddenly remembering the smoke-scented blindfold. "Did Cox ever come here?"

"Why do you ask that?"

"Did he?"

"No." It was a lie. He knew Darya. He was sure it was a lie.

"How far away is full capability?" If Spectrum had really de-existed the newspaper page, how long before it became operational outside the laboratory? Hammond was certain that Spectrum's abilities remained extremely limited. If not, Darya would have been de-existing enemies left and right.

"Not far, Jack."

"Years? Months?"

"Maybe less." She was playing with him. "I'll tell you when I get to the West."

This whole presentation could have been a charade. Certainly the KGB had engineered other elaborate hoaxes in the past. But given the consequences if Darya was telling the truth, who in Washington would bet against her?

"Well," Hammond conceded, his head throbbing, "I'd say you just bought yourself a ticket to the West."

22

THE FOLLOWING MORNING Hammond was shaving in George Cox's bathroom when the telephone rang once and stopped. He put the razor down and listened. Ten seconds later the phone went again. Hammond let it ring. It rang eleven times and stopped.

Hammond finished dressing, borrowed an embassy car, and went for a drive. The number of rings had given him half a message, now he needed the other half.

He cruised past the Defense Ministry, took the ring road to Petrovka Street and drove by Militia headquarters, made a left on Marksa Prospekt to Dzerzhinski Square, and went slowly past the high, brass-handled yellow doors of KGB headquarters. He circled the building three times, slowing in the back as he passed the black, steel drive-in gate and the Gastronom food shop where KGB agents dropped kopeks into vending machines and stood at white Formica tables with their hot cocoa and sausage rolls. The Children's World department store was across the street. When people talked about "the men from Children's World," you knew whom they meant. Rumors said agents and their *stukachi* came and went through a tunnel linking the basements of the store and the KGB building.

Hammond crossed the square and turned left past the yellow stone Central Committee headquarters, flanked by black Zil limousines, then carried on to the old Khodinka Field and the campuslike headquarters complex of the GRU, military intelligence. Driving by the entrance gate, he waited until the sheets of green metal blocking a view from the street gave way to an iron fence. Then he looked up to the fourth floor, counted four windows in from the corner, and noted the position of the two pull-across white curtains, identical to those at the KGB building. The left curtain was closed, the right open.

He continued on to the Academy of Sciences, the Institute of International Relations, and Moscow University. KGB followers, alerted by phone tappers who suspected a signal in the two unanswered phone calls, could do their best to guess his purpose, whether his interest was in all those buildings or only one or none at all.

At ten o'clock that night Hammond slipped a 9mm Walther PPK automatic into his overcoat pocket (the same pocket, he reflected, that used to hold a stethoscope) and drove up Kosygin Street to the Lenin Hills, where

Politburo members in secluded stone dachas with iron-spiked gates drank Courvoisier cognac in front of Sony television sets.

He parked in the darkness next to a snow-covered side-walk with trees and white-slatted park benches. A hundred yards ahead and to the left he could make out the embankment lookout point where lovers came in day-light to gaze down at the Moscow River and the city beyond. Tonight the spot was, or appeared to be, deserted. Hammond's was the only parked car.

He waited for fifteen minutes, peering through the blackness and thinking about Jerry Shroeder's latest hostile act. Frank had at first happily agreed to accompany Hammond tonight, but when Hammond showed up at the embassy to set a time and place to meet, Shroeder's secretary informed him that Frank would be busy.

"Okay," Hammond said, trying not to look too disappointed, "so where can I find a car?"

"Mr. Shroeder didn't say anything about a car."

"Could you ask him? I didn't have any trouble getting one last time."

"He isn't in right now."

"When will he be back?"

"I don't know. Maybe not until tomorrow."

In the end, Hammond had had to get a car from the consular section.

Hammond wondered if he should cable Ralph Whitmore and get the Shroeder problem straightened out now, before it grew worse. But it seemed silly to bother MAG over something as trivial as a car and driver. Shroeder was returning to the States soon anyway, so why make a fuss?

He pulled his wool scarf tighter around his neck and walked to the park on the other side of the lookout point. He watched quietly from one of the benches before strolling up the hill toward the ugly stone wedding cake that was Moscow University. He crossed back toward his car, picked a spot in a clump of trees with a good view of the street and the lookout point, and stood motionless in the dark, listening.

As he searched for movement on the street and sidewalks, his mind went to Darya and Spectrum. If Spectrum really had the potential to de-exist targets, that still did not explain the peculiar skills Darya appeared to possess, such as her ability to transport herself in and out of Cox's locked apartment. Did she herself have some mystical contact with what Burkholzer called the enfolding medium? And what about Valentina? Had she really healed him of the flu, or was that a coincidence? Had she healed the deaf girl?

After another half hour of countersurveillance he approached the lookout point, found a pedestrian path, and started down through the forest toward the river. It was eleven o'clock, the number of times the phone had rung in his apartment that morning.

He picked out a dark shape ahead of him in a clearing next to the path. The shape moved to a bench and sat down. Hammond removed his right glove and gripped the Walther in his pocket. Then he stepped into the clearing.

"How are you, Andrei?" Hammond said.

"Cold. Sorry for all the cloak and dagger."

"What's the point of being a spy if you don't get to act like one?"

Hammond joined Marchenko on the bench.

"It's freezing so I'll get to the point," Marchenko said. "What did you find out from the Leonov woman?"

"Find out about what?" He was pretty demanding, Marchenko.

"Please, Jack, I'm catching pneumonia."

"You wanna be warm, we could go to the embassy."

"Can she heal?"

A full moon was rising over the river.

"You told Cox she could."

"But you saw her. You talked to her." Was it possible that Marchenko had not heard about the deaf girl?

"Don't miss much, do you?" Hammond said. "What's so important about her healing that we have to freeze to death in the middle of the night?"

"There's a Politburo member dying at Kuntsevo." Kuntsevo was the special hospital for Party leaders.

"Who?"

"I can't tell you."

"Dying of what?"

"His heart. Chazov's given up." Yevgeni Chazov was the Soviet Union's top cardiologist. "The patient's a close friend of Andropov's, who wants to know can I do anything."

"*Andropov* wants to know if she can heal?"

Supernaturalism had a powerful tradition in the Soviet Union. Even Brezhnev had tried a healer in his final days. It was said that a dying man, even a Marxist, would grasp at anything. But Andropov—the stoic, KGB-steeped rationalist?

"He didn't say heal. He just asked if I can help."

"You know about the deaf girl, right?"

"What deaf girl?"

"Come on, Andrei, you said you were cold."

"Yes, I know. I hear that didn't raise your status at the embassy."

"I guess I'm not what you'd call the ambassador's favorite."

"That's what happens here. You either go along, or you get thrown out. It's the deceived versus the knowledgeable. You can join up and drink champagne, or stay home and drink Czech beer. The beer's not that bad."

Hammond thought about the hostility of the ambassador, Shroeder, the defense attaché, about how at home Darya had seemed at Spaso House. "No, I guess it isn't."

"Be careful, Jack."

The moon cast eerie shadows across the path. Everything was suddenly colder. Hammond let go of the Walther in his pocket and rubbed his hands together, trying to get warmth into them.

Marchenko said dryly, "Put your other glove on, Jack."

Hammond was embarrassed. He was a good doctor but a lousy spy. He pulled the glove on.

"You know what I think, Andrei? We know Andropov had a heart attack in 1966, he's got a Medtronic pacemaker from Minneapolis. This friend—it's Andropov, right?"

Marchenko shrugged and hunkered deeper into his coat.

"You're sure it's his heart?" Hammond asked.

There had been rumors that Andropov was diabetic. The CIA had even bribed a maintenance man in a foreign embassy to deactivate the flush mechanism in the toilet of a guest suite used by Andropov, then to retrieve the urine when he made repairs. The urine tested negative, but was it really Andropov's? The CIA could not be sure.

"I heard heart," Marchenko said.

"If you want my help, Andrei, it would help to tell me the truth."

"All he does is drink water and piss. Even wets the bed. When you talk to him, his breath smells like shit."

"Losing weight?"

"There's not much left to lose."

Renal failure, Hammond thought. Diabetes has wrecked his kidneys.

"Did he mention healing," Hammond asked, "or is that your idea?"

"He's read a lot of the psychotronics data. He thinks whatever happens it's because of bioenergy. If someone wants to call it supernatural, so what? Savages think transistor radios are supernatural."

Something moved in the forest shadows behind Marchenko. The Russian turned.

"Did you come alone, Andrei?" It could have been an animal or a falling branch.

"One never knows in Russia."

They sat motionless in the cold. Finally, Hammond said, "You didn't answer my question. Would Andropov submit to a healer?"

"I haven't asked him. He might, if I told him about the deaf girl."

"You think that was a legitimate healing?"

"Her doctor thinks so. I saw the records. What do you think? Is there anything to it, really? You're a doctor."

"I don't know, Andrei. What heals? The healing's not in the medicine, it's in the patient. The treatment causes natural functions to overcome the ailment. In the end, every sickness heals itself. I suppose you could say that the biochemical force—whatever that is—that heals comes ultimately from God. So everyone who's healed is healed by him." What was he saying?

"If he heard about the girl, maybe he'd try it."

If Andropov died now, the Brezhnevites might return to power. That would mean the end of the corruption investigations that had Darya so frightened. She would no longer have any reason to seek asylum in the West and to pay for that asylum with Spectrum. If Andropov died, the West's chance of getting Spectrum would die with him.

"What about Darya?" Hammond asked.

"Darya heal Andropov? Never. She'd be glad to see him dead. With his corruption investigation, she could end up shot."

Hammond wondered if Marchenko was aware of Darya's plans to defect again. Did Marchenko know he had visited Spectrum? It would be so much easier, Hammond thought, if I could trust this guy.

"Things could start going better for our countries now, Jack. It would be a pity to see everything handed back to people like Chernenko." Brezhnev's sycophantic old crony had been reduced to virtual invisibility in the Andropov regime. "Perhaps the Leonov woman could be made to understand these things. She has a duty as a citizen. And as a resident of Moscow."

The threat was lightly veiled. If Valentina's residency

permit were withdrawn, she could not remain in Moscow. Life was hard in the capital, but far worse for a young woman thrown out of the city with no job or home.

Hammond looked up the path toward the street and pushed his hands deep into the coat pockets, gripping the Walther. "I'll think about it."

He started back through the shadows toward his car, stopped, and stood motionless in the path. He turned and walked slowly back to Marchenko.

"I'm going to do something very stupid, Andrei."

Marchenko's eyes teared with the cold. "I don't think so."

"I'm going to put myself in your hands."

"Not so stupid."

"Assume the Leonov woman could be persuaded to heal Andropov. What's in it for me?"

"If Andropov stays alive it benefits both our countries, yours as much as mine."

"That's wonderful, Andrei, but what's in it for me?"

"Personally?"

Hammond knew what Marchenko was thinking. Cox said that Marchenko had first taken gifts, then cash. Cox, judging from the contents of his apartment, had been very adept at handing out gifts.

"What is it you want, Jack?"

"I want Darya. I'm not a vengeful man, Andrei, but I owe that lady one for running out on us. She's feeling the heat now and I have reason to suspect that if the temperature goes up she's going to want to defect again. This time, believe me, the defection will be permanent. I want her, Andrei."

"You think I can make her run to you?"

"I know you can." Heavy surveillance, a few pointed threats, and she'd be ready to swap Spectrum for asylum.

"Why should I let you get away with Darya? She's a valuable person."

"Not as valuable as Andropov. And she won't be worth bus fare when Andropov's corruption people get finished with her. It looks like a good trade. Darya for Andropov."

Marchenko tightened his coat collar. "I'll think about it."

"I need an answer now. These cloak-and-dagger meetings take it out of me. I'm going to see Leonov, and what I say to her depends on what you tell me now."

Marchenko hugged himself and shivered. "I told you before that Darya frightens me, and I don't mind repeating it now. She should frighten you too. No one knows what she can do."

"You said she gets a hold on people," Hammond said. "Does she have a hold on you?"

"Not yet."

"I want her, Andrei."

"I'll see what I can do."

23

H*AMMOND AND SHROEDER*
were alone in the embassy snack bar. It wasn't very secure,
which was just another way Shroeder had of letting
Hammond know how unimportant he was.

"What'd Marchenko have to say?" Shroeder demanded, his hairy monkey face twisted into a self-
important frown.

"He wants the Leonov woman to try to heal Andropov."

Shroeder's response to that was a long, empty, now-
I've-heard-everything stare.

"That girl at Spaso House was healed, you know," Hammond said. "I talked to her doctor."

"You believe him?"

"Yes, as a matter of fact, I believe him. I've seen stranger things."

"How many times have you been with Mrs. Leonov?"

"Three times. Counting Saturday."

"That's over the limit."

"Limit?" Shroeder's turf-guarding was getting on Hammond's nerves.

"After two contacts with a Soviet national you have to report further contacts."

"Then I'd better tell you I'm seeing her again today."

"No, you're not."

Two secretaries Hammond had seen in the cultural affairs office arrived at the next table with bowls of tomato soup. They nodded at Shroeder, who ignored them.

"Who's going to stop me?"

"Don't be stupid, Hammond. She's a dissident, a religious freak, a KGB target. She's also female and young. The KGB turns her, gets some happy snaps of you two rolling in the hay. Then they turn you, and—"

Hammond leaned across the table, put his lips into Shroeder's bearded face, and speaking with quiet, controlled ferocity, said, "You want to walk out of here a healthy man?"

"I just said—"

"Or do you want to fly out?"

Shroeder's little body trembled with indignation. "I'm station chief here, Hammond, and DCM, so don't—"

Hammond reached both arms across the table, took a

double handful of Shroeder's collar, and yanked him out of his chair. He stood, moved one hand from the collar to the seat of Shroeder's pants, and turned toward a plate glass window looking onto the back courtyard.

Shroeder's face went crimson. The secretaries looked up from their soup.

"Let go," Shroeder said.

Hammond dropped him sprawling to the floor. He crouched beside him. "Don't ever talk to me like that again, Shroeder. And don't pull rank. I'm here on the orders of your boss's boss's boss."

He walked out.

That evening Hammond spent three hours in taxis, buses, and metro trains to shed surveillance, then took a final cab to the Crimean Bridge and walked five blocks to Valentina's apartment. He wanted to make sure she knew about the deaf girl's healing, and he wanted to know if she'd try to heal Andropov. Also—he just wanted to see her again.

She wasn't home. Not wanting to risk repeated encounters with Mrs. Koblov, the old lady *stukach*, he watched from a park across the street for Valentina's arrival. At midnight, after four and a half hours, he gave up and switched taxis three times getting back to Cox's apartment.

He was worried, and angry with himself. Did Valentina's absence have something to do with Shroeder? It might have been a mistake to rough up Shroeder, but the bastard had accused him of stupidity, skirt chasing, and susceptibility to blackmail. If he let that go, what would be next?

Walking from the cab to the building entrance, Hammond spotted a dim figure standing motionless in the darkness beside a garbage dumpster. It had occurred to him before that the dumpster would make a convenient, though uncomfortable, hiding place for an assailant. He slowed his pace and took a closer look. The man had a black beard and was wearing a beige, canvas, knee-length jacket.

He had no doubt now that Frank had been right—the man was a KGB thug. Hammond thought of challenging him, but remembered that the last time he'd tried that all he'd gained was a blow to the kidney and a kick in the chest.

Hammond entered the building and was going up in the cage elevator when he heard the street door slam closed below. He got out at Cox's floor, drew the Walther from his coat pocket, and stepped around a corner into the dark corridor leading to apartments in the other wing of the building. Footsteps climbed the stone stairs.

Whoever it was must have heard him leaving the elevator, because the steps stopped just below the landing. Hammond held his breath in the stillness.

He heard a faint scraping, shoe leather on grit, and leaned forward to risk a peak around the corner. A figure in brown pants and jacket with a hood covering his head faced Cox's door, left hand in the pocket, gloved right hand touching the knob.

Hammond spoke in Russian. "Hands over your head, don't turn around."

The hands went up.

"Take one step back. Lean forward and put your hands on the door."

Hammond hooked his left foot around the left ankle of

the visitor, ready to pull his legs out from under him. Then he patted the jacket's pockets and reached around to feel the front. What he felt was more alarming than a weapon. He pulled the hood down.

"What the hell are you doing here?"

Valentina's eyes were fixed on the Walther. Hammond put it in his pocket and let them through the door. "I spent four hours outside your apartment waiting for you," he said. "What happened?"

"I'm sorry."

He took her jacket. His hands were trembling. "Have a seat. I'll fix some tea."

She followed him into the kitchen. He turned his back to run tap water into a saucepan. It was the first time he'd ever pointed a gun at anyone. If her left hand had come out of the pocket, he might have shot her. He put the pan on the stove and turned up the gas. Shroeder had ordered him not even to see Valentina, and here she was in his apartment. Shroeder's watchers were probably out in the street now, checking their watches. He had to get her out.

He reached into an overhead cabinet for cups. "What did you come here for, Valentina?"

"I had no where else to go."

He closed the living room curtains and set the cups on the coffee table. His mind was racing.

"What does that mean?"

"The militia arrested Mrs. Koblov. She didn't report your visits. I told you she was kind. If I go back they'll arrest me too. They'll want to know about you."

They were on the sofa. The blue eyes, frank and hopeful, looked straight into him.

"What are you going to do?" Hammond said.

"Whatever the Lord tells you I should do."

"No, no, Valentina, it's up to you. Why did you come here? Why didn't you go to some of your church friends?"

"I don't want to endanger them. They have enough troubles."

"But you don't mind endangering me."

"You are not in danger. You are an American official. They won't send you to a labor camp."

He picked up a teacup, found his hands were still trembling, and put it down. He tried to think. "You can go to a hotel. I'll pay for it."

"Moscow residents cannot go to Moscow hotels. It's not like the West. You have to show your internal passport, you have to have a reservation. And I cannot stay in the metro because it closes at one-thirty, and in the train stations the militia will ask to see my ticket, and it's too cold for the parks."

"How long do you want to stay?"

"It is up to you."

"You don't have any clothes. You don't have—"

She jumped up, grabbed her jacket, and ran out of the apartment.

Hammond did not even have a chance to call after her.

It was two in the morning. The KGB was certainly out there, along with Shroeder's men. She was risking a labor camp. Three years? Six? Maybe a psychiatric hospital. Maybe Serbenov. What was the worst that could happen to him? Relieved of his assignment, called back to Washington, his career broken.

He went out the door and stood at the top of the stairs.

How did he get into this? "Valentina!" His cry echoed down the stone stairs. No answer. He called again. She was gone.

He returned to the sofa and put his head in his hands. He felt like crying. One minute he'd been an Army neurologist in Vietnam and the next minute he was in Moscow throwing a young woman into the snow.

He heard a sound, turned, and saw Valentina in the doorway, a blue plastic suitcase at her feet.

His life had turned upside down.

She put the suitcase in the living room and looked at Hammond as calmly as if they had lived together in this apartment since the beginning of time.

Finally Hammond said, "Where'd you find that?"

"I hid it in the—" She didn't know the word.

"Garbage dumpster."

"They don't collect until six."

He found some sheets and blankets and put her in a small unswept bedroom off the entrance hallway.

She was dusting the night table when he said, "Your healing worked, did you know that?"

Her head snapped around. "How do you know?"

"Her doctor told me. She had a congenital hearing defect, and now she hears."

She turned away from him, said something he didn't hear, and went back to the dusting.

Watching her make the bed, Hammond was almost overcome by a desire to put his arms around her. But when he remembered her in the church house, and in her apartment praying, and when he considered how important she was to his efforts to get Spectrum, he backed toward the door.

"Let me know if you need anything," he said, studying her for some sign that she shared his desire.

"Thank you," she said, and closed the door.

At breakfast Hammond said, "Before we decide how long this can go on, I have something important to ask you."

She glanced up from her coffee. They'd had Kellogg's corn flakes, eggs, bacon, and Aunt Jemima pancakes. She hadn't quite recovered.

"You said once you would ask God to heal anyone who wanted healing."

"Yes." She yawned. He'd definitely overdone it with the pancakes.

"Would it have to be someone who believed in God?"

"God heals whoever he wishes."

"Would you try to heal Yuri Andropov?"

She started to laugh, and almost choked on a mouthful of coffee.

"Would you?" Hammond repeated.

"Would he want me to?"

"If he did."

"Why are you asking this? The questions are unrealistic."

"Perhaps not. Would you?"

"I would try to do whatever God wanted me to do."

"Well, it's true that Andropov is dying, Valentina, and it's true that he's willing to have someone try to heal him."

"Willing? How wonderfully cooperative of him."

"He's dying. He wants to be healed. He does not want to die."

"Why is this important to you? Why do the Americans care if he dies? He is your enemy."

"I have a reason for wanting him to live." He was not ready to explain to Valentina that if Andropov died the pressure on Darya to defect with Spectrum would die with him.

"So it's a political healing. Or an intelligence healing. Something like that." She was taking the matter less seriously than he had expected.

"Would you do it?"

"I would try."

"Fine. More coffee?"

They were putting the breakfast dishes in the sink when the telephone rang. It was Marchenko. "The heat's up."

"What?"

It would have to be important for Marchenko to break their contact procedures.

"You wanted the heat up. It's up. You want to see?"

Hammond wasn't sure what he was going to see, but he didn't want to prolong the call. "Where?"

"I'll pick you up. Dress Russian."

The line went dead.

Hammond showed Valentina how to bolt the door. "I'll knock with six quick knocks, then three, then one. If anyone else comes, don't open the door. And don't answer the telephone. Keep the curtains closed."

"Don't worry." She looked so calm. Maybe living under the eyes of the KGB did that to you. You ended up not worrying about anything.

"Jack?"

"Yes."

"Never mind. Be careful."

24

A WHITE AMBULANCE WITH white-curtained windows stopped at the curb, and Marchenko waved to Hammond from the driver's seat. Hammond climbed in.

"Why the ambulance?"

"Where we're going it reduces curiosity."

"Where are we going?"

"Kashirin. You know it?"

"Only by reputation." The Kashirin psychiatric hospital was almost as bad as Serbenov. "Is Darya there?"

"You'll see. What about your guest?"

"You guys know everything."

"What's she say about the healing?"

"She says she'll try." He didn't want Marchenko to think it was in the bag. "But no guarantees."

They drove silently for a minute, and then Marchenko said, "Let me ask you something. Anybody give you any trouble since you've been here?"

Hammond laughed. "Nothing but. Why?"

"I mean physically. Rough you up."

"Yeah, as a matter of fact. Gave me a good shot in the back. What do you know about that?"

"I've been snooping, and I saw a piece of paper. Someone trying to warn you off Spectrum, is that what it was?"

"The guy told me I was a doctor so to be a doctor."

"It's kind of interesting. The guy wasn't KGB."

"Who was he?"

"MVD, Ministry of Internal Affairs, Militia. Vitali Fedorchuk's the boss."

"Yeah, I read his profile. Friend of Brezhnev and Chernenko."

"Right. Andropov kicked him out of the KGB, bumped him downstairs to the MVD where he could do less harm. He's a tough, ruthless son of a bitch and he's not happy about losing his job. Guess who's his very good friend."

"Who?"

Marchenko looked at Hammond and grinned, the gold molar glistening. "Can't guess?"

"You tell me."

"Darya. She got close to Fedorchuk when he was KGB chairman and Spectrum was its favorite science baby. He's mean and vain, just her meat. Now they do favors for each other. You need to know this, Jack. No matter what

happens with this healing business, don't think just because the KGB's loyal to Andropov you can't get hurt.
Darya can use Fedorchuk's militia to cut your balls off.
Fedorchuk still has his people at the KGB. If he wants to
know something, he has people who'll tell him. And he'll
tell Darya."

Hammond thought about that. Had the mysterious
watchers when he flew from Washington to Nice—and
the driver of that dark blue Ferrari—been KGB agents
doing a favor for Fedorchuk, who was doing a favor for
Darya? There wasn't much she didn't know.

"I appreciate your telling me this, Andrei."

"Don't mention it."

"I have a question. When that guy roughed me up,
there was another man nearby, watching. They didn't
seem to be together. I've seen him since. He's around. I
figured KGB."

"Could be. The militia and the KGB watch each other.
I couldn't really be sure."

Hammond shook his head. The KGB's loyal to Andropov. The militia likes Chernenko, the Brezhnevites. The
militia beats him up, and the KGB watches. The embassy
can't stand the sight of him. Darya's holding hands with
the ambassador. He hoped someday someone would tell
him what the hell was really going on.

They stopped at iron gates, and a blue-uniformed guard
stepped out of a pink stone guardhouse. Marchenko spoke
to him and the gates swung open.

It was like a park—pigeons, birds singing, snow-
covered lawns, red-brick buildings tucked away amid
the birch and cottonwood trees. They drove past men in

ragged coats strolling on the asphalt walks. Farther along, more men lounged on benches behind shoulder-high wire fences.

Deep within the interior of the complex, Marchenko parked the ambulance behind a five-story yellow building with a sign that said "All Union Scientific Center of Psychiatric Health—The Academy of Medical Science of the Soviet Union."

Marchenko, carrying a black briefcase, led Hammond through double doors of frosted glass to an elevator, and down two flights to an underground area with stone floors and gray walls. They passed through two more doors and came finally to an office with three varnished wooden desks and an electric heater.

A blond, acne-scarred man in a white coat shook hands with Marchenko, ignored Hammond, and preceded them into a room that appeared to be made entirely of stainless steel. Darya lay beneath a blue sheet and gray blankets on a narrow, elevated bed. Two thin wires—one red, one yellow—ran from contact points on a two-square-inch shaved patch at the top of her skull to a black control console on a rolling table against the wall behind her head. She was unconscious.

The blond man wrapped a blood-pressure cuff around her arm. Apparently suspicious of Hammond, he spoke in whispers to Marchenko.

"He wanted to know," Marchenko explained in English, "if we were familiar with the reciprocal work being done at Serbenov. I said we were."

Hammond almost panicked. The attendant was fiddling with dials at the console, comparing readings with those in a plastic notebook hanging from a string.

"She told me," Hammond said, wanting to make certain Marchenko understood what might be about to happen, "that they were stimulating Substance P receptors in the septum."

Marchenko, apparently unconcerned, silently watched the attendant prepare the console.

"It induces pain," Hammond said, his alarm growing.

"Yes," Marchenko said. "That's what you wanted."

"It's *not* what I wanted."

The attendant did something at the console, and Darya opened her eyes. Her head turned toward Hammond. Before she could register recognition, her head rose convulsively from the bed and her pupils dilated. She did not make a sound, but the eyes screamed. The pain behind them was naked.

"Stop it," Hammond said, but it had already stopped. Her head fell back flat on the bed, the brow perspiring. The eyes, empty and exhausted, turned again to Hammond.

The attendant whispered to Marchenko.

"Only the head moves," Marchenko repeated to Hammond, "because the body has temporarily been paralyzed from the neck down. The speech center also has been disabled."

"Tell him not to do that again," Hammond said.

Marchenko repeated the command in Russian.

The attendant walked away from the console.

Hammond wondered if Darya could hear. He moved within her vision and nodded. He put his hand on her damp forehead.

The attendant whispered to Marchenko. He was getting on Hammond's nerves.

"He wants to know if you'd like to see the data," Marchenko said.

"No. Is he going to do anything else?"

"Not if I tell him not to."

"Then tell him. Can you get her released?"

"The director won't be back until after lunch. They can do it then."

Driving away in the ambulance, Hammond was silent. He was a *doctor*.

"So did you get what you wanted?" Marchenko asked.

"Andrei, I—" He decided to keep quiet. He didn't want to say something he'd regret.

"There's more," Marchenko said, and reached one hand under his legs for the black briefcase. "Inside you'll find something for you. It's my life. Protect it."

Hammond opened the case and withdrew an inch-thick rectangular package wrapped in newspapers and brown tape.

"Should I open it now?"

"In your embassy. I'll drop you. Darya has tested Spectrum against humans."

Hammond looked quickly at Marchenko to see if he was serious.

"Shocked, are you? She directed Spectrum against the heart of a seventy-three-year-old healthy white male at a distance of a hundred meters. Cardiac arrest. Another test was instantaneously lethal at three and a half kilometers. Direction at the limbic system of a Serbenov patient produced rage. Frontal-temporal targeting, hallucinations. Direction at the caudate nucleus, terror."

Hammond was speechless.

"None of these subjects was immobilized. It didn't matter if they were sleeping or walking around—Spectrum identified them, isolated the target region, and that was that. The neurological subjects rationalized, gave what they thought were valid explanations for their behavior.''

Hammond gripped the package in his lap. ''What's next?''

''They're still testing, want to take it easy, not rush into anything. When they find the right target, the right moment, they'll move. When or who that might be I have no idea.''

''Who is 'they'?''

''Darya and her friends.'' Hammond stared hard at him and waited. ''You can guess,'' Marchenko said. Chernenko probably. Maybe Romanov or Grishin.

Hammond lifted the package. ''How did you get this, Andrei?''

''You know better than to ask that. But I'm not helpless.''

Marchenko stopped the ambulance around the corner of the Arbat Restaurant on Kalinina Prospekt, walking distance from the American embassy.

''I kept my bargain,'' he said, ''now you keep yours. When will the Leonov woman be ready to start? Andropov isn't getting any healthier.''

''Let me know when Darya's out.''

25

*W*HEN HAMMOND RETURN-
ed to the apartment it was gleaming. Looking at the shin-
ing parquet, dusted tables, spotless kitchen, he realized
that the place had not been cleaned since Cox left.

"It's beautiful," he said. "You didn't have to do that."

"Do you know this is really three apartments joined
together?" Valentina said. "It's the biggest apartment I've
ever seen. What's all this?" She waved a hand at the
stacked provisions in the hallway.

"Peanut butter. Americans love peanut butter. And
corn chips. I'm going to lie down for a minute. Did anyone
call?" It had been nearly two hours since Darya's terror-

filled eyes had turned on Hammond, but the shock of it had not diminished.

"No calls, no knocks."

He took off his tie and jacket and lay on the bed, his arms over his eyes, trying to block out the light. He struggled to drive Darya's face from his mind. What the hell had he expected Marchenko to do? Surveillance and threats? The only excuse he could think of was that he had been sent into a world he didn't know anything about. But that wasn't good enough. It was still his fault.

Though he had studied so-called lucid dreaming during his residency, he had never actually experienced it himself until now. He fell asleep and began to dream, but he was awake within the dream, watching himself in the dream. He was flying over the city of Moscow, the embassy, the Kremlin, descending toward Kutuzovsky Prospekt. As his feet touched the roof of Darya's apartment building, a sudden pain filled his head.

He awoke, soaked in sweat. He had never had a migraine, but now he knew what all the fuss was about. The light from the curtained windows sliced into his brain. His stomach turned with nausea.

Head throbbing, he started shakily toward the bathroom. He reached for the doorknob, and missed. He groped again, but the knob was not where his eyes told him it was. Finally he got the door open, faced the sink, and realized he had made a mistake. The sink was not in front of him but on his right. He turned, and discovered the sink was now on his left.

Realizing that his visual orientation had deserted him, he closed his eyes and located the sink by touch. He found the cold tap and splashed water over his head.

He opened his eyes. Nothing happened. He closed them again, opened them, but still he could not see.

Blindness added fear to the pain. He found his way back to the bed and fell across it. He tried to call to Valentina but couldn't get the words out. The pain in his head and stomach grew and spread. Marchenko's words raced through his mind. Was this another Spectrum test? Or not a test—they had decided that this was the time and he was the person?

Hammond had been asleep for five hours when Valentina heard a knock at the door. She turned the knob and the door burst inward, hitting her on the forehead.

"Oh, I'm so sorry, my dear," Darya said, lunging over the threshold, "I must have pushed too hard. Are you all right?" She slammed the door behind her.

Valentina, stunned by the violence, took a step back.

"I have some things to say to Dr. Hammond," Darya announced unpleasantly, striding into the living room. "Where is he?"

"Sleeping." Valentina was shocked and frightened. The confidence she had felt confronting Darya at Spaso House had vanished.

"Good," Darya said. "We can have a little chat." She handed Valentina her fur coat. "Take this, will you? I have some things to say to you as well. We didn't have much time in Serbenov."

Valentina laid the coat over a chair.

"Are you having fun in your little love nest?" Darya said, settling onto the sofa.

"It's not a love nest."

"Don't insult me." Darya's cheeks flushed with hatred.

"You may have Hammond fooled, but you and I both know who you are. I told you in Serbenov what I think of you, and what that God you lie to thinks of you. Sit down, Valentina. Don't just hover there like some wretched little animal."

Valentina sat in a chair.

"Not there," Darya ordered. "Come next to me."

Valentina didn't move.

"Over here, Valentina." Darya patted the cushion beside her. "I want to make you happy."

Valentina felt cold. Darya was watching her, the red lips parted, eyes narrow.

"No?" Darya laughed. "Why not? You sell yourself, why not to me? You want to know what I would pay? One time, and you'd be camped on my doorstep. I could do a lot for you."

Valentina gripped the sides of the chair.

"You're trembling, Valentina. Do I frighten you so?"

She couldn't speak.

"I know your secrets, don't I. Is he paying you well? I hear you got off with quite a bit of money. You should be a very rich little whore by now."

"No one is paying me anything."

Darya laughed, a derisive snort that raised the hairs on Valentina's arms.

"The meek little Christ-lover. What a hypocrite you are. A thief, a whore, a traitor. Don't you make yourself sick?"

Valentina tried to pray. No words came.

"Tell me, Valentina"—Darya lowered her voice— "what do you imagine God thinks of you now? Don't you know how much he hates you? You use him, you lie to him, you steal, you betray. How long will it be before he pays you back? If I ever get you back at Serbenov, I'll do things to you they haven't dreamed of in hell."

Valentina felt herself shrinking.

"Look at me, Valentina. Don't play weak and humble. Your phony little performance at Spaso House, pretending to heal that miserable girl. You make me sick, and if you make me sick, Valentina, think what you do to God."

"The girl was healed."

"Oh, please! I know you, remember? God wouldn't let you heal a cockroach."

Valentina clutched the chair.

"Why don't you be honest for once? Admit what you are."

"I know what I am." Tears filled her eyes.

"Oh, now it's crying. The poor little thing is crying. I am so touched. Valentina, you make me want to vomit."

"Please stop." Valentina put her face in her hands.

"I'll stop all right. But not until I've played a bit. Where is Hammond?"

Hammond was again unconscious, dreaming—inside the dream and outside it too, watching. He saw himself on the bed, and heard a scream. It was Valentina. Fighting the pain in his head and stomach, he pushed himself up, got his feet on the floor, and struggled through the bedroom door.

The living room was in gloom. Something alive was moving, something dark but visible, radiating energy. Everything the darkness touched went to blackness. Hammond was familiar with antimatter, and with antienergy, antiphotons, antilight. It destroyed light. As he watched in the dream, his head and stomach throbbing, he could feel the darkness against his skin—a hot, lightless fire, black fire. A low, resonating growl moved with the darkness. Hammond's nostrils filled with the stink of vomit, feces, decaying flesh.

Wherever light appeared in the gloom, the growl and stench exploded in fury, and the light vanished within a swallowing shadow. Not from anything he saw or heard, but with a certainty he felt directly in his heart, Hammond knew that the darkness was battling for his soul.

He tried to awaken from the nightmare but could not. Suddenly an eruption of fire-orange light enveloped him, intensified, bathed the room in a pure white brilliance as obscuring as the darkness had been. The stench and growl halted abruptly, as if struck by a blow, then returned as the light diminished.

He saw Valentina. Blood was in her hair, her eyes, flowing down her face. The darkness turned on her in a storm of rage. He wanted to help her, but did not know how. Other people were in the room now too, fighting. Hammond was terrified, desperate to escape, but he could not abandon Valentina. He tried to strike out against the darkness. A vision came into his mind of his parents, their neighbors, the Pentecostal offensive lineman at Princeton. Someone he couldn't see held his arm. The restraining hand was wrenched free, and Hammond dashed for Valentina. She flung her arms wide, shielding him. She cried out, dropped to her knees, and disappeared beneath a roiling wave of blackness.

The room fell still and quiet. The darkness approached him—the antiforce, the annihilation of energy and matter.

It lay soft and damp against him. The growl was now a negative noise deeper than silence. He sensed a conscious power pulling at him, willful, impatient, insisting.

He awoke on the bed. The pain was still there. He reached for the lamp and turned it on. Wonderful light. He dragged himself to the curtains, opened them, and lifted the window. Sunshine. He breathed in the fresh, cold air. He could not remember a nightmare, even as a child, more terrifying than the one he had just experienced.

He returned to the bed and collapsed.

The door cracked open and Darya put her head in.

"What are you doing here?" he said. "Where is Valentina?" His stomach was on fire.

"She stepped out for a minute."

He remembered Kashirin. "We have to talk," he said. "It wasn't my fault. I have to explain."

Darya helped him up. "It's all right, I understand. Come with me. I have medicine in my apartment."

He leaned against her and hobbled out to the elevator. Why had Valentina left him?

By the time they arrived at Kutuzovsky Prospekt, the pain was gone and the terror of the nightmare had started to fade. He was tired and hungry. She sat him down on the blue velvet sofa and went to the kitchen for tea.

"I'm terribly sorry, Darya," he said when she returned with a silver tray. "I wanted to make him stop."

She sat beside him. "I appreciate that, Jack. Without your help I'd probably still be there."

She handed him a cup and poured from a silver pot in an embroidered silk tea cozy. A porcelain plate was covered with chocolate cookies.

"I've never had a migraine before." He decided not to mention the nightmare.

"It wasn't a migraine. You know you don't get spatial disorientation with migraines."

"What was it?"

"You saw what we were doing at Serbenov. High-resolution PK on the limbic system. In this case on Substance P receptors in the septum. Sometimes I can do the PK myself, but Spectrum's much more reliable."

"You did that to me?"

"Not me, Jack. Spectrum."

It was true he felt fully recovered now. Marchenko had said Spectrum had been employed against human targets, but that didn't prove his own distress had been caused by Spectrum. The whole thing could be coincidence. On the other hand, how had Darya known about his disorientation if she had not had something to do with it?

"Why did you do it to me?" he asked.

"Why did you do it to *me*?" she answered.

"I didn't do anything to you."

"Marchenko wouldn't have brought you to see me if you weren't responsible in some way. Anyway, it's good for you to understand what Spectrum can do. Firsthand experience is always convincing."

"You want me to know what could happen if—"

"You make it sound like a threat, Jack."

"Isn't it?"

She lifted the plate. "Have a cookie."

To get away from her he stood up and took a couple of steps toward the window.

"Now," she said, "let's talk business. I want to leave."

"You know the price."

"You'll get the Spectrum holodots when I'm in the States with asylum."

"Before you leave, Darya." He returned to the sofa. "You burned us once already, remember?"

"I trust you, Jack, but I'm afraid I can't trust your government. I'll get to Washington and be told there's a problem with asylum. I'll be at the mercy of I don't know who, and there won't be anything you can do to help me. There'll be no work, no legal residency, no travel documents, no official status. I can't take that risk. I want to be in the States with asylum and a passport."

She moved closer to him and put her hand on the back of his neck.

"We don't have to work this out now, Jack. We've both had a difficult time. Stay here with me and we'll talk about it tomorrow."

Was she really prepared to hand over Spectrum?

"I don't think so, Darya. If you want asylum on my terms, say so now and let's get on with it."

She took a sip of tea, those delicate fingers setting the cup back soundlessly in its saucer. "How is your houseguest?"

He had wondered when that would come.

"She's fine, thank you."

"Is she good in bed?"

"I wouldn't know."

"Too bad, she's really quite attractive. But then I forgot. Christians don't screw. One wonders how there can be so many of them."

"Are you going to give me the holodots?"

"We'll talk about it tomorrow."

"Now."

"Are you really in such a rush to get back to that sexless—"

"I guess I am."

He started to rise. The hand went from his neck to his thigh. "I have some caviar and smoked salmon in the refrigerator, Jack, and a couple of bottles of Dom Pérignon. Have dinner with me and we'll watch a film. Don't go back to that miserable apartment."

He laid his head back and felt the warmth of her hand. He had not been to bed with a woman since leaving Washington. It was almost enough to make him forget what he'd just been through at Cox's apartment. Maybe she'd had nothing to do with that. Maybe she was bluffing.

She stretched out on the sofa and put her head on his knees, looking up at him.

"Why don't you move in here, Jack? You shouldn't stay in that rathole. Think of how much fun we could have together. There's really a lot going on in Moscow, a lot of money and people who know how to use it. Live with me, Jack."

"No." He couldn't meet her eyes.

"Are you worried about the embassy? They'll be delighted. Chris Puckett's a good friend of mine. He'd worship the ground you walked on if he knew you were living with me. I don't know everything you're supposed to be doing here, Jack, but I have a lot of friends and if you stumbled—well, I could protect you."

She nestled her head in his lap.

"The world would be yours, Jack. There wouldn't be anything you couldn't have here, no one you couldn't meet, nothing you couldn't do. Think how proud everyone would be of you."

She turned, went up on her elbows, and unzipped his trousers, her voice droning on as if nothing were happening. "I know you think this is an evil government. But you could use it for good. Even God uses Satan for good, doesn't he? Think of the power. You could have Spectrum, Jack. You could take it from the Soviets, use it for good instead of evil. You could get rid of the Soviet threat forever."

Her fingers held him, stroked him. "I want to do something to you, Jack. Something I've never done before."

He felt suddenly sleepy, as if consciousness were draining from him, slipping away. He looked down and saw her face—harsh and lined, the lips tightly drawn and cruel, as it had been when she'd spotted the video cassette in Cox's apartment. He shivered, his body suddenly like ice. He jerked himself awake, knowing why she had wanted him to submit to some shamanistic rite after the nightmare episode with the old woman from the plane. Not to remove a spell, but to cast one.

He pulled her hand free. "Get away from me, Darya."

"Jack, please." She grabbed his arm. "Don't leave, Jack."

It wasn't a plea, it was an order.

"Good-bye, Darya." He got up.

"If you leave now, Jack, you will never get Spectrum. I promise you. You will never get it."

Hammond ignored her and started for the door.

"And you will never have Valentina, either."

He kept walking. She was on her feet now.

"I curse you, Hammond. If you walk out of here now, you will never have Spectrum. You will never have Valentina."

He stopped and turned to her. "Never have Valentina?"
She was insane.

"You are too stupid to believe that? I am cursing you.
If you try to make love, you will die and she will die."

Her face was rigid with rage. He had never seen anything like it before.

"You really think you can curse me?"

"I have cursed you."

He turned, walked out the door, and felt her eyes burning holes in his back.

26

S*TEVE, I NEED YOUR HELP.*"

"What's the problem?"

It was one P.M. in Georgia, and Hammond could almost see Burkholzer settling back in his chair, cradling the telephone against his shoulder, lifting his bad arm into his lap, preparing to lend whatever help he could.

"I'm in trouble," Hammond said.

"Tell me about it."

To get to a secure telephone at nine o'clock at night, after leaving Darya, Hammond had had to pull Frank away from a roast beef dinner with his wife. The agent

escorted him past Marine guards and the CIA duty officer
to his cubbyhole office in the complex the agents sarcastically called the adytum, a sacred temple sanctuary open
only to priests. Frank had discreetly stepped out into the
corridor.

"For reasons I won't go into now, Steve, Darya's in a
rage. She's already given me a dose of what she can do
when she's mad, and I'm not eager for more of it." Hammond had intended to tell Burkholzer of Darya's refusal
to give them Spectrum until she was back in the States.
But now he wasn't so sure.

"What did she do?" Burkholzer asked.

"Migraine, abdominal pain, loss of spatial orientation,
anxiety. It was pretty terrible, Steve, take my word for it."

"How do you know she did it?"

"She told me, gave details. I had a helluva nightmare,
Steve." What if he told Burkholzer about Darya's demand
that she not hand over Spectrum until she's back in the
States, and MAG decided to accept that? Darya would
renege and they'd never get Spectrum.

"Did she say how she did it?" Burkholzer asked.

"High-resolution PK on the limbic system." Hammond
was trying hard to talk and think at the same time. Why
tell Burkholzer? There was no way Burkholzer could
make Darya change her mind. Hammond was going to
have to work this out himself. But how? Impossible.

"Herself or Spectrum?"

"She said Spectrum, but who knows."

"And you think you're in for more of it?"

"I don't know, Steve. Maybe it's not even Spectrum,
or Darya. Maybe it's just me, maybe it would have

happened anyway. But I'm scared, Steve. If it is Spectrum or Darya, there's probably no way of protecting against it, but—maybe I missed something."

"Well, if we're right that Spectrum's based on enfold- ment and Fourier components, there's no protection. It's not like a wave or particle you could shield yourself from."

"So I just have to . . . bite the bullet."

"Pretty much. Or pray."

"Wonderful."

"Ask for protection by the blood of Jesus Christ."

"That's crazy. No offense."

"I'm not kidding, Jack. She believes in the supernatural and if you want to shield yourself from her, you'd better believe in it too."

Hammond realized now that he was embarrassed to tell Burkholzer how convinced he was of Darya's malevo- lence. How could he tell Burkholzer she had cursed him? He was a neurophysiologist, not some medieval necro- mancer.

"There's something else, Steve. I sent a package to the home office. You sitting down?"

Even on a supposedly secure line, he was reluctant to speak openly.

"Yeah."

"They've tested their gadget on humans. Successfully."

Hammond could almost hear the alarm bells going off in Burkholzer's brain.

"On humans?"

"Right."

"What did it do?"

"Call our friend at the home office tomorrow. He'll have something for you."

"I'll do that."

There was something else he had to say. "Steve . . ."

"Yes."

"She just tried to recruit me. She was talking about how wonderful Satan is, use him to do good instead of evil. She tried to make him sound appealing."

"Jack, Satan can't do good and he is definitely not appealing. He hates you. He hates everyone, even the people who worship him. You'd be better off in hell with Jesus than in heaven with Satan."

"I'm over my head, Steve."

There was a pause, Burkholzer thinking. "Jack?"

"Yeah."

"Maybe you oughta come home."

Hammond put the phone down and sat for a moment at Frank's desk. Did Darya really curse him? If he made love, he and the girl would die? MAG had studied voodoo curses, and they worked. No doubt about that. But Jack Hammond and Valentina? Make love and die?

Hammond went back to the apartment, gave the coded knock, and heard Valentina working the locks. He was not prepared for what he saw when the door opened. Her hair was matted with dried blood, she held a blood-soaked washcloth to a lemon-sized swelling on the top of her head, her jeans were splattered with blood, her eyes swollen from crying.

"Valentina, what the hell hap—"

She dropped the washcloth, put her arms around him, hugged, and did not let go.

Had the KGB been here, or Shroeder? He reached behind his back and pulled her hands loose.

"Valentina, what—"

She stepped back into the living room. Broken glass covered the floor. Two chairs were overturned.

"I'm sorry I look like this," she said. "I washed, but I couldn't get the bleeding to stop, and I was so worried about you, I didn't know where she'd taken you, what had happened to you, what she—" She fell against him and sobbed. He held her and let her cry. "I'm sorry," she said, "I'm sorry. I've never been brave. I feel so worthless. I'm sorry."

Stunned and filled with questions, he led her to the sofa and sat down. "It's all right, Valentina, it's all right." He bent her head forward and examined the wound—a two-inch laceration, not deep. There'd have been a lot of blood. "Who did this, Valentina? Where were you? What happened?"

"Didn't you see?"

"I've been gone for two hours."

She walked to the doorway, retrieved the washcloth, and returned to the sofa. "Darya was here." She wiped her tears with the washcloth, smearing her cheeks with blood.

"Darya?"

"We had a fight."

A fight! He saw Valentina falling, swallowed by darkness. "Was I here, Valentina?"

"Yes. Are you all right?"

"Am *I* all right?" He hugged her. "Valentina, I'm fine. I don't know what happened. I thought it was a dream."

She shook her head.

"But there were other people here."

"Not people, Jack."

He looked at her. The tear-swollen, blood-streaked face made him want to cry. He remembered her arms spread wide, shielding him. Who had done this?

"Start at the beginning, Valentina."

"You were resting in the bedroom and Darya came. She wanted to take you out and I wouldn't let her, so we had a fight. She hit me with a water pitcher. I went into the bathroom and when I came back you were both gone."

"That's all?"

"Tell me about your dream," she said.

"I don't know. It was crazy. There was blackness, fighting the light. I saw you. I heard you scream and you fell down. Then the darkness came after me and I woke up and Darya came in the room and I left with her. I thought you'd gone out."

She walked over and picked up one of the fallen chairs. Hammond watched her, waiting. She righted the chair, returned to the sofa, and wiped her face again with the washcloth. She turned to him.

"So it was real," he said.

"Yes, Jack. Real."

It was as if he'd been living like a fish at the bottom of the sea, stubbornly denying wild claims about the existence of air and land. He was accustomed to the effects of evil—lies, thievery, murder—but not to evil itself, evil as a creature. He looked away from her and stared silently across the room. He was confused, disoriented, slightly faint. Now he understood what Carol had been playing with so innocently in their home in Georgetown, what her "spirit guide" was pushing, what MAG's Black group was after.

Valentina left him, and in a minute he heard water

running in the bathroom sink. He got up, steadied himself, and went in. He shaved the hair around her cut, washed it, dabbed it with iodine, and put on a bandage.

"Thank you," she said, looking sadder than he thought it would ever be possible for her to look.

Early the next morning, Hammond walked into the kitchen and picked up a box of corn flakes. It was empty. Looking for another box, he opened a deep overhead storage cupboard. He saw soap, sponges, and bottles of Ajax toilet bowl cleaner. It occurred to him that although he had searched the kitchen when he first arrived, he wasn't certain he had looked in the back of this cupboard. As he pulled over a chair to stand on, Valentina walked in. "What are you looking for?"

"Something to eat. How's your head?"

"Much better. The swelling's down. I'll fry you some eggs."

"No, that's all right."

He groped blindly in the back of the cupboard.

"There's nothing there," Valentina said.

Hammond glanced down at her. "How do you know?"

"I just—" She looked like a boy caught hiding *Playboy*s.

His hand felt a cardboard box, and he pulled it out. It was a Skippy peanut butter carton, two feet square and a foot high, heavy, bound with string.

"That's mine," Valentina said, reaching for it.

"Just a minute," Hammond said, climbing down from the chair. "What's in it?"

"Nothing. It's mine." She made another grab.

He jerked it away. "Let's see."

He put the box on the kitchen table and cut the strings.

He raised the lid, and pulled his hands back as if the cardboard had suddenly become red-hot.

"This is *yours*?"

The box was filled with neatly bound stacks of U.S. dollars, deutsche marks, and suisse francs.

It did not take more than three minutes of riffling through the bundles to tell Hammond he was looking at something close to $250,000.

He said, "I hope you're not going to tell me you're as surprised to see this as I am."

"No."

"So?"

She looked him in the eye, as if trying to measure his willingness to believe what she had to say. Then she pushed the sleeves of her sweater up to her elbows, took his hand, and led him to the sofa in the living room. They sat down, and for the next hour Hammond listened to her story.

It had been a year and a half ago—another age, she was another person. Her grandmother had died and she had lost all interest in Christianity or religion of any kind. Viktor had left his job and become an artist. He was thirty-five, officially unemployed, in the eyes of the authorities a parasite. But his art had won him Western friends, and one day he took her to lunch with a couple of Finnish businessmen at the Intourist hotel. Viktor was different from any other Russian she had ever known. He didn't care about security. He wanted to work by himself for himself. He wasn't drab, he wasn't born beaten.

It was the first time she had been past the door guard at any of Moscow's tourist hotels. They had caviar, crabmeat, roast chicken, and vodka—the best meal of her life.

On the way out, she noticed three stylish, Western-dressed girls in their early twenties standing in the vestibule outside the glass doors.

She thought a lot about that lunch, and about the girls in the vestibule. The girls had looked happy. Viktor said most of them worked part-time, hoping to marry their customers, Western businessmen who would take them away to security, peace, and opulence. Not at all an impossible dream.

Viktor never took her back to the hotel, or anywhere else. Stubbornly refusing to join the artists' union, he had lost his Moscow residency permit and moved to Kursk. She had thought maybe she loved him.

She returned to the hotel on her own and spoke to one of the girls, a third-year philosophy student at Moscow University. She was pleasant, not stupid, not tough. Like Viktor, she wasn't settling for dreariness and death. What kind of a country was it where for light and life you had to go to outcasts and prostitutes? As they talked, two Belgian men staying in the hotel invited them to dinner.

Of the hundred U.S. dollars she made that evening, thirty went to the hotel door guard. Following the practice of the other girls, Valentina changed the remaining seventy dollars—more than double her monthly wage as an interpreter for the Ministry of Trade—into rubles with a young Georgian named Anatoli, who operated out of the backseat of a Zhiguli around the corner from the hotel. The rate was four to one. Tourists got three to one. The other girls said Anatoli got six to one from whoever changed his money.

Seeing an opportunity, Valentina began exchanging customers' dollars herself at three-and-a-half to one. When a West German pharmaceutical dealer exchanged the deutsche-mark equivalent of two thousand dollars with her, she coaxed Anatoli into accepting the money, a relatively large amount, at the increased rate of five to one. The West German's name was Albert Bachmann, and before long, no doubt encouraged by her blue eyes and long, silky blond hair, he was exchanging his office's entire operating budget with Valentina.

Anatoli's black market currency dealer, a fellow Georgian named Ilya, soon demanded to meet the source of all this new wealth. Ilya took over her transactions from Anatoli at a rate of six to one. Bachmann sent Western business friends to Valentina, and soon she had abandoned prostitution and was handling currency exchanges for the Moscow offices of three Western companies.

The incentive for abandoning prostitution was not entirely commercial. Valentina had promised herself that she would continue "to go out with" men she found at the hotel for no longer than one year. It was, in fact, a promise to her grandmother, who, though dead for sixteen months, remained a much loved, and at times inconveniently powerful, moral force in Valentina's life.

Since prostitution was deemed not to exist in the Soviet Union, there was no law forbidding it, and the militia therefore had taken little notice of Valentina. The KGB, typically, was more farsighted. She had been working less than a week when a bald, gray-faced man in a leather topcoat stopped her in the underground passageway from Gorki Street to the metro. He said that unless she was able to provide "useful information" on her Western customers she would be denied further access to the hotel. When she asked who he was and what was meant by useful information, the man turned and climbed the stairs back to Gorki Street.

Noticing a gold Rolex on a Dutch customer's wrist, Valentina asked its worth, and accepted the watch in exchange for the dollar-value in rubles. She thus made money on the currency exchange as well as on the value of the Rolex, which she sold to Ilya for twice what she had paid. After that, making it known that she would give good prices for high-value Western goods, she began buying gold watches as well as jewelry and unmounted gems.

When the visiting boss of an American fertilizer representative asked if she knew where he could get top-quality Siberian crown sables, she took his request to Ilya. Two days later the man had his furs, and a couple of illegal, not-for-export kilogram tins of beluga caviar as well.

Valentina's business continued to flourish, and Ilya introduced her to Nikolai, a slight, pretty, young Muscovite. Nikki wore pastel silk body shirts, Italian shoes, and cashmere jackets with labels from Rome's Via Condotti. He had the nicest manners and the longest eyelashes Valentina had ever seen. He also had a voracious appetite for gold, diamonds, and Western currency, plus an inexhaustible supply of caviar, furs, and privileged friends.

Nikki and Valentina got along like brother and sister. He introduced her to special stores, and to special people, where her Western currency could buy American, Italian, and French fashions. He took her to parties. In the immense high-ceilinged, chandeliered dining room of a white-haired Politburo member, she drank French champagne and danced with Central Committee officials and bright, smartly turned out graduate students from the elite Institute of International Relations. No one doubted where all the money came from. Communism provided extraordinary opportunities for those who knew the right people.

The queen of this party—someone who clearly did know the right people—was a beautiful black-haired young woman whom Valentina recognized immediately. It had been seven years since she had seen Darya disappear into an elevator at Moscow University, but the charm was undiminished. When Nikki introduced them, Darya's hand and smile were as warm and friendly as if she and Valentina had been friends for years. There was no reason to suspect that Darya knew of Valentina's connection to the husband and wife incinerated in Labinsk. Talking with Darya, observing her good-natured kindness, it was difficult for Valentina to believe that she had been responsible.

So many people had competed for Darya's attention at the party that Valentina was surprised the following day when Darya called her at home. What interest could Darya have in a nobody like her?

"We must get together my dear," Darya said. "How could I have gone so long without meeting you?"

"I don't go out much," Valentina said, regretting it immediately. It sounded as if she had no friends.

"Well, we must change that. Can you come to tea tomorrow?"

Valentina went to tea, and to many other parties as well. For the next six weeks Darya wooed her like a lover.

She introduced her to a level of Moscow society Valentina
had never hoped to enter. During a reception in Darya's
own apartment, Darya took her aside and said, "Are you
busy later? Could you stay a moment when the others
leave? I want to talk to you."

Valentina stayed, and when they were side by side on
a sofa in the living room, holding glasses of champagne,
Darya said, "I have a kind of proposition for you."

Valentina felt like Darya's best friend. Was that possible? She was alone in a palatial apartment with one of
the most attractive, influential women in Moscow.

"What is it?" she asked.

"You know, of course, that I work at the Serbenov
Institute."

"Yes." Everyone knew that.

"We are conducting a special study for which we need
a small number of highly intelligent, intuitive young
women. The work will take only a few hours a week, and
it will be well paid. You would not have to give up any
other activities. Would you consider it?"

Unpleasant rumors about Serbenov—that KGB pris-
oners received painful drugs there—were the only disquieting element in Darya's proposal.

"I don't know," Valentina said.

"It will be very exciting. The project is secret so I can't
tell you much about it. But you will have the excitement
and satisfaction of being involved in one of the most advanced scientific projects of our time. We are carrying
science to its last frontier, Valentina, to the point where
we can use the ultimate force in all of us. I know you can
appreciate the importance of that."

"Of course. I'm flattered you would ask me."

"It is not to flatter you. I have looked at many people for this project, and very few have shown the qualities required. You are a very special person, Valentina."

Valentina didn't know what to say.

"Will you do it?"

She was proud and happy, yet something held her back. She was surprised to hear herself answering, "I don't know."

Darya touched her shoulder. "As a special favor to me?"

Valentina looked into Darya's eyes, and saw nothing but affection. "What would I have to do?"

"Nothing unpleasant, I assure you. I can't tell you more until you join the project. But you can trust me, Valentina. You will be pleased. I guarantee you will be pleased."

"May I think about it?"

"Of course. I wouldn't want you to make a quick decision."

Late the next week Valentina had had a telephone call from Darya.

"I'm in France, darling."

"You're where?" It couldn't be true. No one ever went to France.

"Cap Ferrat. I'll be back on the weekend. Can you come to a party?"

"Well, yes." *France.* "I'd love to."

There were only twenty people at the party, in a large apartment on Kutuzovsky Prospekt. Valentina recognized some of the girls from the Intourist hotel. The men were old—no students from the IIR this time. Champagne, vodka, caviar, foie gras. A jazz band. Lots of bedrooms. Darya never appeared. Valentina got the picture and left.

Darya called later and apologized for not meeting her

at the party. "Let me make up for it," she said, and invited Valentina to spend the weekend at a Kremlin guest dacha on Lenin Hills.

Saturday afternoon at the dacha, standing with Darya on a glass-enclosed terrace overlooking the Moscow River, Valentina found the courage to ask about her parents.

"I understand you're from Labinsk," she said.

"Yes." Darya was watching a white motorboat moving slowly down the river.

"My family was from Labinsk too."

"Really?"

"My parents died there." She fixed her eyes on Darya. "They were burned to death."

Darya turned abruptly. "Burned?"

"Yes."

"In a mill?"

"Yes."

"I heard about that. They were your parents? How terrible."

"Yes, it was."

Darya stepped to a green wicker chair but did not sit down. "Everyone said the mill foreman should have been prosecuted. Evidently he was storing inflammables where he shouldn't have."

"Were there any other rumors?"

"Not that I remember. I only heard about the foreman. He was very upset and I suppose being accused of responsibility didn't make him feel much better. People always look for a scapegoat, don't they? What a horrible accident."

She reached out and touched Valentina's hand. "But that's such a stupid thing for me to say. It was certainly more horrible for you than anyone."

"It wasn't pleasant."

Darya paused for a moment. "How curious that we should have that connection. Both our families from Labinsk." She shook her head. "That awful accident."

"Yes."

Darya's eyes went back to the motorboat. After a minute she said, "And now we are about to be partners in a magnificent scientific project."

"Partners? Hardly that, Darya. And really I'm not sure it's something I should do."

"Why not?" Darya appeared startled. "It will change the world, Valentina. It could make you famous. We must never decline an opportunity to probe the . . ."

The more Darya spoke, the more Valentina felt herself withdraw. She wasn't sure she believed what Darya had said about the fire.

"Why do you hesitate?" Darya asked. "Tell me what's holding you back and maybe I can clear it up."

But Valentina couldn't tell her. She couldn't put it into words. Something just said . . . don't do this.

Four days after the Lenin Hills weekend, Darya called Valentina at home and said she had to have an answer.

It was like refusing a marriage proposal from a kind and loving suitor. "I'm sorry. I don't know how to explain. I appreciate your asking me, but I—" She hoped Darya would speak, take her off the hook. "But I just can't do it."

Darya allowed a touch of impatience into her voice.

"Well, I'm sorry too, Valentina. I'm surprised, really. You are making a big mistake. And I must tell you, it hurts me personally."

Valentina thought she knew what that meant. Darya would no longer be her friend. And Darya's friends would no longer be her friends. "I'm sorry," she said.

"Me too."

27

*V*ALENTINA APPEARED AT least as distressed telling this story as Hammond was listening to it. She sat there in jeans and a sweater, her cropped hair giving her a peculiar tomboy look, and the guilt and remorse surrounded her like a cloud. Hammond had always heard that Christians believed they were forgiven for their sins, but this certainly seemed not to be the case with Valentina.

Had she really been a whore? Hammond found it difficult to imagine. The black marketeering bothered him less, though legally it was more important. There was no law against prostitution, but for currency crimes she could be shot.

He was pleased when the telephone promised relief from Valentina's confession. It rang once and stopped. Marchenko. A few seconds later it rang again, and Hammond counted. Ten this time.

"I'm sorry, Valentina, but we'll have to finish this later. I have to go out."

She followed him to the door.

"Hide that money," he said.

"Don't worry."

"And do a better job of it this time."

Hammond drove past GRU headquarters, took note of the position of the window curtains, and met Marchenko at the horse stables in Gorki Park. Nearly deserted during the winter months, the stables were approached on foot, the smooth snow testifying to the absence of unwanted observers. Three horses stood silently in the stalls.

Wrapped in coats and scarves, Hammond and Marchenko sat on a bench in the tack room.

"You're so close to Andropov, Andrei, why do we have to keep freezing ourselves at secret meetings? Who are we hiding from?"

"If the General Secretary had no rivals, my friend, Nikita Khrushchev would have died in office. Did you hear from Darya?"

"Emphatically." Hammond shivered, not entirely from the cold. It was still hard to believe that the nightmare had been real.

"And?"

"Let's just say she has no desire to defect."

One of the horses whinnied, a sound Hammond hadn't heard since weekend rides in Central Park.

"You said if the heat was turned up—that was your phrase—she'd come running to you."

"She didn't."

"So you are learning that she is not so predictable. I told you she was someone to fear."

"We can respect her, Andrei, but that doesn't mean we have to be immobilized by her."

Marchenko grew thoughtful, and Hammond had the feeling the Russian might be way ahead of him. Had Marchenko taken him to Kashirin not to see Darya, but to let Darya see him, so she would know he was the one responsible for her being there, and not cooperate?

"What did you think of the package I gave you?" Marchenko asked.

"I didn't have that much time to study it. I sent it to friends."

"I told you they were looking for the right target, the right moment."

"Yes."

"They've found it."

"And?" He hated Marchenko's coyness.

"Andropov is dying. At his funeral, which may not be very far off, Moscow will flood with heads of government."

Hammond wished he had never gone to Monte Carlo, never met Darya, never come to Moscow. "Give it all to me, Andrei. Don't make me drag it out of you."

"That's all there is."

"What do you mean, that's all there is? They're going

to use Spectrum to massacre heads of government at Andropov's funeral? Take them hostage? Force all the world's governments to surrender to communism? What the hell are you talking about, Andrei?"

"All I know is that Darya is planning to demonstrate Spectrum to visitors at the funeral."

"Which visitors?"

"Use your imagination. Reagan? Kohl? Thatcher?"

"How do you know this?"

"Believe me, I know it. I have heard Darya discuss it."

"With whom?"

"Members of the Brezhnevite clique. Chernenko, Grishin. Don't expect me to tell you everything. You want it all, Jack, but you give nothing."

"Nothing? What is it you want?"

Marchenko scuffed his Russian boots against the tackroom floor. "You know, Jack, the time has come for frankness between us."

Hammond waited.

"I was almost ready to defect, back in Monte Carlo. You know that. In the end—I had a career, a family. It was a lot to lose. But I kept in touch, as you Americans say. I saw Cox. I'm seeing you. I handed over valuable material the last time we met. It's not easy. I'm on your side, Jack. I want what you want. I think I've earned some trust."

"I trust you, Andrei. What are you getting at?"

"I know why you wanted Darya to come to you. You wanted her to give you Spectrum. I too want her to give you Spectrum. You think I want it in the hands of Brezhnevite criminals? But Darya will never give it to you, Jack.

If she gives you Spectrum she has nothing left to bargain with."

"So?" Hammond saw no need to tell Marchenko he had already burned his bridges with Darya.

"Andropov can give it to you."

Hammond almost laughed. "Why would he do that?"

"Because you are going to heal him."

"I am? You believe he'll be healed?"

"I know it's possible. I've seen the data on Mrs. Leonov. She has healed, without question. Whether she will be able to heal Andropov is another matter, but she might."

"So you think Andropov's going to trade Spectrum for his life?" Hammond didn't dare let himself believe it.

"For much more than his life, Jack. He believes that everything he has done will fail if the Brezhnevites return to power. Mikhail Gorbachev must succeed him. To assure that, Andropov has to remain alive through the March meeting of the Supreme Soviet. He wants to trade Spectrum for three more months of life. He offers Spectrum in exchange for the future of his country."

"Does he think the Leonov woman can give him three more months?"

"He isn't sure. But she has healed some people. What other hope does he have?"

"What if Mrs. Leonov tries to heal Andropov and nothing happens? What if there's disagreement about the extent of the healing? Do we have to wait until March to find out if you're going to give us Spectrum?"

"He cannot actually give you Spectrum, Jack. He does not himself have access to the technology. His offer is to destroy Spectrum. And it will be destroyed regardless of the outcome of the healing attempt. After Mrs. Leonov does whatever she does, Spectrum will be destroyed."

Hammond had no doubt that MAG would be happy to settle for Spectrum's destruction. He wondered if Andropov had in mind destroying Darya as well. If so, the Americans would have little trouble developing their own Spectrum before the Soviets could reinvent theirs.

"How will I know it's been destroyed?" Hammond asked.

"You will watch."

"You seem to have anticipated all the questions, Andrei. I hope you're talking with authority."

Marchenko looked straight into Hammond's eyes and spoke firmly. "I am."

"How sick is he, really?" Hammond asked.

"He has only one kidney, and he's on dialysis. He hardly gets out of bed anymore. He's so thin you can see through him. Vomits all the time."

Hammond tried not to think of what Darya might do to him if she suspected he was plotting the destruction of Spectrum.

"How do we do it, Andrei? Logistically. Where is Andropov now?"

"The woman has to be with him?"

"I would certainly think so."

Marchenko dropped his chin into his coat collar. For a moment it looked as if he'd fallen asleep.

"Is there a problem with that?" Hammond asked.

Marchenko looked up. "No one sees him these days except Gorbachev, the doctors, nurses, a personal secretary, and occasionally myself. But don't worry. I'll work it out."

"Well, I am a little worried, Andrei. If there's going to be some difficulty . . ."

"Leave it to me, Jack. I'll work it out and let you know."

Marchenko sounded so confident. Hammond had been right not to tell Burkholzer he'd lost Darya. Now he could tell him about Andropov, and who would care about Darya?

28

*H*AMMOND RETURNED TO
the apartment and helped Valentina make ham sandwiches for lunch. They took them into the living room,
and when they were settled, Hammond said, "Okay. I'm
all ears."

Two weeks after the last telephone conversation with
Darya, the bald, gray-faced KGB man in the leather coat
knocked on her apartment door, escorted her to a black
Volga, and delivered her without a word of explanation
to the Neglinaya Street entrance of KGB headquarters.
Valentina was in a panic. She had illegally exchanged
hundreds of thousands of dollars' worth of Western cur-

rency, had engaged in the black market trading of gems, gold, caviar, and furs. These were capital crimes, never mind that to execute everyone guilty of them would have decapitated the Soviet government.

The bald man walked her through the heavy brass-handled door, past the armed guard in the vaultlike entrance chamber, and finally to a small third-floor office with two threadbare blue chairs and a wooden desk next to a white-curtained window overlooking Dzerzhinski Square.

The bald man disappeared, and she found herself shaking hands with a rotund, elderly, stoop-shouldered official who failed to mention his name.

"You have been having a good time," he said with a smile, as if acknowledging the social success of a favorite niece.

She thought it best to remain silent. Kindly KGB officers were the worst sort.

"Meeting lots of interesting people."

She nodded.

"Please sit down."

She lowered herself into one of the chairs. He settled behind his desk.

"Let me give you some advice," he said, gentle and cozy.

"Please."

"You are a whore." Still smiling. "That is nothing. But you are also a black marketeer. And for that you can be shot."

"I was trying to get information," she said. "I was told that I had to provide useful information."

Sweetness washed over his face, and he raised a chubby

hand. "Of course you were. I have no quarrel with you at all. You have a good job at the Trade Ministry, and it is not in jeopardy, for the moment. You are not here to be chastised. You are here to receive a responsibility."

She had been certain that something truly disastrous lay before her and was now allowing herself a small, tentative sense of relief.

"For some time we have been looking for a certain man. He is intelligent, capable, courageous. Unfortunately, he is also an enemy. When you find him, I'm sure our gratitude will overwhelm any recollection we might have had of your indelicate past."

"Who is he?" Perhaps Ilya or Nikki would know him.

"His name is Enriko Ilich Leonov. He is head of an antigovernment organization, a so-called religious group. If his interests were religious, he would have no objection to registration with the Committee of Religious Affairs. Since he will not register, but insists on remaining in hiding, and since he continues to recruit members for his group, to secure funds from foreign sources, and to publish antigovernment propaganda, there is little doubt regarding his motives and loyalties."

Valentina was not a political person, had never thought about politics for more than three consecutive minutes. There were, in fact, no politics to think about, there was only the Communist Party. Her concerns were for survival and as little distress as possible. That her country had enemies was obvious, and what the outcome would be if the enemies were not opposed was equally obvious. Had not 20 million Russians died in World War II?

She said, "What do you want me to do?"

A week later, on the instructions of the elderly KGB

official, she attended an illegal church "fellowship meeting" in a one-room apartment at a Moscow housing development. She told the two dozen people there that she had been walking past the building and was drawn by the sound of their singing. They liked that and invited her to another meeting in four days at another apartment.

The Sunday after that meeting the KGB man called at six in the morning and gave her directions to an illegal church service in a forest outside Moscow. Fifty people sat on the ground in the July warmth, singing, praying, and listening to talks by two pastors in shirtsleeves. Neither was Enriko Leonov. Afraid of arousing suspicion, she never mentioned his name.

The following Sunday, in a farmhouse to the west of Moscow, she watched as three men and a woman proclaimed their conversion. The pastor, a young man who already had served six years in labor camps, asked them about their faith. In tears they told of how they had "come to Christ." They repented for their sins and were welcomed into the church. She realized that if she hoped to meet Enriko Ilich Leonov, she would have to fake a conversion.

She raised her hand and said that she too had had an experience like the others. The pastor called her to the front of the room. She told about her life as a prostitute, claiming she had started when she was only sixteen and needed the money to buy black market medicine for her grandmother. Telling this story, she felt herself gaining confidence, winning her audience. And then something went wrong. She had gone too far. The faces around her stopped smiling. She was struck with fear. Images of her grandmother leapt from her memory, and with horror she saw the treachery of what she was doing. Her palms and face went cold, sparkles of light filled the periphery of her vision, she felt nauseous and faint.

When she came to, she was lying on a blanket in the kitchen, a cushion under her head, the young pastor squatting beside her. She wept out her story—the true one this time—of prostitution, black marketeering, and the fat, elderly KGB agent at Dzerzhinski Square.

Four days later Valentina was walking from the metro to her job on Marksa Prospekt when a car pulled up beside her. Beckoning to her from the passenger seat was the pastor. He stepped out of the car and told her to get in. She did so. As the car left the curb the driver said, "How do you do. I am Enriko Leonov."

She never again saw the old man at KGB headquarters. She broke off contact with Albert Bachmann, Anatoli, Ilya, Nikki, and all her customers. She shaved her head —as a promise, a gift, a penance, and a separation. Who would want her now?

Valentina finished the story and went to the refrigerator. "May I have a glass of milk?"

"Of course," Hammond said.

There wasn't any question about whether or not to believe her. Certainly it was all true. The anguish on her face removed any doubt about that. He watched her come back to the table with the milk—cropped hair, sweater, jeans—and tried to picture the person she had been. Long blond hair, charming, shrewd, maybe even seductive—a prostitute, black market dealer, KGB informant, ready to sell anything to get out of the squalor.

"What was Enriko like?" he asked her.

She wiped away a milk mustache, and Hammond had another impression, of a timid, struggling child.

"In the Kingdom of God he fit perfectly, but in the world he did not fit at all. He was like a key that will fit only one lock, and no matter what you do to it you cannot make it fit any other lock."

Hammond wondered what lock her own key might fit.

She raised the glass and waited for the last drop of milk to trickle into her mouth. "What do you think about what I told you? Do you believe me?"

"I do."

They faced each other at the living room coffee table. It was as if they had just met for the first time and were finding the experience awkward.

"You haven't told me about the money," he said.

"It belongs to the church."

"Was it yours?"

"The KGB told me to give them the money I had made. I gave them some, but not all. When I married Enriko I gave it to the church."

"What does the church do with it?"

"We buy printing equipment, paper, ink. We get paper from the shops in one-hundred-sheet packs, two packs at a time. When we have a few thousand sheets we print gospels and hymnals."

"And the KGB hasn't found the equipment?"

"They look, believe me—for the equipment, for the money, for our pastors. They threaten people. 'Tell us where everything is and you won't go to prison.' But the people don't know, not many, and the ones who know go to prison."

"It doesn't seem like the KGB would have that much trouble finding the pastors in Moscow."

"People hide them. They sleep on the floor for a night and then move. They sleep in the forests, hallways, construction sites. They don't care. It's a privilege to be persecuted for Christ."

"They can't keep moving printing presses."

"I don't know about that."

"You just keep the money."

"The KGB thinks the money comes from abroad. What are you going to do with it?"

"It isn't mine, Valentina. But you should have told me you had it here."

"Would you have let me keep it?"

"Probably not."

"Are you now?"

"I don't know. I'll have to think about it. Who knows you have it?"

"Not the KGB."

They stopped talking and the awkwardness returned. It was like a first date, waiting for someone to make a pass.

"Are you on my side, Valentina?" Hammond asked finally.

"Yes, I am."

"Will you try to heal Andropov?"

"There wouldn't be any point."

"Why?"

"Because I can't heal."

"I know. Jesus heals, but—"

"I don't mean that. He won't use me to heal."

"You healed the girl at Spaso House."

"That was before."

"Before what?"

"It doesn't matter. I can't heal anymore."

She began to cry.

"Why can't you heal anymore?"

"Because I can't."

"That's not an answer, Valentina. Can't you just try to heal him? Even if it doesn't work, at least—"

"I told you, I can't do it."

He'd lost Darya, been saved by Andropov, and now he was losing Valentina. She *had* to try. "It doesn't matter if you do it or not. But you have to try. I've promised, I've—"

"Then you do it."

She sprang from the sofa and ran into the bedroom. He followed her to the door. She was across the bed, face-down, sobbing. What had gone wrong? Why couldn't she heal? What the hell was happening?

Hammond walked back into the living room, sat on the sofa, and thought about how to break the news to Burkholzer and Whitmore. Darya was gone. Valentina was gone. Andropov was gone. Total failure.

29

THE SUN WAS JUST RISING, and cars on the Baltimore–Washington Parkway had not yet extinguished their headlights. Ralph Whitmore took the exit to Fort Meade, made a right into Savage Road, passed through a barbed-wire-topped Cyclone fence, another barrier of five high-voltage wires strung between wooden posts, and a final ten-foot Cyclone fence. As he approached the nine-story tan tower rising from the center of a squat, green, A-shaped building, he looked up to see television security cameras and an array of antennas and satellite dishes.

He parked the dark blue '81 Chevrolet, unbuttoned his

overcoat, and reached into the side pocket of his brown suit jacket for a laminated, computerized, color-coded plastic card attached to a silver-colored chain. He put the chain around his neck, reached for a black leather attaché case in the backseat, and mounted a dozen steps to the glass-doored entrance of Gatehouse 1.

A blue-uniformed guard with a sidearm said, "Good morning, Admiral." Whitmore moved past him with a nod into a muraled corridor. He passed another uniformed guard with holstered pistol and stepped alone into the second of six elevators connecting the lobby with the executive offices on the sixth floor.

Walking to the end of the corridor, he passed through a blue door marked 9A197. He said, "Is he here yet?" to the only secretary who was working at that early hour.

"No, sir, not yet."

He turned right, entered his private office, and tossed the attaché case onto a brown, GSA-issue leather sofa. He hung his overcoat and suit jacket on metal hangers dangling from a coatrack, slipped the plastic badge inside his shirt, and sat down next to the attaché case. He opened it and removed a black, inch-thick looseleaf binder.

The secretary appeared with a red binder similar to Whitmore's. A buzzing sound came from the outer office.

"That might be him," the secretary said, and hurried out.

Whitmore arranged the two binders on the wooden coffee table separating the sofa from two matching leather chairs. He heard the secretary say, "Go right in, Dr. Burkholzer."

"Good morning," Whitmore said, waving at one of the leather chairs. "Welcome to NSA. Coffee?"

"No thanks." Burkholzer hooked a camel overcoat on the coatrack.

"How was the flight?" Whitmore said. "Sorry to ask you up here so suddenly."

"No problem."

When the package Marchenko gave Hammond had arrived at NSA last night, Whitmore had telephoned Burkholzer, who told him about his conversation with Hammond and promised to get the first plane to Washington.

Burkholzer settled himself in the chair, and Whitmore shoved the black binder toward him. "Have a look."

Burkholzer lifted his bad arm into his lap and did as he was told. The binder contained sixty-six sheets of white paper, the top and bottom of each stamped with two words in red Cyrillic letters a quarter inch high. Russian writing, interspersed with mathematical equations, filled the pages. It didn't take a Ph.D. to guess that the words in red were a Soviet security classification.

"This is what he sent?" Burkholzer asked.

"A photocopy."

Burkholzer skimmed the pages. "Some of the equations are familiar, the sort of thing any quantum physicist would recognize." He glanced from the document to Whitmore. "It would help if I understood Russian."

"Four translators have been up all night to give you that privilege, Steve." Whitmore handed over the red binder.

Not only had each word been translated, every smudge and mark on the original had painstakingly been transferred to the copy. Words crossed out in Russian had similarly been crossed out in the translation. Words added in script in the Russian were added in script in the English. Even penned underlinings were copied with the same slant, width, and apparently inadvertent waverings as the originals. The translators, more than mere linguists, were clearly sensitive to whatever nonverbal codes or meanings might lie hidden on the pages.

Whitmore gave Burkholzer three minutes, then asked, "What is it?"

"Well, obviously it's psychotronic data."

"Is it genuine?"

"It appears to be. As I said, the equations make sense individually. I'd need more time to—"

"Do you recognize the handwriting?" Not all the notes were typed.

"No. Am I supposed to?"

"It's Darya's."

"Ah-*hah*." Burkholzer raised his eyebrows and flipped back a few pages. "Just give me five minutes here, Ralph."

"Help yourself."

Burkholzer got up, laid his suit jacket over the back of the chair, unbuttoned his collar, loosened his tie, sat back down, and lost himself in the pages. Whitmore had the impression that a gunshot would not have disturbed him.

"Enfoldment technology," Burkholzer said after several minutes. "You remember the colored die enfolded in the glycerine at the briefing Hammond and I gave, and the waves from which we hope to extract images of distant objects? Well, what we have here appears to be Spectrum research on the use of various waves to influence physical health and behavior."

Whitmore did not want to interrupt Burkholzer's train of thought. He remained silent and listened.

Burkholzer crossed his legs. "Yes," he said without looking up from the binder. "See here. Listen to this. 'The brain operates as a receptor for portions of the electromagnetic spectrum. EM energy when modulated can act as a stimulus at some point in the sensory systems. There is a physiological basis for the degradation of behavior and for emotional and drive changes.' " He glanced up. "Remember Nixon and Carter?"

Whitmore nodded. He wondered where all this was leading.

"Yes. Here. Listen. 'The degree to which brain stimulation can be limited to a discrete locus is a complex function of the wavelength of the energy, the scattering that occurs as the energy passes through tissue layers, and the nature of the antenna.' " Burkholzer nodded, turned the page, and read silently.

"Air ions . . ." He turned another page. " 'Air ions and electro aerosols have been demonstrated to have physiological and behavior consequences. Effects have been demonstrated on emotions, reaction time, flicker fusion frequency, blood pressure sedimentation rate, serum protein, and metabolism.' "

He looked at Whitmore. "What's Hammond say about this?"

"Nothing yet. He sent it to us as soon as he got it."

The part about flicker fusion frequency had made Whitmore recall the flickering fluorescent lamps in his hotel bathroom. Fearing a lecture, he had not yet told Burkholzer about that episode.

Burkholzer went back to his reading. " 'Charged particles penetrating the alveolar wall are transferred to blood cells and act on the central nervous system by stimulating pulmonary nerves.' " He flipped the page. " 'Photon waves, sound waves, and other oscillatory disturbances of free space, for example neutrinos and gravitons, are under investigation.' I'll bet they are."

He tilted the binder sideways, evidently to examine a graph, then turned it back and continued to read silently. Whitmore waited.

"Yes, here it is. Enfoldment. Fourier transforms. Listen. 'This results in an interference pattern that is either an amplified signal or a scattered wave pattern containing information that was present in the brain wave oscillations or object. The atmospheric carrier wave spreads the interference pattern over the surface of the earth, and certain capable people or devices can perform Fourier transforms to pick off the interference patterns and reconstruct the originals. The Fourier components of entire scenes—buildings, landscapes, individuals, etc.—are directly decodable by the receiver.' "

He turned the page. "Right. Right." Another page. "Yeah. Maybe. 'The result of equation six . . .' " He flipped back a page. "Right. Okay. 'The result of equation six shows that organisms in liquid-crystal-like assemblies of biomolecules exist and are capable of coherent and monochromatic amplification of incoming electromagnetic waves in the kilohertz region by more than a millionfold.' Hmmm. 'Not only can the incoming waves be amplified, but if the liquid-crystal rotation levels are modulated by bioelectrical potential fluctuations induced by the brain of a man, the outgoing field will carry this modulation information.' "

"I'm not sure all this means as much to me as it does to you, Steve."

"It doesn't have to. Just hang on. 'A second person, or a device, capable of perceiving and demodulating this kilohertz wave-modulated information, can then quote read unquote the first person's mind.' "

The telephone on Whitmore's desk buzzed. "Excuse me, Steve, just a second." He took three steps to the side of the desk, lifted the receiver, said, "Put him on."

"Of course, Bill. What's the problem? Right. Who is it?"

Whitmore moved behind the desk and sat down. "Are you *sure*?"

He had to struggle to keep his voice steady. "Okay. Finish the traces and I'll be down in a few minutes."

Burkholzer was watching him.

Whitmore put the phone down.

"Are you all right?" Burkholzer said.

"Yes. It's . . . just some interesting news." He hadn't felt this disturbed since the incident in the bathtub. The caller had been Bill Chub, chief of NSA's Pyramider satellite system, which bounced radio communications from illegal CIA and DIA agents in denied areas to a TRW satellite, then back down to one of four dish antennas on the roof of the NSA headquarters tower, and by cable to computerized decoders in the basement ten floors below Whitmore's office.

One of Chub's people had just received what was called an initiator, a preliminary pulse sent by a squirt transmitter to alert computers electronically that a message would follow in a couple of microseconds. The problem was that no message had followed. Since initiators are sent automatically when the transmitter is turned on, an initiator not followed by a message—they were called widows—was regarded as a sign of possible distress. An agent in trouble had only to activate his transmitter—always disguised as an innocuous personal object like an electric razor or travel clock—to let NSA know that something was wrong. Similarly, an enemy who discovered and activated a transmitter into which a message had not been entered would unknowingly transmit a widow. Two widows not separated by an orthodox transmission were interpreted as an unqualified call for help.

In this case, there had been three widows. And what really gave Whitmore the cold sweats was that Chub had said they came from George Cox. Whitmore had heard a lot of spooky stuff lately, but he was not prepared for agents who came back from the dead.

"You sure you're okay?" Burkholzer said.

"Yeah, I'm sure." Whitmore returned to the sofa. "Let's get on with this. Keep going." Analysis of the widows would provide their geographical origin to within 1,600 square meters. Until then Whitmore could only wait and try to pay attention to Burkholzer.

"Well," Burkholzer said, "let's see . . . Here . . . yes . . . neutrinos. 'Some of the lower-frequency neutrinos can stimulate the deexcitation of biophysical rotationally excited molecules in the brain . . .' Let's see . . . 'Neutrinos can be responsible for the release of coded thought waves. Since neutrinos can travel unimpeded through the earth or other barriers, this is consistent with the independence of psychotronic effects to distance and magnetic shielding.'"

Whitmore fought to keep his mind on Burkholzer.

Burkholzer turned a page. "'As regards macroscopic influences, experimental evidence indicates that will-influenced events actually do occur, for example when tumbling dice are influenced to come to rest in a desired position. By psychotronically influencing the atomic nuclei in the cube a person can generate gravitational forces of the magnitude of about fifteen percent of the earth's gravitation.' "

He flipped the page. "Now we're getting into quantum-mechanical psi-wave interpretations. That's better. Let's see. David Bohm! Bingo. Remember Bohm? I mentioned his name at the briefing. Invented the enfoldment theory?"

Burkholzer didn't wait for an answer.

" 'According to some quantum-mechanical theorists, all matter is indeterminate and dispersed, and actual reality must be described by a wave function with an infinite set of eigenstates extending over all space and time. David Bohm believes that matter must be described by a multistate wave function . . .' Uh-huh. 'The quantum wave is a wave of knowledge or information.' That says it."

He put the binder on the coffee table, readjusted his bad arm in his lap, then picked up the binder and continued. " 'The information of the universe is arrayed not in terms of position and time as we have come to perceive it, but rather as frequency and amplitude information, and the human consciousness essentially performs Fourier transforms on this to order that information into the more familiar form. Consciousness may, by this mechanism, access any portion of space and time to acquire information. Further, since it is known that a particle with wave properties is not located in a strictly determined place, but can be all over the entire universe or at different points at the same time, a generalization from microcosm to macrocosm makes possible the appearance of a macro-object anywhere in the universe.' "

Whitmore was hearing only half of what Burkholzer said. Was Cox—no, not possible.

Burkholzer looked up from the binder. "A few more minutes?"

"All the time you like," Whitmore said.

"Listen to this. 'Each object present as a standing wave in a specific location in space and time is also present at all points in space and time. The table on which this report is being written exists everywhere and at all times simultaneously. It was present last year in the constellation of Alpha Centauri, except that there was less of it there then than there is here now.' "

Burkholzer's eyes scanned down the page. " 'Information regarding physical objects can be enfolded and carried in electromagnetic waves, by electron beams, neutrinos, gravitons, quantum-matter waves, and numerous other forms of movement.' Here, Ralph, this will interest you. 'Planck's equation states that frequency and energy are the same thing. And since we know from Einstein that energy and matter are convertible, it follows that frequency can be matter. Thus, from frequency interference patterns we are able to manifest the physical objects that produced those patterns. This, of course, is the principle on which Spectrum functions. All Spectrum does is bring out, by appropriate focusing, the wave structure of a distant object, which is latently present in any particular point in space. Likewise, human psychological processes have wave characteristics, and the mental images and thoughts of all people are present in every point in space and time. Recording and manifesting images as standing waves that have been ejected outside the brain and externalized is another accomplishment of the Spectrum program.' "

He turned a page. "Etcetera . . ." Another page. "Etcetera . . ." Another page. "Equations . . . Equations . . . Equations . . . You're not interested in those. Let's see. Yes. 'The wave functions of quantum mechanics represent real matter waves that permeate all space and time. It requires only the will of a capable person or a suitably designed device to perform an operation on these waves that would permit the perception of any scene in space and time. It is through Fourier analysis of these waves that objects and events distance in space and/or time can be captured and visualized.' "

The secretary put her head in. "Can I get you anything?"

"Sure you won't have some coffee, Steve?" Whitmore asked.

"No, no, no," Burkholzer said without looking up. "Thanks very much. Now we get into another area. ". . . working on a means to interface human thought and behavior directly through a transducer attached to the head and read directly by a computer. The computer can monitor, modify, and control behavior without the subject's awareness.' You interested in that?"

"I'm interested in everything, Steve."

Burkholzer continued. " 'Serbenov Institute research has established that the most effective psychotronic subjects are highly temperamental and emotionally open female workers and students in the sixteen-to-twenty-one age grouping, though with increased posttesting incidence of blackouts and vomiting. Side effects, including inappropriate behavior, neurasthenia, psychasthenia, and hysteria, were a small price to pay for the desired goal.' "

Burkholzer shook his head. "Easy for them to say."

He took a deep breath, exhaled, and read on. " 'We have demonstrated the psychotronic manipulation of consciousness and correlated it with systematic EEG recordings. Tests include sending to the percipient the anxiety associated with suffocation and sensation of a blow to the head.' Nice. 'After transmitting negative emotions to a human subject, the white cell count decreased by sixteen hundred. Such a psychotronically imposed shift in cell count could be used to alter human health. Control and manipulation of physical health, as well as human consciousness, thoughts, emotions, and will, has been achieved.' "

Burkholzer stopped there, raised his head, and stared in the direction of a large globe next to a window over which a venetian blind had been lowered. A framed sign next to the globe said THERE ARE NO SECRETS, ONLY FOOLS WHO BELIEVE IN SECRETS. After a minute he directed his gaze at Whitmore. "Are you hearing this?"

"I'm afraid so, Steve."

Whitmore waited for Burkholzer to return to the document, but he simply continued to stare.

"Is there more, Steve?"

Burkholzer let out a sigh, dropped his eyes to the binder, and read. " 'During negative healing, field pulsations were noted that were synchronous with the subject's respiration rate, heartbeat, and brain alpha rhythm pattern.' "

Once more Whitmore experienced an uneasy recollection of the hotel bathtub.

" 'Effects on human subjects have included pain, paralysis, burns and other tissue damage, and acute coronary thrombosis. But while electrical fields have been measured successfully between healers and subjects, knowing these field potentials has not yet led to the duplications of human-induced beneficial effects by means of mechanically generated fields.' So they seem to have had more success with negative healing than with the positive type."

"Hammond says one of their people approached him about healing a Soviet official," Whitmore said.

"So they think we may be ahead in that area? I wouldn't be surprised if we were."

"Why?"

"You don't want to hear this, Ralph, but to some significant degree we are dealing here with the supernatural. And positive supernatural entities are superior to the negative. Satan, being a former angel, has far less power than God."

Whitmore, his mind crowded with thoughts of flickering light bulbs and squirt transmissions from dead agents, nodded but did not speak.

Burkholzer flipped a page, then another. He was near the end. "Let's see. 'A device such as Spectrum is impossible to defend against, and its effects, including changes in brain wave characteristics, disturbance of equilibrium, and dizziness, can result in personality changes and/or physical discomfort that, employed broadly against troops, would alter combat effectiveness, and when employed selectively against military and political leaders would reduce the ability to command and govern. Such a device, capable of negatively affecting healthy tissue as well as disrupting fundamental brain rhythms, heart control, and biological-clock mechanisms, would pose a severe threat to enemy command, military, intelligence, embassy, or other security functions.' "

Burkholzer closed the binder. "Well . . ." He placed the binder back on the coffee table and appeared for the moment at a loss for words.

"I have something I want you to hear," Whitmore said, and read a note Hammond had included with the binder. It related everything Marchenko had said about the Spectrum tests on humans—the deaths, the artificially induced rage, hallucinations, terror.

"Do you believe that?" Whitmore asked.

"You mean is it possible? From what's in here?" He touched the binder.

"That's what I mean."

"Definitely. I can't vouch for everything in that binder, and Soviet psychotronic work has been flawed in the past, but no way would I want to bet against what I just read in that binder. No way."

Burkholzer shifted his position in the chair. "When I spoke to Hammond yesterday and he told me he was sending you this package, he said Marchenko told him they had tested Spectrum on humans. Hammond had become sick and wanted to know if there was any way to protect himself from further attacks."

"Sick from—Spectrum made him sick?"

"He wasn't sure. He thought maybe it was just some kind of bug, flu, or something. But he was scared."

"I don't blame him," Whitmore said. "Hammond says in here"—he waved the note Hammond had enclosed with the binder—"that Marchenko told him he doesn't know who they'll use this against first. They're waiting for an appropriate target."

"Who might that be?"

"If they want to debut this thing on someone big, I guess we have to assume they won't restrict their options. Name a chief of state."

"If I were Reagan or any of the others," Burkholzer said, "I'd certainly want to stay close to home. I wouldn't go near any Soviet installation, and I'd stay within reach of good medical facilities."

Both men were silent.

"What are you going to do?" Burkholzer asked.

Whitmore walked over to his desk and punched the intercom. "Margaret, tell the other MAG members I have to see them. Soon as possible. Before lunch. If there's a problem I'll talk to them myself."

He returned to the sofa. "We have to get Spectrum, Steve."

30

HAMMOND KNEW THAT THE
package Marchenko had given him would already have
arrived at NSA headquarters. No doubt Whitmore was
pouring over it now. But he had to warn Whitmore of
Marchenko's latest revelation, that Spectrum would be
used to attack heads of government attending Andropov's
funeral.

Unfortunately, this time it wasn't nine at night and
Frank couldn't get Hammond a secure phone. Jerry Shroeder was on duty, presiding over his CIA kingdom like a
jealous lioness.

"You wanna run things yourself," he told Hammond, "use your own phone."

The embassy medical clinic was a small wooden building in the courtyard. Nothing about it was secure, least of all the telephone.

"Jerry, I'm sorry for what happened in the snack bar. I just need to make a call to Washington. How can that be a problem for you?"

"No problem at all. Use your own phone."

"It's not secure. You know that."

"Write a cable. I'll see it gets priority handling."

And maybe it gets sent and maybe it doesn't. And maybe Shroeder reads it and maybe everybody else in the building.

"You won't give me a secure phone?"

"I'm busy, Jack. Anything else I can do for you?"

Hammond returned to the apartment and retrieved Cox's squirt transmitter from the drain pipe outside the bedroom window. Not knowing Cox's entering code, he was unable to enter and transmit a message. But he knew that by merely activating the transmitter he could send an initiator, and that at least two initiators not followed by a message would provoke a response. He also knew that NSA Pyramider satellites triangulating on the source of the initiator's electronic pulse could pinpoint the transmitter's location.

He turned on the transmitter, waited a couple of seconds, and turned it off. He repeated the procedure twice. One more than necessary.

Then he looked at his watch and went into the living room. Valentina was there.

"What's going on?" she asked.

"I'm waiting for someone. You'd better stay in the bedroom. I don't want them to see you."

"Are you all right?"

"I'm fine. Don't worry. But I'm not sure how long I'll
have to wait. Maybe only a few minutes."

"Are they Americans?"

"Of course they're Americans. You think the Russians
are coming for me?"

She shrugged. "It's Moscow."

Forty-seven minutes later, Hammond answered a heavy
knock at the door. He found Jerry Shroeder dwarfed by
four lanky Marines in civilian parkas.

"Where is it?" Shroeder demanded, pushing into the
apartment.

One of the Marines went to a window.

"Where is what?"

"Cox's toy."

"Who's Cox?" Shroeder was not officially authorized
even to know Cox's name.

"He's still there," the Marine at the window said.

Hammond followed Shroeder to the window. A gray
Zhiguli with a driver inside was parked across the street
opposite the embassy van Shroeder had come in.

"The hell with him," Shroeder said, and turned to Hammond. "You're gonna come with me." He was trying to
sound tough, impress the Marines. "People at home want
an explanation from you."

They went down and crowded into the van. As they
drove up the street, the Marine driver, his eyes on the
rearview mirror, said, "That the girlfriend?"

Hammond turned to see Valentina crossing the street
with her blue plastic suitcase. She climbed into the Zhiguli.

"Well, well, well," Shroeder said, his monkey face giving Hammond a self-satisfied sneer. "What's in the suitcase? Documents? The squirt? Love snaps?"

Hammond knew what was in the suitcase. About $250,000. But in the Zhiguli?

"Your little KGB lady," Shroeder said. "Not that I didn't warn you."

Hammond's heart sank, and he sagged back into the seat.

Fifteen minutes later Hammond was in the embassy, on a secure phone to Ralph Whitmore.

"What's the latest, Jack?" Whitmore said, having been assured it was not Cox who sent the widows.

The latest? Hammond had a sudden urge to tell everything, dump it all in Whitmore's lap. Darya's out, Valentina's out, the whole thing's down the tube. But what could Whitmore do? Hammond had to work this out himself. There had to be an answer. It couldn't just be over.

"I'm told the device will be used against heads of government attending the big man's funeral," Hammond said.

There was no response. He thought he could hear Whitmore talking to someone.

"Are you there?" Hammond asked.

"I'm here," Whitmore said. "We got the package."

"What do you think?"

"Steve's with me now. We just went over it. They're going to use it against funeral visitors?"

"That's what he said. Does Steve think that's possible?"

More muttering between Whitmore and Burkholzer.

"He says he wouldn't bet against it. We have to get the device, Jack."

"I can't go into that on this line." No phone was totally

secure. Whitmore of all people understood that. "We'd better alert counterparts." Other intelligence services, heads of government.

"We'll do that. And Jack, next time you want my attention try something a little less alarming. I almost had a heart attack."

"Not my fault, Ralph. Someone was using the phone."

Hammond was on his way out of the embassy when Shroeder stopped him at the elevator. "Something for you." He handed Hammond a cable and waited to watch him read it.

Divorce finalized today.

It was sent from Santo Domingo and signed by Hammond's wife.

At eight-thirty that night Hammond walked into the apartment's kitchen and pulled a pack of frozen hamburgers from the freezer. He'd checked for the money and it was gone. The squirt—what a sigh of relief—was still in the drainpipe where he'd put it. He unwrapped the hamburgers. Someone knocked on the door.

When he opened it, he stepped into the hallway and said, "Where's the suitcase?"

"What suitcase?"

"I'm tired, Valentina. I saw you leave in the Zhiguli."

"May I come in?"

She followed him back to the kitchen, saw the hamburgers, and put them in a skillet. Just as if nothing had happened.

"Well?" he said.

"The suitcase is safe."

"I'm sure it is. Who was in the Zhiguli?"

"Don't ask me that, Jack."

He turned on her. "Are you kidding? You walk out with two hundred and fifty thousand dollars and get into what looks like a KGB car and I'm not supposed to ask? Just, 'Hi, Valentina, have a hamburger'?"

"I can't tell you."

"Was it KGB?"

Would she admit it if it were? The driver could have been anyone—the guy who hit him in the kidneys or the KGB thug in the canvas jacket. Maybe it was a militia car, some guy working for Vitali Fedorchuk, the militia boss Marchenko had told him about, Darya's friend. Maybe it was Darya. Maybe . . .

"It was church business," Valentina said.

"I'm supposed to believe that?"

"Not necessarily."

She cooked the hamburgers, and they ate them in silence at the kitchen table.

"I have some good news," she said finally.

"I'm listening."

"I can try to heal again."

Had someone sent her back here to tell him that? Get to Andropov and kill him? Valentina couldn't be that treacherous.

"If you still want me to try to heal Andropov," she said, "I'll do it."

Her eyes fixed him across the plates of hamburger.

"What do you need?" he said. He had to trust her. There was no other choice.

"You mean special equipment?" She was amused now. Maybe it *had* been church business. "What's wrong with him?"

Hammond got up and put his empty dish in the sink. "My guess is renal failure, kidney disease. Plus diabetes, which caused the kidney problem. Also heart disease."

"What's he actually dying of?"

"Kidney disease."

"Then I would want to lay my hands on his kidneys."

"How often?"

"Sometimes people are healed immediately. Sometimes it happens gradually, sometimes not at all. It would be good to be able to repeat it as many times as possible."

Hammond went back to the table. "Let me tell you something, Valentina. If he has what I think he has, there won't be any healing him completely. That would be like bringing him back from the dead."

"That's been done too."

"Does it make any difference that he doesn't believe?"

"All that matters is that it's God's will to heal that person at that time in that way."

Hammond called Marchenko, and he showed up in an ambulance at two A.M. On the way out of the apartment, Hammond noticed a heavy sag in the right pocket of Valentina's ski jacket. He pushed his hand against the pocket as he helped her into the ambulance and felt something solid and heavy. Andropov led the assault against Christians in the Soviet Union, and perhaps she held him responsible for the death of her husband. But attack him? She wouldn't do that. On the other hand, who'd been with her in that Zhiguli?

Valentina was on a jump seat next to the gurney in the back of an ambulance, speeding through the darkness along Kalinina Prospekt, Hammond up front next to Marchenko. She could not believe her good fortune. She was going to see Yuri Andropov, the man who had created the KGB's Fifth Directorate, the gang of thugs who beat, tortured, and imprisoned Christians. They had sent her husband to Perm 36.

Six hours ago, when she told Hammond she would attempt the healing, she still had not wanted to do it. She was repelled and scared. But she remembered a man called Ananias, who, recoiling from a similar mission two thousand years ago, had been commanded by God with a single word: "Go!" So she was going. But not unprepared.

Now that he, Valentina, and Marchenko were actually headed for the hospital, Hammond began to have second thoughts. Was he, an American agent, really accompanying Valentina, a Soviet dissident, into the lair of Yuri Andropov? As ambassador to Hungary during the 1956 rebellion, Andropov had invited the Hungarian defense minister to a banquet. Sometime between the caviar and the coffee, the minister was dragged from the table, hauled off to prison, and later shot. Hungarian prime minister Nagy, whom Andropov had promised safe passage from the Yugoslav embassy, stepped outside and was arrested and executed. Andropov's hospitality had a bad reputation.

Kalinina Prospekt veered left into Kutuzovsky Prospekt, and they passed Darya's apartment building. After a few minutes Marchenko made a right turn into a narrow asphalt road, and Hammond could see the dim outlines of new housing developments and factories. They swung into a long straight drive plowed clear of snow with two orange lights at the end.

The former village of Kuntsevo, once a resort area frequented by Tolstoy, Dostoyevsky, and Tchaikovsky, had eventually become the site of Blizhnoye, Stalin's palatial suburban dacha. Stalin was gone now, but the secluded opulence of the Soviet privileged class lived on in what was officially known as the Central Clinic Hospital. Though the name sounded democratic enough, the hospital, unknown to most Muscovites, was reserved for Politburo members and other high government and Party officials. Medical care, meager in Moscow and medieval in the countryside, was state-of-the-art at Kuntsevo. Equipment came from the Siemens Corporation in West Germany, much of the staff was trained in the West, and some of the top doctors, like Andropov's cardiologist, Yevgeni Chazov, had worldwide reputations.

Marchenko braked the ambulance at the orange lights, his way blocked by steel gates extending from beige brick pillars on either side of the road. A man in a full-length sheepskin coat approached the ambulance from a guardhouse next to the pillar on the driver's side.

The guard took a red card from Marchenko's hand, examined it, turned it over, glanced at Marchenko's face, handed the card back, and returned to the guardhouse. The gates swung open. A large building stood against the moonlit sky two hundred yards ahead.

They made a sharp left, curved gently to the right, and two minutes later entered a complex of a half dozen four-story brick buildings set among trees and lawns. They parked in a circular drive. Hammond watched Marchenko unlock the back of the ambulance and swing the door open. Valentina, taking Marchenko's extended hand, jumped down to the asphalt.

They entered a five-story building, rode an elevator to the second floor, and walked down a long hallway to a corner. They had encountered no guards since coming through the gate, a testimony to the strength and reliability of Soviet security. Marchenko pressed a button beside a heavy wooden door. Hammond heard a two-tone chime.

A short, muscular man smartly dressed in a dark gray Western suit and striped Ivy League tie greeted Marchenko, shook hands hastily with Hammond and Valentina, and showed them into a large, ornately decorated living room.

If this was a hospital, it was like none Hammond had ever seen before. The place looked like the drawing room of a nineteenth-century Italian bordello. Richly brocaded purple velvet curtains covered high leaded windows. Oriental rugs lay across the burnished parquet. Hulking mahogany chairs were upholstered in crimson and blue.

But there were abrasive irregularities, evidence of an ostentatious apartment abandoned by its decorator to more pragmatic masters. An antique highboy faced a modern pine desk identical to hundreds of others manufactured for Soviet offices. Other antiques stood side by side with Finnish department-store chairs and tables. Six telephones—white, black, and red—sat side by side on a wheeled metal typing table.

The muscular man excused himself and withdrew. But before they could sit down he was back, beckoning them silently to follow. His eyes fell on the bulge in Valentina's jacket pocket, and Hammond could see him weighing the risk of demanding to have a look. He decided against it.

They entered a red-carpeted hallway, passed closed doors that Hammond guessed contained bedrooms for their guide and other aides, and arrived finally at a door with a gold knob in the shape of a lion's head.

The man straightened, touched his hair, took a breath, and knocked gently. A blond nurse, with widely set blue eyes and skin as white as Valentina's, opened the door and smiled. Andropov was propped like a scarecrow in a purple velvet wing chair in the room's far corner next to a closed double door. His oversized dark suit, white shirt with a half inch of space between collar and neck, and brightly polished shoes framed and accentuated the pathetic body of this emaciated, dying man. Clearly, there had been an insistence that the General Secretary of the Communist Party of the Soviet Union not receive visitors in a robe and pajamas, whatever his condition.

When Valentina walked into the drawing room and saw Andropov, she did what her husband had said he often did with the cruelest prison guards. She looked directly at his eyes, straight at his eyes as hard as she could look, and she said to herself, "I love you." In that instant, she saw his face change. He looked helpless and miserable. Her husband had said, "You see them as God sees them."

Hammond moved as close to Andropov as he dared. The yellow-brown skin, puffy under the eyes, was sloughing off the backs of the old man's hands. Bandages on his neck probably covered puss-filled carbuncles. The left arm twitched. The right hand roamed constantly over his body, scratching. His breath smelled like ammonia. A sediment of urea had produced a faint white frost on the upper lip. Andropov's kidneys were so incapable of cleansing blood that he had, in effect, been sweating urine. The muscular man approached Andropov and with a proper little bow introduced first Hammond, then Valentina.

There was a moment of awkwardness as the muscular man and Marchenko considered how to proceed. The man whispered something to Andropov. The response was alert but slightly slurred. Andropov grimaced, a sign of dialysis dementia, and Hammond guessed he must be spending up to twelve hours a day on the machine. Probably urinating less than a hundred milliliters a day. Can't decide which he wants to do most, scratch, urinate, or vomit.

Hammond turned his back to Andropov, faced Valentina, and mouthed the word "kidneys."

The muscular man exchanged whispers with Marchenko.

Then Andropov spoke again, this time with what Hammond thought might be the trace of a smile, and the words were clearly understood. "Stop whispering," he ordered. "I am not asleep and I am not dead. What happens next?"

Valentina, taking charge, said to the nurse, "It's going to be difficult if the General Secretary stays in the chair. It would be best if he were lying on his stomach."

The nurse and the muscular man looked apprehensively at Andropov. "If that's what she wants," he said, "that's what we'll do." He started to rise and the nurse leapt to help him. He shrugged her off. She opened the double door. Andropov walked through it unaided and removed his jacket.

In the apartment's master bedroom, the bordello motif had succumbed to cutting-edge medical technology. The most advanced intensive care equipment available in the West confronted a massive double bed with inlaid mahogany headboard upholstered in red velvet. Andropov was in no need of the equipment yet, but it was there nevertheless. The dialysis machine was not in the room, and Hammond could sympathize with Andropov for wishing it out of his sight as much as possible.

The nurse took Andropov's jacket, and he sat on the edge of the silk-quilted bed.

Hammond, standing in the doorway, said to Valentina, "Do you want to be alone with him?"

"Yes, please."

Marchenko spoke to the muscular man, who whispered something Hammond couldn't hear.

"They don't want to leave him entirely alone with Valentina," Marchenko said quietly to Hammond. "You can understand why. I think it's reasonable."

"It's all right," Valentina said to Hammond. "Would they let just the nurse stay?"

As Hammond walked out with the other two men, Valentina and the nurse were side by side near the center of the room, about six feet from Andropov, who was removing his shoes. Hammond caught a glimpse of the tape-covered dialysis fistula on Andropov's right ankle.

Valentina watched Andropov take off his shoes. The nurse reached to help him with a knotted lace, but he pushed her hand away. She glanced at Valentina, woman to woman, persecuted to persecuted.

"Do you want me undressed?" he asked impatiently. His speech was clearer than it had been in the drawing room.

"Not all the way," Valentina said. "If you could just

pull out your shirt and maybe lie on your stomach. I want to touch your kidneys."

"I haven't got any kidneys," he said, doing as she had asked. "I have one, but it doesn't work."

Valentina bent over the bed. Andropov's belt was drawn tight, gathering folds of trouser fabric around the emaciated waist.

"Could you loosen your belt?" she asked.

With an effort, he turned on one side, unfastened the silver buckle, pulled the belt loose, and rolled back onto his stomach.

"What are you going to do?" he asked.

"I'm going to place my hands here, over your kidneys, and then I would like you to listen to what I say."

The nurse had stepped to Valentina's side, her head bent to catch every word.

"I heard about the deaf girl," Andropov said. "Did you really heal that deaf girl?"

"No."

He looked up. "No?"

"Jesus healed her."

Valentina closed her eyes and prayed almost inaudibly in tongues, spirit-given words incomprehensible even to herself. She felt an electric tingling in her hands. Then she prayed in Russian, quietly and briefly. She asked Jesus to touch the diseased kidney and make it whole.

"Do you believe he can do that?" she asked.

"If he can, he knows more than my doctors."

"I'm going to say the same words again, and this time why don't you say them with me?"

The nurse fired Valentina a look of shock. Valentina ignored the look, and with a motion of her head and eyes directed the nurse to place her hands on the trouser fabric covering her own hands.

She repeated the prayer but heard no words from Andropov.

"Do you feel anything?" she asked.

"Your hands are warm."

Valentina continued to pray, in tongues again, inaudibly. The heat in her hands increased.

"That feels good," Andropov said. "Better than my masseur."

"Since it feels good," she said, "why don't you say the words with me?"

She again prayed aloud in Russian. The nurse, appearing torn between delight and disbelief, joined her. And this time a few mumbled words came from Andropov.

"Do you believe what you're saying?" Valentina asked.

"I believe you can make my back hot."

"Not me."

She removed her hands and the nurse too lifted hers.

After several seconds, Andropov said, "The heat goes right inside me. Let's stop for a minute."

"I've already stopped," Valentina said.

He lifted his head and saw her by the bed, hands at her sides.

"It wasn't my hands that made you hot," she said.

"What was it?"

"If you feel better and want to thank someone, thank Jesus. But remember that even if you are healed today, someday you will die. It's better to heal what never dies, what's going to be well forever or diseased forever."

She wasn't sure he had heard her. He lowered his head

to the pillow and remained on his stomach, as if not wishing to diminish the warmth in his back.

Valentina reached into her jacket pocket and came out with a bulky, white, cloth-bound Bible. She handed it to the nurse. Then she opened the door and walked back into the drawing room.

31

THIS TIME THERE WERE NO
hasty emergency phone calls, no cloak-and-dagger drives
past GRU headquarters to observe the position of window
curtains. Marchenko called Hammond at the apartment
the morning after the healing session with Andropov and
unhurriedly invited him and Valentina to lunch. He picked
them up twenty minutes later in a Zil limousine with
Politburo plates.

"What's happening, Andrei?" Hammond asked when
they were in the backseat. Despite Marchenko's sociable
chattiness on the phone, or perhaps because of it, he had
brought the Walther.

"Someone wants to meet you. I am not at liberty to say who. I suggest that you relax in this fine automobile and enjoy what will be a short drive."

Hammond glanced at Valentina. She was taking Marchenko's advice, lounging uncuriously in the seat, gazing through the tinted windows at the bleak snow-lined boulevard. It was as if she didn't care, or already knew, where they were going and why.

They pulled up outside the Praga restaurant and were led almost at a run over carpeted floors, past mirrored walls, to a small private dining room. The usual parquet floor was so polished Hammond could see his face in it.

Lace-curtained windows looked over Kalinina Prospekt, and a single square table sat beneath a chandelier.

"Who's he?" Hammond asked, nodding at the empty place to his left. The white tablecloth was covered with silver plates of smoked salmon, crabmeat, ham, and iced bowls of caviar.

"You will see. May I?"

Valentina nodded, and Marchenko dropped two tablespoons of black caviar onto her plate. A tuxedoed waiter filled their glasses with vodka.

"Please begin," Marchenko said. "Our host may be delayed and would be angry with me if I did not take good care of you."

Valentina gave Hammond a grin and a shrug and spread caviar over a wafer-thin slice of brown bread.

Marchenko took a bite of smoked salmon and raised his glass.

"Good health," he said.

Valentina left her glass where it was. Hammond took a sip, deciding to remain courteous but sober.

"No, no, my dear friend," Marchenko scolded, emptying his glass. "One does not sip, one empties."

"I'm not much of a drinker, Andrei."

Marchenko's response died on his lips. He leaped to his feet as a round-faced middle-aged man came through the door unescorted. Before arriving in Moscow, Hammond had read CIA profiles of the twelve Politburo members, but probably would not have recognized any except the balding man who now approached their table. The large red birthmark was like raspberry jam trickling over his right eye.

Mikhail Gorbachev shook hands graciously, sat down, and turned immediately to the hovering waiter, ordering for them all.

When the waiter had disappeared, Gorbachev gave Hammond a smile so charming it would have been the envy even of Darya.

"I want to thank you and the young lady for agreeing to have lunch with me on such short notice. As you know, these are difficult times for us." The voice was soft, gentle, almost docile. Gorbachev clearly had no doubts about Hammond's ability to understand Russian.

"I understand," Hammond said, assuming that Gorbachev was referring to Andropov.

Ignoring the caviar, salmon, and vodka, Gorbachev came to the point. "I have just come from the General Secretary. He has asked me to extend to you both"—he gave Valentina a look that managed to be both serious and cheerful—"his deep appreciation for what you have done for him."

Valentina's smile brought Hammond even more pleasure than the news of Andropov's improvement. Men with Andropov's ailment frequently experienced a dramatic recovery only to sink even lower in the coming days.

"I'm delighted to hear he's feeling better," Hammond said. He would have been more delighted if he could have seen lab tests showing increased urine volume and reduced levels of serum creatinine and urea nitrogen.

"Better is hardly the word. He told me himself he feels like a new man." He turned to Valentina, his manner smooth as velvet. "He wants you back."

Valentina was opening her mouth to speak when Hammond said, "We would be pleased to do whatever we can. I have to say, however, that I have a slight problem with my government."

Gorbachev looked at him, and there was just a hint of steel beneath the velvet.

"I know you want me to be frank," Hammond said.

"Of course."

"We are interested in the potential threat posed by an operation I believe you have code-named Spectrum. We have—"

"Dr. Hammond, Spectrum poses no threat to your country, potential or otherwise. You have my personal guarantee."

Valentina had lost all interest in her caviar. Spectrum was news to her.

"I don't doubt that," Hammond said. "Nevertheless, I have been instructed to require Spectrum's destruction. We had an agreement that Spectrum would be destroyed in exchange for an attempt to heal the General Secretary. The attempt has been made, and if you wish we will make further attempts. But I'm afraid little more can be done until Spectrum is destroyed."

Hammond had to admire the man. Without so much as a flicker of hesitation, Gorbachev said, "Agreed. Spectrum will be destroyed."

"May I ask when?"

"When you like. Tomorrow. Today, if you wish."

If this was true, the decision had obviously been made before Gorbachev came to lunch.

"The doctors," Gorbachev added smugly, "are somewhat puzzled, as you can imagine, by this sudden recuperation."

"They don't know about the healing?"

Gorbachev's faint smile invited Hammond to savor with him the success of their conspiracy.

"You yourself are not puzzled?" Hammond asked, smiling back.

"What works, works. It is not always essential to understand why it works."

Hammond said, "And the next meeting between Mrs. Leonov and the General Secretary will be . . ."

"At your convenience, of course. I had hoped we could go to Kuntsevo immediately after lunch. The General Secretary is eager to proceed as soon as possible."

"Perhaps we could go to Spectrum first," Hammond said, "then to Kuntsevo?"

Gorbachev laughed. "You are very insistent. But you realize that what you ask is not possible. It will take some preparation."

Hammond gave Gorbachev a playful grin. He was beginning to enjoy himself. "We can wait."

327

Gorbachev grinned back. "You can wait, yes." The smile vanished. "But the General Secretary cannot."

Hammond glanced at Marchenko, who had almost succeeded in making himself invisible.

"I have orders," Hammond said. "I have been told, Spectrum must be destroyed first."

"Dr. Hammond, necessity is something not even governments can overcome. I give you the word of my government, and my personal word as well, that if you agree to go first to Kuntsevo, you will be taken immediately afterward to witness the destruction of Spectrum."

Hammond looked at the two large mounds of black caviar on his plate.

"It is the best I can do," Gorbachev went on. "Another meeting with the General Secretary can be done immediately, but for Spectrum we must have several hours preparation. Spectrum will be destroyed, I assure you, this afternoon, but while we wait for those preparations there is no reason not to proceed with the General Secretary."

He paused, but Hammond did not speak.

"You must understand," Gorbachev said, "that we are talking about the future of my country's government."

Hammond was certain Gorbachev knew every word Marchenko had spoken at the Gorki Park horse stables. If Andropov died before the March Supreme Soviet, Gorbachev's succession could not be assured. And if the next Soviet ruler was not Gorbachev, it would be a Brezhnevite. And that would be bad for the Soviet Union, bad for the U.S., bad for the world.

Gorbachev was obviously desperate that another healing session commence immediately. Hammond thought it over—and was struck by an inspiration.

"There is one other thing I would like to ask of you," he said, stunned by the revelation he had just had.

Gorbachev nodded. "I will do my best."

"I want to see Miss Timoshek again. Alone. At Spectrum."

"May I ask why?"

"I will be leaving the Soviet Union shortly. I would like to say good-bye." Hammond did not expect Gorbachev to believe him. But it was take it or leave it.

Gorbachev's eyes studied Hammond across the table, trying to penetrate to the reason for this strange request.

"Let's call it a personal thing," Hammond persisted. "A favor between you and me. In exchange I will agree to an immediate visit to the General Secretary."

Gorbachev's face was as hard and blank as marble.

"Can you get her there?" Hammond asked, trying to make it sound like something between a challenge and a dare.

"I think we can still manage that," Gorbachev said.

"Agreed then?"

The face softened. "Agreed."

"When do we go?" Hammond said.

Gorbachev raised his hands. "Now?"

32

PROMISING TO MEET THEM
in two hours at Kuntsevo, Gorbachev was driven from
the restaurant in a Zil limousine with a Volga chase car.

"What is Spectrum?" Valentina asked Hammond when
they were back in Marchenko's limousine.

"Something that needs destroying."

"But what is it?"

"One of Darya's magic tricks. I'll tell you later."

"Why do you want to see her? What are you going
to do?"

Hammond shook his head and didn't answer.

When they arrived at the hospital they discovered that

Andropov had indeed made a remarkable recovery. His skin had gained a natural color, the mouth odor was gone, the twitching and facial grimaces were less evident, and his speech was not slurred. He greeted Hammond, Valentina, and Marchenko from the same purple wing chair in the drawing room. Standing, he approached Valentina, grasped both her hands, and said, "So warm." Then he turned and led her by the hand into the bedroom. The door closed before even the nurse could follow.

"Do you think she's safe?" Hammond said, intending the remark as a joke.

The nurse said, quite seriously, "Oh, certainly."

Given the general euphoria over Andropov's improvement, Hammond almost found the courage to ask for a urine specimen. Instead, he said to the nurse, "Do you think I could possibly have a look at the latest laboratory results?" Surely they would have done some work that morning.

She mumbled and stuttered and looked at the muscular man, who said, "I will do my best."

Andropov loosened his belt, pulled out his shirt, and lay facedown on the bed. He had not felt so healthy in months. He had no idea how this young lady with the warm, soothing hands had done it. A library full of KGB psychotronic research attributed such things to bioenergy, but the explanations of what precisely that might be were so full of technical double-talk he doubted even the scientists themselves understood it. The only important thing was that he was alive, and since virtually no one but his doctors and Gorbachev had seen him in weeks, the gravity of his illness was for the most part unknown. Only last month, the American magazine *Newsweek*, while correctly diagnosing his problem as kidney disease, nevertheless gave him two years to live. The *Washington Post* gave him "a year or two." All he really needed was another month or six weeks. Already he was winning the generation war. Strong, bright, young leaders in the provinces, honest men singled out by the KGB for jobs in Moscow, had become the new pool from which Soviet leaders would be drawn. They were the future, Gorbachev's men.

Whatever this girl did, it worked. He was better, no doubt about it. If she wanted to pray to this Jesus, let her. And if she wanted him to say the words too, so what? The important thing was how it made him feel.

Again her hands were on his skin, lightly, gently, and she was muttering her prayers. Even the nurse was joining in.

"Would you like to pray with me?" the girl asked.

Heat flowed from her hands, through the flesh, deep into his back, burning with a fire he did not want to extinguish.

"Dear Jesus," she said, "heal . . ."

How could it hurt? He repeated her words.

Gorbachev arrived while Valentina was still in the bedroom. She had been in there more than an hour, and Hammond wondered how much longer it would be before someone had the courage to knock on the door.

Valentina finally came out, Gorbachev went in to speak briefly with Andropov, and ten minutes later Hammond was in the back of Marchenko's Zil sitting between Marchenko and Valentina. Gorbachev had stayed behind with

Andropov, sending one of his chase cars to escort them to Spectrum.

"Where would you like us to drop you?" Marchenko said to Valentina.

She looked at Hammond.

"She can come with us," Hammond said. If Valentina had enough influence with the Almighty to heal Andropov, there was no reason why she shouldn't witness the destruction of Spectrum.

Marchenko shrugged and looked out the window.

When they turned right on Rublevskoe Highway and started back toward the city from Kuntsevo, Hammond began to worry. They hit the ring road without having turned north or south. He was certain the Spectrum installation was well outside Moscow. The only possibility now was that Spectrum was east of the capital. But when they crossed the ring road and continued into the city center, Hammond was convinced he'd been tricked.

"Excuse me, Andrei," he said, "but where are we going?"

"To Spectrum, of course."

"Somehow I had the idea it was out of town."

"You will see." Marchenko smiled at him, the gold molar glistening in the back of his mouth, and for the thousandth time Hammond wondered, Whose side is this guy on?

When they sped into Dzerzhinski Square and approached the yellow stone hulk of KGB headquarters, Hammond seriously considered leaping from the car. The escort car stopped in back at the black iron gate, and by the time the Zil caught up, the gate was open. The Zil moved through without stopping, turned right in the icy concrete courtyard, and bounced over a steel grating onto a ramp.

Four descending hairpin turns later, the limousine pulled into a dimly lighted, low-ceilinged parking garage. The escort stopped beside them. Only six other cars were on the floor, one of them a blue Maserati Hammond guessed had been part of Brezhnev's automobile collection.

Outside the Zil, Hammond confronted Marchenko. "I've been to Spectrum, Andrei, and this isn't it. What's going on?"

Valentina, standing beside him, had both hands on his arm—a Soviet citizen, a dissident, a Christian, finding herself in the basement of KGB headquarters.

"Don't be so suspicious, Jack. Have a little faith."

"And Darya is here?"

"So I was told."

There wasn't much Hammond could do about it now. He took Valentina's hand and followed Marchenko through a steel fire door into a small concrete room with an elevator. As he did so he saw four grim-faced men in identical black quilted jackets, their black trousers tucked into black boots, emerge swiftly from the escort car. They carried gray canvas shoulder bags. One of the men, slightly older than the others and evidently in charge, wore a mustache.

The elevator was larger than the concrete room they had been in. Only two places have elevators this big, Hammond thought—hospitals and prisons. Marchenko put a key into a lock above a vertical row of four black buttons, then pressed the second-lowest button. The elevator descended.

Hammond stared at the door, uneasy with the awareness that unless Lubyanka prison occupied another wing of the building, he was only a few inches from the most notorious prison on earth.

After ten seconds, Hammond looked at Valentina, winked, and squeezed her hand. It was going to be all right. The temperature changes on the way down—warm to cold to warm—were exactly what he had experienced at Spectrum, and the movement and sound of the elevator also were the same. Whoever had brought Darya and him here had done a masterful job of deceptive driving.

The elevator jerked to a halt. A door behind Hammond opened, and he turned to follow Marchenko and the four black-suited men into another concrete chamber. Marchenko faced an elevator opposite the one they had arrived in and punched his finger at a circular row of buttons in a cipher lock. The door opened.

Still holding Valentina's hand, Hammond followed Marchenko into this new elevator, and his fear returned. When he had visited Spectrum with Darya there had been no change of elevator. Either there was more than one way down, or he and Valentina were in serious trouble.

Marchenko, avoiding Hammond's glare, stuck a key into one of two black metal locks, and again they descended. The elevator stopped, and Hammond braced himself, frightened of what might lie on the other side of the door.

"If I may," Marchenko said, and stepped out of the car to proceed them up a fluorescent-lighted passageway to another door. They entered another concrete chamber with a circular cipher lock, stepped into a dimly lighted corridor, and continued along it for what seemed like half a city block. They angled to the left, as Hammond remembered doing during his visit with Darya, then walked about a hundred yards, and waited while Marchenko put his weight against the red pushbar of a black double steel fire door.

Inside Hammond saw a small deserted office containing gray metal desks swept clean of documents, and filing cabinets with combination locks.

A stout man in a green cardigan, waiting rigidly by one of the desks as if he'd been there forever, accepted Marchenko's abrupt nod, stepped to a wooden door, and flung it open. As he did so, Hammond was relieved to hear the distinct clicking sounds the man's shoes had made when he greeted Darya during the earlier visit.

Hammond's reassurance was confirmed by the sight of the small theaterlike room they entered now. He saw the plastic chairs he and Darya had sat in and a hexagonal open space at the center of the room where Spectrum's laser show had taken place.

As Hammond emitted a profound sigh of relief, he heard Marchenko say, "Jack? Over here, please?"

Hammond left Valentina and followed Marchenko into a carpeted area containing the transparent-walled conference room where Darya had briefed him. The easel, minus its display, was still beside the table. Marchenko stopped at the end of the carpeted area, opened a door, and Hammond stepped through into a small cluttered office. The door snapped closed behind him.

Darya sat at a desk strewn with books, documents,

notes, two telephones, and a calculator. The floor was all but hidden beneath old cartons and foot-high stacks of papers. Charts and photographs covered the walls. Disorder was everywhere. Hammond sensed at once that this was Darya's secret retreat, the place where she came to think and brood and do her most important work.

"What are you doing here?" she said, rising.

He had asked to see Darya, but now that she stood before him he was struck by the same feeling of peril and isolation he had experienced when they were alone with Marchenko in the cabana at Monte Carlo.

"How did you get here?" She moved from behind the desk. "Who brought you?"

Hammond drew the Walther from his coat pocket. "Clear off the desk."

"Hammond, what do—"

"We don't have much time, Darya."

"What are you going—"

He stepped forward and swept an arm across the desk. "Lie down and pull up your skirt."

She hesitated an instant, then lunged for the door. Hammond threw his body in front of her. Long red nails slashed at his face. He pulled back, grabbed her wrist, and put the Walther's muzzle against her cheek.

"I don't want to hurt you, Darya, so do us both a favor and don't fight. Lie back and pull up your skirt."

Slowly he released his grip. Watching the Walther, Darya gathered her maroon wool skirt around her waist and boosted herself to the desk. Hammond saw knee-length black leather boots and white underpants.

Sitting there, legs dangling, Darya looked into his face, and he knew she understood what he was about to do.

He said, "I'm sorry, Darya, but you have something I need. It won't hurt any more than removing a splinter. I promise."

"You are going to suffer for this, Hammond. I am going to watch you suffer. There won't be any agony you won't—"

He touched the Walther to her chin.

She leaned back flat against the desk, her eyes straining to follow his movements. He reached into his pocket for the penknife the Marine had given him in Vietnam. He was opening the blade when her head jerked and her right foot came up, the boot aiming for his groin. He turned, caught the blow on his thigh, and swung the Walther. The barrel landed on the side of her head. She fell back unconscious.

When Hammond emerged from the room, Valentina was waiting for him.

"What happened in there?"

"Not now," he said. "I'll explain later."

The four men in black had spread out up the hallway to what Hammond guessed were control areas. They stopped every few yards to remove from their shoulder bags dark-yellow, paper-wrapped packages the size of cigar boxes, which they placed along the floor next to the walls at points indicated by the man with the mustache.

Marchenko stood at Hammond's side. "Satisfied, Jack?"

"Darya's not feeling well," Hammond said. "She may need some help getting out of here."

"Certainly. I meant are you satisfied with what you're seeing."

Hammond stooped to examine one of the yellow packages. Two-inch-long wires connected it to a black plastic detonator the size of a matchbox.

In a white-walled computer room, Hammond asked that additional charges be placed at the bases of three steel support columns. The mustached man, with a glance at Marchenko, found the charges and arranged them around the columns.

"So?" Marchenko asked.

Hammond nodded.

"Come with me."

Hammond and Valentina followed Marchenko back through the office and out the fire door to the angled corridor. The man with the mustache went with them.

"I thought Spectrum was in the country," Hammond said to Marchenko.

"You have been here before?"

"Yes. Where are we?"

"Under Dzerzhinski Square. During the war this was a bomb shelter, connected with tunnels to KGB headquarters and the Central Committee building. When they were looking for a Spectrum site, the security was already here and it wasn't that far from Andropov's office. He liked to walk around and talk to the researchers. Some people said he also liked having the lovely Darya nearby, but they didn't know Andropov."

The mustached man closed the fire door behind them, gave the pushbar a yank, and removed a walkie-talkie from his shoulder bag.

He spoke into it in Russian, then said in English, "One moment."

It was fifteen minutes since Hammond had left Darya's office, more than enough time for her to recover. "Is Darya out?" Hammond said.

Marchenko spoke with the mustached man. "She was not in her office when they looked. He assures me they have searched the facility and there's no one else here."

"You're certain?"

"She is not here. There are two exits besides this one."

Hammond nodded and they waited. After five minutes, a voice Hammond could not make out came over the walkie-talkie. The mustached man answered. Hammond looked at Valentina. Had she understood the words? She shook her head.

Another five minutes passed. A second brief exchange on the radio. Hammond caught Marchenko's eye. He raised a hand. Wait.

Finally a third exchange. This time the mustached man ordered everyone twenty paces farther up the corridor. He remained at the fire door, put his shoulder to it, and pulled heavily on the pushbar. He spoke again into the radio.

The mustached man then reached into his shoulder bag for a black object no larger than a pack of cigarettes. It was circled by two blue stripes. At the center of each stripe was a small rectangular button. The device was a nearly exact copy of one Hammond had seen in a half-day explosives course during his CIA training before coming to Moscow. The top button activated a radio frequency transmitter, allowing the lower button to send a signal to detonators connected to explosive charges.

Marchenko took the transmitter from the mustached man and held it toward Hammond. "You press the top button, wait a second, and press the lower button."

Hammond looked at Valentina, then at Marchenko.

"Go ahead," Marchenko said.

Hammond took the transmitter. "Now?"

"Be my guest."

Hammond pressed the top button. He looked again at Valentina, put his thumb over the lower button, and pressed.

33

A *SINGLE EXPLOSION SHOOK*
the passageway. The mustached man spoke evenly into
the radio, then signaled Hammond to join him. The man
lifted the pushbar and cracked the door. Black smoke
poured out. He closed the door and spoke in English. "You
are wanting to look?"

Hammond searched the man's face for signs of sarcasm.

"No, thanks," Hammond said in Russian. "That'll be
fine."

The man started along the corridor, glancing back to
be sure the others were close behind. Hammond heard a
thud, and a concussion wave hit him in the back. He threw

Valentina to the floor and fell on top of her. Something whistled past his head, the passageway filled with black smoke, and a flash of heat burned his face.

He gripped Valentina's hand and crawled along the floor. An inferno roared behind him. They came to the point where the corridor had angled to the left, made the turn, and the smoke diminished. They stood and ran. When they reached the fluorescent-lighted passageway connecting to the elevator, the mustached man unlocked a steel side door and they scrambled through it, moving at a run along another tunnel, up dark stone stairs, past stacked merchandise crates and forklifts.

Hammond was recalling rumors about a tunnel connecting the basements of the KGB building and Children's World when they suddenly emerged onto the store's ground floor.

Throngs of afternoon shoppers, snow from their boots forming puddles on the red and black tiles, milled around the white, marble-tiled columns, competing wearily for the attention of salesclerks.

Someone shoved Hammond's back. He turned to see the mustached man. "Go! Run!"

Three blue-uniformed militia officers pushed their way toward them through the crowd. Andropov and Gorbachev might have been willing to destroy Spectrum, but the militia—commanded by Vitali Fedorchuk, Darya's friend—was evidently not too happy about it.

Hammond clutched Valentina's arm and rushed for the front of the store. One hand warding off shoppers, he fought his way around a life-size wooden fairy-tale castle that dominated the ground floor. As he burst through glass doors to Marksa Prospekt, a gun fired behind him and he turned to see Marchenko facing back into the store, a machine pistol in his hand.

A milliman, holding a telephone, looked down at Hammond from an elevated, glass-enclosed police booth on the corner. Fire trucks and militia cars screeched into the square. Shoppers, smelling smoke, fought their way out of the store.

Valentina grabbed Hammond by the hand and took off up Marksa Prospekt, past fire trucks and gray militia cars, sirens wailing, headed the other way. They passed the red marble fountain at the Bolshoi Theater, dodged traffic across Sverdlova Street, and dropped into the metro station. Marchenko's footsteps pounded on the stairs behind them. Was he following or chasing?

"This way," Valentina yelled.

Racing across the dirty-white marble tiles, they hurtled without paying through the entrance gates, moving so fast they beat the pop-up wooden barriers. They quick-stepped down the antique wooden escalator, jostled through passengers pouring out of trains on either side, and after what seemed like several New York City blocks, ran up another escalator and pushed through swinging glass doors to a small asphalt park on Revolution Square.

"Where are we going?" Hammond panted. He felt as if they had already covered half of Moscow underground.

"Go to your embassy," Valentina said. "You'll be safe there."

Safe perhaps, but not welcome. The ambassador and Shroeder would no doubt be just as happy if they never saw him again. But it was better than a cell in Lubyanka.

"We'll both go," Hammond said.

"The militia won't let me in."

It was true. Ever since a group of Pentacostals took refuge in the embassy four months ago, the militia guards had become brutally vigilant.

Her eyes scanned the top of the metro station. Hammond looked and saw television cameras—installed, he supposed, to monitor traffic and, when necessary, demonstrations, riots, and fleeing foreign agents who'd just set off Semtex packs under Dzerzhinski Square.

"We've got to get away from here," she said.

"I'll get a cab." Unable to abandon her on a street corner and escape alone to the embassy, he reached in his pocket for the Marlboro pack Frank had given him.

"No," she said, taking his arm, "the driver will tell the KGB where we went."

Dreary-faced pedestrians stood at a trolley stop. Hammond could not see Marchenko or the pursuing millimen. He hurried to a pay phone to call the embassy. He wanted someone to know what was happening, where he was. He didn't want to vanish. The coin would not go into the slot.

"It's frozen," Valentina said. "People spit into them."

"Spit into them? Why the—"

Sirens screamed on the other side of the square. Flashing blue dome lights moved in their direction.

"Come on," Valentina said, starting back toward the metro.

"It'll be filled with millimen," Hammond protested, "and if we take a train they'll stop it."

"There's another entrance," she said. "We can stay underground."

Marchenko, four millimen behind him, charged out through the metro doors. One of the millimen spotted Hammond and shouted.

Valentina yanked Hammond toward an entrance and hurried ahead to the top of an escalator. It was like a ski jump, three times as long and twice as steep as any escalator Hammond had ever seen in the West.

She hesitated, looking down, then made her decision. She climbed onto the two-and-a-half-foot-wide varnished wooden ledge at the side of the moving stairs, gripped the edges, and extended her feet.

The sight of millimen coming through the entrance left Hammond no choice. He jumped to the ledge behind Valentina, put his legs around her, toboggan fashion, and shouted, "Go!"

The gray wall flashed by on his right, startled riders on his left. Narrow aluminum strips an eighth of an inch thick, crossing the ledge every four feet, tore at his buttocks. More and more unbalanced as his speed increased, Hammond spotted a three-inch-high emergency-stop handle in the middle of the ledge at the bottom. He squeezed his ass to the left, raised his right buttock, and lifted his balls over the handle as he and Valentina rocketed off into space.

They hit the marble floor, spun sideways, and skidded across polished tiles toward a row of brown marble archways. Hammond tried to lean around Valentina to protect her from the impact, but he was too late.

When his brain cleared he found Valentina sprawled unconscious across his legs. Blood, gushing so heavily from the top of her head he could not see the wound, formed a small puddle beneath a stone relief of a man brandishing a gun. He felt a stickiness in his trousers and looked inside his overcoat to find blood soaking his crotch.

A shout jerked Hammond's eyes back to the escalator. Marchenko and a milliman were knocking down passengers to get to the bottom. The milliman arrived first, halted, and pointed his automatic at Hammond. Marchenko, standing beside the milliman, yelled something Hammond could not understand.

The muzzle of the milliman's pistol flashed and an explosion echoed through the station. The milliman moved toward Hammond.

Hammond left Valentina, sprinted ahead through the station, then looked back. The advancing milliman had halted at Valentina. Marchenko bent over her. She moved. Marchenko held a handkerchief to her head.

Two other millimen joined the one who had fired. The three conferred for a moment and started toward Hammond with drawn pistols.

Hammond turned and ran.

Valentina saw Marchenko's hand, covered with blood, in front of her face. She tried to get up. Where was Hammond?

"Don't move," Marchenko ordered, and pushed something against the top of her head.

"You're bleeding," she said.

"Not me, I'm afraid."

He pulled off his overcoat, jacket, and shirt. He folded the shirt into a thick square, put it against her head, and placed her hand against it. "Hold that." Then he put the jacket and coat back on. "Can you stand?"

She rose slowly. He put an arm around her and started back toward the escalator to the metro entrance.

"Go after the man," he ordered a militia officer. "I'll get this one to a hospital."

Valentina tried to pull away.

"Don't fight me," Marchenko said. "They'll kill you."

Outside the metro station, Marchenko showed something from his wallet to a man in plainclothes next to a gray Zhiguli. The man hesitated. Marchenko yelled at him, put Valentina in the front seat, and climbed in behind the wheel.

As they drove away, Marchenko said, "How's your head?"

"It's all right." It was throbbing. Her backside felt as if someone had been pounding it with a club.

After five minutes, he pulled to the curb and looked at the wound. "It's stopped bleeding. Keep the bandage on."

Her head hurt so badly she could hardly keep her eyes open. "Where is Dr. Hammond?"

"I don't know."

"Was he arrested?"

"I'm not sure. Maybe he got away."

Hammond had told her Marchenko could be trusted. A GRU agent who could be trusted? But Hammond should know. And Marchenko had, after all, arranged her meeting with Andropov and the destruction of Spectrum.

"Who are you?" she asked.

"Andrei Marchenko."

Did he think she'd had her memory knocked out? "I know your name. But who is Andrei Marchenko?"

"A friend. Where were you going?"

"We weren't going anywhere. We were running from you."

"Not from me. From the militia. I helped you."

She didn't answer.

"You need a doctor," Marchenko said. "You've had a concussion and that cut in your head needs stitching."

"Just let me out."

"I don't think Dr. Hammond would like it much if I did that. Why don't you tell me where you were going?"

"I would like to get out of the car, please."

"Valentina, if you don't tell me a safe place where I can leave you, I am going to take you to a hospital, and they will call the militia."

"Take me home then."

"You don't have a home. You are living with Hammond. His apartment will be watched by the militia. You want me to leave you with them?"

She closed her eyes and fought against the pain in her head. Marchenko could have handed her over to the militia at the metro station. He had lied twice to get her away. She was using his shirt as a bandage. Hammond had said he was a friend. Hammond would want her to trust him.

She laid her head back on the seat. "Dear Lord, tell me what to do. Should I trust this man? Tell me."

Marchenko pulled the car away from the curb. "We can't stay here. I'll give you five minutes to decide where you want to go. If you don't, it's the hospital."

34

AN ESCALATOR AT THE END of the station took Hammond up to a semicircular hall. Shoving through swinging glass doors, he found himself in a quiet two-lane street. He jogged to the corner, turned left at a dairy shop, and entered another street filled with strollers oblivious to the chaos a half mile away in Dzerzhinski Square. He had no idea where he was. He stopped to catch his breath.

What had happened to Valentina? Would he ever see her again? Hammond's training, plus a boyhood growing up on the streets of Brooklyn, had taught him the perils of sentimentality. Still, he could not believe Marchenko had arrested her. If Marchenko was a friend, Valentina might still escape.

Hammond could run for safety inside the embassy, or he could try to find Valentina. It surprised him to discover that he wanted Valentina more than he had wanted Spectrum.

What he needed was a main road where he could hope to flag down a private car whose driver had not heard about the fugitive American. To persuade the driver to take him where he wanted to go he had about ninety dollars in rubles, and if that didn't work he had the Walther.

Feeling the pain growing in his crotch and buttocks— had it been the aluminum strips or the stop handle?—he moved with the crowd to the end of the street and came out unexpectedly into Red Square. The protective screen of pedestrians dispersed, and he was left alone, the wide expanse of gray cobblestones dotted with tourists, soldiers, and militia officers. Two orange buses pulled into the square and disgorged a company of millimen.

Desperate to get out of sight, Hammond hurried along the square's edge and ducked into a food shop, thankfully packed with shoppers. He moved through a mirror-ceilinged opening at the back of the shop into a much larger hall and discovered that he was in GUM, Moscow's largest department store.

He walked quickly along one of the rectangular store's three wide, columned corridors, looking for an exit on the other side from the square. Individual shops lined the walls beneath a four-story-high, curved, windowed roof. The sight of two militia officers window-shopping ahead of him sent him up a stone stairway to a second level of corridors matching those below. Looking over the waist-high metal railing, he watched the officers move slowly to a red-marble, octagon-shaped fountain at the building's center.

Hammond crossed a Venetian-style bridge to the center corridor and again spotted a pair of patrolling millimen. Taking another bridge to the third corridor, he entered a cafe and saw a stairway. Men and women bent sullenly over sausages and potatoes at stand-up tables. The stairs led only up.

Hammond turned back, but the officers had entered the cafe. He turned again and climbed the stairs.

The third and highest level contained offices and work-rooms. Through an open door he saw a half dozen women at tables sewing fur hats. A wizened old woman at a small desk added up figures with an abacus. Beside her on the desk sat a telephone. Could he simply walk in and make a call to the embassy before anyone stopped him? Looking around, he saw a nearby door with a word painted on it: MILITIA.

The militia door opened. Hammond heard men's voices. An officer came out with a walkie-talkie. The man saw Hammond, did a double take, then called, "*Americanski*?"

Hammond bolted.

He made it back to the second-level railing overlooking the fountain and marble floor. He'd already had one collision with marble that afternoon, but if he hung from the floor by his hands he'd have only a six-foot drop.

Militia men now approached him along the corridor from both directions. Shoppers, sensing something unusual, stopped to watch.

Hammond vaulted the railing, dangled by his hands,

and let go. When he felt the marble beneath his feet he fell backward, taking the impact over the flat of his back. He rolled onto his stomach, scrambled to his feet, and ran.

He found a door leading down another flight to a basement delivery area. Shoppers leaving the store squeezed past an unloading truck. Hammond pushed past them to the narrow street behind the store.

Workers with hand trucks jostled pedestrians. A large yellow GUM delivery truck, the driver in the cab, was parked at the curb. The truck's roof bore the same telescoping device electric trolleys used to take current from overhead wires. Guessing that a truck using trolley lines would take him to a major boulevard where he could flag down a car, Hammond jumped in.

He squatted out of sight behind packages at the back, and waited. Unbuttoning his overcoat, he found his trousers saturated in blood from the waist to midthigh. He rebuttoned the coat and took a deep breath. It probably looked like more blood than it was. You could lose a lot of blood and not die. He needed help, but he had plenty of time to find Valentina first. Don't panic. Take it easy.

The double doors swung closed. The truck lurched back, then forward, and gained speed. Fifteen minutes later it stopped and the doors opened. A chubby man in coveralls hopped in, pushed two cartons out to his partner in the street, and jumped back down. Hammond saw an orange trolley idling at the curb of an eight-lane boulevard.

The truck's doors were closing. Hammond leaped for them and pushed. They opened to reveal the face of the chubby man, his eyes widening in fear and amazement.

Hammond smiled as winningly as he knew how, jumped to the ground, and ran past the waiting trolley.

He glanced back and saw the truck driver staring after him. Certain the man would not chase him, Hammond rounded a corner, waited for the truck to drive off, and returned to the boulevard. He realized now that he was in front of the Moskovsko-Leninski department store on the ring road around Moscow.

He stood in the street, waving his Marlboro pack.

There were few cars. None stopped. Trolleys pulled to the curb, loaded passengers, departed. Hammond felt dangerously conspicuous. Who but a Westerner would wave a pack of Marlboros? A trolley stopped, emptied, and waited at the curb. The driver got out, lit a cigarette, stretched, and returned to his seat. It was a two-car articulated trolley, as long as the boulevard was wide.

A militia car passed, stopped, turned on its blue dome light, and backed up. The officer in the passenger seat motioned to Hammond.

Hammond had no choice. He jumped into the trolley, put his Walther against the driver's stomach, and said, "Get moving! Now!"

The man tore his eyes from the Walther and looked at Hammond.

"Go!"

The man closed the doors, and the trolley moved.

Hammond knew he was done for. The trolley could not possibly outrun a militia car, and anyway where could it take him?

"Faster," Hammond ordered.

The driver put his foot down, and the trolley strained to pick up speed. Behind them the militia car turned on its siren. They passed Leninski Prospekt, and the militia car was joined by four others, two with rooftop loudspeakers bellowing commands unintelligible beneath the sirens.

Approaching Gorki Park, Hammond had an idea. He seized the wheel and spun it as hard as he could to the left. The driver screamed and tried to wrench the wheel back, but it was too late. The rear car, unable to follow the abrupt turn, skidded, toppled, and careened across the pavement on its side, showering sparks. The momentum pulled the lead car over and both cars came to a halt crosswise on the boulevard, blocking traffic. Militia cars, trying to avoid the wreckage, spun out of control behind them.

Hammond climbed to the door, leaped down, and ran limping for the park. Inside, he would be safe from militia cars. They'd have to come after him on foot.

He passed a small frozen lake and jogged south over snow-covered paths past trees, an outdoor theater, and a Ferris wheel. He veered toward the river and followed the iron railing, wondering if he could make it down the concrete embankment and across on the ice to the other side. A noise interrupted these thoughts, and looking left, Hammond was alarmed to see a horse and rider trotting toward him. The man waved happily and sped by.

Now Hammond went for all he was worth. He reached the stables where he had talked with Marchenko and collapsed onto the wood floor of the tack room. After lying there three minutes to catch his breath, he threw a saddle onto a chestnut mare, turned up his coat collar against the cold, and cantered away from the river, knowing he would eventually reach Leninski Prospekt, where once again he could try to flag down a car.

Every time his butt touched the saddle he almost passed out from pain. Blood plastered his underpants to his flesh, and when he touched the seat of his trousers his hand came away soaked. He was freezing.

A line of cars had stopped for a red light at Leninski Prospekt, and among them, third back, was a Zil limousine. No safer car existed in Moscow. A militia officer would not dare even to approach such a car, much less stop it in traffic. Hammond could not see through the tinted windows. If there were passengers, he'd have a problem.

He trotted over, trying despite the pain and cold to look as casual as a New York City mounted cop, and inserted the horse between the front bumper of the Zil and the Zhiguli ahead of it.

The light changed, cars pulled away. The Zil honked. Hammond stayed where he was. The Zil backed up, preparing to go around. Hammond advanced to within a half foot of the bumper. The front window came down and a round, crimson face emerged. It yelled at Hammond.

Hammond smiled back.

The door opened and the driver piled out. Hammond waited for him to get several steps from the Zil, then maneuvered the horse between the driver and the car. He slid from the horse's back, darted into the front seat, and slammed the door.

There were no passengers. Hammond put the car in gear and took off, leaving the red-faced driver alone with the horse.

He squirmed in the seat, the increasing pain throbbing in his pelvis. He was sick to his stomach, exhausted, sweating despite the freezing cold. He wondered if he had lost anything between his legs besides blood.

Hammond found Kutuzovsky Prospekt and followed it to the Moscow–Minsk highway. Two militia cars passed him, and a black Volga with official plates and uniformed driver tailed him for a half mile, but turned off. He drove slowly until he had the road to himself, then cruised past the old log house where he had first met Valentina. It sat there in the winter darkness—no lights, silent as death.

If Valentina had escaped, if Marchenko had helped her, she would not be foolish enough to return to the apartment, either Cox's or her own. She would know that this farmhouse was the only place they had in common, the place he would be most likely to look for her. It was his only hope.

Hammond hid the car in a narrow, snow-filled road a hundred yards up the highway and limped back toward the house.

He felt sick and faint, went down on all fours, and was afraid he would pass out and freeze to death before daylight. He pulled himself to his feet and continued toward the house. It had begun to snow.

The piles of old lumber were black shapes in the darkness. He stopped in the snow and listened. Pain burned in his crotch and buttocks. When he moved, his trousers cracked with frozen blood. The ambassador and Shroeder were home warm in their beds. Where was Valentina?

"What do you want here?"

Hammond spun around to find the bearded KGB thug in the beige, canvas, knee-length coat. Hammond didn't dare reach for the Walther.

"What do you want here?" the man repeated.

Hammond knew he had very little left. Invest it wisely. He pulled everything up into his shoulders, took a half step forward, and swung.

Pain exploded in his groin. His knees buckled. "Dear God," he said aloud, and collapsed into the snow.

35

AN ODOR WOKE HIM, THE filthiest stench since Valentina's hallway and his nightmare encounter with the darkness. He opened his eyes to dim light. He was on a dirt floor, wrapped in blankets. He felt for the Walther. Gone. So was his wallet.

He turned his head and saw his embassy credentials in the hands of the KGB agent. The agent stared at him from a wooden, straight-back chair next to a table on which rested what looked like a small, black room-to-room intercom. He was still bundled in his canvas coat, watchful dark eyes staring out over the black beard.

"Feeling better?" the agent asked.

Hammond remained silent. He had nothing to say. It was over. They had destroyed Spectrum, and perhaps Andropov was feeling well enough to continue for the necessary six more weeks. Mission accomplished. But Hammond was finished. Probably Valentina too.

Hammond touched his trousers, stiff with dried blood. Now that he was awake, the pain was increasing, spreading from his groin to his thighs and back.

"What the hell's that stink?" Hammond said.

"Excrement."

The agent returned the credentials to Hammond's wallet and laid the wallet on the blanket. The look in his eyes was out of place, lacking the conquest and superiority Hammond would have thought natural.

Hammond studied the room—unpainted plywood walls and ceiling, a single unshaded low-watt bulb hanging from its cord, a small electric ventilator stuck in a hole at the top of the opposite wall, a circular electric heater glowing orange, a plank door secured with two hasps and padlocks. And the smell of excrement.

Something the size of an upright piano, under a canvas cover, filled a corner next to stacks of paper-wrapped packages.

Hammond began to suspect the impossible.

"Where am I?" he said.

"It doesn't matter."

"It matters to me."

The man shrugged. His canvas coat had a four-inch tear under the right armpit.

"Who are you?" Hammond asked.

"That doesn't matter either."

"How did I get here?"

"Friends."

"What friends?"

"You have many friends, Dr. Hammond." The man's eyes were red and bloodshot. He looked exhausted.

Hammond nodded at the canvas cover.

"May I guess what that is?"

"If you like."

"Printing equipment."

The man's expression did not change. He was younger than Hammond, but his black beard was turning gray around the mouth.

"And the other side of that door—it's the bottom of the privy."

"You'd better rest," the man said.

"Tell me who you are."

The man was silent. The ventilator droned. Hammond stared at the ceiling, his groin throbbing. Then the man said, "Leonov."

There was still hope. "Her brother?"

"Husband."

No wonder she'd kept her distance from him. Hammond was ashamed of his disappointment at finding the husband alive. He wanted her to be happy. But in his heart he wanted Enriko dead.

"I thought you were dead," Hammond said.

"Many people think so." His teeth were so straight they looked false. Had the real ones been knocked out in prison?

"You've been following me, watching my apartment."

"I've been watching my wife."

"Where is she?" Hammond asked.

"I hoped you might know."

Hammond told him about blowing up Spectrum, about the chase, about leaving Valentina.

Enriko nodded, but all he said was, "How are you feeling?"

"I'm all right." It was a lie. The pain was nearly unendurable. He was trembling with chills. He had to have morphine, antibiotics, a doctor. Suddenly, he wanted to cry. "I'm not all right," he said. "My guess, we're going to die here."

The dark eyes watched him. "I'm not. You might."

Was that some kind of threat? Hammond didn't have the strength to ask. He said, "I'm sorry about Valentina."

"She'll be all right."

"I wish I could believe that."

For the first time, Enriko smiled. "So do I."

"What's that supposed to mean?"

"That I wish you could believe."

Believe in Jesus? Hammond didn't need Jesus, he needed morphine.

"If God really wants to help me," Hammond said, "he could start with my ass."

Enriko stepped over to the door and checked the padlocks. "He's got more for you than that. If you're afraid of dying, why don't you give in, take what he wants to give? If I'm wrong, you lose nothing. If I'm right, this will be the first day of your eternal life."

Hammond was almost delirious with pain. Take what he wants to give? "What do I have to do?"

"Nothing. Just believe. The doing comes later. He wants you to know him."

Three sharp bangs—a signal—came from the intercom on the table. "How do I do that?"

362

Enriko raised a hand for silence.

Hammond closed his eyes. Could things get worse?

Enriko whispered, "You pray." They heard a voice. Then motion. A door opened. Slammed closed. Muffled speech. A man talking.

It was Marchenko. Hammond opened his eyes and lay perfectly still, straining to hear. Then a woman spoke. Valentina.

36

VALENTINA'S HEAD HAD stopped aching. Her buttocks were numb. She had had no choice but to trust Marchenko, to tell him to take her to the farmhouse. He parked the gray Zhiguli in front and insisted on going in with her. She couldn't stop him.

Anna, the white-haired owner, unlocked the door in a heavy woolen dressing gown. When she saw Valentina, the blood on her hair and ski jacket, she raised her hands to her face and said, "What happened?"

Entering ahead of Marchenko, Valentina quickly put her finger to her lips. Anna eyed the heavyset Russian.

"So I am safe now," Valentina said to Marchenko, "and you can go."

"Shouldn't I stay? You've had a bad accident."

"Anna can look after me."

"Perhaps I could have a cup of something hot. It's very cold." Snow was swirling down in thick clusters.

Valentina hesitated, then looked at Anna. Anna hobbled to the kitchen.

"I'll be right back," Valentina said, and followed her. In the kitchen, Anna whispered, "Who's he?"

"A friend, I think. Is anyone here?" She'd been praying for a miracle.

"They're in back."

"They?"

"Enriko and the American."

Valentina returned to the living room, struggling to hide her delight from Marchenko. Anna went with her, carrying a cup of ersatz coffee.

The makeshift wooden benches had been removed. They kept their coats on and sat on chairs with mended upholstery.

"How's your head?" Marchenko asked.

"The bleeding's stopped. I'm afraid your shirt is ruined."

"It doesn't matter."

Marchenko sipped the coffee. The women watched him.

"Where is Hammond?" Marchenko said.

After a moment, Anna said, "I am alone."

"I don't doubt that," Marchenko said, "but where is Hammond?"

No one answered. Marchenko returned the cup to its

saucer. He was rising to his feet when they heard the sound of a car stopping in the road.

Enriko's head was two inches from the intercom, eyes closed, listening or praying.

"What are they saying?" Hammond asked. He couldn't believe it. He'd been right. She was here.

"Marchenko wants to know where you are."

So she had told Enriko about Marchenko.

"Will she tell him?" Hammond asked.

"I don't know."

Had Marchenko forced Valentina to bring him here? Increasing pain was robbing Hammond of the ability to think. He was near the end of his rope, and he knew it. He had to hold on, not give up. He shivered with cold and fever. Even if he did get out of here, where would he go, what would he do? He had no apartment to run to, no assurance he wouldn't die in some rat-infested Soviet hospital or rot in a Lubyanka cell. The pain echoed and resounded through his body. It was an agony he had never known existed. He closed his eyes, and moaned.

Enriko looked up. "Can I help?"

It's over, Hammond thought. I can't do any more. It's finished. He let go, and in his mind whatever it was he'd been clinging to fell away. A tingling began in his hands and feet, increased, began to burn. He was light-headed. He tried to raise his knees, hoping to get more blood flowing to his head.

The burning increased, power surging up from his feet, filling his brain, ready to explode through the top of his skull. He was certain the power was visible, a blinding white light illuminating the underground chamber. What the hell did Enriko think?

His insides shuddered. Another presence filled the room. He was terrified, defenseless. Something black and suffocating squeezed him, tightened, pushed him down. He was crushed, plunging. He grabbed at the floor. "Stop!" he screamed. "Jesus, help me!"

Two car doors slammed. Valentina looked quickly at Marchenko. When the knock came, he nodded. Anna lifted the latch, and Darya burst in past her without a word. When she saw Marchenko and Valentina, her face lit up.

"Well, well, well," she said. "What a delightful surprise."

Valentina felt instantly that Darya had changed. Fear showed behind the sarcasm. She had lost something.

"Why are you here?" Marchenko demanded, and now his tone bit with the hard authority Valentina had come to expect of Soviet officials.

"Spectrum has been attacked, as you know very well," Darya said, brushing snow from her fur coat but not taking it off. "And I am looking for a certain Dr. Hammond." She had a swelling just above her left ear.

"So?" Marchenko said.

"Don't make your stupidity more evident than it has to be, Andrei. Our militia is not so incompetent as you would wish. Hammond is here and we all know it." Darya turned, and Valentina felt the chill of her eyes. "What does your husband think of your little love affair, my dear?

I thought Christians frowned on that sort of thing. Or haven't you actually done it yet, just a little fantasizing? But you don't allow that either, do you?"

Valentina stiffened.

"Perhaps you've forgotten what you're missing, Valentina," Darya went on. "Americans are so much better than Russians. Russians screw as drearily as they do everything else."

"Be quiet, Darya," Marchenko said.

"Except you, Andrei. A little uninspired, perhaps, but at least you take instruction well."

"Get out of here, Darya. Hammond's in militia custody."

"You know better than to tell me that, Andrei. But I will find him. And if I don't, the militia will. If they have to tear this shack apart."

"There is no one here," Anna said.

"We shall see."

So Darya had called the militia. Now it was just a matter of waiting. Darya stopped talking and crossed her legs. But she refused to meet Valentina's gaze.

Hammond lay on the blanket, overcome with a sense of peace. In the moment he had called out for help, help came. Not from a vague, abstract force, but from a Person he could know, someone who had been calling to him, waiting for him, someone who could cleanse him, make him what he was supposed to be. The nightmare in Cox's apartment had demonstrated the reality of the supernatural, and now he had met the One who created it. An awareness of love and forgiveness—of an indescribable need eternally filled on a cross—had grown so powerfully in him that he had had to ask for it to stop. Valentina was right. God was alive. His son was alive.

"You're smiling," Enriko said, still at the table with the intercom.

The chills had gone and the pain was down to the level of discomfort.

"What happened?" Hammond was sure the light had filled the room.

"Nothing. You've been asleep for an hour."

"You didn't see anything?"

"Should I have?"

"No."

"Darya's here," Enriko said.

Hammond didn't care. His peace could not be disturbed even by the threat of Darya's arrival.

"What's she doing?" he asked.

"I don't know. I think they're in the kitchen. They might be waiting for someone." Enriko sat up straight and smiled at Hammond. "You're better."

"Much, thanks."

As he spoke, the light went out.

"The militia's arrived," Enriko said.

"How do you know?"

"They turn off the power. They figure the darkness confuses us and the cold saps our strength."

The ventilator stopped whirring, the intercom went off. Without the heater, the temperature plunged. Hammond curled his body into the fetal position, hugged his knees, and shivered.

"How long will we be here?" he asked.

"Depends how long they stay. The only way in here is down the hole. If no one tells them where we are, they'll never find us."

Hammond had grown accustomed to the stink, but now with the ventilator off it reasserted itself. Soon the smell was as overpowering as the cold. Was there water down here? Food? What if the militia decided to hang around for a few days?

They arrived in three cars—six uniformed militiamen and a man in plainclothes the others called Major.

The major talked briefly in whispers with Darya. Tall and good-looking, he stood erect in a fur-collared leather overcoat with a fit and quality that could only have been achieved abroad. Clearly a bright young man on the rise, no doubt with privileged relatives and an elite education at someplace like the Institute of International Relations, he was very much in charge.

When he had finished with Darya, he turned to the others.

"Where is Hammond?"

"He is not here," Marchenko said. Wind hurled snow against the windows. The room was freezing.

"You have searched?"

"Of course."

"That's ridiculous," Darya said angrily. "He hasn't left this room."

"You—" The major looked at Anna.

"There is no one here," she said.

His eyes went to Valentina. "What do you say?"

"I haven't seen anyone. We are the only ones here."

"He is here," Darya said impatiently. "You don't expect them to admit it."

"I would expect him to admit it," he said, nodding his head at Marchenko.

"He is a GRU officer working for the Americans," Darya said. "He is no friend of yours nor of your country's."

"A traitor?" The major smiled at Marchenko, making a joke of Darya's accusation.

"This woman is crazy," Marchenko replied. "The man she looks for is in militia custody. He is not here."

"I am the militia," the major said, his tone hardening. "Dr. Hammond is not in custody."

"You see," Darya said triumphantly.

"But that does not necessarily mean that he is here," the major said.

He directed Marchenko to a chair in a corner of the living room, led Anna to the kitchen, then went with Valentina to a small bedroom. He closed the door, perched on the edge of a wooden table next to a window, and politely told her to take the upholstered chair.

"You've had a nasty accident," he said, waving a hand at her blood-clotted hair.

She didn't answer.

"Don't be afraid. We're just looking for someone, and we'll be out of here in a few minutes."

He waited for a response, but Valentina gave none.

"You know an American named Jack Hammond."

She stared at him.

"Is he here?"

She held the stare.

He grinned, as warmly as if they'd been on a date. "I

told you, you don't have to be afraid. No one's going to hurt you. I just want to ask some questions."

It was the way her husband had told her they began with him. Just a friendly chat.

"You're not going to tell me about the American? Is he here?"

She met his gentle, inviting eyes but did not speak. After twenty seconds his smile broke, and he went to the door.

"Don't leave," he said, but not harshly, and left the room.

Then the lights went out.

Valentina bent forward in her jacket, hugging herself against the cold. It was hardly more than twenty-four hours since Enriko had picked her up in the Zhiguli outside Hammond's apartment, but it seemed like a month. They had driven into a forest west of the city. She had told him about her feeling for Hammond, about her conviction that she had lost her healing gift.

"I feel so guilty," she had said. "I can't even pray. I don't know where God is. He's gone."

In the darkness she could just make out his beard.

"You know where he is, Valentina. He's inside you."

She put her head against his shoulder and wept. The canvas coat had been her present to him when they married. "Not anymore."

"Who told you that?"

She wiped her eyes but didn't speak.

"Who told you that, Valentina? Someone told you that."

"Darya."

She pulled away from him and sat up.

"I'm not surprised," he said. "She takes a little bit of

truth, and she uses it. She poisons you. She tells you you're weak, unworthy, hopeless. She manipulates you. It's witchcraft."

"Do you have a handkerchief?"

He pulled one from his coat pocket and she wiped her eyes.

"Valentina, you've resisted evil before, but this is the first time God's let you fight it face-to-face."

"Well, I lost."

"You did not lose. When God looks for people to do a job he looks for nothing, and he finds it in all of us. The things the enemy tries to use to disqualify us are the very things that qualify us. God doesn't use the powerful, he uses the weak."

They were parked on a dirt road. Car lights streaked by ahead of them.

"Satan takes our unworthiness and places it before us and says, 'See, this is why you can't do what you used to do, what you hoped to do.' And actually it's that very unworthiness God uses to fulfill his destiny for us."

She handed back the handkerchief.

"They want me to try to heal Andropov," she said.

That did not surprise him either. "Then do it."

"I can't."

With the engine and heater off, the car was like ice.

"God doesn't revoke his gifts, Valentina. Darya wants you to believe you can't heal. Satan wants it. Remember, 'If we confess our sins, God is faithful and just and will forgive us and purify us.'"

She saw the outline of his face against a passing light.

"You have to believe that, Valentina, and live on the basis of it."

They sat silently. Then he prayed with her.

"We've been here too long," he said when they had finished. He started the engine. "Don't tell anyone you saw me. I'll drop you at the metro."

That had been hardly more than a day ago, and now here she was, only a few yards from Enriko and Hammond. What were they talking about down there under the privy?

Valentina went to the door and cracked it open. The hallway was empty. She stepped out and peeked around the corner into the living room. Four boxlike metal lamps with handles cast a dim, eerie light. Darya was at a table, bending forward, her forehead supported on clasped hands. The major and a uniformed man stood motionless beside her. Marchenko sat in the corner.

Another militiaman entered noisily through the front door and was immediately hushed. His eyes swept the room and fixed uncertainly on Darya.

Without lifting her head, Darya said, "What's in back?"

The major said, "Get the old woman."

Valentina ducked back into the bedroom while a militiaman brought Anna from the kitchen. Then she returned to the hallway.

"What's in the back?" the major demanded. He was less polite now.

"Nothing," the woman said.

"Something's back there," the major said, "even if it's only dirt and snow. What's in the back?"

"Dirt and snow."

The room fell silent as a church. Darya did not move or raise her head.

After half a minute she said, "There is something back there. A shack. They are in the shack."

The uniformed men exchanged glances. The major said, "They?"

Darya stood. "Let's look."

He did not like Darya's giving orders. "What do you mean by *they*?"

"I mean there are more than one."

"How do you know that?"

"I know it. May we please look?"

"You don't have to," Anna said. "It is only a privy. The shack is a privy."

"We will look anyway," Darya said.

The major's men edged away from the door. They could see themselves searching a privy.

"You expect me to believe that people are hiding out back in a privy?" the major said.

"I expect you not to be a fool. If you do not want to do as I say, we can discuss the matter with Vitali Fedorchuk." Boss of the militia.

"We will look," the major said.

"And bring the girl," Darya ordered.

Valentina saw Marchenko rise from his chair. "This is enough," he said. "We will not search a privy."

"I beg your pardon?" The major faced Marchenko.

"I said we will not search a privy. I am in charge here."

The major's voice became brittle. "You are mistaken. These are my men, I have orders, and we will do whatever I think necessary."

Marchenko withdrew from his pocket a crumpled white envelope. "I am a colonel in the GRU. I report directly to

Chairman Andropov." He extracted a sheet of paper and handed it to the major.

The major read the paper, looked at the back, and read it again. He handed it back to Marchenko. "I appreciate your position, Colonel." His voice was a good deal more respectful. "But I ask you to understand that we have had a report that Dr. Hammond is here. I have orders to search. I must carry out my orders."

"This is an intelligence operation, Major. You and your men are to return to your cars and depart. If you wish, you may take Miss Timoshek with you."

The major thought it over. "With all respect, Colonel, I must insist that I be allowed to carry out my orders."

Marchenko's hand went back into his jacket with the envelope. It came out with a small black pistol.

"You will depart," Marchenko ordered. "With your men."

The major's eyes moved from the gun to Marchenko's face. His tone hardened. "I will carry out my orders."

Darya found her voice. "Don't let him—"

"Be quiet," the major ordered.

Marchenko leveled the pistol at the major's chest.

For five seconds no one breathed.

"Your decision?" the major said.

Marchenko waited another ten seconds, then put the gun away. Watching from the hallway, Valentina thought she saw him grin.

"Stay here with the old woman," the major ordered one of his men. "And you—get two more lights from the car."

When everyone was finally behind the house, standing with lights in the snow and frozen slush, Darya pulled up the collar of her fur coat and said to Valentina, "This is going to be a reunion. The wife, the long-lost husband, and the lover. Go ahead, please. Lead us to the privy."

Valentina walked back through the snow and tugged at the privy door.

"It's frozen shut," she said. "There's no one here."

"Miss Timoshek," the major said, his patience fading as the snow and cold added to the absurdity of searching a privy. "This is really—"

"Shut up."

Darya pulled at the door handle. It gave way and she stumbled back. The major put out a hand to steady her.

She stood behind him as he stuck his head in. He said, "I don't think—"

Darya pulled him away so forcefully he had to grab the arm of one of his men.

She stepped inside. "Give me some light."

The major, standing in the door, aimed his flashlight into the privy. Steam rose from the warmth at the bottom. Darya yanked the light from him and pointed it into the porcelain-ringed hole. She leaned forward. Something down there held her attention.

"Let me have your gloves," she ordered, removing her own and stuffing them into the pockets of her coat.

"Miss Timoshek," the major said, "there couldn't possibly be anyone down there. This is ridiculous." What did his men think of him, taking orders from this woman?

"There's no one here," Valentina said. "You can see that."

The men shuffled and turned, ready to head back to the house.

"Give me your gloves," Darya repeated.

He didn't move.

"If you do not . . ."

The men looked at their commander.

"Yes?" the major said. "If I do not?" He stepped all the way into the privy, and Valentina, joined by Marchenko, took his place in the doorway.

"Do you know who I am?" Darya's words were filled with menace.

The major stood his ground. His men watched him. Valentina watched him.

"Do you know who I am?" she said again. "Do you know what I can do?"

"I am not afraid of your friends, Miss Timoshek. I am an officer of the militia." Was *she* going to pull a gun on him too?

Suddenly Darya whirled on Valentina. "Tell him what I can do. Tell him what I did."

It was a confession. Valentina thought of her parents, of the mound of sawdust ignited at the timber mill.

"Tell him!" Darya shouted.

Valentina said nothing.

Darya turned furiously and aimed her gaze at the roll of paper fixed to the wall with string. Valentina felt heat, a hot stinging in her face and hands. She prayed, and in response the room became occupied by a presence she could think of only as love enraged. She was aware of a perfect, pure power that would have been capable of absolutely anything. But she was amazed and moved by what that power did. It allowed Darya to have her way. There was a small, silent flash, a tongue of flame, and the paper fell to the floor in a black, smoking ash.

The major, speechless, handed over his gloves.

Darya pulled them on, bent to grip the edge of the porcelain, and again stuck the light into the hole. She seemed unaffected by the stench.

She moved aside and said to the major, "Lift it."

"Lift what?" the major said. His eyes were still on the smoking paper.

"The porcelain, of course."

The major looked at Darya but made no move toward the porcelain.

Marchenko smiled at her from the doorway. "Allow me."

He squeezed into the privy next to Darya and the major, and with both hands gripped an edge of the porcelain. He raised it on end, exposing an oval-shaped hole a meter wide.

Darya kneeled and thrust her light back into the hole. Then she removed the hand with the light and reached in with the other hand, trying to grab hold of something. Whatever it was, she couldn't quite get a grip on it. She needed both arms in the hole, one to hold the light, the other to grab what she had seen there. She adjusted her position and stuck both arms and her head into the hole.

Marchenko put out his hands, apparently to hold Darya's waist. Her knees slipped on the edge. She called out, her legs flailed, and she vanished. Valentina heard a brief shout, then sudden silence.

The major shoved Marchenko aside, lunged forward over the hole, and looked down. Marchenko stepped back out of the privy, his face suddenly radiant in the beam of a flashlight.

To Hammond in the cold and darkness of the underground chamber, Darya's cries sounded like the screams of demons dying. Faint blows shook the wooden door. The screams stopped abruptly. The blows died. The room filled with silence.

The light went back on. The ventilator roared to life. Men's voices poured from the intercom.

"They're back in the house," Enriko said, tearing keys from his pocket. "Can you move?"

Hammond reached for the Walther. He wanted out of there so badly he could have moved with two broken legs.

Enriko unfastened the locks, pulled the door, and a freezing stench struck Hammond in the face. He waited for Enriko to make his way up the iron ladder, then reached out, gripped the sides, and put his own feet on the lowest rung. He took one step up the ladder and stopped.

"Are you coming?" Enriko called.

"Yes. Just a moment."

Hammond stepped back into the chamber and reached into his pants pocket for a blood-soaked handkerchief. He unfolded it and looked at the tiny patch of red, ragged flesh adhering to the fabric. Near the center of the flesh, surgically inserted just below the surface, was a small black speck. Making love to Darya in his Georgetown apartment, Hammond had thought it was a mole.

He took a long look at that obscene black speck, considered the evil it contained, and recalled Darya's words about using evil for good. The holodots were the answer to Spectrum, to how it worked, how to make it. They were what Hammond had been ordered to obtain, what his mission, the danger and pain, had been all about.

He folded the handkerchief around the holodots and stepped back onto the ladder.

"Are you there?" Enriko called.

"Yes, I'm coming," Hammond said, but something held him on the bottom rung. He thought of MAG and Whitmore, of his own responsibilities and loyalties.

"We have to get out of here." Enriko was shouting.

"Coming," Hammond said. His fist tightened around the handkerchief. He looked down. The hole was so black he could not even guess its depth. Whatever else Spectrum might be, it was not from God. When man knows God, it's God who has done the revealing, not man who has done the discovering. He closed his eyes and said a prayer. Then he opened his eyes and his hand at the same time, and watched the handkerchief fall from sight into the darkness.

Forgetting what remained of his pain, Hammond climbed to the wooden shack. Enriko helped him up through the hole.

When they were side by side Enriko whispered, "You okay?"

"Yes," he said. "Okay. Very okay." For the first time since taking the job with MAG—for the first time in his life—Hammond felt whole and safe.

Enriko eased the door open, listened, looked, and stepped out. The snow had stopped falling, the sky was bright and still. Followed by Hammond, he moved cautiously around to the front of the house. Three militia cars were parked in a line along the highway. With Hammond at his back, Enriko crept silently to a lighted window. They looked through and saw Valentina, Marchenko, three uniformed militiamen, and a plainclothesman on chairs in the living room. Marchenko was talking to the plainclothesman.

Enriko walked quickly but silently to one of the Volgas, found the keys in the lock, and left both front doors open.

"Give me the gun," he said.

"Enriko—"

"If you want to help Valentina, give me the gun."

Hammond gave it to him.

"Go back to the Zil," Enriko ordered, "and get to your embassy."

Hammond shook his head and followed Enriko toward the house. He stood back and watched from the darkness as Enriko kicked in the door, shouted a command, and stepped inside. Waiting in silence, his heart pounding, Hammond saw Enriko step out backward through the door with Valentina. She ran for the street, jumped into the Volga, and started the engine.

Enriko backed away from the door, and the plainclothesman, pointing a machine pistol, came into the lighted rectangle. Enriko leveled the Walther at him, yelled something, but did not fire.

With horror Hammond realized that Enriko was bluffing, that he was not going to shoot. Hammond dashed for the house.

Marchenko threw himself at the plainclothesman, knocking him into the side of the door. The plainclothesman fired. Enriko hurtled backward into Hammond's arms. Hammond tore away the Walther and sent three quick rounds into the lighted doorway. The plainclothesman's gun fired again. Marchenko fell. Hammond felt as if someone had hit him in the stomach with an ax.

Automatic weapons fire filled his ears. Hands grabbed him under the armpits and dragged him back to the dark highway.

A voice said, "Steady. Take it easy. Relax and let me do the work."

He was lifted and spread across the backseat of a car. He looked up and saw Frank. "Take it easy. Don't move."

Doors slammed. Frank disappeared. The engine revved, tires screeched, and the acceleration pushed Hammond into the backrest. From the front seat Frank called, "Can you talk?"

Hammond wanted to shout Valentina's name, make Frank go back, but his mouth and throat were filled with blood. He tried to reach for the door handle. His arm wouldn't move. He spat, swallowed, coughed, struggled to clear his throat. She was back there, alone, and he was racing away.

"Everything's gonna be okay," Frank yelled. "Just take it easy. We'll be at the embassy in fifteen minutes."

Hammond lay choking on blood, praying, seeing Valentina.

37

A LEATHER-GLOVED HAND
went over Valentina's mouth and she was dragged kicking
across the seat of the Volga through the open door onto
the snow. She had been behind the wheel, the engine
idling, waiting for Enriko to come running from the house.
Her arms and legs were pinned and a needle stung her
right buttock. Running men carried her across the snow
and lifted her into a car trunk. She heard an American
voice say, "Close it and wait. I'll be back with Hammond."
The trunk door slammed shut.

She awoke in a double bed, under a quilt, with her
clothes still on. Her head had been bandaged. The tall,

skinny man named Frank who had been with her and Hammond at Spaso House was in a chair next to the bed, smiling. He said she was in the American embassy. He showed her where the bathroom was and told her he'd see her again in the morning. She slept for ten hours.

The next afternoon Frank took her to the embassy snack bar for a tuna salad sandwich and a Coke.

"What happened?" she said. "Why am I here? Where is Jack?"

"You're here for your own safety. Jack's in Helsinki, in a hospital. He's all right. He said to tell you he'll call as soon as he can."

She knew from the way he said "he's all right" that the answer to her next question would be bad.

"And my husband?"

"Dead. I'm sorry."

"Do you know what happened?"

"The militia says it was a single round in the heart, fired as he was trying to escape from militiamen at the house."

"And Marchenko?"

"Also dead. The problem there is that the militia claims the slug was a hollowpoint. They don't normally use hollowpoints. So it had to be ours."

He was talking to her as if she were a colleague. She hoped that meant he was telling the truth.

"Hammond's Walther was loaded with SuperVel hollowpoints. We didn't tell them that, of course."

She went up to her room, a spare bedroom in the north-wing apartment of the cultural affairs officer. She closed the door and sat on the bed. She had a view of the ten-story building across the boulevard, columns on the balconies of the top three floors. Frank had said it was loaded with electronics, "so don't talk in your sleep."

Enriko was dead. She ought to rejoice. No more pain for him, no more adulterous desires for her. In the fourteen months they'd been married, they had been together seven weeks. If only she could have seen Jack before he left. What was going to happen now? The Americans would hand her back to the Soviets.

At five o'clock the next morning a man knocked on her door.

"Get dressed." He was short, wiry, bearded. "I'll be back in five minutes." And rude.

She pulled on jeans and a sweatshirt. When he returned he was wearing a heavy, wool-lined leather jacket and carrying an attaché case. He was with a crew-cut young man who didn't speak.

"Should I get a coat?" she asked.

"This way," he said without answering, and she followed him into the elevator, down to the ground floor, and across a back courtyard to a large unheated garage. Inside the garage, he turned on an overhead light, opened the back of a van, and gestured to her to climb in.

They sat on facing seats in the cold and half darkness. The other man got in the driver's seat but did not start the engine.

"Tell me about yourself," the man in the jacket said.

"Are we going someplace?" she asked. "Who are you?"

"My name's Shroeder, I work for the embassy, and that's the last question you get. Tell me about yourself."

"My name is Valentina Leonov." She was freezing. That was no accident, of course. These two Americans could just as well have worked for the KGB.

The man said, "Albert Bachmann."

She closed her eyes and said a short prayer. She asked for guidance and strength. "I used to know a man by that name."

"Unless you want to freeze to death, Valentina, you'd better speed things up. I'll help by telling you that I already know about Albert Bachmann and your whoring and everything else. But I want to hear it from you. So get started."

She felt a sudden strength, a heart-dwelling toughness, and remembered the first time she had met Enriko. She had shared his spiritual confidence but not his physical courage. She had longed for that gift.

She told Shroeder about Bachmann, about her currency dealings, the black market in furs, gems, gold, caviar. She told him about Anatoli, Ilya, Nikki, the parties with Darya Timoshek, and about her association with the KGB.

"The Soviets say you were the biggest hotel whore in Moscow," Shroeder said. "You robbed your customers. One guy lost eight hundred dollars?"

"That's not true."

"Shacked up with a terrorist, helped him hide from the cops."

"Terrorist? He's a Christian."

"They want you back."

"I'm not surprised."

"Prostitution. Economic crimes. Treason. If the situation were reversed, we'd be screaming to have your ass."

She looked at him, straight at his eyes, and in her mind she said, "I love you."

He opened the van and led her back to her room. "Don't leave."

She stayed in the bedroom. She couldn't go to the snack bar, didn't see Frank. Short-haired men in civilian clothes brought her food on metal trays. Why didn't Jack call? Maybe he had. It was out of Jack's hands now. She stopped wondering what would become of her. She knew. They couldn't keep her here forever. They certainly were not going to send her to the West. She asked for a Bible and one came with her next meal. She memorized verses. Enriko had told her, "The only Bible in the camp is the one in your head."

38

H*AMMOND CAME TO WITH*
a delicious sense of drowsiness. He settled gently, eyes closed, into a half sleep, and floated. Eventually he became aware of a low humming sound. Opening his eyes, he saw a gray curtain not ten inches from his nose. He turned his head, looked up at a curved blue ceiling, then rolled onto his other side and found himself facing something so familiar he was annoyed not to be able to identify it.

The curtain rustled open and a man said, "So you're awake. How do you feel?"

"Fine." What the hell was that thing?

"Any pain?"

"No."

"Don't be a hero. Does it hurt?"

"No. Where am I?"

"On your way to Helsinki."

Something pricked his butt, and as he sank back into deep sleep he remembered. An airplane window. With the slide closed.

Ralph Whitmore's plane landed in Helsinki at eleven A.M. on Wednesday, and an embassy Ford was there to drive him to the hospital. Hammond was uncomfortable but alert. A tube from somewhere under the sheets emptied into a container beneath the bed.

"Where is she?" Hammond asked.

"In the Moscow embassy."

"What's going to happen to her?"

"I'll be frank, Jack. I've been on the phone with Shroeder twice a day since this happened, including from the car on the way over here. The consensus is that Andropov went into a uremic coma two days after you and Valentina saw him last. We can't be sure. Even most of the Politburo members probably don't know what's going on. I want to get Valentina out as soon as possible. When things—"

"*You* want to? Meaning others don't?"

"There's some thinking, Jack, that when Andropov dies, if Gorbachev takes over she won't have to get out. From Gorbachev's point of view, she'll be a national hero."

"And if Gorbachev doesn't take over? If it's someone like Chernenko?"

"It won't be Chernenko. He's an old man, almost as ill as Andropov. But if it's someone like that—Romanov or

Grishin—then, yes, she'll be in trouble. But not many people think that's likely to happen."

"You mean not many people give a damn."

"Getting someone like Valentina out of Russia isn't that easy, Jack. It's not something we do every day. There are only so many exits, and when you use one you can't use it again. I'm not suggesting we throw her to the wolves. As I said, I want her out. And getting others to agree with me may become easier as more details become known about Andropov's health and the succession struggle."

By the time Whitmore finished this speech, Hammond's head was flat on the pillow, his eyes closed, pain and anger written all over his face.

"I'm sorry about Marchenko," Whitmore said.

That didn't help. Hammond had heard about Marchenko.

"He was a good friend," Hammond said. Too bad he had to die to prove it. And Enriko Leonov. A lot of good people dying. "How's Burkholzer?"

"Fine. Getting promoted."

Hammond opened his eyes. "Promoted?"

"Why the surprise?"

"I thought he was in trouble. Pfister hates him. Buford too."

"You ought to have more faith in my intelligence, Jack. I'm joining the Black and White teams, putting Burkholzer in charge."

"That'll be the end of Black, the end of anything he thinks doesn't come from God."

"I don't know that?"

Each morning Whitmore called Shroeder in Moscow and NSA headquarters in Fort Meade. In the afternoon he went to the hospital. Every conversation with Hammond was the same.

"When are you getting her out?"

"I'm doing everything I can. It's not in my hands. It's up to State and the CIA. And they—"

"Have other interests."

"Well, they do, Jack. You know that. They're—"

"They're not in love with her."

"I didn't mean that."

"She helped us destroy Spectrum, Ralph. Doesn't that count for anything?"

"It counts for a lot. It's the reason they're fighting over it. Otherwise no one would care."

On Wednesday night, one week after Whitmore's arrival in Helsinki, NSA monitors heard telephoned preparations for a plane to fly Andropov's alcoholic son Igor back to Moscow from a disarmament conference in Stockholm.

"That means he's finished," Hammond said.

"Probably."

Thursday afternoon Andropov died. Late the following morning it was common knowledge Chernenko had been elected chairman of the funeral commission.

"Now what?" Hammond said. "Do they need more proof than that? The chairman of the funeral commission becomes general secretary, right?"

"They're not stupid enough to elect Chernenko. I spoke with the ambassador two hours ago. He thinks they're just trying to mollify the conservatives. It'll be Romanov or Gorbachev."

"That gives our guy a fifty-fifty chance. Why don't they just get her the hell out, Ralph?"

"If it were as easy as putting her on a plane at Shere-metyevo, she'd have been gone last week. How many people do you think need getting out? It's a competition. Everybody has someone."

"What happens now?"

"There'll be a Central Committee plenum tomorrow to elect the new man. If Shroeder's people are as good as he says they are, we should know by late afternoon."

Two weeks ago it had seemed so important, who succeeded Andropov. The future of the Soviet Union and the West had depended on it. But now it wasn't politics, now it was Valentina. If Chernenko won—and if Shroeder won—she'd be handed back and disappear into the labor camps.

"This is all in Shroeder's hands, isn't it, Ralph? He's the guy who's there, calling the shots. He'll decide."

"I hate to say it."

"And I almost threw him through a window."

After a week, the bearded man called Shroeder was back at Valentina's door.

"Bundle up, you're leaving."

"Where am I going?"

"Five minutes."

When he returned, he led her to the rear courtyard. Through an archway to the street she saw two militia guards and a makeshift van like the one that had taken her from the militia station to the court. She followed him past a low wooden building with a sign that said MEDICAL CLINIC to a small basement room beneath the garage.

She saw a lawn mower, a plywood crate, empty beer cartons, an old wooden chair.

"Sit down," Shroeder ordered.

Then her eyes fell on a sight that confirmed her suspicion. Shroeder had picked up a heavy web-strap restraining harness. They used those in the camps.

Coming through the door of Hammond's hospital room Sunday morning, Whitmore said, "Good news and bad news."

"Go ahead."

"The bad news is that we still don't know who it'll be. The good news is that they did not hold a plenum yesterday, which means they're having problems. There's a fight. Shroeder and his people were up all night, we've got traffic analysts on every signal going and coming from every East Bloc installation in the universe."

"And?"

"My best guess—I still don't think Chernenko can win. He's older and sicker now than when he was beaten by Andropov after Brezhnev's death. He's uneducated, he has no industrial or agricultural expertise. His only recommendation is that he was Brezhnev's buddy and he's supported by most of the Politburo."

"And Gorbachev?"

"He's been groomed by Andropov. He'd be Andropov's choice. Unfortunately he's the youngest man in the Politburo. It's hard for some people to think of him as leader of the Soviet Union. But he's got the armed forces, Marshal Ustinov, behind him, and the KGB. He's the wave of the future."

"The wave of the future."

"I know, sounds like an epitaph. Hard to see the Central Committee electing a wave of the future."

That night, Whitmore returned with more news.

"Vice President Bush has been told not to arrive for the funeral until late tomorrow. That means they can't sort out the airport reception apparatus because they don't know who the hell's gonna be boss. Can you imagine that? They've got seventy national leaders on the way and they don't even know who their general secretary will be?"

The next evening, Monday, Hammond was on his back, eyes closed, trying not to think about what the nurse was doing to his belly. She was in the wound with a swab—it felt like a shovel—prodding and cleaning, meddling with the drain. He heard footsteps and opened his eyes to find Whitmore at the foot of the bed. He was trying, unsuccessfully, to look cheerful.

"I don't need bad news right now, Ralph."

"Sorry."

"Chernenko?"

Whitmore nodded. The nurse bathed the wound in something cold, put on a fresh bandage, and wheeled her torture cart out of the room.

"Is Valentina still there?"

"I'm afraid so."

"What's going on?"

"They self-destructed. The Brezhnevites had five of the eleven Politburo seats. Romanov's vanity kept him in the fight as long as he thought he had a chance, then he kicked in with Chernenko. Ustinov stayed with Gorbachev. What happened in the end, everyone agreed to go with Chernenko as long as Andropov's policies weren't slaughtered. Chernenko had to guarantee he wouldn't rehabilitate Brezhnev and go back to business as usual."

Hammond laid his head back on the pillow and stared

at the ceiling. He and Valentina had never made love, never held hands, never even been out to dinner together, but just thinking about her gave him more pleasure than—he thought about it—yes, than whole-body sex with Darya.

"The Central Committee," Whitmore went on, "elected Chernenko this morning. His acceptance speech had a promise to stay with Andropov's programs. Brezhnev's name never came up. Gorbachev rounded things off with a speech of his own, letting everyone know he's the number two man."

"And all the corrupt old fools breathed a sigh of relief." Whitmore shrugged.

"So we failed, Ralph. Heal Andropov, help him hang on until the March Supreme Soviet, and Gorbachev takes the throne. That's what we thought. But the Brezhnevites won. Marchenko's dead. Enriko's dead. Valentina's—"

"They didn't really win, Jack. They bought a little time. Chernenko's a sick man. When he dies, it'll be Gorbachev. We won, we just didn't win exactly the way we wanted to win."

"Screw all that, Ralph. What about Valentina?"

Whitmore reached for his attaché case. "On the way over from Washington I had a change of planes in Paris. Jean-Claude Chapelle, the SDECE chief, came out to the airport. You remember they found a phone call from the lobby of Cox's hotel to a villa on Cap Ferrat?"

"Yeah." Whitmore was preparing him for something.

"The villa belonged to Darya. Subscriber checks on the villa's phone tolls turned up a call to Valentina's apartment house in Moscow."

"And?" Hammond had never told anyone, including Whitmore, about Valentina's criminal background.

"Shroeder's been talking to Valentina."

Hammond's stomach tightened. "Go ahead, Ralph."

"The Soviets handed over a dossier on Valentina. They seem to think they have a better chance of getting her back if they convince us she's a criminal."

"And you believe the dossier?"

"She confirmed it, Jack. Most of it."

"To whom?"

"Shroeder."

"What did she say?"

"This isn't going to be easy, Jack."

"It doesn't have to be. Let's hear it."

Whitmore repeated what Valentina had told Shroeder.

"All of that has only one importance to me, Ralph. Does it reduce our resolve to get her out?"

"No, I don't think so. She gave us Spectrum. What she used to be doesn't matter."

Whitmore opened the attaché case. "Are you interested in Darya's villa?"

"Not really."

"Chapelle's people took it apart."

He handed Hammond nine eleven-by-fourteen color photographs. They showed a high wrought-iron entrance gate, a rambling three-story stone villa, two swimming pools, stables, caretaker's cottage, guesthouse, narrow beach, and a boat dock.

Two of the pictures were of the interior of the guesthouse. At the end of a large room an upside-down cross stood on an altar draped in red. The walls were decorated with paintings and drawings of rams' heads, triple sixes, circled stars, and other satanic symbols. Some of the drawings, in red, appeared to have been done with blood.

Another photograph, taken after a fire, showed the exterior of the guesthouse in ruins.

"How did it burn?" Hammond asked.

"Chapelle said they don't know. When they went the first time, the whole place was empty. They went back the next day, and that's what they found. The other buildings were still intact. Fire officials are carrying the case as accidental, possibly a short circuit. In the main house they found records of bank and security transactions, receipts for the purchase of gold and diamonds. A bedroom wall safe contained four and a half kilos of cocaine."

"Arrests?"

"The only individual associated with the villa was Darya. The only clothes on the premises appeared to be Darya's. Obviously, she did a lot of entertaining. The wine cellar and kitchens were heavily stocked."

"The caretaker?"

"Gone with the wind."

"Have you told Burkholzer?"

"Haven't had a chance. What do you think he'll say?"

"Satanism, the supernatural. Whether you'll want to believe it is something else."

Hammond believed it. The Soviets had tried to recruit the devil, but the devil was the one who did the recruiting.

"Put this on."

Shroeder held out the harness. Valentina was not going to let him come near her.

"Come on, no one's going to hurt you."

"I don't need that."

"Believe me, you'll need it."

"For what?"

"You're taking a trip. Trust me."

"Trust you? Why should I trust you?"

"I'm an American. I'm on your side. You trusted Hammond, right?"

He stepped toward her. She rose from the chair. "Don't come near me."

"Listen, Valentina, this isn't Hammond, okay? Save the innocence for him. I'm the guy who knows you're a whore and a thief. So let's make it easy. Either you put this on or it gets put on for you."

A man in a white smock came through the door carrying a small black valise. He nodded at her. To Shroeder he said, "Trouble?"

"Not really. She's gonna be nice, aren't you, Valentina?"

"Who is this?" she asked, her voice shaking.

"He's a nurse. He's going to give you an injection."

She picked up the chair and held it in front of her. Shroeder laughed. "Hey, come on, what do you think we are? We're the good guys."

The man in white opened the bag and filled a hypodermic syringe.

"I don't want that," she said.

"Look, do you want to get out of here or not?" Shroeder said. "We're doing you a favor."

"That depends on where I'm going."

"You're going West, okay?"

"You're lying."

"Do I look Russian?"

The nurse said, "This'll help you rest during the trip."

"You're going to give me to the KGB."

"Now why would we do a thing like that?" Shroeder asked. He glanced at the nurse. Both men stepped toward her.

She lifted the chair. "Stay away from me with that."

Tuesday they buried Andropov. The only Politburo member who had accompanied Andropov's family to the lying in state at the House of Unions was Mikhail Gorbachev. Limousines deposited mourners beneath a massive portrait of Andropov at the light-green stone building's black-and-red-draped four-columned portico on Marksa Prospekt, not far from Andropov's old KGB office, the Central Committee headquarters, and the Kremlin. Inside, beneath glittering chandeliers in the Hall of Columns, where Lenin and Stalin had themselves lain in state, Andropov, ringed by red flags and flowers, stared dully from the bier.

Speaking from the mausoleum in Red Square, huddled against the snow and stinging wind and fatigued from the previous days' succession struggle, Chernenko addressed his countrymen and a worldwide television audience as the new leader of the Soviet Union. It was a pathetic, embarrassing failure. Soviets who had seen in Andropov a hopeful explosion of youth, ambition, and rectitude were once again confronted with debility and decadence.

Chernenko's energy faltered every few words, and he appeared to gasp for breath. During the funeral parade, he raised his arm to salute, then dropped it, tried again, and once more found the effort too great. Escorting the coffin the few yards to its grave in the Kremlin wall, Chernenko could not even lift an arm to give the impression that he was helping to bear the weight. And with him at the head of the cortege, erect and robust, his physical and political power standing out against the new leader's infirmity, went Mikhail Gorbachev.

It was the moment Hammond dreaded. The nurse rolled her instrument-laden trolley into the room and went to work. He laid his head back, closed his eyes, and tried to think of something else. The pain never made him want to scream. It was a groaning pain, deep and visceral.

He heard footsteps. Whitmore was back. Why did he always come now? And always with bad news.

"Can you wait a minute, Ralph? Not right now, please."

Hammond smelled something new. Not the ether odor the nurse usually brought. Puzzled and disbelieving, he took a deep breath. It was the smell of Moscow, the smell Frank had called tears, the smell of strong, industrial, Soviet soap.

He dared not open his eyes.

39

TWO WEEKS IN A HOSPITAL
in Helsinki, two more weeks convalescing at a U.S. Air
Force base in Frankfurt, and now here he was, feeling like
a million dollars. Two million. All the money in the world.

The sun's warmth was suddenly withdrawn and Hammond opened his eyes to see Valentina shading his chest.

"This is beautiful," she said, looking happier than anyone he had ever seen.

She had climbed the ladder from the sea to the stone edge of the swimming pool where Hammond lay on a *matelas*. They had arrived two nights ago, stayed in separate rooms, and the pastor of an Anglican church in

Cannes had married them this morning. She swore the white bikini Hammond gave her was the first bathing suit she had ever owned.

"Not bad," he said, sitting up. "Glad you like it."

In half an hour it would be late enough to go up to the terrace, watch the Mediterranean sparkling below, and lunch on grilled sea bass and a bottle of Bâtard-Montrachet. He'd told the reception desk they'd be needing only one room for the rest of their stay.

Hammond had thought long and hard before bringing her here. But there were things he had to see put to rest—bad tastes, foul odors, ugly sounds. He needed to demonstrate that he was forgiven and knew it, that he was saved, that this was, really, one more day of his eternal life. And he wanted to do it with her, share it with her, give thanks with her.

"Have you been here before?" she asked, stretching out beside him.

"Only once."

He reached over and buried his face in her shoulder, inhaling the sweet Mediterranean aroma of salt and sunshine. The flesh still bore the fading blue bruise of the web-strap restraining harness. Shroeder's diplomatically protected personal effects as he departed Moscow had included more than furs, caviar, and antique furniture. Valentina, lightly tranquilized, had come out in one of the heavy wooden crates, lifted gently onto an Air Force C-9 jet for the ninety-minute flight to Helsinki. The restraining harness, fastened to plastic-covered bolts, integrated her as solidly into the crate as if she'd been a fifteenth-century Rublev icon.

"With a girl?"

"No." He raised his head and kissed her. "With a colleague. The man who used to have the apartment in Moscow. We ate his peanut butter."

She nodded.

"It wasn't very pleasant, but he was the kind of guy who would have loved our beginning our honeymoon here. I'll tell you about him someday."

After lunch, drowsy from the sun and wine, they strolled up the lawn to their room. They were on the second floor, somewhere over the room Cox and Whitmore had had.

Hammond undressed, put on one of the hotel's white terry-cloth robes, and called to Valentina in the bath.

"Tell me something."

"Yes?"

"Do you believe in curses?"

The bathroom door opened. She came out wrapped in a towel.

"I believe in blessings." She walked over and hugged him.

"But not curses?"

"Not for us. Why?"

"No reason. Let's go to bed."

ACKNOWLEDGMENTS

Research for this novel was conducted in the United States, France, and the Soviet Union. I am particularly indebted to the several people, perhaps better not named, who helped me in the Soviet Union; to Philip Buechler, a spiritual-warfare expert; and to Arthur Hartman, ambassador to the Soviet Union at the time of Yuri Andropov's death.

Publications named and quoted are real, including the scientific paper attempting to demonstrate the power of a human mind to control tumbling dice and the Surgeon General's report citing an intelligence gap in our knowledge of Soviet astral-projection research.

The fundamental details of the peculiar behavior of Presidents Richard M. Nixon and Jimmy Carter, as well as the CIA's involvement in assessing the possible paranormal significance of Nixon's symptoms, are factual, as are the statements of Nikita Khrushchev and Leonid Brezhnev that the book relates to those events. Brezhnev's misfortunes with the falling scaffolding and incorrect speech also are factual.

Research attributed to actual institutions did not necessarily occur at those institutions. Pan Am did not actually begin serving Moscow until 1985.

Of the hundreds of books and other publications contributing to the research, I would especially like to name: *Andropov*, by Zhores A. Medvedev; *The Holographic Paradigm*, edited by Ken Wilber; *Parapsychology and Contemporary Science*, by A. P. Dubrov and V. N. Pushkin; *The Puzzle Palace*, by James Bamford; *Shadows and Whispers*, by Dusko Doder; *The 3-Pound Universe*, by Judith Hooper and Dick Teresi; and *Wholeness and the Implicate Order*, by David Bohm.

All characters in the book, except for well-known historical figures, are fictional. Moscow embassy personnel mentioned in the book, including the U.S. ambassador, deputy chief of mission, station chief, defense attaché, and others, are fictional and bear no resemblance to individuals actually holding those posts.